PRAISE FOR THE ERSTWHILE TYLER KYLE

"*I came for the terror but I stayed for the love. This bewitching novel perfectly nails the vibe of a low-budget, high-gore monster/slasher flick, but deftly uses the genre to tell a moving fable of self, and love, lost and found again*"
— Daniel Maidman, visual artist and author of *The Exile of Zanzibar.*

"*The amount of absolute batshit in this story is a character of its own, I swear.*"
— Mary Ann Marlowe, author of *Some Kind of Magic.*

"*Engaging and original,* The Erstwhile Tyler Kyle *manages to balance humour and horror with a great big helping of heart. It's impossible to put down and equally impossible to describe, not so much read as experienced. I wish I could do so for the first time again.*"
— Alistair Reeves, author of *A Spell for Heartsickness.*

"*The small town claustrophobic atmosphere was incredibly well done and the behavior of the eclectic townspeople was deliciously creepy and off putting.*"
— Mel, Tome Raider

about psychology, and our fear of the unknown, and the cycles of pain that can be created by one heartless act. Also it's about gay sex."

– Seann Barbour, author of *The Maw*

"You don't know who or what to trust, what's real and what isn't, or anything else, quite frankly. This story is a brilliantly constructed game of Jenga and you never know what piece will be the key, or how the entire tower might come down when it inevitably does. I can't emphasize enough how well done this is!"

– Tasha Reynolds, *The Sinister Scoop*

"Blended horror tropes, podcast vibes, unreliable narrators, and comedy, making this book unique and an overall good time."

– Bookaholic Reviews

"The emotional stakes are high throughout this story with themes of unrequited love, a mother's abandonment, platonic love and dangerous obsession. There is an atmospheric, fever dream-like/drugged feeling to many of the scenes and for good reason . . . at times I found myself physically cringing with my toes curling up."

– Sue Bavey

"I highly recommend this one. It's great. It's fantastic. It's darkly humourous in some places. You just have to read it for yourself. It gets out there. It gets real out there and I absolutely loved it."

– Horror Reads

"Surprising at every turn. Hot when it needed to be hot; dark when it needed to be dark. A Solid five stars from me."

– Scott Roche

thing is written first-person present, but there is so much flair that makes it unique. Some people may be put off by the use of bold words, crossed out words, emojis, etc, but it adds such a unique feel to the book."
    – Timothy Wolff, author of *Platinum Tinted Darkness*

"I'm pretty sure this was the most unique and original book I've ever read - and I mean that in the best way possible."
    – Sarah McKnight, author of *Carousel*

"Steve's not just a writer testing his luck. He's the game maker."
    – Gerard Howard, author of *The Fractured God*

"Tyler is a seamless blend of comedy and tragedy. One second, he's larger than life, a supernova of Charisma, Uniqueness, Nerve, and Talent, then perspective shifts, and he's a Richard Siken poem made flesh, a roiling sea of shame and desire. Outside of Tyler, every other character puts in an absolute shift; if there were Oscars for books, this one would win 'Best Ensemble Cast' as well as a host of others."
    – Paul, Queen's Book Asylum

THE

ERSTWHILE

TYLER

KYLE

ALSO BY STEVE HUGH WESTENRA

The Wings of Ashtaroth (Book One of *The Sands of Hazzan*)
So Sing the Barrows (forthcoming, 2024)
For One Night Only (forthcoming)

STEVE HUGH WESTENRA

THE ERSTWHILE TYLER KYLE

SGP

Cover art and interior design by Steve Hugh Westenra
No AI was used in the making of this book or its cover.

ISBNs: 979-8-2237569-2-7 (ebook), 978-1-0688433-0-3 (paperback), 978-1-0688433-1-0 (hardcover)

Spoon God Publishing

To Mom and Dad. Mom for telling me I'm funny and asking why I never write funny things, and Dad for reading the (possibly) funny thing I tried to write.

And to Lucas, who sat there while I played Rihanna's "Umbrella" on repeat for an hour.

Content warnings can be found at the back of the book or at Stevewestenra.com.

THE

ERSTWHILE

TYLER

KYLE

ACT 1

Seven thirty, fingers dirty
Dig into the soil thick
Drink the juice and swallow thunder
Feed the groundworms with your spit

Seven thirty, fingers dirty
Pomegranate in the vein
Lick the blood and swallow songspell
Whisper to the old wolfsbane

Monkshood medley in the belly
Skin the flesh and sunder shell
Peel the rind that's turned to jelly
Heed the night bird's wanton call

Eight and second, that's the catch
Cinch the suit and pin the latch
Walk the streets of Echo Island
Bury summer's naked thatch

The Echo Island Diary: Entry 1
Tyler Kyle Went to the Island

July 12ᵗʰ, 2019: 10:00 AM

It is a truth universally acknowledged that a man in possession of the name **Tyler** is definitely an asshole. Combine that with the name **Kyle** and you've got yourself not just an *asshole*, but a serial *killing* asshole. **Tyler Kyle**, serial killer. **Tyler Kyle**, a knock-off brand of women's underwear. **Tyler Kyle**, the name of some nineties garage band who picked the name because *it sounds like a fucking serial killer.*

Tyler Kyle. B-movie vixen Virginia Kyle's only child. The name of one half of cryptid-hunting YouTube duo, Discovery Bang. The Scully to Josh Likens's Asian-Canadian Mulder on our stupidly popular channel.

Tyler Kyle.

~~Me.~~

Remember that name, because it'll be on the test.

Okay, there's no test (not unless you backed this project at the $100 level, in which case *thanks as always for your support, please share this Kickstarter far and wide. Tell your friends, tell your grandma*).

Or maybe you won't need to, because **I** did it everybody (woo!). **Tyler Kyle** went to the island.

And the island has no internet.

At least it has this notepad. Josh could milk an episode or eight out of this journal alone:

"Hey guys! Today we'll be digging into the unresolved mysteries surrounding the authorship of the Echo Island Diary and whether Ty wrote this or if it was Sasquatch. I've contacted noted bigfoot scholar Dr. Wylie Earp of the University of Western-Skidoo, California, and he has some interesting theories about the pictograms on Page One. Tangentially, we'll also examine theories that **the manuscript could in fact be an elaborate hoax** , conjured into being by a crazed Batman fanatic who wrote it all in an adderall-induced haze. With me today is my new co-host, joining me for five months now since the untimely disappearance of **Tyler Kyle**. Take it away, Pam!"

Josh would never say *tangentially* though. Is it weird I know that? It's probably weird. Sorry,

Josh, if you're reading this.

Sorry for a lot of things. Turning up dead after following a fake video of my vanished celebrity mom to an isolated murder island in the Canadian wilderness, for one thing.

That's got to be the worst mistake I made since ignoring the fan~~stalker~~ who posted it.

1

FAPPING INTO GOD'S SOCK

I t's 10:30 AM and I've arrived at White Sails Cabins and Resort. Both the *white sails* and the *resort* parts of the name remain conspicuously enigmatic given the lack of sailboats on the lake surrounding the island, and the absence of the usual accouterments typical of a resort: a pool, a playground, a restaurant, tourists to, you know, *tour*.

The resort is at the edge of town, which is a five-minute walk from the middle of town. Already I feel both like I've seen everything I need to see, and like this is the kind of place that probably has a hidden network of tunnels underneath it to accommodate the otherwise short-for-space Lovecraftian cult and their Tuesday-evening virgin sacrifices. In a small town like this the local cult is probably low on virgins.

And if you're thinking, *well, I know where this is going,* I'm sorry. You'll have to wait to live out your Nicholas Cage bee fantasy realness. I'm about the level of pure that McDonald's 100% real beef is 100% real anything.

I'm just saying, if I end up dead, sans one Josh Likens who couldn't get permission from the island's mayor to enter in time for us to shoot, it probably wasn't a cult.

At least the room's cozy, for a murder resort. We have plain wood walls, simple floral sheets tucked tight around the bed. A lamp. A small table. Only an analog TV, but I brought my laptop. It smells a bit like vanilla potpourri—dated, but, you know, *nice*. This would be a relaxing place—the kind of setting *Tyler*-made for my usual cracks about how pleasant and scenic and normal the home of Devil Man Cryptid Face Who Skins Tourists And Wears Their Hands As Mittens is and how I'd like to settle down here. It would be, except for the part about there being a real-life stalker crouching in the picturesque saltbox houses and charmingly abandoned storefronts.

I grab the receiver of the rotary phone on the side table and plunk it back in the cradle. Josh would get a kick out of it. It's not even one of those fake-antique ones you find at flea markets, but a utilitarian beige box like Mom and me rented when I was a kid. Josh would still get a kick out of it. He'd latch onto it like a drowning sailor, assuming it was a clue to, well, whatever this mystery is. Maybe my stalky e-mail friend is a pissed off phone-salesman, driven to despair over the collapse of his rotary empire, blaming me and my mom because she didn't pay our bill that one time.

I mean, she presumably paid all our bills, but I'm not gonna lie and say she wasn't sometimes overcome by the oblivious whimsy fans fell in love with. Funny how in the real world, whimsy has consequences.

I had to make my reservation by phone because Echo Island doesn't just not have internet, I'm not sure it's seen the business end of a graphing calculator. I was able to swing a ticket on the biplane to Echo Island based on Virginia Kyle's infamy, and the fact that—at least based on the hand-annotated map me and Josh found tucked inside her copy of *Interview with a Vampire*—Mom has a genuine connection with this island.

I smooth the map out on the dresser.

Mom's handwriting litters the page. Jumbled letters in a probable code are scrawled beneath several of the buildings on the island, and another that sits alone in the surrounding forest.

Weirdly, the name on the map isn't Echo Island, but Saint Serge's. For whatever reason, the name got changed–maybe because the mysterious camp that used to exist here took its name with it when it closed in the 70s.

Echo Island is like other small towns until it isn't. Its mayor, an aging millionaire called Conrad Uphill, wields substantial power over who and what comes and goes. Surrounded by acres of forest, accessible only by plane, Echo Island is practically his private fortress. The lake that surrounds it is more like a moat, and the fir and spruce that dominate the forest are a cryptozoologist's wet dream. *Who knows what terror lurks in them thar trees?*

Maybe our stalker knows. Their harassment started with hundreds of e-mails begging us to investigate a vague canine cryptid on the island. Until the last e-mail, the one with the attached video of my presumed-dead mom.

I fall back on the bed, which dips and creaks under me. It's a bit small, but again, *cozy*. Do they keep all the rooms so neat, despite the lack of guests? Or maybe there are guests—famous people who pay Conrad Uphill to let them disappear. That's one possibility of what happened to my mom.

When people used to spin their pet theories about how Virgie Kyle ran off to start a new life I'd get this stabbing feeling in my brain. It's there now, but deeper, because suddenly it could be true. It's the happier of the two endings I can imagine as having played out, the one part of me has always wanted to believe.

My mom, missing, but out there. My mom, who packed a suitcase and vanished off the set of *Plutonium Blonde* in 2001 at the height of the revival of her career, on the eve of her fiftieth birthday. My mom, who left her twelve-year-old son alone in a dark apartment with no note and no supervision. It was a long weekend. The production was taking a break. I waited for four days before I ran out of Spaghettios and banged on a neighbour's door. Sometimes I wonder if I hadn't run out of food, if I would've stayed there forever. As long as I was inside that apartment, she could still walk through the door.

I know from "investigative" videos online that I told the police I saw her go, that she bent down and whispered something in my ear, but I don't remember it. Every video claims she said something different: *wait for me, I'll be right back, I'm sorry baby doll, be good now.*

Wait. I'm coming. Be good. I couldn't do the first thing, but I didn't completely fuck up the last. Probably. Josh might disagree.

I slide my phone from my pocket and flick through my files till I land on the video. My thumb hovers with a will of its own above the play button. It hits.

The clip is black and white—not the true black and white of early cinema, but the black and white of later imitations. She's young, twenty-something, which makes me think this is one of her early roles, back when she was what the industry called a triple threat and before they put her out to pasture at thirty. She sashays into the frame from a room that's out of view. The set's decorated like a wealthy home out of a 30s or 40s Universal picture, and she's dressed in a silk negligee and dress coat, her black hair pinned in a complicated hairdo that may be a wig. Her grin splits wide. She always had the same grin, and I still don't know if that was because she was an excellent actress, because she was always genuinely smiling, or because I never saw her real smile. Whatever the truth is, she looks happy as she approaches the camera.

"Hey, baby doll," she says, something she used to call me. Something she *only* called me. But it's not me she's talking to. She grabs a martini glass from a side table as she passes it, plucks the cherry out by its stem and pops it in her mouth. She swallows. When she pulls the stem out, it forms a perfect knot. She puts the glass down, then grabs a newspaper from the table. She holds it up. The date of the *Echo Island Gazette* is April 5th, 2019—over three months ago. The headline reads: "Dog Days Ahead: Uphill Looks Back on 100 Years of Summer."

Mom wiggles the paper. "Seven-thirty fingers dirty, Ty. Come for me, baby doll."

Off-screen, a woman's husky voice murmurs: "The world's not ready yet."

The video ends as Mom exits the frame and steps out of the way to reveal her dog-eared copy of James Blish's *A Case of Conscience* on the table.

Hundreds of Discovery Bang fans have poured over this footage, zooming in as much, and sometimes more, than its quality allows. Still others have ordered copies of Blish's out of print sci-fi novel and dissected every page like it'll offer up the secrets of the universe—or even just *me*. Suddenly I'm the subject of dissection:

Why does Virgie Kyle knot the cherry stem when she's talking to her son? *Slice*. Why did she ever call you baby doll? Isn't that pretty fucked? *Cut*. Fingers dirty? Sounds like a weird sex thing. *Snick,* and there goes the skin over the rib cage.

Theories abound, each more laughable than the last: my mom's a time traveller. My mom's an alien. I'm my own dad. I murdered my mom and her ghost sent me this video. Seven-thirty, fingers dirty refers to the time of her death, and the blood on my hands from when I jabbed my twelve-year-old fingers into the hole I'd made.

When your channel courts viewers who believe a walking penis stalks central Florida, you get what you ask for, I guess.

I'm too smart by half to think my mom's alive, that this isn't the work of someone with basic photoshop skills playing a cruel joke, but I couldn't *not* come. At the very least, this island may have something to tell me, even if it's just what her real smile looks like.

I close the video, flick through the master folder where I keep Discovery Bang's raw footage. Most of these clips won't make it in. We have, in no particular order: the gas leak in that basement where me and Kayla—our camera girl—nearly passed out; Josh *actually* passing out after being chased by a *literally* feral raccoon; Josh trying to convince me we can afford a visit to Loch Ness, which he seems to think will be cheaper because my mom was Scottish; our Fresno Nightcrawler trip, so, in a nutshell, four hours loitering in parking lots.

There's only one complete episode. A file I have yet to delete. The last episode to go up on the channel. Maybe the last episode we'll finish. As I think it, it's like someone's taken a shovel to my diaphragm.

I hit play and immediately my phone bombards me with Ennio Morricone's "The Ecstasy of Gold." It's our theme song—Josh's choice. We started using it around . . . I dunno, episode seven?

As usual, Josh opens the episode. As usual, Josh does basically everything.

JOSH: Welcome, Bangers, to another episode of Discovery Bang. I'm here with my co-host, the erstwhile Tyler Ky—

TY: *Erstwhile?*

JOSH: Yeah, you know. You're an erstwhile kind of guy.

TY: I guess I better dust off the old resumé. [Mimes taking out and dusting off a piece of paper]. Whoa, looks like I haven't held a real job since, uh, "2011, concession stand operator." It means, like, *former*, like I used to be your co-host but you've replaced me.

JOSH: [Sighs. Faces the camera] Guys, if you're as interested in replacing Ty as *I* am, get your audition tapes ready and sound off in the comments. But for now [Eyes Tyler, who's still miming], let's get right to our investigation. In today's episode, we'll be reviewing our footage from our trip to Paris, Michigan in which we attempt to answer the question of just what is the Michigan Dogman, and what does he want?

TY: Is it directions to the furry convention, or to be told once and for all that he's a good boy?

JOSH: This is serious [He smiles]. Actual patrons helped fund this trip so you could spend your days snarking instead of shoveling popcorn into tiny paper bags.

TY: That's the hard part, is it? The tiny bags? [Holds up hands]. Well, maybe. I just think, part of the appeal is, you know, maybe the snark. I'm giving the viewers what they want. [Grins] Speaking of, later, on our OnlyFans, you can watch me spank Josh for flunking his vocab test.

I'm a fucking ass.

"*Fuuuuuuck.*" I close the video with the same intensity as if I were throwing the phone against the wall. "Fuck."

With my eyes closed, I can pretend it didn't happen. I can take back what I said and everything that followed. I can avoid watching a simple joke snowball in our fanbase till Josh's girlfriend got so upset she dumped him after I doubled down on that lovely piece of shtick during a liveshow. I can undrink the tequila we downed before jumping in the hot tub at the awards show months later. I can unpeel my lips from his. I can unfeel his twenty-ton petting, and I can especially unsay the fucking heartless joke that stopped him dead in his wandering hands, the: *maybe we should rethink an OnlyFans.*

With my eyes closed, Josh doesn't pull away. With my ears shut he doesn't tell me he doesn't want me. When I'm pretending, I can erase Josh's deadpan *we need to talk about the show* from the vacant lot between my ears. I can fix things between me and my best friend. I can forget that the real reason he's not with me now probably isn't that he couldn't get permission, but because he wanted an excuse not to be alone together.

I swallow, eyes closed, and the garbage doesn't go away, but for a moment as I brush my fingers over my lips I can remember what those first minutes were like, when I held something I'd wanted so long in my hands and crashed into it so hard I could have cracked straight down the middle.

I'm hard, and I pop the button on my jeans and undo my zipper, the one and only fucked-up asshole who gets horny thinking about the time his life imploded.

The phone rings. Not the rotary phone, but my cell. I blink and fumble to answer.

"Fuck." Ugh. "I—*hi*." Discovery Bang here, and in this episode, we'll be investigating the piece of sentient trash known as Tyler Kyle. Sightings are common, but somehow the true extent of his madness remains unknown.

"You okay, man?" asks Josh, a kind of distance in his voice, or maybe that's my imagination.

I rub my hand over my face and spring off the bed, very ready not to be the sorry-ass loser masturbating in a cabin and picturing the man he's talking to deep-throating him in the woods. I'm not that far gone. Yet.

"Tired." Which is true. I barely slept on the bus ride to the plane, and the flight was too bumpy for a nap. "Acres of gorgeous forest and the promise of weeks of peace and solitude really wipes me out."

Josh laughs. It's forced. "Have you spotted this canine cryptid yet?"

"Not unless it's a tree. This has to be the least exciting non-existent monster we've ever not encountered. You're lucky you couldn't make it."

We don't do this, this searching for something to say because we can't talk about the only thing that matters. When you struggle through theatre school side-by-side with someone you lose all sense of shame.

Almost.

Maybe I should come out and tell him I'm not gay, but that has to be the single stupidest thought I've ever had and he's not going to swallow it. I'm not sure I swallow it.

"I'm still working on that Conrad Uphill guy," Josh says. "It's real weird, man. According to the Way Back Machine, he had this page all about a summer festival called Dog Day. It doesn't sound normal. I've been cross-referencing it against regional histories, but there's nothing. I think it's related to Sasquatch."

I head to the bathroom and pin the phone between cheek and shoulder while I wash my hands. The water comes out peaty, and there's no bath, only a shower. Josh would hate that.

Ever since he saw *Psycho* as a kid he can't take showers with the curtain closed, and I'm pretty sure White Sails Cabins would be less understanding than me about water damage.

I shake away the image of Josh showering as I shake off my hands. "Only you would cross-reference a harmless small-town dog show with Big Foot."

"Sasquatch. Anyway—watch your back until I get there. Don't join any cults or climb inside giant wooden men."

So he's still planning to come. "This isn't a show, Josh. I'm not out here hunting anything."

"*Besides answers,*" he says dramatically. "Sorry." He pauses, and we sink back into the mire of a minute ago. "Are you going to see Uphill about the movie?"

"Not first thing—maybe tomorrow." I tried to press Uphill to set a formal date for our meeting over the phone, but he pretended I hadn't asked the question. It's a tactic I'm intimately familiar with at this point.

I head back into the main room and start unpacking.

There's a long pause, so deep I can hear Josh's breath. "You shouldn't be doing this alone."

"With my keen sense of humour, I'm never alone. It's like having a whole extra person in my brain." And this is real life. Not the show. This isn't me yukking it up as we chase Josh's monster of the week.

"I'm being serious, Ty. The really real kind of seriousness."

I pace the small square of room not overtaken by luggage and furniture, gesticulating as I talk. "Yeah, I could tell by your concern I might get eaten by Big Foot that this was serious, really real business. Have you ever heard the one about the boy who called wolf?"

"*Sasquatch.*"

I can see Josh shake his head and it's like we're on camera again.

"I'm pretty sure the story's about a wolf, but okay. If a big hairy man in a suit stomping through the woods and shedding plastic body hair is what does it for you, I'm happy to play along."

"You wouldn't have to wear a suit."

It occurs to me suddenly that if it's possible to queerbait *yourself*, that's exactly what we've been doing for five seasons.

I don't know how to take the comment, so I assume it's a crack about how I look like Big Foot. Maybe I do, since Big Foot isn't real and can look like whatever the hell Josh wants him to—in this case, a spindly White dude with curly black hair.

"All the way out here, alone in the dark. The call of the wild's calling me home, Josh." I stretch out my leg, admiring my sneakers. I kick one of them off like it burns and grip my knee, like Josh can see me. "Oh god, Josh. It's happening. My shoe size expanding—I'll never fit back into my Docs. Those were expensive. And there's hair. Hair where there wasn't hair before." I collapse onto the bed.

And scene.

"You're an asshole."

"An asshole with no shoes. I'll need a tetanus shot when I get back. Scratch that, rabies." I stare at the ceiling, calmer than I was, drifting between the safety of the set we've constructed. "I'll be fine. The only thing I'm worried about is whoever sent that e-mail, but maybe they just wanted our attention. Someone who knows something and that was the only way to reach out."

It sounds dumb as I say it.

"Maybe it was that Uphill guy. If he knows your mom, maybe he knows about you."

I sit beside the suitcase and untie my remaining sneaker. "Guess I'll find out when I meet him. He wanted to talk in person." I pause. "This isn't some swamp creature; it's my mom. You don't have to be here. I'll ask some questions, maybe get some answers, probably discover nothing at all. It's not really Discovery Bang material." Even though all we do is discover *nothing at all.*

"Yeah, maybe it's a good thing." Another pause, and I can feel the words building up in him. "I thought—I thought we could talk about the show. We need to figure things out."

My chest doesn't just hitch, it's made of hitches. I shove a pile of shirts into the bottom of the dresser, trying to cauterize the part of my brain that gives a shit, which, unfortunately, is most of it. I could fool myself thinking this is the beginning of some grandiose gesture, some declaration. I could do that, but it would be cruel, and even I don't hate myself that much. Still, the possibility floats in the silence, and part of me reaches for it because if there's a way in which Josh and I are equally stupid it's that we're both romantics.

I swallow, try not to spit out the first asshole thing that comes to mind. Sometimes I need someone to tell me when to shut up. "I thought you figured it out at the pool."

Fuck.

There's the cold, creeping over me like a sheet. The part that would rather cut him off now than listen to the precise, real, true way he's going to do it himself.

And he's silent again, because he's good and I'm bad and that's all there is to it.

As I unpack my bag, waiting for him to say something terrible and hoping he'll say something else, Mom's photo slips from between two pairs of pants. I'm here for her, for me, not for Josh. Maybe the space is good for me. Maybe I need to be on my own. Maybe Josh and I were always one fuckup away from splitting apart.

"Listen, Josh, I'm sorry, I have to go. There's a Sasquatch howling at the moon and I have to make a barricade."

Hanging up is easier than anything that comes after.

2

WEIRDO IN A WEIRD WORLD

I t's the heat of the day in mid-July, and even some distance from the forest, the air is sticky with the smell of hot spruce sap, moisture evaporating off the surface of moss, and lichen-encrusted bark peeling off stubby, pressed-close trees. There's an undercurrent of putrefaction beneath the tang of the woods, the stagnation of the moat-like lake. I can smell the ocean, but the Atlantic is at least eighty kilometers from here.

Echo Island is human design white-washed onto the surface of the wilderness. The saltbox houses are painted every shade you could ask for as long as it's white, pastel, or fire-engine red, and each one stands hunched beneath the shadow of Conrad Uphill's McMansion at the centre of town.

When you make a living on nonsense like me and Josh do, you travel to a lot of weird and wacky small towns. I've seen everything: Giant Turnipville, Michigan, where every gift shop—and there are at least five, plus enumerable corner stores and gas stations that triple as the same—features snowglobes filled with to-scale models of town and turnip; Mermaid Bay, Maryland, where the cryptid du jour isn't *homo aquaticus* as the name would suggest, but yet another Big Foot rip-off, whose proud simian visage can be purchased in mask or burger form from a hundred seaside stalls; Alien, New Mexico where—well, that should be obvious. Point is, all of them are wacky in this uniquely manufactured way. Every Bumfuck, Nowhere is some

variation of artificial, and the artificiality is always necessitated
by the genuinely heartbreaking story of how the town slowly
suffocated from the death of [insert industry here] till all its
young folk moved to Baltimore, or Albuquerque, or whatever
passes for a moderately-sized city in Michigan.

Echo Island—Saint Serge's—*whatever*—is nothing like that.

The island is man-made, nearly perfectly rectangular like the
lake-moat that provides a slim border between the town and an
ocean of trees. It's also flat as a crêpe, with pine-clad hills rolling
in the distance as though God designed this place with postcards
in mind. Classic New Ossory, Canada, at least once you drive
past the capital city of Avalon.

Walking out from White Sails, which sits on the southern
side of the rectangle scenically facing the forest, I'm met by a
series of pot-holed grey roads disappearing round the sides of
abandoned-looking houses.

It's unclear how or why anyone lives here. The website gave
no indication that there was ever industry in the town, despite the proximity of the forest, and unless—Josh would love
this—everyone here is a ghost, they have to eat. The site claims
Conrad Uphill founded the town on the back of an inherited
fortune, but presumably the "Conrad" referred to is a long-dead
ancestor.

The only possible clue to the island's purpose was a sub-page
on the website called "Island Song," featuring a rambling description of the resonance of the natural environment, and the
sonic power of the trees. The eau de hippy is strong.

Part of me itches to explore, as if walking the perimeter of
the town would peel back its skin and reveal my mother's face
beneath, but as I glance up the road to my right, my stomach
rumbles.

Red, yellow, blue houses. I pass each one, trying not to stare
too hard at the floral-patterned curtains. Slender fingers slide
open the fabric from inside the blue house, and an elderly
woman's face, framed by brown Farrah Fawcett curls, spies on

me—this new stranger who's come to town. This weirdo in an even weirder world. And because I'm a weirdo, I raise my hand, smile like the creepiest of creepers, and wave.

Like a character out of one of Mom's so-bad-they're-good movies, the woman snaps from the window and the curtains fall back into place.

To be fair to her, I'm kind of a jackass. I'd snap away from the window too if I saw my smile. From the outside, maybe my smile's like Mom's—brighter than the sun as long as the sun's a plastic model.

I'm staring.

Residual guilt clings to me. These are people, not set pieces. Whatever drew Claudia—it just seems like her name is probably Claudia—to this island is more complicated than my flippant dismissal of her suggests. There's a story behind her face. And who knows, maybe she, too, is the lost child of an even loster Hollywood starlet. Maybe she, too, came to Echo Island chasing a cryptic video. Maybe I, too, will be drawn to stake my claim to a prim little saltbox house overlooking the moat.

The house disappears behind me and a diner comes into view, recessed behind a parking lot. The lot has painted parking spaces and everything, like a human town with human people. Every one of the spaces is empty, of course. The *idea* of car exists, but the reality remains elusive.

Outside the diner, an electric pink sign flashes *Ziggy's* off and on. The neon monstrosity clashes with the folksy atmosphere, utterly useless in daylight.

Josh'd love it.

I grip my phone. I never should have hung up on him. It was a childish response to an adult situation, and eventually I'm going to have to call him back and stop being an asshole. Of the two of us, I'm supposed to be the sensible one.

I stand in the empty parking lot with my phone in my hand, staring at the screen. If I'm so set on getting this over with, why not call him? Here's as good a place as any for a friendship break-up.

"Okay, Tyler. Okay. Press the button. Just do it, friend. Just do it. And stop talking to yourself. Claudia's going to see you and call the cops. Fuck." I stare at the screen, and I swear I'm about to hit *call* when *no signal* pops up.

No signal. I choke a laugh. Josh being Josh, he'd call it fate, or kismet, or karma. I hold the phone up like I'm scanning for alien life, but neither aliens nor the phone company are eager to make contact.

My chest is buzzing. I can't tell if it's relief, or the buildup of anxiety finally boiling over. There's nothing I can do now. Josh's call came through fine at the cabin. I can try again after lunch.

The bell on the door to Ziggy's jangles as I step inside. The interior is accented in pastel pink and baby blue, not just veering toward the kitschy side of nostalgia, but doing a cannonball into the centre of the pool. A matronly woman with perm-burned eighties curls is wiping down the glistening counter-top. The round, red-cushioned barstools are empty—all but one.

A Black woman around my age, maybe a little younger—say, her late twenties—pokes at a slab of quiche on a paper plate, staring into her meal's gelatinous surface while her mind surfs the stars. She's got a black leather jacket with metal studs on the shoulders, skin-tight leather pants to match, and dangling silver moons for earrings. Her natural hair's pulled up in a faux-hawk, and as I approach to get a closer look at the menu I glance sideways and catch a glimpse of Gothy winged eyeliner and white-painted nails with tips sharp enough to put somebody's eye out. She stares sidelong right back at me and looks me down and up again. She smirks, like I'm a catch.

The kind she throws back out to sea.

On the wall behind the counter is a large, gilt-framed portrait of Conrad Uphill. Black and white versions of the same image decorate the laminated placemats in front of every chair. In the portrait, he's wearing a cowboy hat and shades, smirking so a crack of teeth is visible. Picture an older Giancarlo Esposito making a face like he's about to take a shot at a nearby spittoon.

"What can I get for you, Ducky?" asks the waitress. She's smiling, but there's an edge to it.

The menu on the wall is one of those slatted boards where you slide the letters along. We have: " uiche" on one line, "q iche" on the next, "qui ," and even a "   he."

"Do you have anything that's not quiche?" It's possible she'll find my acerbic tone charming, but based on past experience, that won't be the case unless she's high. She does not look high.

"Brown soft drink."

"I don't like quiche."

Goth Girl snorts.

The waitress stares at me, smacking the red-striped washcloth onto the counter in a way that suggests she'd like to do the same to my face. Completely deadpan, she says: "Why are you here?"

"Honestly, at this point I genuinely have no idea." This was a bad move. Not just my quiche-based dining experience, but everything: taking the video seriously instead of as someone's fucked-up joke, the plane ride into the middle of a forest so dense it failed pre-school, coming to the island alone, hanging up on Josh instead of being an adult, thinking a town that smacks its mayor's face on restaurant placemats is a good place to vacation.

I force a smile, like that'll get me out of this, but the waitress isn't having it. She stalks away and disappears into the kitchen. On the wall behind where she was standing there's an old-timey metal sign that reads *Real Men Don't Eat Quiche.*

"I guess I'm a real man after all. Gepetto's going to have egg on his face."

A hand closes around my arm. The Goth girl slides off her stool. She's staring at me like murder beneath her thickly lined eyes. "Come on, Ben Whishaw. Let's find you some Real Man Food."

I'll state for the record that if I were played by anyone in a movie he'd be someone solidly straight—not because I'm homophobic or—well, whatever. No one's playing me in a movie. I'm not even playing anyone *else* in a movie despite my long-dashed theatre-school dreams, and well, yeah, I guess the straightness is up for debate.

"It's Tyler," I say, as I follow her out the door. She seems like the kind of person who'll keep calling me names if I don't correct her immediately.

"Tia." She smiles at me and heads across the parking lot. The back of her jacket has *Sisters of the Moon* written in Gothic cursive around an image of a foxglove in silver thread. She shrugs off the jacket and ties it around her waist, revealing a black tank. "You must be Virgie Kyle's son."

"Should I act surprised you know that?" In a small town, it's very possible Uphill's gossiped to all five residents that I was coming.

She glances at me over her shoulder. "Everyone knows about Virgie." She bends and picks up a stone, then pelts it real hard at a rusty mailbox at the end of a driveway. "The only Echo Islander whoever made it."

"My mom's from Edinburgh," I explain, "Scotland, not, you know, Nova Scotia or whatever."

A dog howls up the road, followed by a series of sharp, discordant yaps. The noise stops me, some primitive instinct rising to the surface and telling me I should walk in the opposite direction.

Tia snorts. She doesn't seem worried about the dogs, so I follow. There's sensible precaution and then there's tilting at windmills.

"Is there a kennel around here, or . . . ?"

"It's *or*," Tia answers, like it was one of two options.

We round the bend at the corner of Allenby and Rivers. I guess that makes the road with Ziggy's Allenby. Neither of them is a name on my mom's map, like the names were changed when Saint Serge's became Echo Island.

On Rivers Road, a pack of mutts is clustered on the lawn of one of the houses that backs onto the moat. I'm not scared, but I exercise a reasonable amount of caution and slow my stride.

"Are there a lot of feral dogs on your tiny island in the middle of the woods?" I ask.

"It's not *my* island. But yeah. It's kind of a thing." She reaches into her pocket and pulls out a rolled cigarette. She lights it with a match. She doesn't offer me one.

We're getting real close to the dogs, but Tia isn't even looking at them.

"What kind of *thing* involves feral dogs running around small towns and no one calls the pound? And how did they get here—did someone, like, sit down and decide they wanted to airlift in a bunch of strays? 'Oh, hey, Pete, yeah I'd like a hundred cute little puppies so I can let them loose on my island and watch them get rabies.'"

Tia puffs out a trail of smoke and coughs, brows raised. "You talk a lot."

"And you don't answer questions." God, I sound like fucking Josh. Tia's just a girl. She's not a suspect in the global conspiracy to keep the truth about Big Foot from the world.

She hands me her cigarette and I take it, though I quit five years ago. Her cheap black lipstick stains the rim. I take a puff and my exhaustion blows out with the first exhale.

"You looked like you wanted it," she says. "You owe me five bucks."

"For a cigarette?" I hand it back to her, not exactly Midas over here.

"It costs a lot to get things in—we only have two planes."

We pass the pack of dogs as they hurtle down the side of the house toward the moat and the forest. They didn't seem interested in us at all.

"So tell me about the dogs," I say. The stalker who e-mailed Josh about Echo Island mentioned dogs in the wood, but the e-mails were vague. We assumed TraughtDog01—some kind of pun on Naughty Dog, beloved developer of the Crash Bandicoot series?—was trying and failing to describe a canine cryptid.

The dogs zigzag behind the house, but their howling rings in my ear.

"Not much to tell," says Tia. She hands me the cigarette, watching my face. "You know about the Dog Days, right?"

"Some kind of pet show?"

She laughs and it lights up her face. She wiggles her fingers for the cigarette. "Give it here." She takes a puff, smirking. "It's a hunting festival on the 30th. We all take our rifles and hunt the feral dogs in the woods. I guess it's pretty fucked, from the outside."

It's beyond fucked, which must show on my face, because her smile fades. "What happens to all the dead dogs?"

She flicks her tongue over her bottom lip. "What did you think the surprise was in Colleen's Quiche Surprise?" She laughs again. "I'm fucking with you. We just burn them. Connie tried turning them into boots and exporting them, but it turns out no one wants dog-skin thigh-highs."

The vegan slash pet-owner in me is utterly horrified, and the curious cat is just as utterly fascinated. "So where did the dogs come from?"

"Just around, I guess. The founders probably brought them here and it got out of control."

There's so much wrong with that, so many questions I still have—like how the population never drops, and why anyone let their pets go feral when the island's so small, and who the founders are if it's not Uphill's family?—but then Tia stops in front of a second diner.

The Thunder Moon is basically a log cabin. Its sign is hand-painted, faded, and features a thick coating of literal grunge to add to the atmospheric grunge it's aiming for. The motorcycle out front is the cherry on the sundae. It's also the first vehicle I've seen.

I slip Mom's map out on a hunch, *and yeah*, it's one of the buildings with code underneath.

"So who flew you in?" Tia flicks her cigarette butt onto the asphalt parking lot and crushes it.

I tuck the map in my pocket and flash back to the flight. "Uh, Gary. No, Greg."

"Gord." She smiles. "Not great with names?"

"Great with names, bad with mornings."

"Besides Connie, Gord and Pam are the only ones with money around here. Pam gets us stuff off-island. Contraband music, cigs. If you've got cash, she'll help you out." Tia pushes open the door and The Thunder Moon hits me like a bolt of lightning: its stale cigarette smell, the earthiness of the beer and the wood and the sweat. The log walls, the wooden bar, the low lighting even in the middle of the day—it's charmingly homey. Somewhere I'd sit and drink with Josh—pals, buddies, bros.

The fact he's not here is an ache in my chest. He *should* be here, and my bones know it. I slide my phone out, glance at the screen.

Still no signal.

"Is that a tablet?" asks Tia.

I look up, put the phone away. "It's my cell?" There's no sign on her face that she's joking.

She shrugs and approaches the bar, practically bends in half leaning over the counter. "Geeeeeeene!" she calls. "I've got fresh blood for you. City boy, thinks he's funny, might be cute I don't know. You'll never find out if you don't get your ass out here and serve us. Okay, time's up, I'm stealing your beer!" Her boots plunk back onto the floor, and she strolls past the saloon gate. I hear her filling a glass with something, but I'm too busy taking in the rest of The Thunder Moon to notice what it is.

The same portrait of Conrad Uphill hangs on the wall and the same placemats grace the booths along the window. The diner extends back to the right of the bar, where there's a small, curtained stage.

"What's your poison, Kyle?" Tia's voice is lighter. She's really in her element here. She hollers back into the kitchen again: "Geeeeeene. Get the fuck out here. City Boy's hungry and he hates quiche."

"What the fuck, Tee? I'm taking a *shit*," someone—Gene, presumably—hollers back.

The walls are cluttered with photos in small frames, taxidermied deer, and stray antlers. There's an honest-to-god squirrel cut in half, with its backside and tail mounted on one frame and its front jutting from another. Someone's engraved *Mr. Nuts* in goofy letters underneath.

Tasteful.

I scan the photos for familiar faces—scratch that, for Mom. And I find her. A signed promotional photo from *Planet Zombie*, one of her early flicks. I reach for it.

Tia snaps her fingers. "*Kyle*. I said what's your poison?"

She's hovering at the counter. I dart a look at Mom, but my stomach growls. I can always ask Tia about the photo while we eat.

I walk over, scrolling the chalkboard behind her. "What's the 'monkshood medley'? I didn't know you were talking literal poison here."

Tia sighs, pouting at the sign. "Mostly grape juice. Wouldn't waste the change if I were you."

"It is *not* grape juice!" yells Gene from the belly of the beast.

"*Sorry*," says Tia, not sounding sorry at all.

"I'll have what you're having." I cock my chin at the beer.

Tia smiles. "Good choice. And cheap."

"Doesn't have to be cheap as long as it's cold. What do they have for food here?" There's no sign of a menu.

Tia gestures at the door behind the counter, where the kitchen must be. "Fries, nachos, border collie."

I give her a look. "I'm not the only comedian in town."

"You're the only *bad* comedian."

If the Josh call doesn't go well, maybe I should hit Tia up with pitches for new material. *Tee and Ty Crawl Bars, Tee Rakes Ty Over the Coals, Tee and Ty Ruin Alliteration for Normal People*.

Tia slides my beer over on a mat with Conrad Uphill on the base. His grin distorts through the liquid.

"Fries are fine." It's simple, hard to ruin kind of food, and I'm craving carbs. "So what did you mean earlier, about my mom being the only Islander who made it? Her picture's over there on the wall."

The kitchen doors swing open and a hulking troll of a man with carrot-orange hair and a black tank like Tia's heaves over to the bar. Gene's drying his hands on a towel that's carrying the weight of the entire hand sanitizer industry on its shoulders.

It's dirty, is what I'm getting at. I should probably rethink the fries.

"*Fuck* Arcadia to the sun, that was a shit." Gene slaps Tia playfully with the dirty towel, grinning.

"Gene?" She nods in my direction, eyes wide, clearly holding back a smile.

He holds out his hands to indicate the impressive girth of said shit. "It was *this*—"

"GENE." Tia shoves her hand out in my direction. "Meet City Boy. City Boy, meet Gene."

Gene jumps back against the chalk sign. It wobbles against the wall. From the expression of horror on his face, I must have blended into the haze of The Thunder Moon like a second Mr. Nuts.

"Oh my goodness," he says. "I thought you were joking, Tee." He slumps back down, but he's still tall and huge, and now that I look at him, he's wearing an earring like Tia's.

Probably a local craft fair around here or something. I should pick up something for Kayla. She's one of those people who gets feelings from stones. Put her and Josh in a room together and they start communing with ley lines.

Gene shoves out a paw. I want to pretend I didn't see it, as per the towel comment, but he's a big dopey-eyed basset hound and I just can't do it. I grab his hand. His shake could turn coal into diamonds.

"I'm Gene, uh. This is my restaurant—there's karaoke Wednesday and Thursday, live music Fridays." He reaches behind him and tears a poster from where it's been stapled to the wall. "There's a show tonight if you want. Echo Island's own Queen Cee doing her hit song, 'Umbrella,' and a lot of the classics."

I take the ripped poster. A glammy Black woman in a glittery purple bodice holding a striped parasol is posed at an angle. Beneath heels that could puncture a lung are the words *Queen Cee* with pastel pink hearts bubbling from the letters.

I smile and take the poster. "Tyler Kyle. City boy. I think I'm funny. I might be cute I don't know."

Tia rolls her eyes.

Gene winks at me. "You're all right."

It occurs to me that Tia's brought me to a gay bar. Maybe it's my lack of experience on this front, but it seems to me that there's some physical transformation that must happen when you realize this thing about yourself, and other . . . *possibly not straight people* sense it the way sharks do blood, and then they swarm around you and start biting off rainbow chunks—or taking you to meet other very nice and perfectly friendly *possibly not straight people* who want to say kind things to you and fumble around their bar.

Wow, I just described gaydar. How 2003.

"He wants some fries, Gene. Get on it." Tia's giving him that under the liner look she gave me at Ziggy's, so maybe I'm not as special as I thought.

Gene zips back into the kitchen, only to resurface, wave, then disappear.

"Don't worry, he's harmless," says Tia. "You're not really his type."

"He's in good company." I sit on the stool and lay the poster down.

Tia drums her ceramic-white nails against the counter, then grabs her beer. "Cheers."

I clink my glass against hers and take a sip. It's a pale ale. Fruity. It's not bad.

"So my mom." The thud of my glass against the counter punctuates the statement.

Tia straightens. "There's not much to say. She lived here for a while, I guess. Left. Came back."

"*Came back.*" As in, she was here. Really here. I chug back another drink. It's hard not to glare, but I do try. "When?"

Tia shakes her head, looking at the counter. "I don't know. I was a kid. She was a movie star, so the town made a big deal of it."

"Was it 2001?"

Gene chooses this moment to bustle in with a heaping basket of greasy fries. He lays it on the counter, but vanishes almost as quickly. I definitely look more intense than I meant to.

But Tia meets my gaze. "I don't know. Maybe." She purses her lips. "She didn't stay here long."

She's lying. I know she's lying and I can't think why except that she knows my mom better than she's saying, and maybe it's that Virgie Kyle really did want to disappear. Maybe she really is hiding, and Tia's protecting her. But if that's true, why did Tia ever admit she knew who I was? Why did Uphill invite me here?

"I don't believe you."

The door opens behind me, but I don't turn to look. Tia and I play don't blink, until finally a woman's voice calls out.

"Hey, Tee—this guy bothering you?"

Tia breaks our staring contest and smiles over my shoulder. She takes a last swig of her beer, then walks from around the counter to join her friend.

I turn around, and there's a skinny White woman with the same jacket as Tia's and a motorcycle helmet tucked beneath her arm. Her brown hair's pulled back in a messy ponytail.

Tia clasps the woman's hand and leans in for a kiss. "He's fine, Nor. Just an out-of-towner I was helping."

Nor's still staring like she might drag me outside and grind my face into the dirt.

I've never been great at self-preservation. "Please, give me something. I flew all the way here." I pause, let some of the hurt into my voice. "She's my mom. She was all I had."

For a moment, Tia looks like she might say something. Her forehead creases. Her lip twitches, pained. But then she shakes her head. "You seem like a nice guy, Tyler. You should get out of dodge before the big bad wolf eats you up."

The Echo Island Diary: Entry 2
Tyler Kyle Makes a Phone Call

July 12th, 2019: 8:00 PM

Here's a life lesson, viewers: if you want to not come off like a total jackass loser, don't awkwardly stand in an enclosed space curling a phone cord round your finger while telephonically vomiting your emotions into your best friend's voicemail as Cathy the receptionist pretends not to hear you while she reviews financial statements (what finances this place has is a mystery it'll be up to Josh and his new co-host to solve).

In the best Discovery Bang fanfiction, my replacement on the show is a pure little vixen called Brenda. She gets Josh in a way I never could, holds him close as he cries over my body that was just decapitated by the Chupacabra I was too stupid to believe in. Josh holds his Bren Bren tight, whispers in her ear sweet nothings and also the lyrics from "Frozen," which I really relate to because Elsa, like me, is all alone and no one understands her. No one but Josh. Brenda and Josh. OTP forever. The dream team. Something my phonecall makes it clear I'll never understand.

The phonecall:

Hey, Josh. It's Tyler (*obviously* it's Tyler). That was fucked earlier, and immature. I wasn't thinking straight. I shouldn't have snapped at you and we do need to talk about the show (Cathy watches me pace from beneath her glasses, I card my hand through hair I ought to cut, purse my full lips). We've been doing this a long time. Maybe too long (more pausing, like I'm auditioning for William Shatner's Days of Our Lives. I twine my finger round a stray curl). I don't think I want to anymore. Look. Fuck. I'm in love with you, Josh (**shut up, shut up, shut up**, I wish Tyler would just **shut up**. Cathy barely looks at him, shakes her head at his grade-school confession and the choked sound in his voice). It's not a joke for me. I need to step away. Just try and call back when you get this so we can hash it out. The rental's phone should work. If you leave a message, we can set up a time to talk. Or we can wait till I get back. Don't bother with Uphill. I think I need to do this alone. Talk soon.

Cathy smiled patiently at me when I handed her back the phone. Was I imagining things, or did she linger her attention on me a little? I'm no Brad Pitt, but given the right weather conditions and astrological convergences, I don't clean up bad. My shirt today's fitted in a way that makes me look reasonably impressive, I've got facial hair

that gives off grad school philosophy genius, and
my locks (though too long, and slipping annoy-
ingly into the brown orbs of my eyes) are the right
side of tousled at the moment, ♥**onyx-black**♥
and layered in a masculine cut that somehow
still screams I'm in touch with my feminine side.
I don't hold a candle to people like Josh, who
could give Steven Yeun a run for his money:
nerdy but cute. He's the aster to my disaster.
Genuine. I'm like a nasty snake, slinking through
the garden grass, ready to bite your ankles. I glis-
ten in the light, but my underbelly's caked in ~~drit~~
dirt. Something beautiful turned hideous as soon
as it opens its mouth.

Maybe I've always been a little fixated on myself. I
do spend a lot of time staring in the mirror. More
than most people do. More than seems normal.
But I don't think about me when I'm doing
it. That's the truly fucked part. The part you
don't admit to others, or even sometimes yourself. That when I slide my palm over my cheek,
my forehead, my eyes, it's Josh I'm dreaming of.
It's Josh's face, Josh's skin. Is he as soft as me, is
he softer? What would it feel like to wear him like
a nice tight Josh onesie?

Maybe I've always secretly wanted what Josh has,
like my body could not just sit beside his, always,
but like I could fold into him, flesh to flesh. And
whatever that thing is—this Brundlefly fusion of
us that's stuck on the other side of the glass—it
could be reached if I had the guts to punch out
that mirror and get my paws a little bloody.

Mirror mirror on the wall, who's the fairest of them all?

Maybe Echo Island's getting to me.

It'd be cleaner if Josh never took me up on the call. I wouldn't have to hear about him until five years down the line when his face pops up on a recommended video, where he's flirting with some beautiful new stranger with strawberry blond hair. He'll speak, and she'll speak, their voices forming a harmony so perfect it *silences*.

After the call I headed back to my room, slumped down on the bed, and started writing.

Or did I? Maybe Tyler Kyle didn't sit down to write at all. Maybe this isn't Tyler writing. Maybe Tyler shouldn't have forgotten about the stalker who sent that e-mail.

Or maybe I'm bullshitting

Is it my words you're reading now, viewers?

Did I make it?

3

First–Rate Sorcerer

When I can't get through to Josh, I wait in my room, scrolling through our old videos, *this* close to deleting them because holding on feels unhealthy. It's so easy to look back on even the unused footage and trace the moments that made a pattern in my head: stray words from Josh that I interpreted as flirting, casual remarks meant not for me, but for the viewers we both knew on some level would eat that shit up. That Hallowe'en episode when we dressed as Dracula and Mina Harker from the Coppola adaptation—not my idea.

As I'm idling through the folders, I hover over an app Josh installed on my phone last Christmas–one of those novelty gifts he likes. It's a tiny obnoxious icon of his face with a speech-bubble that reads *Joshbot*—some kind of soundboarding app that responds to my speech. I haven't opened it since the day he gave it to me at that Christmas party. All it said back then was, "Tyler, you're an asshole."

So, accurate.

I fall asleep waiting for Josh's call. When I wake up, the air is humid, the window is dark, and crickets are fiddling like the devil's come down to Echo Island.

I check my watch—still two hours shy of the concert Gene mentioned, but I make the executive decision to stop waiting and head to The Moon.

When I arrive, Gene's sitting at one of the tables near the stage in the back, snapping his fingers while Tia and Nor karaoke their off-key hearts out to "We Go Together" from *Grease.*

There's something wholesome about the moment, until Nor hits a high note and my ear drums burst.

I take a seat beside Gene. He turns to me and smiles, slaps my shoulder. "You made it."

I smile back—it's actually impossible not to. I'm pretty sure it's medically *dangerous* not to. "How could I miss Sandy and Danny as performed by Bob Dylan on coke?"

Gene's smile disappears, his expression grave—*haunted* actually. Like Josh when he sees a raccoon.

"You have to stop talking about that," says Gene.

I furrow my brow, a piercing belt from Tia shooting through me like the vibrations from a dentist's drill. "Talking about what?"

Gene darts a look at the stage, then in a hiss says, "*Bob Dylan.*"

"I've only mentioned Bob Dylan né Zimmerman twice, and one of those times is right now."

Gene smooths his hand over his face like it's putty he can mold into a shape that doesn't have to deal with me. "We don't talk about things from the old world here. Everything in Arcadia is new, made for us."

Made for them?

Tia and Nor's singing degenerates into laughter as they fall into each other. Nor grabs Tia's shoulders and kisses her forehead, and for an instant I'm on set, watching Mom discreetly slip her fingers through those of whatever crewmember she's designated Girlfriend of the Week.

I swallow.

"Is that something Conrad Uphill tells you to say?" I ask.

Gene smiles. "Oh no, not at all. It's part of our culture."

"Echo Island culture or Saint Serge's?"

Gene shrugs. "Saint Serge's is long gone—some fundy retreat that ran out of cash and disbanded." He slaps the table. "Why don't I get us a refill before people start arriving and run me off my feet?"

Fundies, huh? I stare at the names—not just *Serge*, but the road names the current islanders changed: Evening Light Avenue, Saint Sebastian Street.

The song on the karaoke machine changes, but the Sisters of the Moon are laughing too hard to sing. Pretty sure a little lady called Mary Jane is up there enhancing the melody.

"You need any help?" I ask Gene. It seems weird that he wouldn't have anyone working with him, especially if he's expecting a crowd.

But Gene points at the stage and gets up. "Why don't you relax? Have some fun with the girls. You look like you need it."

I smirk. "I don't think they want to play this game with me."

Tia hops off the stage. "Big words, City Boy."

"Fighting words," says Nor. If I hadn't heard her get slaughtered by the *Grease* soundtrack, I might be intimidated. She glowers worse than Tia, like she needs to throw her weight around near me, like I'm gonna piss on her lawn and steal her woman, even though it's devastatingly obvious how into her Tia is.

She looks at her the way Josh always seemed to be looking at me.

Well, maybe I'm not the best judge of this stuff.

If Josh does show up, he's going to think I did all this on purpose. Brought him to this big gay bar on this isolated getaway island. And he'll be thinking how this is where I belong, how I've found my place. And it'll be this cheap, sad story, and it'll be all over the internet—my corner of it anyway—and I'll get to choose between being a poster boy for living your truth or an asshole for wanting any kind of privacy, and Josh can be the supportive no-homo friend who doesn't know what his BFF is going through but *he'll always be there to listen*. And I can be mourned, in one way or another. And worse, I can be fitted into a box, and it'll be the kind you fold shut and shelve out of sight.

What I'm feeling, it's definitely some kind of shame, and then on top of that is the shame of feeling ashamed for my shame. A big ol' shame casserole with shit icing.

Tia grabs my hand and pulls me off the chair. "Come on, I thought you were going to kick our asses, not sit there like a sad sundae."

I let her drag me to the stage as Gene returns with drinks. He sets a beer on the stage and Nor jumps off to grab it.

Gene slaps her hand. "*Hey.* That's for Tyler."

Nor holds both palms up, still gripping the mic. She shoves it at my chest. "How's he going to drink while he's wailing? Fuck it, I'm getting shots."

As Nor stomps off, Tia gives my sleeve a tug. "Sorry my girlfriend's a cunt. She doesn't play well with strangers."

"I heard that!" Nor calls from the bar.

"Tyler's not a stranger," says Gene. He plunks himself back down in his chair. "He's family."

Tia looks me up and down. She laughs. "*Distant* family."

"Because of my mom, right?" Virgie Kyle's photo *is* on Gene's wall. This place meant something to her.

But they both go quiet. Tia's gaze is boring into Gene's. It's a stare that says *I'll set you on fire and dance on the ashes if you speak.*

Gene clears his throat, drums his fingers against his beer glass. He takes a long swig and sets it down. "You're one of us. That's all. This place is home to anyone who wants it to be, and that means you."

"Gooble gobble, gooble gobble," I mutter into my drink, though to be honest, if there's anywhere I feel truly at home it's with fellow freaks.

Theatre school was a bubble world of weird. The place where suddenly everything *off* about me was not only desirable but needed to be louder, bigger, faster, faker. YouTube magnified all of that.

Not that I'm the worst by a long shot, but there's something that dies in the brain—or maybe *clicks on*, is a better way to put it—when you commit wholeheartedly to the production of yourself as a commodity. You don't realize you're doing it at first, and you can convince yourself it's only an extension of your stage performance, or your auditions, but it picks you apart in dangerously specific ways.

I slide my phone out of my pocket.

"He's a saa-aa-aad Sunday," Tia sings, off-key, obviously. *"He wishes it was Monday."*

"Sorry. My brain's . . . . " I twirl my finger beside my head to let her know it's not the company. I'm just cuckoo for cocoa puffs. "I've got some friends I'm hoping to hear from. Our last conversation was a bit rough."

Josh and Kayla—the only stable faces in a sea of evil exes and booty calls.

Gene smiles with a tenderness that has its own gravitational pull. "Never leave things unsaid, and never say things you'll regret."

I want to agree, but I can't. "I'm the kind of person who needs to learn to say significantly less."

Tia smirks at me. "Not here. Say away."

I find it hard to believe that when she's barely answered any of my questions, and the answers she has given are probably horseshit. But maybe there are avenues of investigation she'll be more open to. There's mine and Josh's stalker, for one—whoever it was that sent those e-mails and posted Mom's video. TraughtDog01.

"Does 'Traught Dog' mean anything to you?"

Tia looks clueless. "Trot? Like a horse?"

"Forget it."

Gene takes another long chug, finishing the pint. "We have a dog problem around here."

"It's the name of this person who told me I could learn about my mom on the island." Well, that's more or less what happened. The video was clearly meant to get me and Josh here, anyway. I wonder what they'd have done if I'd replied with, "Sorry, Virgie's a complete deadbeat and I couldn't give two shits."

But I didn't do that, and even if I had, you can bet Josh wouldn't. Of the two of us, he's the only investigator. Kayla makes our footage look pretty, and I—I really just stand around snarking.

"She did come here," Gene edges, a little too carefully.

"Be careful," Tia adds. "Not everyone here plays nice."

It's like she knows our stalker is, well, a stalker. "As in?" I ask.

She shrugs. "You might not have noticed, being an outsider, but this place is pretty isolated."

I roll my eyes. "Oh really, do tell."

She taps the stage. "Stick with the Sisters of the Moon and we'll see you through, that's all I'm saying. We don't do anyone dirty."

I'm about as easy to bait with banter as the fabled *banter-snatch* of . . . Okay, I'll stop. Shun me in my frumiousness. "What do I have to do to become a Sister of the Moon?"

Nor's already on her way back, balancing a platter of a dozen shots. "You have to beat us at karaoke." As she passes Gene, he grabs a shot glass. She strides up to me and Tia and holds them out.

I take one, hoping it inches me closer to Nor's good side—assuming she has one of those.

"I don't remember that rule," says Tia.

But why the hell not. Why not have fun and why not also butter them up.

"Okay," I say. "So how are we doing this? Two against one? And who's judging?"

Tia and Nor yell out "*Gene*" and "*Not Gene*" at the same time.

"He's the only one not participating," says Tia.

"Yeah, and all City Boy has to do is take off his shirt and he wins," Nor snaps.

Gene's every shade of red, and staring into his shot like it's a well he can dive into. He bends over and grabs some garbage, presumably to hide his blush.

God, poor Gene.

I hold out my palms. "Hey, no need to slander the man pouring the free drinks. I'm completely confident in my ability to win on my own merits." I move to help Gene pick up the debris.

It's a crumpled draft of a novel or poem.

Nor grins. "So confident I get to judge?"

I give a little shrug, wink. "Exactly that amount of confident." I smooth out the paper.

Echo Island Diary – Entry 2

—but like I could fold into him, flesh to flesh. And whatever that thing is—this Brundlefly fusion of us that's stuck on the other side of the glass—it would be reached if I had the guts to punch out that mirror—

Scratch the novel thought—looks like someone's journal. Gene grabs it out of my hand, so maybe it's his.

Tia elbows Nor in the side. "We get to pick the songs."

"I pick my songs."

Normally I'd find the suggestion hilarious, but I don't want to end up singing anything about love. Or cults. Or parents.

I'm having a sensitive moment.

The door to The Moon swings open and a middle-aged couple enter, holding hands. Gene twists in his seat, waves, and gets up. Soon they're yammering back and forth with so much local specificity it may as well be another language. Gene scoots to the bar, ignoring us completely.

Gene the Machine indeed.

"He really doesn't need help?" I ask Tia.

"One man army," Nor confirms. "And he hates it when people touch his grills."

Tia smiles at me. "It's true. He's a big baby anytime one of us suggests we help him cook. He keeps a lock on the freezer and everything."

Now that is weird.

I'm wearing my emotions on my face again, because Nor holds out her hand, palm downwards, as though to calm my troubled mind.

"That's cause of that time Ru got shut inside," she says. "He's super paranoid about it now."

They go quiet, share a look like they got caught talking about Bob Dylan past curfew.

"So how about this contest?" I hold up my shot glass and Tia and Nor clink theirs against mine. We sling them back and Tia let's out a *woo!*

"I'm going to kick your fucking ass, City Boy." Like Nor pre-planned it, she reaches smoothly inside her jacket pocket, pulls out a pair of black 90s shades, and slides them on.

Everything she does seems so seamlessly cool that I'm relieved it comes off as at least a little affected. Tia plucks the glasses off, rolls her eyes, and tucks the shades onto the closest inch of bar counter—out of reach.

As even more patrons shuffle in, I leap on stage. I reach down and grab a second shot glass and drink, ready for some theatrics. "Okay, let's see what we have. If Gene won't let us help at the bar, we can at least provide some entertainment."

Well, *I* can provide some entertainment.

On the assumption that Josh might walk in any second, I avoid "YMCA."

As soon as I think it, it's hard not to let that thought overwhelm me, like maybe he will walk through the door—that next patron, no, the next. And what? He'll hear Tyler Kyle singing "Ain't No Mountain High Enough" and my voice will hypnotize him with some ineffable magnetic quality, and he'll be compelled to reveal that, yeah, actually, he always loved me after all, and we'll solve the mystery of Virgie Kyle, escape the sinister clutches of our stalker, and everything will be fine like it hasn't been in so very, very long?

Right.

Scrolling through most of the options reveals a long list of titles with only two names next to them: V. Kyle and Queen Cee.

I wasn't expecting a clue on the karaoke machine, but I'm guessing that "V" doesn't stand for Vernon. As far as I know, my mom didn't sing any songs—well, she didn't *write* any songs, anyway. But then again, apparently she was the mastermind behind "Dancing Queen," so what do I know?

A few tracks have generic enough titles that it's impossible to know what they are. I reject all the ones my mom supposedly wrote, and between that and my moratorium on anything with love in the title, I'm stuck with a very short list.

I select Queen Cee's "Ironic," and it doesn't disappoint, as Montréal's own Alanis starts up, sans vocals.

Here's the thing about me. I may not be quite what my mom was, but if Virgie was a triple threat, I'm still a double. And after more than a few musical leads in theatre school, I know I'm—if not hot shit—then way past tepid. The other thing I should note is, no matter how much I hate being scrutinized, there's a substantial part of me that's a glutton for attention—no surprise there, I'm sure. Put me on stage and it's hard to get me off. Put me on camera and I'm insufferable.

I start singing without any introduction, let Tia and Nor drown in the knowledge of their own defeat as soon as I possibly can. I want them to have no fucking hope. I want them to regret their life choices immediately. I want to not feel like shit for five minutes, and yeah, if Josh and Kayla should happen to stroll through those doors, I want to be knocking it not just out of the park but off the fucking island.

So I'm prepared for Tia and Nor's stares when I hit that chorus, but what I'm not expecting is the way the whole bar goes fucking silent. I close my eyes, open them, thinking it was a trick of the light, but even Gene is bent round the bar, frozen where he stands as foamy beer runs down his hands to gather on the floor.

Hypnotized wasn't too far off.

And the swell in my guts—this high—is something I haven't felt since I graduated, so even though the intensity of the way they're all staring should probably freak me out, I milk every minute till those last soft notes end the song.

The atmosphere in the bar is tense. The lighting's low, sultry, but considering how everyone's eyes are dilated, it's still too bright. The roundness of their stares sends a shiver down my spine. Too big. Too bright. Too full of hunger.

The world's turned luminescent, iridescent—every *escent* I can summon. It's beautiful in the way being drunk is beautiful when your hangover starts while you're still several shots away from sober.

So, not beautiful at all.

The lights in the bar cast their mirror images into the eyes of the audience: a dozen moons reflected in bowls of water. Everyone and everything is stillness and silence—a bated breath given physical form.

The next song auto-plays, and the bar is full of sound—not just the music from the karaoke machine, but clinking glasses, laughter, cheers, and creaking chairs.

Did I miss something?

My fingers are sweaty around the mic, like I've been holding it a long time. It's only been minutes.

Hasn't it?

Panic floods me—I've blacked out, or someone's spiked my drink, or–

I don't know what could have happened. I don't know what that rush of euphoria was while I sang. Every sinew in me is screaming to have it back.

It's got to be exhaustion. The brain does backflips at the most unexpected little spikes or dips in this or that chemical. And I know I'm pushing myself, not only with this trip, but I'm pushing myself around, the way Josh tells me not to.

Everything will be fine.

"Tia?" I look down at where she and Nor were sitting, and, thank fuck, they're still there.

Tia has her arm around Nor's shoulder. A tear slides down her cheek. She doesn't even try to wipe it away.

"Is she okay?" I ask Tia.

Tia turns to Nor, smiles, and kisses the tear away. "Yeah." She looks up at me. "Sing another, okay? That was good."

The compliment isn't exactly comforting, but I pick something. "Crazy," which should be Seal, or Britney Spears, but is apparently another Queen Cee hit, blasts from the speakers.

This time when I start, everyone cheers. The tables seem fuller, the voices louder. A couple of patrons sway back and forth, that same glassy look in their eyes, but most of the others get raucous, pushing against each other, raising their arms, clawing the air.

Nor's not the only one crying—not the only one crying to Britney fucking Spears.

I guess I win the contest?

My head spins. I'm drunker than I thought. I'm riding a wave of . . . it feels like the vibrations of the earth, like soil between my toes, like the shivers of trees: barely felt but ever-present. The environment's listening to me, and it's singing back.

I feel good. I've never felt so good. Adrenaline's pumping through me. The song ends and then it's another and another. My voice is raw as nails. I feed it with another couple shots. I could keep doing this all night. I could do this forever.

My brain is on fire.

In the audience, lights dance in blank eyes. Those same lights are in my eyes, I can feel it. That thought again, buzzing like a fly I can't swat: did someone slip something in my drink?

And then a V. Kyle song starts. "Knowing Me, Knowing You." And I stop, and the miasma of feeling that shuddered through me vanishes.

I want it back, and so do they. They're staring, screaming, waving arms, clawing. Tia and Nor smash their lips together, bodies pressed against the stage.

"You want me to sing something else?" I yell into the mic. I can't stop grinning.

"*Sing*, fucker," says Nor, before burying her face in Tia's again.

Tired of retreading pop tunes, I plug in my phone and select the practice audio I used during my rehearsals for *Chicago*. I hit *play* on "Razzle Dazzle."

And I sing.

Here I am in my moment, maybe not a first-rate sorcerer, but a second-rate liar, a failure not only as an actor, but as a small-time YouTube host, as a best friend, as the only member of Virginia Kyle's family seriously investigating her disappearance, as a professional asshole.

And The Thunder Moon drinks up every syllable like liquid diamond.

The Thunder Moon drinks up every syllable until the music cuts off near the end of the song, and suddenly "Umbrella" by Rihanna is playing from every speaker inside—and seemingly some *outside*—Gene's fine establishment.

The door to The Moon slams open so hard it bounces. Standing in the centre of the entrance is a drag queen in six-inch glittery purple heels; a purple boa; a top-hat; and a sequined, corseted Bo-Peep gown. Queen Cee stomps into the bar and the crowd parts for her like the waves before Moses. She swipes a beglittered cane in front of her.

And tells me I can stand under her umbrella

ella
ella.

4

CONTROL

The tables move out of Queen Cee's way like it was chore-ographed, and she hiplets her way toward the stage. Every movement is perfectly synchronized to the beat, every syllable is matched to the snap of heel or hip or cane. Her voice resonates like a solar flare.

Listeners roll the karaoke equipment out of the Queen's way and I back up. I'm very ready to disappear behind the curtain at the rear of the small stage.

But she's not singing to the other bar patrons; she's singing to me.

Queen Cee's brown eyes shimmer with a light that dances in the eyes of everyone in the room. The air is buzzing like the sound of insect wings magnified a thousand decibels, and the haze that clouds the bar is the colour out of space, almost purple, to match the Queen's gown. It's a wave that rolls over me, a heady perfume thick as a hot-boxed bathroom.

As she reaches the centre of the room and hits the bridge of the song, she sets her cane aside so that it's standing upright as though by magic. She unbuttons the corset-gown, drops into a crouch, clicks her thighs together as she strips down. She emerges from the carcass of the purple dress as though from a cocoon, black-leather-clad, with the boning of her Bo-peep skirt still attached. When she pops out of the crouch, she swivels the cane in front of her and unclasps the skirt, hooking it into the cane so that it forms *an umbrella*.

Tia and Nor are dancing to the side of the stage while Nor balances the tray of shots. As the Queen passes she takes the platter, sashaying up the stairs to the stage. She holds the tray out to me.

I smile. I take a shot.

Queen Cee hands the tray to someone in the audience.

She's singing up close, stepping around me, dragging her talon of a fingernail across my chest, my arm, my back. It's undeniably sexual, a frisson that tides across the peaks and valleys of my skin. From behind me, she reaches for the mic I'm clutching in my sweaty palm and presses it against my shirt.

Her voice is loud in my ear. It's a nice voice, and she's got a nice body, a nice face, oddly beautiful make-up. She's clearly older than me, maybe her fifties? Done up like a lady, it's hard to be sure.

My smile all but tumbles out of me, like he's his own man with his own needs and what he needs is to make Queen Cee happy.

"Sing," she mouths, between words, and it's impossible not to obey.

I add my voice to hers, and for a moment that's almost too painful to bear, it's like we're not two voices, but one. The sound shears barber-shop-close to the skin—the *snikt* of hairs mowed down like grass, the feel of insects tiptoeing across your wilderness, a needle prick, a loose tooth worried in the gum.

And I'm not just inside it, I *am* it. I am the machine. The instrument. The song.

She gives my shoulder a playful shove and I sense that I'm to face the audience. We're here for them after all.

Echo Islanders crowd the bar so tight they form a mushroom cap outside the door.

When the song ends, the audience erupts in half a pack of wolf howls.

I scan for Tia, Nor, and Gene, but Tia and Nor are completely out of it and Gene's vanished round the side of the bar. But

I do glimpse the receptionist from White Sails headbanging to the now non-existent music like the world's grungiest Karen.

It's none of them that grabs me though.

A beautiful blonde hugs the wall like she's hoping to phase into it if only her tight red dress will let her. She's staring at me with something I'm hard-pressed to call anything but hunger, like she's still caught in the hangover of the song, only when she realizes I'm staring back she buries her face behind her raised palm and turns away. The push-pull of bodies swallows her.

Queen Cee reaches her arm around me, squeezing me against her side. She'd be taller than me even without the heels, and those put her over me by a full foot.

"Another for the road, Sweet Pea?" Her voice is artificially high and sugary sweet.

It takes me a moment to realize she means another song. And I want to. I want to so bad.

"My throat's kind of sore."

There's a flicker of disappointment past her fake lashes. She masks it well, bends down all dainty-like, and pinches another shot glass between her pastel purple claws.

"We can't have that now, can we, Sugar?" She hands me the shot, then slides her hand around the side of my neck and down the front.

I can't stop looking in her eyes, and for a moment panic sputters in my chest, a brief spike of fear alongside the anesthetizing warmth of the alcohol and the fog of the music and the high of the crowd's love.

Something's wrong, it says, but no—no, how could anything be wrong? We're singing Queen Cee's songs together. We're safe in the glow of The Moon.

So I drink my medicine.

I close and open my eyes as another song starts—it has a familiar little intro—could it be another of Queen Cee's tracks? Did I hear it on the island?

My eyelids open to the sight of the Queen drinking a shot of her own. Then she leans forward, kisses her mouth to mine, parts my lips with her tongue, spilling liquor against my teeth and down my throat. It fizzes in my mouth. I swallow fast, terrified I'll choke or spit or embarrass myself in some other way.

I don't.

Hot and bothered, I kiss her back. My ears and brain are buzzing. The air is buzzing. Her hands are all over me, just like, just like—I can't remember. There's someone I should remember.

Her lipstick tastes like raspberries.

"*Tyler, you're an asshole,*" blares Josh's voice over every speaker in the bar, cutting into the music.

I snap away.

Josh. Josh's stupid app on my phone, and my phone plugged into the speakers still, and Queen Cee staring at me in confusion.

All I can do is stare back as the instrumental beat of "Baby One More Time . . ." plays in the background. The crowd is looking at me not with adoration, but with hate.

I can't find Tia and Nor in the crowd. I don't recognize anyone.

I ruined it.

The spark of panic I thought I'd smothered blossoms into a flame and I mutter "Sorry," while backtracking to the speaker. I snap my phone free and—without knowing where it'll take me—flee offstage past the curtain.

The cramped storage area behind the stage is full of ladders, lights, props, and a dad's worth of broken electronics.

I stop to fumble with Josh's stupid app.

Fuck, that was embarrassing. I'm not even sure what part of *that* I mean. Was it the way I got so into the karaoke? Was it kissing Queen Cee? Was it Joshbot and the scathing looks from literally every person on the island? It's like I ran over their collective puppies.

There's a door to what I assume is outside and I shove it open, still messing with the fucking app, still drunk.

Someone must have slipped something in my drink. Otherwise, none of this makes sense. And that means Nor, or Gene, or . . . fuck, it could've been anyone. Nor's tray of shots was sitting wide open for anyone to mess with. There was that fizzy feeling in my mouth when Queen Cee kissed me, but no, I felt off way before she showed up.

The cool night air sobers me up enough that I'm able to lean against the brick wall outside the bar and close Joshbot.

Josh's obscene grin disappears from the centre of the phone and I shove it into my pocket. I hang my head against the wall and close my eyes to stop the alley from spinning.

I could really go for one of Tia's five-dollar cigarettes. Where's a tone-deaf lesbian biker when you need her?

It should be a matter of catching my breath, assessing the situation with a clear head. This mire I'm stuck in is only temporary.

I take inventory, thinking if I lay it all out it won't seem so insurmountable.

1. Someone's drugged me. Which, well, that fucking sucks, but at least nothing really bad happened, and whatever else Joshbot did, he snapped me out of it. I just need to return to my cabin, lock the door, and go to the cops come morning.

2. Mom. So my mom might be here. Look for her, investigate, keep my eyes out for a stalker with an evil twisty mustache. I know Virgie Kyle came here and that's something.

3. Me and Josh are over. Move on and suck it up. If I'm alone, I need to either make a fucking friend or get used to it. No one's alone forever.

The door clicks open.

"You all right, Sugar?"

I breathe in, out, in, out. I open my eyes. "Just overheated."

Queen Cee's face is all concern, though her big bright eyeshadow is working overtime to try to disguise it. She walks right up to me, so we're not even a foot apart, facing each other. She raises her hand, brushes a curl out of my face. She smells like makeup and sweat. It's the smell of backstage, of theatre school.

"You've got quite a set of pipes." She smiles. "Sure you're okay? Got anyone I can call? What about that friend on your phone?"

I kiss her.

She falls into it immediately, closing the narrow gap between us, running her hand up my shirt and pressing me against the wall. I grip her round the waist, feel the hardness of her back, the man beneath the padding. I find her cock as she unzips my fly.

I don't know what she wants, really, apart from me in a vague sort of way. It's enough. It's all that matters. It feels good to be wanted.

But I've never fucked a man, never been fucked by one. I'm drunk out of my mind, but I'm still smart enough to know that several shots past passing a breathalyzer, behind a bar against a brick wall with no lube and no clue and with a complete stranger is not an ideal first time.

So I push her hip, nudging her till she gets what I'm doing and reverses our positions. She leans against the wall.

I get on my knees and shove her cock in my mouth.

Any worry I wouldn't still want this disappears as she fills my mouth: thick, and hard, and warm.

She grips my hair, scrapes her nails gently across my scalp. She moans as I lick my tongue along the base of her, wobbles on her heels as I drink up her sweat. The taste of skin is almost sour in my mouth, mingling with the raspberry flavour of her lips and the sting of the shots. I pull back, working the head, my brain alternating between thinking nothing at all, and thinking in encyclopedic detail about all the things my exes did to me that I liked. I stroke her balls with one hand, left hand palm-down-wards against the dirty ground, gravel and dirt buried in my skin, digging into my knees.

I don't care. I don't fucking care about anything.

I suck her like I'm starving, and she swells and tenses in my mouth, and there's something powerful about knowing that's all me, that I'm in control.

I'm so in control.

She grips my hair, groans.

A recording of Gowan's "Strange Animal," starts to play inside the bar, but the voice is all Queen Cee.

From the open side of the alley a woman gasps, and I turn enough to see the pretty blonde from the audience standing there, wide-eyed beneath the glow of a blinking streetlamp, her hand covering her mouth in shock.

Queen Cee cums in my mouth and I—well I hadn't thought too much about that part, which was possibly a mistake.

Especially when I try to swallow, gag, and puke all over her. Fuck.

I slide back on my ass, wiping bodily excretions off my mouth. "God—uh." I can't look at her, and from how she's standing there, skirt still clutched in one hand, her vomit-covered junk hanging out, she's also at a loss.

"Fuck, I'm sorry. I'll get something to–to clean you up." Tongue tied, and all it took was a back-alley blow-job. That's one way to get me to shut up, I guess.

I scramble to my feet, very conscious of the gravel buried in my palms, the dirt staining my jeans, the woman watching all this from the mouth of the alley.

This was, I'm realizing, a poor life choice.

Queen Cee lets out an awkward chuckle. She grabs an old-fashioned handkerchief from her purse and wipes herself off, then hands me another.

I dab at my mouth, brush off my knees.

She pats my cheek. "Don't worry about it, Sugar." She pushes herself off the wall, snaps the straps of her bra, then leans down and kisses me.

I glance at the alley entrance, but the blonde's vanished.

Queen Cee clucks her tongue. "She's no one you need to worry about. Got more lip than sense."

What's that supposed to mean? It's not like the woman said anything—she just looked embarrassed and surprised which, considering, is about the best I could hope for.

I wave my hand at her crotch. "Are you sure you don't—"

Queen Cee locks eyes with me, smiling. "Such a polite young man. But no, Sweet Pea, I'm fine."

I step away from her, my arms shaking a little, the cold night air grabbing me. "Then I'd better head home."

I snap round and march out of that alley like the rabid dogs of Echo Island are hot on my tail.

5

WHAT MUSIC THEY MAKE

It's almost pitch black, with only pockets of light where a scarcity of working streetlamps spotlight the cracked road. Wind gently bows the tops of the firs, and the sound of the tree trunks is like the creaking of an ancient ship on a calm sea. If you're gonna run away, it's a beautiful place to run to.

I've never minded the dark, not like Josh. Night is special. It smells different, like if *cool* had a scent.

It's so quiet that when I pass the house of the woman I named Claudia, her open door swinging back and forth has the resonance of a thunderclap.

I stop in the middle of the road, watching it thud against its jamb. As I approach, patchwork lawn crunches beneath my sneakers.

What if she left the door like that on purpose? What if she turns the corner and I freak her the fuck out?

"Hello?" I holler.

No answer.

I turn around . . . and stop.

Claudia's all the way at the end of the road, walking toward the moat and the forest in a flimsy white nightgown, alone and ploughing toward the water and the woods beyond.

I've never been scared of demons, or aliens, or cryptids of any kind, but those hidden roots'll do a number on you, especially if you're as out of it as our sleepwalker.

So I suck it up and run after her. The water should wake her once she hits it, but what if it doesn't and then not only am I the asshole who killed Discovery Bang for Josh and all our fans, I'm the human excrement who watched a woman drown herself?

I run for the bank.

Claudia nearly trips as her skin makes contact with the water—believe me, I can tell. You know that feeling, like someone's wound an ice-hot wire between where your skin is above and below the water and your torso might actually slide off your bottom half, and your balls retreat so far it's like they're soldiers in Napoleon's army and winter's just hit Moscow and oh god you're all destined to become tragic human-cannibal popsicles—sorry, history nerd.

She shudders *like that*, and even though I'm winded I keep going because fuck if something was ever wrong this is it. She's either so asleep she doesn't notice, or so depressed she doesn't care, and neither is a state in which you go wandering in the forest alone.

For a second she's gone, but then she's up and walking again, striding unevenly into the forest as her *probably*-bare feet tread on roots and rocks and those rigid spikes of grass that are almost as bad as Legos.

I've spent a lot of time in the forest.

I dart a look at The Moon. I could race back, grab help, but it only takes minutes for someone to get lost in the woods. I'm her best shot.

I reach the moat, but the blackness between the trees has swallowed her whole. Or maybe it hasn't, and it's just that I can't see shit.

My sneakers wobble atop the peak of the mound before the dip leading to the moat, and I reach for my phone for the flashlight function. The sudden glare is blinding.

"*Welcome to Joshbot, Tyler Kyle. Your one-stop shop for not being a douchebag misanthropist—*"

"It's *misanthrope*, actually," I blurt without thinking, because—okay, at this point if you're lost on the fact that I blurt things without thinking, there's no hope for you.

After I've white-mansplained Joshbot, I flick past the app to the settings, hit the flashlight, and immediately the black water of the moat churns in front of me like it's filled with anthropophageous eels.

Anthropophageous is man-eating, for those who hate search engines and also don't want to be spanked on the OnlyFans.

The water looks deep, but then it's night. A sixty or seventy-year-old sleepwalker just waded across and was fine. I'm an able-bodied, thirty-year-old man. I can handle it.

I skid on my way down the small slope, then charge right in, because again, no self-preservation.

"*Uh, Ty, are you dead? You haven't said anything in half a minute.*"

Joshbot's still on, but my balls are chilling like the Grande Armée, and I'm fighting to hold onto the phone. The waist-high water has sucked in all the sunlight summer had to offer and it's still frigid.

"*Ty? I can't hear you. Ty?*"

I flash the light across the trees ahead of me. Its yellow-white beam doesn't illuminate much beyond the bank. There's no sign of Claudia. The creak of the trees is still the only sound. Maybe I should be making *more* noise, so she hears me. I amp up the volume on Joshbot, so next time he—it—speaks, it might wake Claudia.

The base of the moat is soft and squishy beneath my sneakers. As I push against the water, reaching the midway point, large, sharp rocks nick my shoes.

"*Earth to Tyler?*" prods Joshbot's tinny voice.

Maybe I should drop the phone in the water.

"I'm fine," I say, because that might shut him up. Only I don't want him to shut up. I need him to talk. "Uhhhh. Ogopogo is bullshit and all the witnesses were drunks or evil capitalists."

I can sense its motors chugging.

"Where's your joy? You have absolutely no magic in your life, Tyler. It must feel awful being you. Seriously."

I build up a little speed, skipping and floating toward the shore. Getting up the other side of the slope is a scramble.

If I thought it was dark on the island, if I thought it was dark*er* near the shore, then it's dark*est* in the woods. Full on Blair Witch, with branches, and pinecones, and needles all fighting for their chance to scratch me.

I shove the branches away, sucking back the sting when they slap my face. After marching a few feet, it's clear this is a hopeless cause. The balsams and spruce are too dense, and Claudia's gone too far for me to find her by bulldozing through. Better to listen.

There's all kinds of noise in the woods when you really listen: owls, the rustle of small mammals, the groaning of the trees. They're all *quiet*, soft noises, sounds that manage to co-exist happily without canceling each other out. If you stand still, you can hear sticks snapping underfoot pretty clearly.

I hear sticks snapping underfoot pretty clearly.

"What was that?" asks Joshbot.

I'm impressed my phone's microphone is that powerful.

"It's nothing."

"Pretty sure nothing doesn't make a sound like that, Ty. Pretty sure nothing doesn't make a sound at all. That's kind of the point."

"Yeah, yeah, I'll give you that, but if the something's a raccoon, or a squirrel, or a lady with night terrors, I still get my point."

Or feral dogs. That's something I didn't consider. The pack from earlier would have been much louder though. The *crack, crack* I'm hearing is too measured, too human.

I hang my neck back and stare at the patches of sky, hoping for stars, but it's only void. I peer behind me in the direction I *think* I came from, but I know from reading too many survival stories that however close I am from where I came, I'm still a hair's breadth from becoming another doomed hiker, found mummified in the hills ten years later. If I wanted, if I were *smart*, I could turn back and probably find the moat. But I'm not smart, not really, and if I leave now, it could take a search party hours to find Claudia, if they ever do.

"*Ty? Say something. It can be anything.*"

"Anything."

Crack crack. Crackcrackcrack snikt

In the distance—at least I think in the distance—there's a low frequency rumble, something like a bike engine but throatier, a vibration I can feel in my feet.

There must be a generator out here. I try to fix on its direction so I can walk toward it, but the sound's omnipresent.

The footsteps of a giant.

"*Can I hold your hand?*" asks Joshbot. "*Not in a gay way, in a . . . friendly comraderiely way.*"

Oh. *Oh.* I wasn't expecting this bullshit. I stomp through the trees, my commitment to stealth abandoned, the strength of my footsteps fueled mostly by anger. "Fuck you, Robot Josh."

The forest has gone silent, except for the generator sound. It's like the weighty hum as the orchestra's starting up, but before they open the curtains. Like a video on mute when you thought you'd hit the sound.

White-barked branches spear out of the darkness, thicker-packed than they were near the island. One of them slices my shoulder and I gasp, flinching back, nearly impaling myself on yet another branch.

Joshbot chooses this moment to grace me with its flirting. "*Tyler? I'm serious man. Can you just—*"

"NO." I didn't know you could cut off a program, but turns out you can, if you're the erstwhile Tyler Kyle. Explorer. Adventurer. Failed saverer of wandering Claudias, and talkerer to himself. "Fuck it, I'm turning you off."

Joshbot laughs. *"But you only ever turn me on, Ty."*

Ugh. *UGH.* That's the face I make. Picture that word as a face.

I turn Joshbot off. Claudia will have to make do with me.

"Hey!" I call. I've been too slow, that's the problem. If I speed up, I can find her. I wasn't that far behind.

But in the darkness, where your mind isn't at its most sensible, my brain starts asking questions, like whether I could have imagined Claudia, or what if the figure I saw was someone tending their backyard and I missed them going back inside. What if I'm walking, walking, walking because I don't ever know when to stop? Josh jokes I could walk halfway around the earth and not even notice, and he's not wrong.

Another branch rakes my side while one more buffets my forehead.

Snikt. I turn toward the sound, or where I think it came from. That's one of the true dangers, that I'll head off following wildlife by mistake. The thought adds another layer of potential tragedy to my future biography: "Tyler Kyle Confesses Unrequited Love to Friend, Hours Before Vanishing Forever into the Woods in Presumed Suicide. Today we talk to the last person to see him alive. Tell us, Queen Cee, what did he do during his last few minutes as part of civilization?"

My toes are wrinkling in my waterlogged sneakers, my chest feels tight and cold. Every step is a crunch and a squelch, hardly graceful.

"Claudia?" My flashlight planes across a bright white figure in the woods. When I raise the light again, I can't find her.

Oh, come on.

"Hey? Woman in white?"

There's no movement, and by that I mean not only that I see nothing—besides darkness and trees—but that I hear nothing.

My sneaker snags on hard metal and I go flying. My knee slams down on a perfectly flat slab, pain ricocheting up my leg to my hip, but I catch myself with my palms.

I ease myself into a crouch. The phone is face-down, glowing beneath some shrubs. I grab it and beam its light over the raised metal square that tripped me.

It's an access hatch.

Grooved letters are embossed on the surface: Dan. 4:25. I'd say a biblical reference, if sewer contractors were known for signing their work in Old Testament. There's a handle, but when I give it a tug, it doesn't budge—welded or rusted shut. No way Claudia accidentally opened it and fell in. But at least if there's an access tunnel out here, we—*I*—can't have got that far from Echo Island. And maybe it explains the generator's rumble, the one that's got louder as I walked.

"Seven-thirty, fingers dirty. Dig into the soil thick." It's a woman's voice, the rest of what sounds like a poem mumbled and lost to the forest. Those first words are the ones Mom spoke in the video.

Seven-thirty, fingers dirty.

I'm on my feet, following the sound of her voice, my aching knees barely registering. I shine the flashlight back and forth like a siren.

The beam lights up Claudia like she's an angel glowing at the Hellmouth, her brown hair turned yellow—almost as pale and bright as her nightdress. She's got her back to me.

"Hello!" I don't want to startle her by slinking up unannounced. Maybe she's got Alzheimer's. If she sees me suddenly she could bolt.

But Claudia doesn't even turn around. She sways from side to side, the way Josh's pet rats do when they can't see but know something's in front of them. And there *is* something in front of her: a flat grey wall. Could be some kind of power station related to the access hatch. If I'm lucky it's unlocked and there's a phone inside.

I try to make as much noise as I can, but it's no use.

A shape darts through the trees to my left, real fast like a wolf, but bigger. Taller.

Probably an owl my sleep-deprived brain misinterpreted.

My heart thumps nearly to the rhythm of that fucking generator.

"Seven-thirty, fingers dirty . . . ." she repeats.

Leaves rustle ahead of us, to Claudia's left, and it's a big enough patch that unless this is the King of the Owls we're talking about, it has to be something larger.

"Claudia?" I reach for her. The sound radiates through me. I can practically feel the vibrations in my ear drum.

"*Seven-thirty, fingers dirty. Seven-thirty fingers dirty, seven-thirtyfinger—*"

My hand clamps down on her shoulder.

Claudia screams. She lunges at me. Her nails rake my cheek, drawing blood. I hold up my hands defensively, and her fist hits my phone, hits the flashlight, sends it flying.

She throws—*throws*—me to the ground, and my head narrowly misses a small log and probably serious brain injury.

"Hey. Hey," I groan.

She's standing above me, feet splayed, staring into the woods and swaying. "Seven-thirty, fingers dirty, seven—"

"Seven-thirty, fingers dirty. Yeah, I know. Your watch is off, and I'm out of handkerchiefs."

Her refrain lowers to a whisper.

My phone's screen flashes—it's not far. I reach for it, careful not to make any sudden movements so She Hulk doesn't decide to stomp my face into the ground.

Claudia starts up again, seemingly knocked out of the repetition by the sound of the phone. "The trees are calling. I need to go out to the trees."

"Have I got great news for you, Claudia." I pull the phone over, jab the flashlight button. "*And then there was light.*"

And he saw that the light was not good at all, because it glances off the eyes of whatever animal rustled the leaves earlier and, well, I thought only black bears lived this far east, but that thing has to be a grizzly, because it's . . . it's eyes are really far up, even considering it's about twenty feet from us.

No. Don't be a Josh. It's in a tree. Whatever owns those glowing headlamp eyes is in a tree.

And you know what climbs trees and is surprisingly limber? Bears.

I didn't know I could stand up as fast as I do. I grab Claudia by the shoulder and haul her as hard as I can back the way I think I came, and personally, I'm impressed I manage that fucking much.

Claudia swings at me and misses.

Behind us, the bear's trampling undergrowth, branches, whole *trees* by the sound of it. The entire forest is cracking to kindling in its path and it wasn't that far away to begin with.

The generator sound is like waves crashing right next to me, only now it's joined by this high-pitched Nazgûl shriek, the sound of rutting elks.

One or both of me and Claudia is screaming. I'm leaping over roots and logs, struggling to drag her along.

There's this show, *I Survived*, that Kayla's a big fan of. In it, guests who've overcome extremely traumatic, usually violent, events share their stories. I guess it's uplifting, hearing how all these little Davids managed to fell their respective Goliaths: Sandra escapes the serial killer who trunked eighteen women before her; Rick and Sydney beat the home invader who turns out to have been their murderous landlord; McKartee avenges herself on the Whitest parents in America for her war crime of a name.

I wouldn't put money down on me joining their number is all I'm saying.

In the distance, there's a fuzzy electric glow.

The bear screeches, so maybe it *is* an elk—but who really gives a fuck because it's bearing down on us and Claudia is pulling so hard she's threatening to dislocate my arm.

The vibrations from the generator, the screaming of the elk, the rumbling of the ground beneath our feet as if something huge and hungry is chasing us. It's a sound I don't just hear, but feel.

And then I *do* trip on a branch.

I lose my grip on Claudia, and she flies backwards as I fall. There's a *thuthunk-thuthunk-thuthunkboom*, and for one desperate second I think the thuthunkbooming is me and I've fallen and a sex-mad elk has speared me with his antlers and decapitated me. I'm dying, accompanied by the background music of my own head rolling across the forest floor.

The generator sound's gone now, and I can hear normal forest noises again. The elk or bear is nowhere to be heard.

I turn around, and *oh hey*, that pile of logs wasn't there before.

A woman groans from beneath them. Claudia is—fuck. Claudia's pinned under one of the logs, in what must have been someone's boobytrap.

"Claudia?" I kneel beside her.

Her right leg's completely buried, but her left is free. She heaves, using her arms to try and drag herself free. I swear I can hear her flesh scraping against bark like nails on a chalkboard. I fight the urge to vomit, close my eyes, drink in the calm, ordinary, normal night sounds.

What was it I said? The night is special? The sounds of the trees are like an ancient ship creaking on a calm sea?

Words from another time. An earlier, more innocent hour.

And the generator is back.

"Fuck, let me help." I cup the log at one end, grinding my waterlogged shoes into the dirt for leverage. Claudia reaches to help, and embarrassingly, her push is what rolls it off.

Her scream is more like a growl, low and with teeth, but her leg looks . . . There's a stick poking through it, just above the bone so that her skin puffs out in an unnatural curve.

I scramble to her side and slip my hands under her armpits to pull her away, but the stick I thought was free-floating is still attached to a buried log. When I try to snap it, it's too elastic.

I'm 99% sure the elk are what's making the low frequency sound, which means we have very little time. I'm not going to outrun a stampeding cervid in his own back woods.

"We need to get out of here, Claudia." I move to pull her.

Claudia swats my shoulder. "No, you leave me be, young man. And who's Claudia?"

Her tone isn't what I'd expect from a woman with a beat up leg with bears hunting her through the woods in the middle of the night. "I can't leave you be, because we're being chased and you're injured."

"My name's Mary," says Claudia.

"Mary. Right. Nice to meet you. We're still being chased."

Mary scoffs. "Are you Virgie's boy?"

I stare at her. "Did Conrad Uphill tell you that?"

She waves her hand. "Connie didn't tell me nothing I can't see with my own eyes. You've got her look." She nods, matter-of-fact, assessing me. "But that hair looks Jewish to me."

I have no idea how to respond to that, so I don't. Should I be offended, or would being offended be offensive, given that I know zero about my mom's sperm donor?

The rumbling is getting closer again—and am I crazy, or is it multivalent now, like there's more than one and the sounds are echoing in and out of each other? I clamp a hand over my ear, but it does nothing to stop the reverberations in my bones.

I move to slip my arm under Mary's shoulder, but she pushes me off.

"We need to go!" I say. "I'll try and carry you."

My arms are fucking shaking. Fuck. This is not good.

"Do you have a knife?" Mary asks.

In the distance, trees crack.

I glance up at the darkness, patting my pocket. "Yeah, I do," I stutter. I grab my pocketknife and flick it open. What the fuck is this going to do against a bear? My hand is sweaty against the handle. I didn't realize my palms were so sweaty.

"Good," says Mary, in a tone that's distinctly teacherly. "Now cut my leg open."

"*What*?"

Mary grimaces to the sound of breaking trees. She reaches toward her leg, having to yell to be heard. "Just cut the skin away. Skin grows back, heads don't."

"*What*?"

Fuck. Fuck fuck fuck.

The Nazgûl screech returns, and I can't move. I can't move. I can't move.

Fuck.

"*Tyler, you're an asshole,*" says Joshbot, helpfully.

Mary grabs my arm, calm as an ancient ship creaking on the sea.

She stabs my knife into her leg and slashes—*deep.*

Blood sprays across my face and I'm blinded. It's in my nose, dripping down my face, my lips. I taste her blood in my mouth.

I drop the knife and throw up.

"Pick me up." Mary sounds so stern, so in control. How? She didn't even scream. Her blood is pouring out—it's on my, in my—

I puke again, wipe my mouth, wipe my face, clear the blood away, or spread it around, or—

I heave. This time I keep it in. I let out a whine instead.

I reach for her, holding out my phone's flashlight, shaking, forcing myself to examine the wound. It's gaping and red, like a big crescent grin cut in her skin revealing raw red muscle.

The branch is still on top of her, covered in the flap of discarded skin she forced me to slice away. I grimace and tug her leg out from under it.

"We need to bind it, right, for blood loss?" I pat her nightie, try to tear it. My arm is *rattling*. Fuck I'm a wreck. I can't even tear her dress, so I reach for my shirt and tear that instead. I point at her leg. "Lift it up."

She obeys, and I wind my shirt tight around the injury.

"You're doing fine, Tyler," says Mary. She pats my hand.

I'm pretty sure I'm crying. I'm not doing fine at all. I'm complete shit actually.

"I'm going to carry you," I say. Giving myself a command makes the tunnel vision of my panic recede a little.

When I stand, I pan the flashlight over the woods.

The trees are filled with eyes.

Fifteen feet off the ground, all around us, they don't even blink. This time, they're completely silent. When I stare into the perfect white circles, it's like a movie hypnotist is swinging a pendulum back and forth, back and forth—

They're creeping in, twigs cracking beneath even their tenderest footsteps. The generator rumble starts again, almost like a very low warbling, deep in the throat. The sound is followed by a sharp keen, the screech of before, and then a breathy huffing, like someone whispering *heyheyhey* right in your ear.

Heyheyhey, stay right where you are. I want you to stay right there. *Heyheyhey*, that's right, that's right. Be good. Be good, baby doll. Just

like

that.

6

IT'S ALL IN THE EYES

M ary punches my leg. I feel it like a pea beneath a hundred downy pillows.

The glow of the bears' eyes is so beautiful, so peaceful. And how bad would it be, really, to be devoured? To know your small death would feed an army of forest critters? What other meaning could I hope to find out there in the big scary world, being alive? Living is hard. It takes so much effort. To die, all I have to do is stand here and wait.

And beautiful. Dear God will it be beautiful.

Jaws clamped around my neck, the *beatbeatbeat* of my heart, the *beatbeatbeat, the beatbeatbeat* of *my heart, the beat beat beat of my heart, the beat beat . . . .beat . . . hey*

The jaws closing, the puncture of thin skin, the pulse of blood down the neck, claws raised to swipe open my chest, my ribcage, my heart

Swipe right for supper

And I'll melt over time into the earth and the pine needles, diffused into root and moss, and the trees will sing songs of me, and the words they make will sound like *heyheyhey*.

6 1/2

RUNNING

"*Uh, Ty, are you dead? You haven't said anything in half a minute.*"

"*Ty? I can't hear you. Ty?*"

"*Earth to Tyler.*"

Hard nails sink into the calf of my right leg and then pull.

I slam onto the forest floor and the wind's knocked out of me.

The ground is rough, the spikes of the pine needles sharp. The revelation of texture is like the moment when the camera focuses and everything is detail.

I groan, remembering where I am and whose hand is scrabbling at my poor soaked sneaker.

"Mary—"

Her sigh of relief is audible. "You need to listen, Tyler. You're in shock, but everything's going to be perfectly all right as long as you do what I tell you."

I close my eyes, listening to the generator rumble. "Uh huh. I'm listening."

I feel calm, actually. It's kind of weird. Maybe it's bad-weird. Maybe that's a symptom of shock.

Mary is snapping her fingers. She hisses. "*Tyler Kyle.*"

"Uh huh."

"*Listen*. You need to get up and carry me. We're going to walk out of the woods now. Can you hear the dogs?"

I *can* hear barking. "Yeah."

"They're coming from town. Run toward them."

I stumble to my feet, start to turn around and look at the trees again. She punches my foot.

"I thought we were walking." I hoist her up. She's somehow both lighter and heavier than anticipated.

She pats my shoulder and smiles. "I lied."

Something creaks behind me and I turn—

Heyheyhey.

Mary slaps me. "Don't look at the trees."

But I want to look. I *have* to look. I can hear the bears creeping toward us: the crack of branches, the rustle of bushes.

It's so dark with my cell in my pocket.

The dogs are barking wildly. I squint and make out the shape of at least two packs of them, cavorting toward us. I don't have to turn around to know the bears are receding. The rumble has changed, a retreating sound, I guess. I don't blame them. I want to run away from those dogs too.

Instead, I run toward them.

It'd be nice to say that this time I'm more careful, but there's no room for careful when you're covered in blood, bolting for civilization-*ish*, praying there's a doctor who can see to the nice old lady who's been very patient while you almost accidentally let her bleed out, in very real danger of being eaten by bears or elk or whatever they are, and feral dogs are careering toward you like they're Tonya Harding and you're Nancy Kerrigan and you're the only thing standing between them and that Olympic gold.

Fortunately the dogs don't baton me in my leg.

Two groups of dogs part to either side of me as I run, like Mary and I are the prow of a ship piercing the waves. They veer left and right, and then we're past them. Their yaps are met by the shrieking of the elk.

Branches scream past.

Mary's arms loosen around my neck. I jostle her to snap her awake and she raises her head slightly. She was so grounded before that I half forgot she was the one in real danger, that the blood on my face I've been cracking nervous jokes about belongs inside her body.

Things like this are why I'm an asshole.

"Almost there, Mary." I have no idea how close we are, or if I've been turned around and I'm thudding deeper into the vast acres of forest between Echo Island and the real world.

"Talk to me, Mary." I stop briefly, surveying the woods. I'm in the tightly packed conifers again.

She clutches the neckline of my shirt, as though for comfort. "I'm very sleepy, Tyler dear."

That's not good. "So you knew my mom." I pick a direction and resume running.

"We used to meet for bridge every Friday," says Mary. "I trounced her every time." She laughs.

I wish I could laugh. I wish it felt good like it should. The first piece of solid information about my mom since I got here and it's from a woman who's dying in my arms while we exit pursued by bear.

"Do you remember playing bridge together?" Mary asks, and for a second I think she's spaced out again, that she's confused me with Virginia Kyle. But then I realize she means do *I* remember playing with Mom. And . . . yes. Yes, I do remember.

"I'd forgotten," I say.

Is that water in the distance? Please fuck let it be water. Even a stream—I could follow a stream.

"She talked about you all the time." Mary chokes up a bit, or is it only that she's about to pass out? "Called you her baby doll. The last thing she wanted was for you to turn up *here*."

Huh. Huh. Right. Talked about me all the time, after abandoning me. Prayed I'd never come looking. Perfectly normal, sane, maternal behaviour.

I've always known what she did was wrong. I've always known I should be angrier than I was. Instead of anger there's an empty space I tiptoe around. I've made room for it in my thoughts. Too much room. Too much I just don't think about and too much mental energy expended thinking about not thinking about it.

"Well I'm here," I say. "So where's she?"

Mary doesn't speak.

We burst onto the top of the ditch, and I wobble dangerously above the moat. I roll my feet back as much as I can, catching my back against a tree. I close my eyes, breathing out hard. I could cry again, or puke, or both. I don't though. I plunge toward the moat.

And Claudia—*Mary*—sighs.

"I'm so sorry, dear." She rubs my back as we wade across, and I know, from deep within that empty hole in my thoughts, from the way she says it—the same way Josh says *we need to talk about the show*—what the next words out of her mouth will be. "She died two years ago. She's buried in Arcadia."

Some days it's like the depths want to plumb me. There's an ache in my chest like I've swallowed a bucket of wood chips. A finality, maybe a hopelessness. What am I doing here? What did I think I'd find?

"How?" The water drags at my legs as we pass the halfway mark.

"Stroke," Mary says. "It was very quick."

Her palm is warm and kind as it paints faint circles on my back—this woman who knew my mother longer than I did, who shared her final years, bent over a bridge game every Friday night. Virgie Kyle, B movie bombshell and cult darling, wasting away in the middle of the forest with no audience to light her up. It's not like the mom I remember, but then, the mom I remember wasn't real to begin with.

We make the shore and I start hiking up the bank. "I'll take you to the doctor. Which way?"

Mary's passed out against my shoulder.

Fuck.

Fuck.

Okay. Where am I? Allenby and Rivers, where I started. If my earlier guess was right, I'll find stores and other amenities closer to Uphill's mansion at the centre of the island.

I bolt up the road. As I enter the range of one of the street-lamps, my arm glistens red where Mary's wound now lies open. My shredded t-shirt must have drifted off in the moat and she's been bleeding out all over my arm for fuck knows how long.

The wound looks pale. Dead meat on a butcher's block.

Sneakers slap the road behind me, slowing to a jog. I speed up on instinct, but a woman calls out.

"Hey! Wait."

I swerve round, clutching Mary to my chest. It's the beautiful blonde from The Moon, no longer in a red dress but wearing sweats and a pink bomber jacket.

"Help me. I—I—" I swallow. "Mary's hurt. And there were bear *things*."

The blonde's already taking Mary's legs, hefting probably more than half Mary's weight. "Let's get her to The Moon. They'll call for Connie."

I swallow a gag, clutching Mary tight under her shoulders, ready to collapse. Me and the blonde hurry up the road.

The lights are still on inside The Thunder Moon. A record-ing of "Baby One More Time" blasts within from male vocal cords.

I give Mary a light slap on the arm, then a harder one when she doesn't respond. Her eyes snap awake as I shove open the bar door.

The place is almost emptied out, no Queen Cee on stage, no crowd.

At the sight of Tia, Nor, Gene, and about five strangers all clustered at the bar, I almost collapse.

Almost.

The blonde takes up the slack, and we lay Mary on a table. I stand there, shaking, wanting to fall or sit or fucking faint, but unable to stop standing.

"Help," I say.

The music on the radio cuts off, and Tia and Nor rush to catch me.

7

THREE WOLF MOON

Tia and Nor shove me into a chair. Considering I almost died, they could be nicer.

Mary has propped herself up on her elbows, and is staring at me nonchalantly, like *I'm* the one bleeding out and she's enjoying the show.

"Someone get her a popcorn," I mumble.

"Hey, Gene," calls the pretty blonde who helped me. "Call Conrad. We need the car."

"And Colleen." Nor's voice is sad, tense. "She should be told."

Someone's hand is on my shoulder. It's Tia's. That's pretty nice actually. She's nicer than I thought. A good person. Not like—

I fumble after my phone, and in my eagerness to reach my pocket I slam my forehead into the table. "Ahhhh, fuck." I pin my hand to my head.

"Take it easy," says Nor. "What's his problem?"

"He's in shock," says Mary, snapping her fingers at someone off-screen—I mean out of view—

"My phone," I manage. The relief that fills me as my fingers curl around it is embarrassing.

"Tyler, you're an asshole."

"You too, buddy, you too." I clutch it and lean back.

The blonde's staring at me, horrified by Joshbot. She's not alone.

"He's sent a driver." Gene walks over with an overflowing shot glass. It *clinks* on the table.

I point to it. "What's that?"

"Booze," says Gene.

I nod. "I know, I meant what kind."

"Booze," Gene repeats, shrugging.

"Ah, so, moonshine then." I reach for it.

Tia swats my hand away. "Should he . . . ?"

"Best thing for it," grunts Nor.

Tia holds her hand up, fingers splayed. "How many, Kyle?"

I make a face then meet her worried gaze. "All of them."

"Does that even work?" asks Nor.

"No idea," says Tia.

I frown past Tia and Nor at Mary, who's still lying on the table. "She's really hurt. You have to help her. These logs fell on her leg and I had to cut—" I'm so fucking tired of puking that I suck it back out of sheer spite. "She was wandering in the woods, totally out of it." I gesticulate with my arm, narrowly missing Nor. "Some bears or elk showed up, and I ran, but she was hurt, and those feral dogs we saw earlier—" I wave at Tia, but she's staring at me like I'm ranting in the subway about Jesus. "You remember, right? The dogs, the ones you kill on, on—" I snap my fingers. "Dog Day, that's right."

Nor picks up the shot of Booze and holds it out. I take it, and alcohol spills over my hand, stinging in the scratches that I'm now noticing crisscross my skin. No wonder I'm shaking.

"I remember," says Tia. She glances at Nor, like I can't see her, but I *can*, and I'm angry.

She told me she didn't know where Mom went, but there's no way that was true. Tia is a fucking liar.

I sling back the shot.

Outside, a car pulls up.

I twist in my chair, ready to get up and get out. *Uphill's* out there, or his car is. Booze in my belly and fire in my head, I'm getting answers. Now.

And also I want to make sure Mary's okay. Yeah, that too. And I learned my mom died and I'm two stupid years too late, and I've got no shits to give and I'm walking out of this bar and no one's going to stop me!

Nor slams me back down. "*Sit.*"

"Is it me, or do all the women on Echo Island lift?" I ask, but no one responds—well, Gene titters a bit. Thanks Gene, you're a pal.

The blonde and the extras all support Mary beneath her head and legs, carrying her toward the door.

Mary smiles at me. "Everything will be all right, Tyler."

As the blonde passes me, she leans in and whispers: "Tomorrow. Ziggy's. Your mom."

Seemingly sensing I'm about to make a run for it again, Nor squeezes my shoulder in a way that's deeply threatening.

The rest of the strangers clear out, leaving me alone with Gene, Tia, and Nor. After what I learned tonight, I'm not exactly comforted.

In the background, Gene's on the phone. "Yeah, Colleen. She'll be at Uphill's. Want the girls to come get you? You sure? It's no problem. Okay, okay." He hesitates. "I've been there, so if you wanna talk or anything . . . ."

Tia wipes a cloth soaked in iodine down the side of my face where Mary scratched me and I scrunch my eyes shut at the sting.

Tia meets my eyes. "If it scars, just pretend you got in a knife fight." She smiles. It's frightening.

"Well that sure beats 'Oh, yeah, this old thing? A septuagenarian raked her nails into my flesh and handed me my ass.'" I glance at the door. I really do hope Mary's okay. She was pretty A+, beating me up aside.

Tia and Nor share another look.

What is it about me that provokes such intense reactions? Am I really that tedious? I'd say I was too used to receiving a sea of adoration from our fans and so my view of reality is permanently warped, but I do exist in the world outside the show, unlike, say, those Ticky Tockers at places like Omega House.

I'm not totally impervious to negative reactions.

Many is the time I've had a proverbial cone of shame placed on my head at Josh's family dinners. His nice, upstanding, White, intensely Protestant dad will do that under-the-brows glower in Josh's direction, and Josh'll give me a signal to shut up by offering me more potato and mayo casserole. Or his nice, upstanding, White, intensely Protestant mom will purse her lips into a smile so prim it's got its own bonnet and parasol, and Josh will spill tang over her nice, white, Protestant tablecloth to redirect her ire toward her failure of an adopted son.

Josh talks more than I do, and you get us together and it's like a stream of two consciousnesses.

Was. Was like that.

It's not like I'm not used to raising hackles, is what I'm saying, but these shared looks between Tia and Nor are weirding me out. They step away and start talking heatedly in a whisper.

Gene interrupts, clutching the phone's receiver against his chest. "Hey, girls. Colleen changed her mind—she'll take a ride."

"I'll go," says Tia. "I need some fresh air and silence." She sounds mad—not at Gene, but at Nor, maybe?

Nor grabs Tia's wrist as she's turning away. "*We'll* go."

Suddenly it's the two of us. Gene and me. Me and Gene. He stares at me from behind the counter, then hangs up the receiver. My internal Josh is wailing about how that's suspicious. Was there never anyone on the other end? Why didn't he hang up before? Was it an excuse to get Tia and Nor to leave us alone?

But Josh is paranoid, and contrary to what he thinks, most people are perfectly nice. Quirky maybe, disturbing sometimes, but ultimately well-meaning.

All the same, I stand up, jab my thumb at the door. "You know, Gene, thanks for the Booze. It really helped. If Mary's all right, I better head back to my cabin. I've had kind of an exhausting day."

Gene frowns. "Nuh uh. Mary said you're in shock. I'm not letting you out of my sight."

Those are serial killer words if I ever heard them. But hey, I don't judge. It's probably a rough hobby on an island this small. 'Oh him? He's just Gene the Machine. Guts a tourist every now and then. Mulches up the good parts for burgers, tosses the rest. The feral dogs love all the free bones.'

I stroll to the counter, showing off my ability to, uh, walk.

It doesn't go well.

I catch myself on a bar stool, my hip swinging in the opposite direction to the stool—never good this side of 30.

"I'm fine," I get out, before Gene can ask. It takes the air out of the embarrassment. "Maybe I need more Booze."

Or less. Fuck that shot was strong, and it's only hitting me now. And I've eaten barely anything today. But good ol' Gene pours me another. He slides it across the counter as I try to clamber onto the stool.

"Come on," says Gene, walking and pointing in the direction of the kitchen. "You're . . . uh, a bit dirty still, and there's shorter chairs out back."

I glance at the tables and booths of equally normal height out here, but what odds. I shrug, grab the shot glass, and wobble through two sets of saloon doors into the kitchen. The slap of the wood against my legs flashes me back to the branches whipping me in the face as I ran.

For a moment, my chest feels like poprocks and soda.

"Nice place you got here, Gene," I say, conversationally, normally, before I've even taken it all in.

The shorter chairs are here as promised, beside a metal counter that's slightly more industrial than I would have expected from The Moon. Gene's full of surprises, I guess.

He gestures to the sink and a dish rag beside it.

"You can clean up if you want. I'll get a bottle." He wanders off, leaving me to dip my entire head under the tap and rinse.

The water runs pinky orange for a good minute. Ploughing my hands through my hair brings up leaves, dirt, and a couple caterpillars. I mop my face with the dry rag, then dampen it and start on my arms with a bar of soap.

When Gene returns he's clutching the promised bottle. He sets it on the countertop and squats on the plastic chair beside where I'm washing. He pours two shots, watching me wash.

"You've got a bit of—" He makes circles in the air with his finger, clearly uncomfortable saying it.

I twist my back, catch sight of a chunk of stomach acid and fries on my jeans. "Thanks." I need a shower, but Gene's obviously taking this babysitting gig seriously, so I settle with the tolerable amount of gross I am and sit across from him.

I grab the first shot glass and drink. Then I reach for Booze 3.0. Gene clinks his glass against mine. "Cheers."

Almost as fast as I lower my glass, he pours another. I'm gonna have to peel myself off the floor tomorrow.

"So, do you work out?" asks Gene.

That has to be a first. "Sure, for the first three weeks after every New Year's."

I guess Tia was lying about not being his type.

Gene scratches the back of his head. He laughs nervously, his cheeks beet-red. "You're really funny, you know?" He reaches for my glass and holds up the bottle questioningly.

I nod, trying to rub the soreness out of the back of my neck. The Booze is helping. I sling back another, missing slightly so some of it runs down my cheek. I dab it up with the remains of my shirt.

"Sorry—your shirt. I've got some spares." Gene pries himself from the chair.

I twist my neck to call out to him and *rrrrr* that wrecks. "I don't know how to tell you this, Gene, but we're not the same size."

Gene is what we in Hollywood call a chonky boy, and I'm like what a skeleton would look like if it decided to cosplay a human and ran out of padding.

Gene waves like it's not an issue, and hurries upstairs. When he comes back, he's holding—no joke—the actual Three Wolf Moon. He tosses it to me.

I grin. "Where'd you get this?" I hold back on making a crack about it in case he owns it in earnest. It's my size, too. A little snug, actually, when I pull it on. Maybe it's from his youth? It's kind of an ancient reference at this point, another reminder of how Echo Island is trapped in the past.

Gene rolls his shoulder. He looks kind of sad. "People leave all kinds of stuff here."

The way he rubs his thumb back and forth across his shot glass is warning me off a line of follow-up questions, and anyway, I'm not sure I want to know if my Gene the Machine serial killer theory was correct, so I smile. "Lucky me, I guess."

"Looks good on you," says Gene, but somehow it's not creepy, not in the slightest. It's just . . . kind.

Makes me feel bad for what I'm about to do, which is use his tipsiness to question him about the town. "Mary was really out of it when I found her." The words tumble out—I thought I was being savvy, but part of me obviously needs to get what happened tonight out of my system. That or it's the Booze.

No filter, no filter. I never had one anyway, and what was there is shot—shot, get it? Eh? Eh?—to pieces.

I meet Gene's friendly blue eyes. "Does she have anyone?" Uphill, presumably. There must be a reason he was Gene's first call.

"Her wife, Colleen. She waitresses at Ziggy's." Gene pours himself another. He clears his throat. "Mary's been wandering for a while. It's not the first time." He doesn't look at me while he talks, keeps staring into his drink.

I'm no psychoanalyst, but there's something bugging him, some personal connection to what's happening—or maybe he's just close to Mary. Maybe everyone on Echo Island is close as peas in a pod.

I nod at Gene like I understand what he's going through. But I don't. I have no family who could suffer from dementia. Mom only ever took me on one trip back to the Old Country, and we spent it wandering around Edinburgh sneaking after ghost tours so we didn't have to pay the fee. I guess we were there to see her parents—my grandparents—but we rented a place the whole time, and I never met them. I was five then. As far as I know, it was the last time she went back.

"Is Mary getting help?" I ask.

"There's a clinic at Arcadia." Gene leans back in the uncomfortable plastic chair, which creaks beneath his weight. "She doesn't have long." He looks up at me. "She's lucky she met you. Those traps aren't supposed to be up so late in the year."

I swallow. The trap was probably my fault. But there were also the bears.

The glowing circles of their eyes beam bright in my vision, like I'm still in the forest. I shiver. I've never frozen that badly before. I couldn't get moving, couldn't look away.

What did Gene say? Something weird. It gnaws at me till I remember it. "What are the traps for?"

"The bears," Gene says. "We take them away around now for the hunt. I guess Clegg missed one."

I snort. "Clegg."

"Are you sure you're all right?" asks Gene.

I wave. "I'm just drunk. And whose fault is that?"

Gene's face transforms with his grin, eyes lit up, the whole works. The guilt at the flirting stabs me right between the ribs. Is this what it's like for Josh?

When you scrape away the thin patina of my public image, I'm a sore schmuck, drinking in all Josh's little lines, consuming them till his lyrics saturate my blood like heavy metal poisoning.

But at least I made Gene smile, right?

"I'm sorry," I say, and I watch that smile melt in real time. I've got the serious tone in my wavery, drunk voice, the one we all use to let people down. People who don't deserve it, except when they do. "I'm—" Booze Brain searches for an explanation, but there isn't a good one. "I'm in love with someone. Back home. It's about to not work out."

Unwanted, drunk tears prick at my eyes. Are they for Josh, or for Mom, or for me, or even Mary? Take your pick. Everyone's a winner.

If I were anywhere else, it's Josh I'd call to come get me right about now, when the warmth of that early buzz wears off and I turn into sad Tyler puking into a stranger's toilet at 3AM. The name at the top of the speed dial.

What a weight to wear around your neck.

Gene's staring at me, confused. Fuck. Why did I say that? Why did I assume anything about what Gene wanted, or how I made him hurt, or . . . ?

"I'm an asshole," I admit with a shrug.

"*Where's your joy?*" comes Joshbot's voice, straight from pocket to ear. "*You have absolutely no magic in your life, Tyler. It must feel awful being you. Seriously.*"

"What's that?" asks Gene. "Hello?"

He leans toward my pants.

I laugh, frenzied like the dogs.

Gene frowns quizzically. "Your pants made a sound."

I take my phone out. "That's the voice of the guy I was talking about. It's an app he made me."

The phone clearly troubles him, based on that grimace, so I slip it back in my pocket, flicking Joshbot off.

For some reason, out of everything, turning off Josh's stupid app that seems to have five total phrases is what does it. Maybe it's the fact that it somehow convinced me I was really talking to it in the woods, like part of Josh was here and I wasn't alone. Maybe it's that by shutting it off I'm shutting out the real one.

Maybe it's the reminder that I'm the one who ran away, and now that I know about Mom, there's not even a reason to stay.

Whatever the cause, I break. I start sobbing and hang my head in my hands. It's pathetic.

Gene lays a big meaty hand on my shoulder, a gentle giant. "Everything's going to be fine," he says, with the wisdom of a queer who's been and seen it all.

I wipe my nose off on the back of my hand. "Why does everyone keep saying that? I'm fine already. Peachy."

Having a mental breakdown.

The door of the saloon clatters. Gene removes his hand from my shoulder and heaves to his feet. "I'll be right back."

But I'm done with this. I follow Gene out, patting my way along the metal counter until I'm certain I can walk unaided.

Tia's in the diner wearing a motorcycle helmet. "Thanks, Gene. I'll take him home."

"He can stay here," says Gene. "It's no trouble. The spare's done up and everything."

I do my best impression of a sober person, standing tall—hard to do next to Gene—and gesturing sophisticatel-ly—catedly at the air. "I need to be alone. I should shower also."

Tia gives me that look from earlier, from before Mary. "That second part's definitely true."

"You sure?" Gene asks. All the sorrows of my world are reflected in his big, dopey eyes. High-octane empathy.

"Yeah." I stumble to Tia to demonstrate the potency of my readiness, and Tia catches me, holding me round the waist to stop me colliding with a table.

"I've got him," she says. "Catch you tomorrow."

And Tia whisk—wicks?—whips? me into the night.

8

RIDING ON BIKES WITH GIRLS

Tia shoves one hand into the front pocket of her jacket as she supports me with the other and we walk toward the motorcycle. "Sorry about Gene." Her keys jangle.

I shake my head. "It's cool. Seems like a nice guy."

She gives me a look. Does she think I'm some kind of heartless asshole? Except I guess that's a lot of how I sell myself so, yeah, probably.

"He must really like you to give you that shirt."

"Yeah?" I stare down at Three Wolf and wince. I can sense the sad story about to slip out of her. Is he old enough to have a kid who died? He's got about ten years on me—early forties—it's possible.

"Yeah." She sounds annoyed, which means my tone or my face must have been off. Not too surprising after the moonshine, but it's unfortunate and unintended.

"Are you going to tell me why?" I press, some irritation slipping into my own voice. I'm not a mind reader, and I just saw a woman get her leg crushed.

I'm a little jittery.

Tia sighs as she helps me onto the back of her Franken-bike—Harley and Yamaha logos competing for space. "Gene's partner died last year. They were head over heels for each other. He used to do stand up at The Moon in that shirt."

I guess that's why he asked about the comedy. "I'm sorry." I grip the sides of the bike, then the sides of Tia once she's on. No point being shy—I'm not entirely convinced I won't fall off even gripping her jacket. She doesn't offer me a helmet. Guess there isn't one.

"That's how it is," says Tia. "He's lonely and he won't move on. That's why I introduced you earlier. You look lonely too."

I laugh, nervous. "I don't look lonely. How does someone even *look* lonely? I'm tired."

Tia revs the engine and I tighten my legs around the bike. She says something, but I miss it. Probably for the best.

The exhaust smells weirdly of fries and methane, the same fries I puked up all over myself in the woods. *Ugh.*

She pulls out from The Moon and immediately my stomach crawls up my throat to escape. The vibrations from the bike rattle up my legs and, uh, crotch. It's actually a lot like the low frequency sound from earlier.

Mist rises off the surface of the moat, glowing red beneath the haze of her novelty-coloured headlights.

As she makes the Allenby/Rivers turn I squeeze her side. "Uh, Tia. Slow. Slow down, please."

"I'm going 10." She says. Flatly. Yet somehow also loud, to be heard over the engine.

I pull my legs back, and one of them nicks the tail pipe and *ow*. I really hope I'm not adding third-degree burn to tonight's list of injuries.

She slows anyway. What a trooper.

Then she speeds up.

"That better?" she calls over the *rrrrrr* of the engine.

And yeah, actually, it is. "Yeah, actually." I hesitate. "Why didn't you tell me my mom died? She's buried here. I could visit her grave and you pretended she left."

Tia doesn't answer as we zip smoothly past the houses. And I'm so fucking tired of silence, of fucking lying, of everything.

"Stop the *fucking* bike. I said stop."

Tia stops. My stomach does a backflip. "You can't walk back by yourself."

I wish me getting off the bike was a smooth, controlled thing, but I stumble, almost falling. Only some of that's drunkenness. Most of it's clumsiness. "It's, like, two minutes," I spit, already storming away. "Or am I in danger of getting mauled by a bear, since there's apparently so many of them you need a safety wall of deadly traps?"

I can feel Tia rolling her eyes behind me.

"I didn't tell you about your mom because I didn't want to upset you." The suckiest of sucky responses.

"Yeah, much better to make me think if I scour the earth I'll find her living it up in Seoul. You're a real boon to the tourist industry."

"You're drunk," says Tia, which is correct, but also not an invalidation of my point.

I spin round, facing her. "And what the fuck is Arcadia? Everyone keeps saying that—*Arcadia*—and you took Mary there."

Tia parks the bike and gets off. She crosses her arms. "It's Connie's house. It's important on the island. Nothing to freak over."

I snort. "Nothing to freak over. Right. Just like me in the forest watching Mary bleed out. And—and why the fuck is everyone here gay?"

Tia arches an eyebrow, mid-my-rant.

"I mean," I continue, "I'm probably a way more than bi-curious heterosexualish man, but everyone I've met so far is a wife of a wife, or a girlfriend of a girlfriend, or a husband with a dead husband. And while we're at it, why are there so many dead people? I get it, people die, and sometimes they die young and it really fucking sucks, but for a town with like twenty people it seems like kind of a lot. And I'm not some conspiracy theory weirdo like Josh—"

"Who's Josh?"

"—but I'm not a fucking idiot. Fucking bears don't fucking hypnotize people and make sounds like the footsteps of T-Rex out of *Jurassic* Fucking *Park*." The italics I'm imagining in my head are because it's a title and not for emphasis, though that too.

"It's just bears," she says. "What do you want me to say?"

I waggle my finger. "Oh no. I'm the skeptic here. I make a living out of this shit—depressing as that may be. I know my owl from my *sound of Josh stepping on a stick and screaming like a five-year-old girl*—"

"Who's Josh?"

"—and something was fucking off at karaoke. And what is *Seven-thirty, fingers dirty*? Is that a sex thing or—"

"It's a poem."

"—or is it some fucked-up cult thing and I was wrong when I said this wasn't about to get all *Wicker Man* on me and when Josh shows up it's going to be—"

"Who's Josh?"

"—all sacrificial murder and *where* is *Rowan Morrison slash where* is *Tyler Kyle and*—"

Tia's walked up to me—unnoticed. She presses her finger to my lips. "Be quiet." She cocks her head to her left.

I stare at her. The night bugs are cricketing, or the crickets are night-bugging. Suddenly everything is absurdly peaceful, and I'm obscenely drunk, making a spectacle of myself in the middle of the street. I turn, and yeah, there are a few lights on.

All but Mary's.

Islanders peer out at me and Tia, their beautiful mundane dreams disrupted by my rambling drunk thoughts.

"I'm sorr—"

Tia shakes her head. "You're drunk, and in shock. Get on the bike and shut up."

Some of my uneasiness must cross my face because she smiles consolingly, then kisses my cheek.

When I touch my face I feel her cheap black lipstick on my skin. "What's that for?"

"For getting on my bike and letting me drive you home. For going after Mary. Whatever you want it to be for."

What to say to that? So I don't say, and instead I do as she commanded and I'm quiet right up to the moment we pull into White Sails.

My disembarkation is smoother this time. "Thanks."

Tia leans against the parked bike, arms crossed, staring at the gravel. "Don't thank me." She presses the gravel beneath her boot, rolling the rocks against each other. "I'm sorry, okay? I should have told you about your mom, but I thought if *you* thought Echo Island was her pit stop you might leave town like I told you to."

"Are you going to leap onto your hog and put-put-put into the night if I ask why it's so important I leave?"

She looks up, glower snapping into place as if she's fully automated: the Tia-1000 Series. "Echo Island's not always kind to outsiders."

I snort. "Vague."

"But true."

I swallow. "Was my mom one of those outsiders?"

Tia's lips crinkle. She unclasps her arms. "I really didn't know her. I promise. She hung around with the other seniors most of the time, kind of kept to herself unless Connie dragged her to one of the bars to perform."

"Perform?"

"Sing. He liked it when she sung his songs."

Tia says it like it's so normal, but it's not normal at all, not the fact that she chose *dragged* of all verbs, and not the creeper vibes I get imagining Uphill lurking behind my mom like a demented cowboy Ursula while she sings her heart out.

Like me. Tonight.

"Did he have something on her? Is that why she came here? Is it why she stayed?"

Cool air blows my hair against my cheek, and the smell of the forest travels with it. I should be wasted—I probably still am wasted—but the conversation and the crispness of the night are sobering.

Tia shakes her head. "I promise I don't know, Tyler."

"Am I in danger here?"

Tia stands up properly, but if I thought it was because she was ready for some real talk, I'm quickly disabused of the notion. Tia slips back onto her bike. "Stay away from Conrad. He has a way with people, especially people he likes."

I laugh. It feels raw and savage in my throat, grating against the burn of the Booze. "He doesn't know me."

"Doesn't matter." She revs the engine, and for a moment I'm worried she'll wake the other White Sails guests. But I haven't seen any other guests. I'm the only one. "He'll like you," she continues. "And when he likes someone, he does everything he can to keep them."

"Tia—" I follow as she pulls onto the road, but she ignores me, and she's not wrong about the shock or the drunkenness or the exhaustion.

I glance back at the blackened windows of the hotel office. Inside, an electronic device blinks off-on-off-on like a flickering modem light. Something about this struggling machine on an island technologically trapped in the 1850s compels me. I stand in front of the window, press my palm to the glass. I stare inside, and though I can't place why, for only a moment, it's like someone's staring back. Like the machine is an eye—blinking, assessing, watching.

The breeze ripples against Three Wolf Moon. It could be Echo Island's breath, a deep exhale after years holding it all in.

The Echo Island Diary: Entry 3
Tyler Kyle is More Void Than Substance

July 13th, 2019, 11:15 AM

Dear Diary,

Fuck, I'm hung over.

Josh does hangovers so much better than me. He can drink me under the table and still come out looking artfully disheveled. He never gets puke stuck in his cobalt-black hair, and he never gets the shits afterwards or anything gross at all really. It's sexy as fuck. ♥ He's all loose tees and tender whines and delicately closed eyes as he lounges on the couch, or his bed, or even the floor. It's so whelming when we're together.

Sometimes I watch him while he's sleeping, watch the moisture beading on eyelashes so downy they could be crows' feathers. I want to kneel at his side and scoop that moisture up and paint my tongue with it. I want to squeeze the oil from his perfect little ~~pours~~ pores and fill my mouth with those tiny worms of flesh.

There's a whole hell of a lot you can make out of human bodies (candles, soap, clothing). Throughout all of history, humans have made medicine from the deceased (dust that's actually ground mummy, mellified man). I read about mellified man on a website called Wikipedia dot com. People would volunteer to eat nothing but honey till it killed them, then they'd be shut up in a honey-lined coffin to decompose for a hundred years, until they entirely liquefied. You could buy it and eat it and it would heal all kinds of things.

When I watch Josh, his body is like a mellified man—a sweet, sweet death I could suck and swallow and consume until it cured all the badness inside me. Did he know all those times we walked side-by-side I was imagining his body, immortalized in honey, in wax, in soap? Perhaps even my body could be rarefied, purified, transformed, if I only knew the recipe. My body could be useful.

Looking back to all those moments it's no wonder I've been in funnylove with Josh all these years. The kind of love that's bad for everyone, but mostly for him. The kind of love that infects, contorts, deforms. The kind of love that makes you say fucked up shit you shouldn't (and makes you want even more fucked up shit).

If Josh were here now I'd take back all those times I dragged him on the show for being better than

me. If Josh were here, there's so much I'd take
~~back~~.

All those times I called you stupid for your
adorable wordification. All those times I didn't
believe you saw what you said you saw in the
woods. You heard it here first—Tyler Kyle is admitting he was wrong. If only I'd wanted to believe earlier, we could have been so much more.
Now we never will be, and whose fault is that?

I tip my hat to you, future new Discovery Bang
co-host, for recognizing and admitting what I
never could. For taking us next level. When you
bag your first Sasquatch, I'll be looking down on
you from purgatory. The only question is, which
circle?

You're got your gluttons, your greedy, your
slothful, your lusty, your prideful, your angry,
your envious.

I weigh about ninety pounds soaking wet so it's
probably not gluttony. Sloth maybe? I could buy
that. I've always ridden on Josh's coattails, plus
I've always wondered if you could tie a guy to a
bed for a year like the killer does in "Se7en." By
the end he was shrivelled like a corpse, still alive,
but insane. And lust—I wouldn't have guessed,
but after praying on my knees at the altar of a
drag queen's cock, it's obvious I'm a trashy fucking whore. Then again, pride and envy work too.
Cut off the nose to spite the face.

Yeah, yeah.

What's in the box? What's in the box, Josh? What's in the motherfucking box?

Yeah, yeah, yeah, yeah.

Envy is my sin.

Discovery Bang was Josh's brainchild—I mean, how could it not be? Josh was a dean's list prodigy in theatre school and I was lucky if the creative director used the sketches of my set ideas as toilet paper.

Josh saved me. Now it's my turn to save him from myself.

Even most of our fans have me all figured out. Sure, there's some shitty smut about me and Josh—I'm looking at you Pornstar Popsicle, and your normie Tosh fic—but I know what our audience has really been waiting for is to see a real team on-screen. Brenda x Josh (Brosh!).

But I still can't stop wishing he was beside me for one last fucking hurrah. I can't stop hoping he'll appear to solve the mess that is Echo Island. I need him, the way I've always needed him, only I'm finally catching on that Josh doesn't need *me*.

This has always been a two-player game, and I'm riding solo.

9

NEVER GIVE UP ON THE THINGS THAT MAKE YOU S MILE! MOTHERFUCKER

It's Saturday. Thanks to Gene's paint thinner and my own terrible judgement, I spent the entirety of Friday in bed nursing the worst hangover of my life. At least by supper I could eat, and I polished off the last of the snacks I'd packed as emergency vegan supplies. Once I'm done at Conrad Uphill's Arcadia, I have to find somewhere that sells real produce.

But the weirder things get, the less I expect of this place. Does it have stores at all? Does it have a police station or a hospital or a library? Or is it quiche-only restaurants all the way down?

And if that's true, why did Mom come here? It can't have been the attraction of Friday night bridge with old ladies, no matter how sweet Mary is. I'm adult enough and distant enough from the event to see why a single mom pushing fifty might snap and see leaving her kid as the only way out, but what I've never been able to track is Virgie Kyle giving up her work. Those terrible movies were everything to her. Her fans were everything to her.

I haul on a fresh t-shirt, then think better of it. I'm meeting Uphill today. The Big Cheese. The Head Honcho. Discovery-Bang-casual's not going to cut it. So despite the heat I grab a plain black long-sleeve.

Black buttons on black shirt. Black hair, black sneakers. Like I'm about to join Tia's Sisters of the Moon. Like I'm dressed for a funeral.

Will Uphill let me walk the grounds to the cemetery Mary mentioned? Fuck it—I don't care if he doesn't. I don't care if he sets his dogs on me. I have to see. When I see, I'll be sure.

I catch myself in the mirror. My skin's pasty, I've got shadows under my eyes. Maybe I should ask Tia to borrow her eyeliner so I can complete the look. I really do wish I had something more theatrical, a cape or fangs or plastic claws. Mom would dig that.

I crumple at the waist, hand clamped to my mouth, vision blurred with tears. "Oh, fuck. Oh, god."

And almost as abruptly as it comes, it goes. I wipe my hand over my face, grab a tissue to clean my nose.

This is it. This is why I came. To bury old hurts, to move on. I'm one graveside visit away from putting this to bed. Well, half of this. There's still more to learn, like whether there's anything of Mom left here, like who she was talking to in the video—this mysterious *other Ty* who she presumably named me after. I still have a million questions.

I slip my phone into my pocket. I may not have anyone here with me—and yeah, okay, Josh was probably right that I shouldn't be doing this alone—but at least I have Joshbot.

Wow.

So that's what a wave of shame mixed with self-loathing feels like. I can't wait to get the fuck away from here.

Before I head out I check in with the receptionist in case Josh called. As if I timed it, Cathy's at the door kissing someone I assume is her wife—real shocker there. Cathy's wife or girlfriend leaves and I wave to her like we've met, already forgetting how to be human after a day off the clock.

"Did anyone call for me?" I ask, flat out, no pleasantries. I can't summon them today, especially when I still have the image of Cathy headbanging to "Umbrella," tattooed onto my memory.

She smiles, because she's nicer than I am. "Sorry, no calls. Want me to take a message in case they phone back?"

"Tell him I'll be back in a few days. The investigation's over."

That should stop him begging Uphill for access to the island. Worse than Josh showing up and wasting his time so we can listen to my awkward voicemail together would be Josh turning up after I've left and listening to it with Kayla in the cabin I've just vacated.

'Yeah, that's right, not only did I end the show over voicemail after confessing my undying love for you, but you also wasted $1000 and 8 hours to fly here for no reason.'

Not a follow-up conversation I relish.

I'm heading out the door when something catches my eye—a glossy pamphlet peeking out from beneath some papers. There's no way to take it without Cathy noticing, so I play it cazh and peruse it in front of her.

It's an honest-to-god tourist brochure, complete with an anime version of Conrad Uphill dressed in a lupine fursuit and gesturing to the pristine wilderness on the pamphlet's cover. A speech balloon reads, "Welcome to Arcadia! Welcome to Freedom!"

Cathy stretches over the desk and taps the brochure with her pencil. "I'll need that back when you're done."

"Uh, sure?" I mean, I wasn't going to take it home and pin it to my wall. Still, it's kind of weird.

"They're expensive to print," she says, obviously sensing my confusion. "And we only got so many in for the newcomers—I have a couple extras, but we sometimes need those for orientation."

That's new.

I unfold the pamphlet. On the interior flap there's another cartoon drawing, this time of young people in aggressively normal beige outfits, each perfectly gendered—long plain skirts for the girls, ties and tucked-in dress shirts for the boys. The girls wear pigtails, while all the boys are clean-shaven with crew cuts. It's like something off a 1950s recruitment poster. On the opposing flap is a second picture, structured so the two images become a *before* and *after*. The second image features the same kids, but this time they're all dressed uniquely. It still kind of looks like a recruitment poster, but maybe one from the 90s instead, when educational programs started trying to sell themselves as models of diversity. Several of the *after* kids wear leather and metal studs, others look like hippies or have dyed hair. One of the *before*-boys is a girl in the second image.

Looks like Echo Island never stopped being a camp.

The center of the pamphlet's triptych features a modern, cartoon map of the island.

I turn the pamphlet over. Where I'd expect to find a list of things to do while vacationing on the island, it's all bullshit motivational phrases: "Don't be Afraid to be Yourself!," "Dream!," "When Life Gives You Lemons Make Lemonade . . . on Echo Island!" and even, "Life. Laugh. Love" complete with typo.

Oh, and "Seven Thirty, Fingers Dirty." That ol' inspirational classic.

I hold the pamphlet up to Cathy. "Uphill runs a summer camp?"

Maybe it's the real reason Josh was having so much trouble getting here—the rooms were booked by parents chomping at the bit to send their teens for a summer hunting feral dogs through the woods and making boots from their carcasses.

Again, classic.

"A hundred years of summer and counting." Cathy's smile is painted on. "Is there anything else, hon?" she asks, Stepfordly.

"Yeah, actually. I'd like to know why no one on the island can answer a straight question." Or a bent question.

Cathy purses her lips. "I'm really sorry. Connie's looking forward to seeing you and explaining it himself."

After Tia's warning to me two nights ago the statement carries an extra level of threat.

I wave the pamphlet again. "I thought coming to Echo Island was meant to deprogram you or whatever. Welcome to Freedom, right?"

"That's just a line, Sweetie."

"Yeah, thought so." But she didn't tell me I was wrong about the deprogramming.

And not that it'd be weird to have some kind of LGBT-themed go-get-'em-champ summer club—at least not any weirder or creepier than those are by default—but from what I saw on the website, Echo Island isn't big on advertising that service. If the island were really trying to provide an opportunity for the gay youth to find themselves, they'd probably want to make sure the gay youth in question could find Echo Island first.

As Cathy predicted, it's summery outside. I shield my eyes and look up at the endless blue sky, suddenly wishing it would rain. Already I'm regretting the long-sleeve.

According to the pamphlet I can reach Uphill's by walking past The Moon again, taking Rivers Road and turning onto Talbot Avenue, but I'm craving variety and walk up Dubrovna instead. The part of the street I walk on is purely residential, but some of those squat cement buildings I noted from the plane dot the streets that slash horizontally to connect Rivers with Dubrovna: Glendon, Old Thiess, Kessler, Fitzgerald—are they the surnames of the mysterious founders Tia mentioned? I'd have expected Uphill's mansion to sit on Main Street or King or Queen, but it's another random last name.

Whatever truth lurks behind Echo Island's roads will have to remain unsolved, because as soon as I reach Talbot it's like I'm someone's tiny plastic toy and they've tossed me into a playset that's a couple inches too big.

I can only describe Arcadia as an estate. Fifteen-foot metal fences stretch the length of Talbot to either side of the Mc-Mansion, curving onto Dubrovna and extending so far up the road I can't see where they end. Towering pines clutter the corner so I can just make out the mansion's masonry beyond them. It's big enough that the graveyard Mary told me about becomes entirely more plausible. And somehow, all the roads I've passed have hidden it from view, despite how massive it is. It's as though the layout was designed to disguise the place, only it seems counterproductive to hide a building so obviously conceived with ostentation in mind.

The opposite side of the road is fenced backyards stretching from behind the houses on the street I just passed. In and of itself it doesn't sound that weird, but the visual of all those homes back-on to Talbot, with Arcadia looming behind them, makes my teeth ache. Like Arcadia can't tolerate anyone—even another building—looking it face-on. Like Arcadia is a prison watchtower overseeing everyone and everything on the island. A panopticon.

The ditch that runs alongside the yards is filled with purple foxgloves, same as the ones on Tia's jacket. Maybe someone's got a dictionary of symbolism lying around somewhere.

I straighten, swallow, push down the worry churning in my guts. I run my fingers over my phone case, retreading the questions I typed in the phone's notepad to ask Uphill, in case I forgot one of the many millions. This isn't a place I want to visit twice.

I stop across from a metal gate that stands dead centre in front of the mansion, the one so large it's like it was built to keep something out. *Arcadia* is written in metalwork in an arch over the entrance, and as though the head archivist at the world's premier museum of kitsch leaned back and admired the design and said, 'No, that's not enough, give it more flash!,' there's a painted sign arching beneath it. If you've ever received a copy of *The Watchtower* in your postal box, you'll have zero problems picturing it.

In the image, Conrad Uphill, black cowboy hat and all, stands at the front of a parade of racially diverse Echo Islanders. Two children cling to him from left and right, gleefully looking up at him like he's Christ Jesus and he's leading everyone off to eat Kraft Dinner and dance with tigers in the promised land. The line of people curves back so far you can't see the end. Everyone's smiling, the pearly whites revealed by Uphill's grin so sharp they could cut cement.

Behind the gate, a long driveway extends to the pillared white doorstep, then branches left and right.

It's totally fucked, and I'm totally about to die, or at the very least be forced to convert to Uphillery, or Uphillism, or Uphillianity, but I cross the road and walk straight up to the buzzer beside the gate. So what if I have to drink a little Kool Aid or handle a few snakes or speak a few tongues? It's only temporary. Everything is only ever temporary.

The speaker outside the building croaks into action before I can speak and an artificial yet somehow still charming twang statics from inside. It's Conrad Uphill's voice, welcoming me as the gates to Arcadia creak open.

"Seven-thirty, fingers dirty, baby doll," says the voice with a laugh. "Come find me."

10

CONRAD UPHILL'S PARLOUR

"Fuck off," I say into the speaker.

I'll go find someone sane to question, and if I can't find any of those—increasingly likely—I'll call Gord and fly home.

I glance at the fence—too tall for me to climb, but I bet I could squeeze through, especially if this radical no-food diet continues.

"I know what you're thinking, Tyler Kyle," says Conrad.

"Tacos."

There's a pause. "Excuse me?"

"Tacos." I turn to face it and cross my arms, since he's obviously got cameras on me, and since I've obviously embraced talking to electronics. "I was thinking about tacos. The perfect summer food—easy to make on the go, or down at the beach, or with a group of friends on a picnic in the murder woods. Customizable, if unlike me you hang out with more than two people at a time. Or if, like me, you have a bestie whose idea of culinary panache is cooking his frozen dinners in the oven and not the microwave. Plus, easy to veganize. Or not! You do you with Mr. Taco."

My stomach rumbles.

Conrad Uphill chuckles. "Very nice, Mr. Kyle."

I'm not impressed with his affected, southern Dracula routine. "Unfortunately, you don't eat . . . tacos. Right? Well, I hate to break it to you, but I'm already a vampire. You really need to catch up on your Discovery Bangisodes. That was like, so last season."

"Oh, I'm all caught up on everything you do, Mr. Kyle."

Great. "Let me guess, cameras in the cabin, right? Yesterday was probably boring. Sleep. Sleep. Shit. Sleep. Shit."

He laughs again, like maybe he doesn't know what else to do. "Come now, Mr. Kyle. You must think I'm an evil mastermind. Whatever made you so frightened of little old Connie Uphill?"

I wrinkle my nose at the speaker like it's done a massive fart. "I wouldn't call it fear exactly, more like a justifiable hesitancy when it comes to getting in mansions with strange men, even when they do have candy. And so far, where's my candy?"

Uphill's voice drops several octaves, and the twang vanishes.

"Here's your candy, Mr. Kyle. Everything that comes in or out of Echo Island comes and goes by my discretion. Every speck of dust, every idle little squirrel, every bratty, overgrown child with something to prove."

I widen my eyes, point to my chest, do a little mimery. Who, me? *Me?* Aw shucks.

"All I need is to make a single phone call," Uphill continues, completely ignoring me, "and flights out of town go from negligible to non-existent. I'm no survival expert, but as I admire you from the vantage of my estate, I can't help but be left with the impression of a man unused to roughing it."

So he thinks he's pegged me. Fine. I *wouldn't* survive a trek across the wilderness all on my lonesome—or probably even as part of a togethersome, especially if my other thirds were Josh and Kayla—but you don't give hammy speeches like his if you genuinely have any self-confidence in your ability to intimidate. Real tough guys don't need to talk it up, they do the do. And as a mighty fine talker and a terrible doer, I should know.

And knowledge is power.

Or something.

"Don't body shame me!" I say. So much power.

But Uphill has a trump card. The one thing that could convince me to step into the parlour.

"Your mother had a beautiful body." I can hear the creepy smile in his voice. "Don't worry your vacant little head, I don't mean it like that. I know you've been snooping around town, asking your cute questions. I prefer my conquests with a little more testosterone than Virgie could provide. You know, I'm sorry, Tyler. I think we got off on the wrong foot. It means a lot to Echo Island to have a Kyle back on home soil, and like any old queen I'm a veritable *glutton* for a bit of drama."

For once I'm quiet. He likes to talk almost as much as I do, which means if I'm silent he'll probably keep talking, and the more he says the better chance I have of learning something useful.

He continues. "I don't get much opportunity to show off anymore—I'm sure you understand, with your little TV show."

Why is everything about me "little?" I'm staunchly average height, and if anything, my dreams tend to overreach a little . . . I mean, *a bit*.

"You get internet at Arcadia?" I ask.

"I get everything I want." He shifts back into speech mode. My legs are starting to ache. I hope he convinces me to come indoors soon so I can sit down. Also, *air conditioning*. What a miracle. Totally worth being murdered for. "Your arrival is very important to me, and I'll be frank, I'm even a little starstruck. Your mother and I were great friends, and I got overexcited setting this whole show up for you. You do like a bit of mystery, isn't that right? Isn't that what your TV show is about? The one you make with your boyfriend?"

Uphill couldn't possibly know enough about me to have anticipated how that would cut, could he? No one knows about what went down between me and Josh. Sure, watch ten out of ten of our videos and you'll catch a veritable cascade of innuendo, but neither of us filmed Tequila Hot Tub Funtimes, so he can't possibly know his comment will hurt. And it does hurt, stupidly. It hurts that even this megalomaniacal cartoon TV villain can hit play on our channel and draw the same conclusions that started to blossom in my chest like emotional cancer.

"He's not my boyfriend." I'm falling into something like a trap, probably, but even if it's discount Lord Summerisle we're talking about, I'm not going to let someone believe things about Josh that aren't true.

"Oh, I'm very sorry. I shouldn't have assumed. I take it though, that you do love a mystery, and I *do* love to entertain. I suspect we share that in common." He sighs. "Please come in. It was never my intention to cause you distress, and now that you're here I'll be happy to answer your questions."

I hesitate. I mean obviously this is deeply fucked, and I wouldn't trust him even if Tia hadn't straight up warned me not to fucking trust him. But I don't honestly think he's going to murder me. It's more like he wants to suss me out, to convince me of his way of seeing things, to collect me. He thinks he's playing me, thinks he's the smart one and I'm, as he put it, *a bratty, overgrown child*. It's something I can use. And while I chickened out using the extremely minimal "wiles" I apparently possess to interrogate Gene, I don't give a flying fuck about leaving Uphill with blue balls and a broken heart.

I shrug. "Yeah, fine."

I mosey through Arcadia's gates, with barely a glance at the avenue of pines to either side of me. I hope my nonchalance uneases him, but if he's watched as much Discovery Bang as he implied, he's probably not phased at all.

The electronic gate scrapes shut behind me, which would be concerning if I couldn't squeeze through the holes.

At the tops of the pines, cameras spy on me from their arboreal perches like one-eyed birds. Weirder than the cameras, which are honestly not weird at all for a rich asshole's house, are the big metal speakers on telephone poles. I can perfectly imagine Josh spying one in the dark and mistaking it for Siren Head.

The pristine white door creaks open as I reach the grand entrance, and I can't say 100% that the creak doesn't come from the speakers hidden between the trees. The artificiality is comforting. It's haunted carnival level stuff, campy and obvious. When I approach the door I'm fully expecting a plastic skeleton to leap out at me from a bizarre angle.

It's more of a surprise that nothing happens, that when I open the door and walk through there's no one waiting for me—only a silver platter on a cocktail table, laden with pornstar cocktails and animal crackers. I know the drinks are pornstars, because my obscene love of what's unequivocally the worst cocktail invented became an in-house meme for about a month.

The table stands beside a curved grand staircase—the only obvious path to follow, even if there wasn't a sign with an image of a pointing hand directing me upstairs.

A notecard with *eat me* is folded in front of the drink and crackers. Not exactly encouraging. Still, I take one of the drinks and pocket some of the crackers. I'm not eating anything Uphill gives me until I have some evidence they're not laced with rohypnol, but I am starving.

I mount the stairs slowly, to the clink of the ice in my glass. At the top, a narrow hallway stretches to either side of the stairs—not what I'd expected from this fancy a building. Sure, it's got red velvet carpeting, gilded baroque accents on its cream walls, but usually you'd expect wide open spaces, room for multiple guests to prance upstairs showing themselves off. It's almost like this building wasn't originally styled this way, like Uphill converted it from something more utilitarian.

My black sneakers mothball against the carpet as I follow the signs down the right-hand corridor. The doors lining either side of the hallway are spaced at perfect, even intervals, like a prison or a hospital or an apartment building. They're painted red so they bleed into the carpet.

Uphill hasn't bothered to turn on the lights, and with only the natural sunlight filtering in from the windows in the entrance and a wider area further up, the shadowy white walls and prevalent red are disorienting.

I reach for the pamphlet in my pocket and unfold it to examine the cartoon image of the mansion and get a better idea of its shape. When I flew in it looked rectangular, and that does seem to be the case on the map, but the drawing gives me no sense of how far it extends, of its original purpose. If it were a hospital, that would explain why Gene called Uphill to come get Mary.

I pass a recessed window with a little chair tucked into one corner. There's a picture on the wall, and for once it's not of Uphill. It's an engraving of some kind. There's a man I assume is a king, given the crown—usually a solid indicator. He's seated at a table with a naked Greek statue lady, and someone's hiding under the table. The second most prominent figure is a monster, or a guy in a donkey mask. He's running out of the frame as the king beckons him back.

Maybe he's not into pony play.

There's foreign writing beneath the picture—Latin maybe?—I only catch a glimpse. It's kind of neat. But then, my tolerance for *off* is high.

I snap a picture of the etching. Maybe on the way out—assuming Uphill hasn't locked me in his sex dungeon—I can take a closer look. If the internet were working, Josh'd already be cross-referencing this shit.

I round a sharp corner, only to be met with more identical doors. Geometric Tiffany lamps hang from the ceiling, lighting up the corridor. The lights—too large for the space—only increase the sense of wrongness.

The signs lead me to a break in the wall. Large, unpainted wooden doors dominate the alcove, framed by two huge deer. Their antlers are twined round with dried, pale blue foxgloves. The stags are an almost perfect mirror of each other, their necks arching toward the door so they're watching me as I approach. I spare a glance at the stag to my right, then depress the handle and push one of the double doors inwards.

Inside smells of wood paneling and old house. If you've never been inside an old house, I'm not sure how else to describe the odour. It's not unpleasant, maybe a little musty, the combination of leather and ancient fittings and whatever chemicals they use to polish and preserve antique furniture.

The room's bigger than I would have thought, but it's so packed with antiques that a distinct wave of claustrophobia washes over me.

A giant taxidermied swan looms in the corner—no, not just a swan. A swan's head and wings sewn onto the body of what looks like a goat, or maybe a sheared sheep. It's posed so its avian head is bent toward a lifted front leg, like a cat cleaning itself.

It probably says a lot about me that my first thought isn't *fuck, run*, so much as "where the hell did he get the swan?"

I guess to most people though, this would be extremely weird and at least mildly upsetting.

What *is* weird, is Conrad Uphill sitting at the desk, clad in black cowboy hat, black-rimmed glasses and matching black suit, with a chocolate cake sitting directly on the desk in front of him, and his hands buried right inside the cake. I mean, *right* into the centre of the cake like you always wanted to do as a kid only you got your hand slapped every time.

A huge wood panel frames him, cluttered with curios in glass cases—more taxidermy by the looks of it. Two tusks stick out from the wall behind him, above what looks like a fireplace. The patterned green wallpaper covering the rest of the room reminds me of something you'd see on the set of *Arsenic and Old Lace*. $100 says there's a trap door.

"Mmm. Hmm. Mm. Hhn." Uphill, sucks the icing off his fingers one by one.

Behind me, the door shuts with a dull thud.

"Good cake?" I ask, approaching the desk, very conscious of my untouched drink.

"Delectable. Mario's. Best cake in town." He gives a chef's kiss, then grins. There's something familiar about his smile besides its resemblance to the portraits hanging in every restaurant. He gestures at the mess in front of him. "Care to try some?"

The cake's sides have collapsed onto the desk like a mudslide devouring a steep, winding road.

"Thanks. I'm vegan."

I should probably find him frightening or gross, but there's something magnetic about his face. He's also very handsome, for a guy over twice my age who's covered in cake.

Uphill waves a cakey hand. "Oh, I know. A lot of us are on Echo Island. I had it made special for you. But I couldn't resist, you know?"

I smile, willing my empty stomach not to growl. Right now it would be perfectly happy to eat Uphill's desk-cake.

"I already ate," I lie.

Uphill laughs. Judging by the lines at the corners of his eyes, he laughs a lot. "Is that why you've hardly touched your drink?" He wiggles his fingers and I hand him the pornstar. He takes a gulp. "*Ahh.* See? Perfectly safe."

And then it hits—I *do* know him. I've seen that face up *real* close before, hidden beneath ten layers of foundation and contouring. And not just his face, but . . . well, I think that's one memory I'm going to bury under cement after dousing it in lime.

Queen fucking Cee.

I take the pornstar back, trying to disguise my recognition, or my failure to recognize him, or whatever would make this situation less horrific, which I'm swiftly realizing is nothing. "I want to keep a clear head."

"Don't worry." He tilts his head to look up at me beneath a heavy brow. "They're virgin." He grins wide, grabs a handkerchief from beside him, wipes off his hands, and dabs his cheeks.

I could throw up all over again, though mostly I'm disgusted with myself. "Like me, is that it?" I ask flatly. "You'll be disappointed if you try and use me to summon the Great Old Ones or whatever."

Uphill casually swipes the cake off the desk so it falls to his right, like there's a garbage can beside him, only I'm pretty sure there isn't.

"I doubt very much they would be disappointed, Mr. Kyle. You're a fine specimen. But I didn't call you here to sacrifice you. I know what you must be thinking about this place, *about big bad Conrad Uphill*." He smiles, all teeth.

I grimace. "You could have said something back at The Moon, but I guess it didn't occur to you I might have acted differently if I'd known I was making out with L. Ron Hubbard."

It's viscerally satisfying to watch the smile melt from Uphill's face. "I do apologize, Mr. Kyle, but I wasn't under the impression you didn't know who I was. We were both a little intoxicated, if I recall, and *if* you'll recall, it was you who kissed me, you who—"

I close my eyes and hold up my hands. I don't want it repeated, more than aware of what I did and who I did it to. "Let's just—fuck. We can forget it. I wasn't even there. It's probably number negative 1000 on the list of fucked up shit you're responsible for."

Conrad wipes down his desk. "I promise you don't have half the story yet. Echo Island means a lot to the people who've called it home—your mother among them."

I place the cocktail on his desk, and he snatches it up and shoves a coaster under it. Which, *okay*, but I did just watch the dude eat a literal cake off the literal surface.

"Why don't you start by explaining why my mom came here and how she heard of this place." I shift my attention from Uphill to the animals behind him.

The taxidermy's displayed in small cases built into the wood paneling. It's more hybrids like the swan-goat, only fun-sized: rabbits with ravens, voles with juncos, a fish with a squirrel. If I'd looked closer at the deer outside, would they have had salmony lips?

Three sets of tiny legs in red skirts hang above Uphill's head, trapped inside a rectangular picture frame. The flesh of the legs—calves made to seem like legs, really—looks oddly human, until they end in animal feet: hooves and paws.

"Admiring my girls?" he asks.

I refocus on Uphill. "Yeah, I was thinking I could take them dancing at The Thunder Moon."

Uphill chuckles. "It's nice to see your charm isn't all for the cameras."

Isn't it? I'd bet my life Uphill's filming this whole conversation. "It's for whoever I think is worth it." I feel like Gollum trying to seduce Saruman the Wise.

He smiles, but it's hollow.

"Are you going to answer my questions, Mr. Uphill?" I hop up so I'm half sitting on the desk.

Remarkably, I don't fall off. Round of applause?

"Conrad, if you please." Uphill looks me up and down. His face is stone, his eyes dull as shark eyes. It's what murderers must look like, just before the killing blow.

"Are you going to answer my questions, Conrad?" I smile. I do the intimidating thing with my face, hoping it matches his expression measure for measure and knowing it doesn't. I'm just not going to pull off the gravitas of a seventy-year-old in a black cowboy hat.

He walks around the desk to stand beside me, then grabs my hand, tracing his thumb over the ridges and pads of my fingers. "You have long fingers," he says, like maybe I've somehow lived my whole life without this knowledge.

"You don't say," I reply, because why the hell not at this point? If Uphill was going to banish me for being a mouthy little shit he'd have done it already.

As predicted, he ignores me. He rolls his thumb over the joints of my fingers and I can't fight a shiver, can't help but be drawn back to the not totally awful parts of kissing him.

"Do you know the violinist Paganini?" he asks. "From the eighteen hundreds." He raises his thick brown eyebrows above his round-rimmed glasses. "They say he made a bargain with the devil to be able to play so well, but that's just a story. In reality, he simply possessed very long fingers. He was probably double-jointed as well. What might have been a deformity made him a virtuoso."

Uphill slides his fingers back over mine. I swallow, staring him in his face. On the surface it's so I can keep an eye on him, but there's something else underneath it, something like a song calling me, like the night at The Moon. I don't want to look, but I can't stop. The whole forest seems to live inside his eyes, and despite the casual ableism I'm momentarily hypnotized.

"His was a life to envy," Conrad finishes, receding behind his desk so the great tusks of his post-modern taxidermy jut to either side of him: spears pointed right at me.

"Didn't he die of syphilis?" I ask, joking, distancing.

Uphill grins, and it breaks the spell my wisecrack couldn't. "There are worse ways to go."

"I mean, I guess on a technical level, yeah. It probably sucks worse to get stretched on the rack."

"Your mother started off her life here," he says, like the whole Paganini monologue never happened. He strokes his desk. "Have you ever heard of conversion therapy, Mr. Kyle?"

"Straight camp, right?" I've read some articles, watched a movie.

"Camp, yes." Uphill chokes a laugh that's as scathing as a rusty metal fence. "Those places were—*are*—torture. Well-meaning Christian parents sending little Bobby or Suzy to unknot the tangled parts of themselves and scrape from their bones the desires that sleep beneath their skin. They believe if you scour the veins, the nerves, if you strip the flesh you can fill it back up again with something clean and pure."

He reaches toward one of the stuffed monstrosities tucked into the wall panel, the smallest bird I've ever seen sewn together with the head of a fieldmouse. It looks vulnerable. The way Uphill smooths the back of his hand down the glass that surrounds it is gentle and loving.

"But the dirt doesn't live in the skin." It's like he's no longer in the room with me, like he's not talking to *me* at all. He plucks his glasses from his face and rubs his eyes. "Dirt lives in the heart. It poisons with words and songs and beautiful lies. The voice that silences, the caress that stings, the kiss that bites and tears.

"They believe they can shove a man—*a boy's*—head underwater and drown out his desires, that a stick, *a stick*, can knock away his hopes and dreams like they were teeth. Yes, a straight camp. But what do they do with us, Mr. Kyle, when the stick doesn't work? When the water meant to cleanse only inspires us to drink more deeply? They send you to a worse place, and then another. They tell your parents it's not working. You're a tough nut to crack and it's a fallacy of the modern age that we should be so tender with a disobedient child. Spare the rod, spare the isolation, spare the torture—you spoil the fag."

He slips his glasses on. "What happens when there is no more worse? Where do they take Suzy when even the worst place can't tame her?" He turns to face me. "They brought her to Saint Serge's, where they took so many of us. And once upon a time I would do my darndest to break them." He clutches his hands, rubbing them. "But I didn't break them. They broke me. And I found enough of us broken men and women who were tired of the charade, of sending our own to the slaughter, and we made Echo Island ours. Arcadia. A world where anything is possible. A world where you can fly from that *worst place,* with its rules and its codes and its lies, and you can wake up here. Free."

I swallow as his wide eyes catch mine. I think I know what he's saying, despite the layers he's wrapped his answer in to turn it into a grand speech worthy of unpacking. A monologue made for the stage.

"You used to work at a conversion camp," I say, because it's like he wants me to say it.

He smiles. "Yes." He goes back to cleaning his desk. "And now I run Echo Island as an escape from such places. When parents send their children from camp to camp, they've already given them up. I have some good friends in one of those *worst places*, and so when the time comes for Suzy and Bobby to be broken and tortured somewhere new, I pay for them to come here instead. Echo Island is a sanctuary, Tyler. Small recompense for what I've done, but I am paying."

I couldn't care less about Uphill's personal guilt for whatever atrocities he was part of. I came here for one thing. "And my mom?"

"Nice Scottish lass, siphoned in the early days. Oh, we were young then. She helped me, you know, when we overthrew the founders. Then one day she decided she wanted to see the world." Uphill's grin springs back to his face like the smile of a customer service rep. "We all missed Virgie Kyle. Who wouldn't? You knew her. A bright star in a lonely sky. A comet shooting across the sunset. And that *voice.*"

My heart's swimming in my throat. I know my face is all tells—nose twitching, brow creasing. All my little ticks. Her ticks. "But you let her go. And she had me. And she came back to Echo Island anyway. Why?"

Uphill takes my hand again, but I snatch it back and slip off the desk. "Her own business, and she dealt with it as she saw fit. We don't ask a lot of questions on the island, Mr. Kyle. It's antithetical to our mission statement."

"*Your* mission statement." His tone doesn't sit right, setting fire to an anger I'd left simmering. "It's your face plastered all over walls and place mats and guidebooks. It's you who's painted on the front of this mansion, about to graduate your cultists to the Galactic Confederacy."

Uphill sniffs. "It's only ego. We all have one. We're not a cult, or if we are then I think you severely misunderstand what that word means. But I thought you wanted to learn about Virgie, didn't you? Isn't that why you flew all the way here?"

"So tell me."

He holds his hands out. "I can't read your mind. What do you want to know? You told me you had questions, Mr. Kyle. Did the dogs scare you? What about the bears? I heard you had an awful time out there in the woods when poor Mary got crushed by that trap."

I have questions about each of those, about . . . whatever that was in the forest, but he's trying to break my calm, scatter my thoughts. I stop. I breathe. I think. I even pretend for a moment I'm not *me* me, standing here still half-panicked from two nights ago and grieving the deaths of my mom, my friendship, and my career. Instead I'm Discovery Bang me. I don't take people's bullshit. I don't crack.

I stare him down, let out a breath. "Who's the other Ty my mom names in the video you sent?"

A flicker of confusion crosses Uphill's face. "I didn't send a video. Don't get me wrong, I'm very pleased to have a real celebrity visitor, but I wouldn't have reached out to you if you hadn't called first."

I try to read his face for an indication he's lying, but he's inscrutable. I'd assumed, based on the evidence so far, that Uphill was the stalker. If he's not, we—*I*—may have bigger problems. Unless the stalker was trying to do something altruistic—lure me here so I could find out about my mom.

"Tysha was your mother's partner before she left. Virgie returned to us every summer for the Dog Days. The last time she came, it was Ty's funeral that brought her home. Not even I can say why she stayed, but if you want my honest assessment of your mother, she was always running from something. The something didn't have to be real for it to feel urgent to her. Her feet wouldn't stay still. She made a nice little home here, but eventually she ran from that, too. A place didn't have to be bad for it to seem like a cage. It was only a matter of time, I think, before she packed up and left us again. I'm sure she would have if the stroke hadn't taken her." His frown deepens. In the moment, he looks genuinely sad, like he truly is mourning a dead friend. "And for that you have my sincere condolences, Mr. Kyle."

Caught in the quagmire of his words, I'm temporarily quiet.

Sure, Uphill's told me all about this conversion camp, some rebellion he supposedly orchestrated with my mother to turn Echo Island into a queer paradise, but when it comes to learning anything about my mom's motivations, I'm nearly as clueless as when I stepped past that tacky metal gate and into Arcadia. All he's told me, though not in as many words, is that at some point my mother decided I was the cage she needed away from. Nothing I hadn't thought myself a thousand times.

Not that it doesn't hurt. It's an old wound: one glimmering star in the constellation of my life. It fucked me up back then, sure, but I was generally pretty sane until I set foot here. It hits differently coming from someone else's mouth, like a knife taken to a scar that's already healed over and had its stitches removed.

"She's buried on your estate," I say, because whether or not Uphill's grief is genuine, I don't have the energy to engage with it.

He nods, solemn at least. "You can follow the signs to the graveyard if you like. Tysha's buried there as well, along with the rest of us."

"Makes it sound like you're all already dead," I say, because in saying it I'm temporarily removed from the source of any discomfort.

"I'm very much alive, Mr. Kyle," Uphill assures me.

"Phew." I wipe my forehead. "That's a relief." And without taking a breath I add: "So what about the monsters in the wood?"

11

THE MONSTERS IN THE WOOD

"Oh, I don't know what you mean, Mr. Kyle." Uphill smiles, incredulous. "My understanding is that you're the voice of rationality on your little show. Surely you understand how the mind plays games when it's faced with the unknown? Shadows in the forest, dangers the mind converts to supernatural events to make the unspeakable palatable. When we experience true horror, real violence, our brains produce endorphins, adrenaline—" he flicks his finger against my glass, "—a veritable cocktail of mind-altering substances. But you know that. So why don't you tell *me*, Mr. Kyle, what you think you saw in the forest?" He raises his eyebrows. "What monsters did your sweet endorphins conjure for you in the darkness?"

He's not going to tell me anything. This was hideously pointless.

I step back from the desk. I prowl around the room, ogling paintings in frames I hadn't noticed were hanging on the wall behind me, letting my gaze roll over every poor mounted animal with glass beads for eyes. It's all so much garbage, a perfect match for the garbage person sitting behind me.

I keep my back to him until I hear his chair creak. Then I keep my back to him some more. I reach for a framed, black and white photograph and unhook it from the wall.

In it, Uphill's standing next to a frumpy Middle Eastern woman who could be auditioning for the role of Baba Yaga, and a smiling straight White couple in lab coats. You can tell they're a couple from their clasped hands, and also the obnoxious shirts they're wearing underneath the lab coats: "Future Mommy" and "Future Daddy."

I remove the photo. *June 17th, 1976 - Conrad, Meg, Angela, and Eric* is written on the back.

"Are you finished vandalizing my property, Mr. Kyle?"

"No." I fold the photograph in half and slide it into my pocket. "Now I am. Maybe."

I pop out my phone and open my list of questions.

I sit down on the floor directly in front of his desk, cross-legged. "Okay. Number one." I hold up a finger in case he's a visual learner.

"What are you doing, Mr. Kyle?" He stands up and leans forward across his desk like he couldn't see me.

Oops.

I clear my throat. "Number one. What are the monsters in the—Okay. Number two. What's Dan. 4.25?" I look up expectantly.

"Would you like a chair, Mr. Kyle?"

"No. Number two. What's Dan. 4.25?"

Uphill steps out from behind his desk. I hear him scuff his shoe against the carpet like there's cake on his foot. "Why, it's a biblical verse, Mr. Kyle."

"Great. Figured that out. What one? I'm guessing as an ex-minister for the church of heteronorma-nativity you've got the whole book memorized."

Uphill sucks his teeth. "That one was rather tortured, Mr. Kyle. I'm afraid I don't recall. We don't keep Bibles on the island any longer. It's from the book of Daniel, if that helps. Do you know the book of Daniel?"

I look up at him. "Makes friends with lions, has visions, heals some friends who get trapped in Nebuchadnezzar's Easy Bake oven—that about the gist?"

Uphill grins. He drums his fingers against his desk. "That's about the gist. I'm afraid I've let my knowledge lapse."

I shrug. "Can I use your internet to look it up?"

"No, Mr. Kyle, you cannot."

"Aw shucks, that's not suspicious. Anyway, moving on. Number Three—"

He uncrosses his legs. "How many of these are there?"

"Twenty-Seven."

"Really, Mr. Kyle, this is a bit much. It's as if you don't *trust* me. Truthfully, I do have work to attend to."

I glare at him from beneath thick black eyebrows. "How about some follow-ups. You said my mom came here every year for the Dog Days. Why?"

I'd like to say I would have noticed Mom making a trip to Echo Island every July, but she was always getting flown places and leaving me with the camera crew, or the producers, or even other actors. That's basically what happened after she left for good. On-set orphan, Tyler Kyle.

Uphill smiles this time, the tension in his brow relaxing. That's not exactly good for me. "Tradition means a lot to us on the island. It meant less to your mother, but she had Tysha to come home to."

In the video, after Mom's little dance with the paper, Tysha says, "The world's not ready yet," as though they're planning to leave together. So why didn't Ty come with my mother? And if Mom wanted to leave as badly as she makes it sound in the tape, why did she ever come back? All I can figure is Uphill had a way of keeping Tysha here. By his own admission, he has a massive ego and participated in an inhumane social program that gave him total authority over his charges and their movements. People like Uphill don't give that up.

And both of us have seen the video, even if he's not the one who sent and doctored it. So he knows I have good reason to doubt his happy camper story about how Mom couldn't wait to return. He knows that, and he doesn't care, which means he thinks I can't touch him.

I push myself to my feet. "Why didn't Tysha leave with Mom?" Now that I'm standing, we're unnervingly close. I lean into the weirdness.

"They didn't consult me about their plans, Mr. Kyle. If Tysha intended to leave, she didn't inform me."

I frown. "The video—"

An alarm at the volume of an ambulance siren blares from a speaker in the upper right corner and I swear I jump back several feet.

Jesus.

Christ.

Uphill doesn't flinch. "I'm sorry," he yells over the noise. "It's my reminder to take my pills." He hurries behind the desk, bends down, and the alarm cuts off.

I glare at the speaker, which looks an awful lot like the ones along the driveway. If this is a converted conversion camp, they probably had communications systems all over the island.

Like a prison, because I guess it was one. It probably still is, only I can't figure how Uphill manages it. Tia and Nor and Gene don't seem like cultists and no one's in literal cages. Sure, trekking it out of here would be hard, but it's not impossible, and Tia talked about the pilots like they were friendly.

Uphill slides open a desk drawer, pulls out a generic white pill bottle, and shakes it. I walk to the desk, read the label as he pops the lid.

"Persephone." I frown. Something about it gives me déjà vu. Mom was always taking pills—were they the same ones? To be honest, I'd always assumed she was an addict.

He slams back a couple pills. I catch a glimmer of purplish ovals inside the container before he closes it. "Keeps the ticker in tip-top shape." His southern twang is back—is it meant to signal the end of our meeting? The hand he raises and gestures at the door with is a less than subtle hint.

"I'm not done with my questions," I say.

"That's too bad." He walks from behind the desk. "But I'm afraid I'm done with you. For now. You have my permission to see Mary, if you'd like. I warn you, she's less than coherent today." He leads me to the door, hand on my back. There's a surprising amount of force behind the push for a man his age. "The hospital is on the ground floor. You'll see the door from the graveyard out back."

I don't like his hand on my back. I don't like his strength. Like all along he's been holding back. I don't like the way he talks about me, or about other people like we're toys.

I may as well be that stuffed swan in the corner.

12

PAM

Almost all the graves are grown-over with weeds. Tall grasses and creeping vines smother granite slabs and stretch like grim green fingers toward gently sloped mounds. My hindbrain deliberates the likelihood that most of those buried here predate the island's liberation, but then, why would the organizers of a conversion camp bother with tombstones? An unmarked pit is surely good enough for delinquent bones.

Maples and choke cherries enclose the perimeter of the cemetery, and a few young saplings sprout from some of the graves. There are a lot of graves—hundreds, I'd say— considering how low the population must be.

I crouch before one of the stones and brush the weeds from its surface. Some people would probably consider rubbing gravestones creepy, but to me it's like . . . I don't know. Reaching backwards in time and saying hi to someone. Only sad in the sense that, yeah, they can't reach back and one day every one of us will be unable to reach back, but for a little while at least, we can try.

Selena Daniels. 1981-2006. I trace my fingers over the letters. Fuck, she was young. There's no *Beloved Daughter* or *Beloved Sister* or even *Beloved Queer Orphan* beneath her name. Like she's nobody and she had no one.

"RIP, Selena." I stand up, moving to the next. *Electo*, obviously someone's chosen name. The dates are *1965-2006*. The same year—and I guess that makes sense really. People who died around the same time getting buried together.

As I walk, my attention's drawn to the dates. A lot of really young people die on the island.

A lot.

1978-1997, 1972-2001, 2002-2018

I snap some photos. *If*—and that's a massive fucking if at this point—I can get my phone working and contact Josh, I can send him some of this shit. As I walk I type out another note to myself to ask him to look up that Bible verse while he's at it.

I'm nearing the centre of the cemetery, where a huge apple tree arches its branches over a patch of grass. There's a woman sitting with her back against the trunk, reading what looks like a single-issue comic. She's biting her nail like she's on the edge of her seat, so engrossed she doesn't turn around.

A kindred spirit, maybe? Not too many weirdos hang out reading comics in graveyards. Then I recognize her: the blonde who helped me carry Mary. The blonde who told me to meet her at Ziggy's . . . yesterday.

Fuck.

She's *deep* in whatever she's reading and doesn't look up even though I'm making a ton of noise. There's a very slight, almost non-existent, breeze and it gathers a few stray strands of her long hair. When they tickle her cheek, she tucks them behind her ear, the upper corner of her comic bending gently. I catch a glimpse of the Superman logo on the chest of—well, presumably Superman, but it could be any number of characters: Supergirl, Superboy, Superdino.

"Hey!" I call out, trying not to sound threatening.

She bolts to her feet, scattering the contents of her backpack across the grass: lipstick, tampons, a notepad . . ..

She adjusts her thick-rimmed square glasses, staring at me with wide, Amanda-Seyfried eyes. She's about my age, my height. Her pale skin's turned beet-fucking red as she stares at me.

I hold my palms up. "I'm Tyler Kyle. Virgie's son. Who you helped the other day? I'm sorry about missing you at Ziggy's. Gene kind of plied me with moonshine."

"Pam," she spits out. "Pamela. Pamela Anderson." She scrunches her eyes closed. "No. I meant. I'm not—my name's Pamela *Matheson*."

Fuck, I scared her. I'm still scaring her. I can practically see her heart pumping in her chest. And wait—wasn't Pam the other pilot? Tia mentioned that she snuck in contraband.

"I'm really sorry. I didn't mean to creep you out—I wasn't sneaking up on you or anything." I point at the mansion. "I was here talking to Uphill, and I came out here to . . .."

She glances behind her briefly. "For your mom? She's over there."

I start picking up her stuff. She steps out of the way, opens her bag and sets it down, crouching beside it.

"I'm really sorry," I repeat. "And, uh, I'm sorry about what you saw in the alley. I was really drunk."

"I-It's really okay." She pauses. "Tyler."

There's a hint of something   recognition?—in the squeak of her voice. It's no wonder, I guess. She told me the other night she knew about my mom, which means she knew about me.

I place Pam's things as gently as I can in the bag: nail polish, a Mars bar, the lipstick and tampons, a pack of condoms. When I reach for the notepad, she darts out a hand and we grab it at the same time.

"Sorry!" we blurt, looking up. And, no joke, our foreheads collide.

"*Fuck*."

"Ow."

I draw back, rubbing my head and laughing.

She rips the notepad out of my hand and shoves it into the bag. It accidentally tears one of the pages and I'm left holding a small scrap with *cobolt-black* written across it. I'm guessing it's her stock list. That'd explain her panic. She might even think I'm Conrad Uphill's spy, here to confiscate her contraband.

"And, sorry again." I hand it to her and smile, but as she takes it, she stares like a deer in headlights.

"You're really pretty." She clamps her hand over her mouth.

Now *I'm* staring. I swallow, raise an eyebrow. "Right back at you?"

What is this. What is my life. Who is this person. Who am I. *Fuck.*

I laugh, force myself to my feet.

There's a book in the grass. When I pick it up, it's an old Bible. I leaf through it. While I'm doing that, Pam collects her comic—*Young Justice* #15—from the grass. She smooths her hand over it, then carefully slides it back inside its bag and board. She must be a collector.

"Uphill said they didn't have Bibles on the island."

Pam darts a nervous look between me and the Good Book. "You won't tell anyone, will you?" She bites her lip. It's painfully cute. I'm suddenly thinking about the lipstick and whether it's hers and what colour it is and *fuck.*

"Uphill and I are on what you'd call opposing sides," I say with confidence. "You said you had information for me about my mom?"

"Did you check out the museum?" Pam perks up, some of that nervousness gone. I kind of miss the flustered blush.

"Museum?"

Pam stands up, shoulders her brown bag, which is covered in pins and badges, mostly superhero stuff. There's an *I Want to Believe* badge with a UFO behind it, and like *that* I'm thinking of Josh.

I slide the folder with his name on it back into my mental filing cabinet, letting myself get a little lost in Pam's blue eyes.

"The Virginia Kyle museum," she says. "It's in Arcadia."

I flick through the Bible for the book of Daniel.

"Could you show me?" I ask, still searching. "And the hospital too. I'm supposed to visit Mary."

"Sure." Pam inches a little closer as if to see what I'm looking at. "Daniel 4.25, right? You saw it on the hatch in the woods?" She indicates a passage with her finger. She's reading it upside down, so when she recites the words it must be from memory.

"You will be driven away from people and will live with the wild animals; you will eat grass like the ox and be drenched with the dew of heaven." Her voice cracks. "Seven times will pass by for you until you acknowledge that the Most High is sovereign over all kingdoms on earth and gives them to anyone he wishes."

She looks up at me and smiles. She has nice teeth, especially considering the likelihood of competent dentistry on the island.

"What does it mean?" I ask.

"It's about the Babylonian king, Nebuchadnezzar. He had a dream that he was visited by an angel, who described a man cursed to live in the wilderness. When Nebuchadnezzar asks the prophet Daniel to interpret for him, Daniel explains that the angel is talking about Nebuchadnezzar himself. The king goes crazy and lives like an animal in the desert until he acknowledges god."

I smirk. "So, bullshit."

Pam snatches the Bible back. "It's not bullshit." She shoves it inside her bag and closes the zipper. "You're just like everyone else." She pulls away as if to leave.

"I'm sorry. Please don't go. You're the first person I've met who's answered my questions." I pause. "I'm kind of famous for talking without thinking. And I'm a professional asshole."

She hesitates. If I were her, I'd run. She clearly doesn't need more trouble in her life, and for the people on Echo Island, I'm a big heaping plateful of trouble.

Her eyes narrow. "What's professional about being an asshole?"

I cross my arms, scuff the grass. "Uh, nothing really. I make videos on this thing called the internet? It's when computers talk to each other over long distances. You can put movies and music on there where anyone can access them. I make videos for a living with my friend and for some reason people like them and give us money to watch us do stupid shit. Being an asshole's kind of my schtick, I guess."

Pam mirrors my pose, raises an eyebrow. "Oh please, tell me more about this human thing called the world wide web."

"That wasn't me trying to be a tool, or even accidentally being a tool. But everyone I've met here has a panic attack when I take out my phone."

She relaxes, and there's that subtle breeze again, blowing her hair across her face, her neck. The sunlight glints against a gold cross that's mostly hidden beneath her cardigan. "We must seem really backwards to you."

"Not *backwards*," I say, thinking how totally backwards they are. "Quaint, quirky, charmingly off the wall."

She purses her lips and grips the bag straps. "Come on, I'll show you where your mom is."

I walk behind her at what seems like a respectful distance. Maybe it's the nice Christian woman-vibe she's giving off, the pale pink sweater, the floral print skirt, the Bible, but she makes me want to be nice. She makes me want to treat her more delicately.

Is it sexist to say that? I hope not. I mean, she seems like a powerful, independent, and intelligent woman. I just . . . want to be nice to her. Nicer than usual. Watch my Ps and Qs. It's probably not anything but nerves and guilt. She obviously came here to be alone.

I'm overthinking this.

"Why *is* everyone so different here?" I ask. "Uphill told me he brings conversion camp kids—" Oh, fuck. I've been reading this wrong. Pam's a lesbian. She's not flirting with me, this is . . . she's awkward probably. Suddenly there's a cold heavy stone in my stomach. It sounds and feels like Josh pushing me away in the hot tub.

"I get that he brings people here," I continue, "but does no one ever leave? Some of you guys are pretty young, but no one knows anything about the rest of the world."

Pam powers on, talking as she walks. "You seem smart. Haven't you already figured it out?"

I warm at the compliment, but the feel-good moment is tempered by the answer I know she's looking for. "They're not allowed to leave."

"Except me and Gord," Pam confirms. "Uphill keeps everyone here, for our safety."

I snort. "From *what*? You're all adults. If you flew Tia and Nor and Gene out of here, it's not like their parents could snatch them up and put them in another camp. And the world's not—I'm not saying everything's perfect out there, but it's getting better. You can be gay and be okay."

And this is a PSA, hey!

Pam runs her fingers along the tops of the stones. I can feel the roughness under my own hands. Her fingers knot in a clump of vine and she stumbles.

I catch her, only she wasn't *exactly* falling, not *exactly* in need of saving.

She's right up against me, her bag scrunched between us. She looks over her shoulder, right in my eyes, cheeks pink. She doesn't pull away at the feel of my hands on her upper arms.

"I'm not like them. I didn't get sent here." She starts walking. "I was born on the island."

"Right." I catch up to her. "So why don't you all leave? Especially you."

"You wouldn't believe me if I told you."

"I don't believe a lot of things, but I've seen some shit since getting here. I'm suddenly a lot more open. Unless you're about to tell me it's a Big Foot conference and everyone's here to trade secrets on how not to be seen."

She stops before one of the stones. It's a stately grey, plain as all the others. She steps away, revealing *Virginia Kyle*

1951-2017 Echo Island Nightingale. Not, *Beloved Mother,* or even, *Beloved Friend.* But *Echo Island Nightingale,* like a bird in a cage. In Uphill's cage.

I picture Queen Cee's lips mouthing "sing" at me and shoving the mic against my chest.

"Do you want some time?" Pam asks softly.

"No." The sadness I expected never arrives, and I'm left at an airport with a sign reading "Filial Grief," and a whole lot of anger in the place of my no-show client.

Pam eases up to me, lays a hand on my shoulder. "My parents died on the island." She swallows.

The comment tears my attention from the grave. She's staring at her feet.

A bee or a wasp or some other buzzing critter zips past our faces. Pam doesn't flinch. She reaches for a thick blade of grass and runs her finger over its surface.

"How did Uphill keep them here?" I ask. "And how did he keep my mother here?"

She shakes her head, removes her hand from my shoulder, starts pulling apart the grass by its fibers till it's pulpy green string. "He didn't keep my parents here. They were founders, and he killed them. They're not . . . *here* in the graveyard. They're out in the woods, with the others."

Pamela Matheson and I are in a bubble, all the sound around us muted till it's nothing but a fuzzy background soundtrack.

I wish I was better at this kind of thing.

She closes her eyes, tears brimming at her lashes. Her nostrils flare, lips trembling. She tilts her head toward the sky, like she's waiting for the hand of God to reach down and kiss away her pain.

I give her shoulder a squeeze.

"I'm sorry," she mumbles from between suffocated sobs. She wipes her eyes, then holds out her hands like they're poised to grip a stone. "I—I know what the founders did. And I know—I know that makes them bad. It makes me *so bad.*"

She falls to her knees in front of my mother's grave and I crouch beside her, rubbing circles on her back. I think it's the right thing to do, that it's maybe what Josh or Kayla would do. I've never been good with crying people.

As if seeking comfort, she presses her finger against the groove of the dates on my mom's headstone, tracing the shape of the numbers, saying hi across a two-year gulf.

I can't bring myself to do the same. I can't bring myself to say hi.

"You're not bad, Pam. Whatever they did is something *they* did. And yeah, it sounds like what they did was pretty shit, but maybe there was some good too." I pause. I don't know this woman. Who am I to guess what she needs? But I try, because I get the feeling no one's tried for her in a very long time. "We don't know whether Uphill's story can even be trusted. It seems like he's got everyone feeding out of his cake-covered hands."

She sniffs. "You have no idea."

"I'd like to." I shake my hand at Mom's grave. "I came here to find out what happened to my mom, so anything you can tell me, even something small."

Pam twines more grass around her finger, eyes glazed over. "It's the drugs, I think. Or maybe it's the water. It's not that we *don't* leave, it's that we can't. When we try, we have seizures, or strokes, or it's so painful we turn back." She *snaps* the grass, then tosses it aside. "Me and Gord can go a little further, but I've *tried* stepping past the air pad on the other side and it hurts like my whole body's about to explode." She bites down hard on her lip, shaking. "I know it sounds insane, but the founders did something to this island. They made this place so it was born broken, and now we're all broken too."

What Pam's describing isn't possible. Maybe there is something in the water, or something in the drugs she mentioned—*Persephone* at a guess—but it has to be psychosomatic.

"My mom got out." What did Tia call Mom? The only Echo Islander who ever made it. It carries a totally different meaning now.

Pam lays her palm flat against the grave. "Your mom was like me I think, but stronger. But she still returned in the end."

It's like I've been bowled over by the logs that crushed Mary's leg.

Whether there's any medical truth to what Pam's told me, my mom believed it. It's why she never came back. It's why she never called and why she told Mary that the last thing she wanted was for me to come here. Virgie Kyle never abandoned anything. Not because she wanted to anyway.

I feel the fizz of something—one of Uphill's purple pills?—bubble in my mouth as Queen Cee kissed me. Has he already poisoned me with something he thinks could trap me here? Whatever it is, it won't work unless I believe it will.

I could fucking scream. I could burn Uphill's house down. I *will* burn it down.

"Let's get out of here. I have to see Mary, and I have to get off this island."

"You're not staying?" Her eyes are pleading. She shakes her head and stands up, and I rise alongside her. "I'm sorry. That sounded crazy."

"No, I get it." I think I do anyway. "I'm not staying—actually, I came to talk to you to see about booking a ticket out of here."

I hesitate—it's been like ten fucking minutes, but how can I *not* ask? She's crying in front of me believing all there is for her is this tiny fucked-up world where anyone who tries to leave has a fucking heart attack. It doesn't really matter if we're close, or if I know her. She's trapped in this place, the same as my mom was. And she's begging, if not with words, then with her eyes, for me to help.

"You could come with me. I'd help you get papers if you need them. I promise you won't have a stroke. And if there *is* something keeping you here, my mom must have figured out how to bypass it. If we follow her tracks, we can work it out. I just need to get a message to some friends on the outside first. Josh was supposed to come with me, but I can't get hold of him to tell him to cancel, and I'm afraid he'll show up after I'm gone."

I don't like the look on Pam's face, like she's a vet about to tell me Mr. Snuggles isn't going to make it. "Gord's bringing someone back to the island." She stares in the direction of the landing strip, past acres of trees and yard. "I talked to him this morning and he said some guy got a ticket. He didn't give me a name."

Josh will be here in a few hours. But then it hits me. "Wait—one ticket?"

"Yeah." Pam frowns. "Why?"

"There's no way Josh wouldn't take Kayla—she's our camera person, and Josh'd film himself 24/7 if he could." I swallow. No, it can't be Josh, which means I could still stop him. And if it *is* Josh? Well, I'm here, and as soon as *he's* here we can hop on Pam's plane and get the islanders some help.

Pam honestly looks . . . consternated. Or maybe thoughtful? "It's hard to get Conrad to let you in. I doubt he would have given this other person permission. He probably only let one of your friends through. I'm really sorry."

And like that I'm fucked again. I can't leave the island with Josh even *maybe* coming here, but if whoever's on that plane *isn't* Josh, then I still need to e-mail him, and I can only do that on the mainland.

I frown at Pam. "Is there a phone here that works? I left him a message at the cabin, but I don't think it got through." He hasn't answered, anyway. But then, Josh never checks his fucking messages. He can't remember his password half the time. Me and Kayla had to make him a google doc with all his logins.

Pam frowns. "The closest cell tower doesn't reach us most of the time, and the landlines only work across the island in July.

But I could e-mail your friend from the mainland, if you give me his address. I'm doing a run tomorrow."

It's nearly impossible not to ask her to take me with her, but I have to be here for Josh. Whatever fucking happens between me and him once this is over, I'm not letting Uphill sink his claws in. Josh is a smart man, but he's a bleeding heart and gullible as all hell. All Uphill has to do is weave the right story, and Josh'll be his.

"We have a plan." I stalk toward the mansion, beckoning Pam to follow. "I need you, Pam. I know nothing about this island, and if we're going to break this hold Uphill has on everyone, we have to be clever. Make Uphill think I'm here for the long haul. I need to ask you some things. I found Mary in the forest, and there were these monsters. I thought they were bears, but they made these low frequency rumbles, and they were massive."

Pam's brow furrows. "We do get bears here. Are you sure it wasn't the dogs? There's a lot of them around before the Dog Days. We cull them at the end of the month."

A pained laugh escapes me. "Yeah, sure, dogs."

"Sorry." Pam's watching me with an expression like she's disappointed her professor. It makes me feel awkward, like I might be taking advantage of her.

"Not something you need to be sorry for. Maybe I did hallucinate." I don't think that's true, but what good is making her think I'm crazy?

The mansion windows stare out onto the graveyard. I half expect to see Uphill's silhouette, or Mary's, or even a ghost's. There's no one, and I can't say why, but the emptiness is worse.

13

THE VIRGIE KYLE
INTERPRETATION CENTRE

P am leads me down a low-ceilinged corridor on the ground
floor. It's lined with more identical red doors, the walls
painted the same pristine white. The tacky red carpet's gone,
replaced by square tiling in bad need of repair.

At least it's light down here—daylight pouring in from some
windows at the far end of the hallway.

"Tyler Kyle," Pam muses as we walk, sing-songy. "Like Selina
Kyle."

"You really like DC, huh?"

"You know who she is?" Pam swings round, walking backwards as she faces me. She's beaming like a famous superhero
is the equivalent of an obscure Renaissance painter and this is
kismet. Fate. Karma.

"Catwoman," I say. And then, because she's looking me up
and down like I'm the Michelin-star meal the maître d' wheeled
out: "But out of the two of us, you're the better Michelle Pfeif-
fer."

This is my brain on flirting. After years of canned banter with
my straight best friend, a cheesy, 'you're hot like Famously Hot
Woman,' is apparently all I have.

And what if she's not flirting? What if this is another "*You
wouldn't have to wear a suit*"? Another "*I don't want you*"? I'm
being stupid, but that's just it. My brain is stupid.

"I don't know about that." She turns back around, and it's like the rush after your plane lands safe and sound. People don't hit on me like this. I don't hit on people.

As we walk, I rattle the handles of a few doors—all locked. What could Uphill possibly be keeping in these rooms that he cares enough about to hide? Unless it's medical equipment. Since the hospital's housed in Arcadia, it's possible.

"How extensive is this clinic?" I ask.

Pam's gripping either strap of her backpack. Her pins glint white under the light. She tosses her hair as she glances back at me. It's dizzying, like I'm in a shampoo commercial and every strand's in slow-mo. What a dope.

"Not very," she says. "We have what we need, but it's not a big town."

"What happens when there's an emergency? Or someone needs a specialist?"

"We pray one comes along." She clears her throat. "Or Uphill sends for someone, as long as it's off-season."

"Off-season?"

She chuckles. "Any time besides the Dog Days."

"And the people who come here—no one thinks this place is weird?" I hate grilling her like this, but I'm starved for answers and Pam is practically a buffet.

Not . . . not like that. I mean, not that I'm thinking about her like she's food, or, or sex, or.

She called me pretty.

Fuck.

"Conrad keeps visitors to himself most of the time." She rattles a doorknob. "He doesn't like people snooping around."

A woman's scream interrupts us. We freeze. It's the sound of nails on a chalkboard, of a dying animal hurling itself against the bars of its cage.

I find my courage swimming somewhere around my toes and approach Pam. She's still as glass. "I suppose there's no chance that's not where we're headed?" Silly quips usually do the trick when I need to bring Josh down after a close call with some bushes. Fingers crossed, Josh-whispering works on Pam.

She relaxes. "It sounds like Mary."

It did sound like Mary. "She screamed like that in the forest. I'll go check on her. You stay here in case Uphill shows up."

I jog down the corridor. It's not hard to tell which is Mary's room. There's this terrible scraping noise like tearing paper, and a tumbling, slamming sound like hardcovers cascading from a shelf.

Hopefully I'm not the only one checking on her. The last time I had to hold her down I lost the fight and the only sedative I have on hand is a bad Ben Stein impression.

I open the door quickly, figuring if I have to subdue her, it's better if she can't prepare.

Mary's going *Hulk smash* on the hospital room. There's a hole the size of her head—I really hope she didn't use her head—bashed through the drywall.

Before I can reach her she rams her body against the wall, and when it doesn't break, she punches her hand—fingers splayed—right through it and *shreds*. Striped, green floral paper rips off in strips, catching in her bloody nailbeds.

Colleen—the waitress from Ziggy's Quicheopolis—is wailing on the bed, clutching a broken wrist, and calling Mary's name.

Mary shrieks and rushes in for another attack. "THE TREES. OUTSIDE OUTSIDE OUTSIDE. I NEED TO GET OUTSIDE."

I must have done something really fucking awful in a past life to deserve this.

"No, don't!" Colleen screeches at me as I'm coming at Mary from behind.

Mary's elbow jabs my chest. I don't feel myself flying this time, but I do feel the crash as my back meets the legs of the metal hospital bed. I scream.

Colleen's at my side, pulling me by the scruff of my shirt with her uninjured hand. "Connie?!" she yells.

The door bangs open as though on cue—knowing Uphill it really could be on cue. Black-booted feet stomp inside, but I'm still curled in a pathetic man-ball and don't see much besides the boots. That, and Mary's body as it slumps against our rescuers, knocked or tased out.

"Get him out of here!" Uphill screams.

Pam's skirt and white sneakers inch toward me. She helps me up, pulling my arm over her shoulder, and ushers me out of the room. The door slams behind us, and men's muffled voices roll from inside to the accompaniment of Colleen's sobs.

Pam walks me ten feet and sets me against the wall. She brushes my hair out of my face.

"Someone's going to have to notify the Olympic ethics committee," I say. "I'm pretty sure Mary's on steroids."

"That's not funny." Pam blinks her big blue eyes. She's real close, her hand probing my face for injuries.

Today's apparently petting day at the Tyler Kyle enclosure.

"I'm fine." I push off the wall, with the unfortunate consequence that Pam's arm falls from my shoulder.

A deep ache radiates across my chest where Mary's elbow landed, but nothing feels broken.

Pam's face is a wasteland of concern. "We should wait for Conrad so he can get the doctor to look at you."

I'm not waiting anywhere for Uphill's anything.

"I want to see that museum." As I start walking, I stumble. I kick my leg out, unkink it, and then I'm fine. I'm fine.

Pam falls into step beside me, hovering in a way she didn't before. I pick up the pace—I want to be out of sight by the time Uphill remembers me.

"I'm fine." I give her a look. "But we probably don't have much time. I'm guessing Uphill doesn't want me in that museum or he would have rolled out the red carpet."

Pam shoots me a look. "You think you warrant a red carpet?"

I'm not sure what it is about me that provokes incredulity after, like, five minutes of meeting people, but it's probably not a compliment. "Well, you know, only because gold isn't typically available."

She's frowning. It's not entirely clear she realizes that was a joke.

"What, you don't think I deserve the good china?" Doubling down is *obviously* the way to go here. I mean, name a time when that hasn't worked in my favour?

But she breaks into a smile. "Are you inviting yourself to my house?"

Her fingers grasp mine, soft skin against . . . well, I guess my palms are pretty soft and unmanly too.

She pulls me down a frighteningly narrow hallway to her left. A single red door stands at the end of the corridor, lit by a single, flickering fluorescent light. With every beat of luminescence, a metal keypad next to the door shines silver. It's painful to look at, frenetic.

The universe is telling us something, and it's that we should save our game first.

I jerk Pam's wrist, stopping her. "On second thought, let's not go to Camelot."

Pam presses her finger to my lips. She slides her backpack off and lays it on the floor at her feet. "Keep watch."

I turn around as she rifles through the bag, peering over my shoulder as she holds up a black device with a red light to the keypad. Something clicks, and she starts punching in numbers—or maybe she's typing into her gadget.

The door beeps, low and long. She shoves her device back into her bag and hauls me through the door by my shirt. The autolock clicks behind us.

Windows spill bright light across the floor to our left.

"Here she is, Ty." Pam holds her hand out indicating a door at the other end of the hall, but the introduction isn't necessary.

An arch of black and white checkered tiles frames the door. The entrance to the Virgie Kyle Interpretation Centre and Gift Shop—not its official name—is painted white on one door, black on the opposite.

"Virginia Kyle Memorial Museum," I read off a silver plaque beside the door. There's another keypad beside it, and Pam's already breaking out her little black box.

She works her magic, muttering to herself incoherently the whole time. As before, the door beeps. Pam smiles at me and puts her gear away. "You ready?"

It feels like we're a team. A duo. It sends a thrill through me, but guilt rolls in hot on its tails, like I'm cheating. Like it's bad. Like Josh should be here, by my side as we blast the mystery of Virgie Kyle wide open.

I swallow, feel my phone in my pocket. How embarrassing would it be, on a scale of 10 to 900 if I turned on Joshbot for the two seconds it takes to open the door?

JOSH: [a squeeze of my hand where the camera couldn't see, just like I've done for him so many times] You okay, man?

TY: Who me? *Fine.* Pssh. What's a dead mother's creepy indoor mausoleum owned by a megalomaniacal wannabe cowboy cult leader on an isolated island conversion camp when you've faced down the Lizard Man of Scape Ore Swamp?

JOSH: Are you admitting we faced down the Lizard Man?

TY: We faced down some weeds, anyway.

JOSH: I distinctly remember *your* face down in the weeds [Maniacal laughter].

If I survive Echo Island, maybe I can play both characters.

But right now, we're Tyler and Pam, Pam and Tyler. And she's looking at me, waiting. She's not Josh, but someone new who smiles at me, and seems to like me, and cares enough to ask if I'm okay.

"I'm ready," I say, leaving Josh behind.

It's weird that what I'm feeling now is so much worse than when I stood at Mom's grave, but it is. Maybe because all that's in the graveyard is a body she left behind two years ago, and inside these rooms part of her is still alive. I need to see that part, and I'm not sure I want to.

As we push open the doors, Conrad Uphill's voice blasts from the corners of the room. I nearly have a heart attack, until I realize it's a recording.

"Welcome, to the Virginia Kyle Memorial Museum," Uphill's voice crackles. "Inside these walls you'll learn everything there is to know about the woman affectionately known as the Echo Island Nightingale, known to those who loved her as Virgie."

I phase out the generic museum narration as the weirdness of the décor hits me.

Everything—and I mean *everything*—is coloured in greyscale. If this were any other time, and I were happily touristing a museum dedicated to someone else's absentee movie star parent, it would be incredibly cool—a trompe l'oeil that's more of a trompe de corps. It's like we've walked inside one of her movies—not just the sets, which I visited when she was filming, but inside the screen itself.

"This is . . . ." I'm lost for words. It's probably a miracle or something.

Pam grins at me. Looking at her—all in colour—is a shock to the retinas.

"Cool, isn't it?" She approaches the rounded information booth beside the entrance and picks up a black and white pamphlet. She unfolds it as she talks. "Most people are probably whelmed these days when they come here but being here with you I'm totally *over*." She looks up and smiles. "Your *face*."

I have no idea what half of that meant—Echo Island slang going its own way and doing its own thing, I guess. "It's certainly an artistic statement."

The walls are covered with framed stills from Mom's movies, blown-up block prints of newspaper articles, and even glossy photos of her singing live. Glass display cases line the walls—normal museum shit made strange by its subject. Across the room is a door framed by glazed windows—clearly the main entrance, and at a guess accessible from the garden.

There's an opening to the left leading into a second exhibit room. As I walk toward it, Pam takes the pamphlet and follows.

Uphill's affected twang provides the soundtrack. "Virginia Kyle was born in Edinburgh, Scotland, but she was reborn on Echo Island in a temple of sky and spruce and smooth pine smell."

I pause beside a display case. The items themselves—a paperback copy of *Dune* along with Le Guin's *The Left Hand of Darkness*—are recessed into the panel to maintain the illusion of the greyscale room. There's an artistically open journal inside. One page describes a concert Mom performed at The Moon, but the next page is a string of code, just like my map.

Pam sidles up to me. She taps the glass. "I got her some of these books. She could never get enough. And movies too."

"Yeah, she was always a big ol' nerd." And in the video posted to that channel, she had *A Case of Conscience* by James Blish on the side table. I wonder what happened to that one. I step around the side of the display. "Can you help me open this? I need that journal."

There's a metal slot for a key at the back of the case.

Pam leans forward. "We'll have to break it."

Is it worth the risk we'll trigger an alarm? Maybe not, but I'm low on both clues and fucks. "Hand me your sweater."

Pam slips it off, wary. "Please don't—"

She doesn't get the words out before I've wrapped my hand and smashed my fist through the case and *ow, fuck* the sweater was *not* thick enough.

"Ty?" Pam's cringing.

"I'm fine." I grab the journal and draw my arm out, scattering glass. I gingerly unwrap the sweater and examine the damage to my hand—a few shallow scratches to add to the collection, a small puncture. I pluck a shard from my skin with a wince.

Pam frowns at her sweater, gives it another shake, then unzips her bag. She shoves the sweater and my mom's journal inside.

"Thanks."

Pam smiles a little tightly and we keep walking.

"Did they put all her stuff in here?" I ask, stepping beneath an arch and into a darkened room—well, it's sort of dark. The walls are painted dark grey, and the only light comes from four pale lamps illuminating more block-print photos. It's small and round–a kind of vestibule.

"I don't know," says Pam. "Usually when someone dies it gets divvied up, unless there's a will. Conrad did a drive for keepsakes for the museum."

The centrepiece of this room is a massive picture of my mom and a Black woman I assume is Tysha. It's a headshot of the couple in profile, and judging by the lace ribbon streaming down Mom's hair, it's also a wedding photo. They're laughing, hands clasped, two gold rings—the only colour in the whole room—engraved with each other's names.

I step right up to it, processing that laugh, the reality of her happiness. Is that what she looked like when she laughed with me? It's been so long I can't remember.

Tysha's a handsome woman with shaved hair and a strong jawline. She looks sporty, but it's impossible to know from a picture.

"I knew them. You can ask me anything you want," says Pam. She's beside me again, real close. I can feel her breath on the back of my neck.

I step away from both the photo and Pam, and when I turn around I'm met by an opening into another room. A crystal chandelier so huge it hides whatever lies beyond it glitters above, outrageously big for the space. I walk forward, drawn by a pinch of colour reflected in the dangling glass: the peach of skin, the purple and black of a dress.

It feels like someone's grabbed my heart and stretched it out.

"Ty?" Pam's shoes clip along behind me.

"Virginia Kyle did so much for this town," Uphill says from the speakers. His voice cracks, not with static, but emotion. "So much, and we can never repay her. Our sweet nightingale. My friend."

I step from the thunder-grey arch of the photo room and into a round white chamber. More photos line the curved walls, but I'm more interested in what's obviously a statue of some kind on the opposite wall.

Until a photograph I recognize catches my eye.

It's a close-up of me from one of mine and Josh's expeditions—Josh has been cut from the frame. It's a nice shot, too. A picture I might have picked myself if I were cycling through potential profile pictures. It looks better than I usually look, is what I'm saying. A display case stands in front of it. I peer inside and find the original, coloured image, recessed like the books in the main exhibit room.

"That's from the show." I turn around, pointing to the black and white screen grab.

"Those videos you post online?" This time Pam doesn't approach, maybe sensing the shift in my mood. It makes me feel bad, but I can apologize later. Right now I'm feeling too many other things to waste time on guilt.

"It's a cryptid investigation show. We hunt monsters." I rest my hand on the glass, reading the description of the item. "It says this photo was found with her private possessions. How the fuck did she get it?"

Pam frowns. "Conrad? He gets stuff online all the time, stuff no one else can."

And Uphill already knows about the show.

"Fuck." I turn to Pam. "She ever ask you for anything like that?"

Pam shakes her head. But then she gets a look on her face like she's remembering something. "She asked me to buy her tickets to a live show once. It had a weird name—"

My throat is as dry as instant ramen fresh from the packet. "Discovery Bang?"

Pam nods. "I think so. Yes, Discovery Bang. She did that sometimes, buying tickets to movies or plays she couldn't ever see." She looks me straight in my eyes, covers her mouth with her hand like a shocked cartoon character. "Were you in all those movies? Were you in *Guardians of the Galaxy*?"

I mean, I *could* lie. But I don't. I shoot her a modest smile. "No movies. Josh and me—my friend, Josh, who I do the cryptid show with—we were in theatre school together. Our careers weren't really taking off like we hoped I guess, and Josh got the idea for Discovery Bang. But I was in a few shows, even had some lead roles. Slim in *Cowboy Mouth*, Billy Flynn, Puck—"

She looks bored. I stop.

"That's so cool." Her words have the tone of a babysitter feigning interest in a scribbled drawing. I'm sure Pam will be a sweetie and pin my resumé on her fridge.

I glance at the display. I've never wanted to be that asshole, rambling about himself to the first woman who'll put up with it. And here we are, in a big ol' museum dedicated to my mom, with a stupid blown-up photo of me on the wall and I'm talking about how cool I am to a captive audience.

"I'm sorry," I say. "I guess I'm overwhelmed, you know?"

She grins. "Totally." She walks up to me, takes my hand, then leads me round the chandelier. "Come here. You need to see this part." The sound of a smile fills her voice, and it obliterates the bad feeling from before. It's like we're ordinary people visiting an ordinary exhibit. Pam's dragging me along to see her favourite painting, or the funny animatronic prime ministers, or the fossilized dinosaur turd she loved as a kid.

We step round the chandelier and Uphill's background narration snaps off, replaced by the opening notes of Céline Dion's arrangement of "All By Myself." Instead of Céline though, it's my mom singing.

The colourful figure I saw beyond the chandelier is Virginia Kyle, frozen in wax atop a low platform. She's crooning into a mic, her hand raised as though reaching toward someone in the audience, her unblinking glass eyes staring into the middle distance.

She looks so real it's like if I touch her, I'll find her skin warm. Dramatic black curls frame a face with eternally perfect make-up. She's Isabella Rossellini in *Blue Velvet*, Marlene Dietrich in *The Blue Angel*, younger even than I remember her, like Uphill made this model long before she ever left the island that first time, like he already knew one day he'd build this room.

I shudder. Mom's voice cuts through me as she hits those high notes.

"Are you all right, Ty?" Pam asks.

Whatever the expression is on my face, I get the feeling it's not what Pam was hoping for.

I rub the side of my forehead. "Sorry. Is there a way to turn it off?"

Pam lets go of me and approaches a panel in front of the wax figure. "Umm. It's just more songs. Sorry!"

I walk up beside her. There's a list of tracks on the panel beneath a header that reads, "Virgie's Hits." My mom never released any songs and these ones are all covers, despite what the display reads. Along with "All By Myself," is a host of power ballads and sentimental tracks. I hit "Dancing Queen," for something less emotional, and immediately it blasts from the speakers.

The bright light of the chandelier clicks off, and disco lamp colours aurora across the ceiling. They whirl across my mother's wax face, catching her glass eyes so they flash red, then green, then purple.

"You forgot the mood lighting," says Conrad Uphill.

This time his voice doesn't come from the speakers.

14
LET'S SPLIT UP

"You know, Pamela," says Uphill, "you could have asked before giving Mr. Kyle the tour." He steps around the chandelier and stands with his arms crossed as disco lamp polka dots vault across his face.

Pam walks toward him, a contrite slump to her shoulders, but I speak before she can open her mouth to apologize to the asshole.

"Not that in the grand scheme of your creepiness it fucking matters, but I made her take me."

Uphill flicks the main light on, and the music disappears. He sighs. "I apologize, Mr. Kyle, but I'll have to ask you to leave. The museum is closed. We had an unfortunate break-in last month and the sheriff's office is still investigating."

"What, so he could steal my mom's forty-year-old panties?" I meet Uphill's gaze. He doesn't flinch. "Is there anything you don't have of hers? How about I leave you a lock of genuine, Kyle-family hair for the collection?"

Uphill slides off his glasses to clean them. "Really, Mr. Kyle. Is now the best time for theatrics?"

I wave my hand, encompassing the room.

Uphill walks toward us. "I don't want to have to call the police."

"Please do," I say, which is stupid, because at this point it's obvious they must work for him. I scowl. "Fine. I'll leave. Have fun jacking off to 'I Will Remember You.' That's by Sarah McLachlan by the way, not Virgie Kyle."

I march to the other side of the room and, in what I can only call a sudden fit of pique, grab the block print of my face off the wall.

Or try to.

It's glued on or something, so what actually happens is I pull really hard and kind of end up spinning on my heel as I hold on. It *does* come free, under the droll gaze of Uphill, but unfortunately so do I. I fall flat on my ass with the print clutched in my hands.

Pam hurries toward me with a look of intense pathos on her face. "Tyler, are you okay?"

"Fine." I let her help me up, and then I continue storming out. I storm all the way to the glazed glass door in the main exhibit room.

Uphill is slowly walking toward us like we're two five-year-olds who've threatened to run away from home and he's waiting to see how far we get before we break down and call him to pick us up.

I haul the door open and Pam runs out. I linger in the open doorway, block print awkwardly shoved under my arm, figuring I should leave Uphill with a clever retort or something. "Fuck you, I'm going to the cops."

Not exactly clever.

I dash into a greyscale cafe and an honest-to-God gift shop. As much as I'd like to peruse the variety of notebooks and magnets featuring my mom's face, I follow Pam through a second set of doors and into the garden.

"We should get out of here," says Pam, adjusting her backpack. "He could stop me leaving the island if we wait till my flight tomorrow. You'd better write down your friend's e-mail and your message. Do you have any paper?"

"No—what about your notebook?"

We're at what looks like the side of the mansion, and we start back toward Talbot, past the massive conifers lining the driveway.

Pam bites her lip, like she's confused for a second, but then she brightens. "Right." She laughs. "I'm such a ditz." She slips her bag off, riffling as we walk, and takes out the notebook. She tears off a blank page and hands it to me along with a pen.

I stop and use the print of my face as a support for the paper, scribbling Josh's name and e-mail, along with his cell number just in case.

What do I write? What kind of prohibition will he take seriously?

"You know," says Pam, "Uphill *is* the cops. He has this stupid alter-ego at the police station—Alphonse Downstream? They won't help you."

My heart sinks.

And Uphill knows I'm with Pam now. He knows she could get me off the island, or call for help.

"Then we really don't have any time." I start writing.

> *SUBJECT LINE: Josh it's Tyler—Read this e-mail.*

No.

I hesitate. "I'm going to write down my password. That way he'll see the message is from me. Okay? Just log into my account."

> *I'm leaving the island ASAP. ~~DO NOT COME.~~ Don't come. The mayor is a crazy cult leader who's convinced the townspeople they can't leave or they'll die. ~~There's a weird hatch and animatronics in the woods and~~ I'm getting off the island and going to the cops but I need to know you won't come. There's*

no monsters. It's not Big Foot or vampires or the chupacabra. It's just evil weird humans and they will kill you. There's no internet or phones, so a pilot named Pam is sending this for me. I've cc'ed Kayla so listen to her please when she tells you NOT TO COME. Remember, she's smarter than you.

- Ty

P. S. You taste like lime.

I scrawl Kayla's e-mail alongside Josh's, then snap the pen closed and reread the note. It's . . . crap. I sound out of it, not like me at all. Am I really that panicked? Is there something else I could say that he should know? Honestly, the less he knows the better. If he knows too much he'll think it's something he can fix or investigate. I want to cross out the *P.S.* but that's the key. Something only the two of us know. The thing he said to me before I fucked everything up. There's probably something *else*, something better, but—

"Ty?" Pam taps my shoulder. "We have to hurry."

I shove the paper and pen at her. I tap Kayla's address. "Make sure you cc Kayla."

It doesn't honestly matter if Josh hates me. It doesn't matter if reading that *P.S.* makes him puke his guts out. It doesn't matter if he never speaks to me again. What matters is he's safe.

Pam takes the paper and reads it over. "What's the last line about?"

"Just an inside joke. He's . . . prone to paranoia."

Pam slides the message into her bag and we head out. "Paranoia of limes?"

"If only."

We stop outside Arcadia.

I point in the direction of White Sails. "I'm headed this way." The landing strip's in the opposite direction and to the north.

Pam squeezes the straps of her bag. She's looking at me intently, like she doesn't want to stop looking. And I like looking at her, too, but this isn't the best time, and that e-mail really hooked its claws in and dragged my silly flirty head out of the clouds. I hate being fixated like this, thinking about Josh all the time, but it's pretty normal really, isn't it? The most important relationship of my adult life is imploding right in front of me and I'm not even there to deal with it.

"Be safe, Tyler Kyle. I really like you." Pam bites her lip, and then she turns and leaves like she's too embarrassed by what she said to wait for my reply.

Her confession's a bit sudden, but there is something there, something between us. So I can't blame her for saying what she said, even if I'm more circumspect. At a guess, she probably hasn't had much of a social life on an island where everyone hates her for what her parents did and even bisexuals are probably a rarity.

A few minutes into my walk down Talbot though, and I'm shooting myself for not planning where or how to meet up once Pam returns. As long as I know Josh and Kayla aren't about to show up, I'm happy to leave, and in a few hours I'll be sure. Then again, even if Josh isn't Gord's scheduled passenger, I wouldn't put it past him to hike to Echo Island through the woods.

For once, Josh, please don't decide to be brave.

The Echo Island Diary: Entry 4
Tyler Kyle Falls in Love

July 14th, 2019: 2:00 PM

Pam. What a name. No one young is named Pam.
It's a name that materializes and attaches to you
when you hit 45. Picture a frumpy middle-aged
woman in a gym suit with back rolls and a bad
dye-job, then picture everything *but* that.

When Pam turns around, the sunlight catching her blond hair blinds me and her sap-
phire-blue eyes melt me with their pale fire (that's
a Nabokov reference btws). Pam's lips are where
kisses go to die and she's got this adorable almost poodle skirt with a cute little pink sweater
that most girls couldn't pull off without looking
prudish. Pam's not wearing a whole lot of make-
up, giving off more of a natural vibe. It's a lot
more tasteful than, say, Tia or Nor, with their
heavy liner and everything.

I fall in love with Pam immediately, like some-

thing out of a movie only this is real. Pam reminds me of Josh, not in terms of their looks,
which are very different, but in personality. Right
away, I'm picturing us at a party, Pam on my arm,
everyone staring with barely disguised jealousy as
I introduce her to Josh. He'd smile, unable to take
his eyes off her, unable to take his eyes off her all
night even though I was the one who brought her
with me and **she's mine she's mine she's mine**
and only I can taste her.

Pam lays Josh down on sheets as soft as dreams
and he's all moans and touching and wanting and
hunger and Pam rides him like an angel falling.

Finally, I'm almost not alone.

Pam is Ariadne planting her life-saving string.
Only I can never be her hero. For Pam to be truly
free I have to ~~die~~stay.

And if I'm not Theseus, I must be the minotaur.

I press the curve of my horns to her ~~porceline~~
~~porcelin~~ porcelain skin, prick her thighs with
their knife-sharp tips till the blood runs red on
white. I want to fuck him so bad, hot and heavy.
I want to crush ~~him~~her with my weight. I want
to split her apart with my meaty bovine girth and
fill her virgin belly till she swells like a whore and
whelps a thousand mongrel pups.

Do you know the story of the minotaur?
Daedalus made a bull so beautiful everyone
wanted to fuck it, and Pasiphae (the wife of king

Minos) wanted to fuck it most of all. So she dressed up like a cow and seduced him and he fucked her and made her his thirsty little slut and fulfilled all the dirty secret desires that tormented her every night. Pasiphae was a bad dirty girl and for her crimes she burned inside the belly of a golden calf, consumed at last.

She wanted it all along, and that's fine, because I want it right back. SHhe wants to do what I tell herhimher. SHhe wants not to have to think anymore. Selina wants Max to push her out that window or why does she spill her guts out in the first place?

I want to fuck her senseless so she's dazed and useless and then I want to wrap razor wire round her neck and pull and pull and pull till it slices right through and his pretty head comes off and so I can bury it and watch it rot and take it out to look at over and over and over again, watch the worms impregnate his eyes until they finally burst and his ichor runs out like punctured egg yolks and I can drink it up and see what she sees and dream what she dreams.

And her liquefying body will taste like Josh.

I'll stuff her empty throat with monkshood to ease the ache of what I've taken (you should always give a gift in return for a favour, or else it's bad luck). I'll sew his lips shut and finally he'll be silent as a winter night, and who knows, maybe I'll do that last part before the head thing so I can hear her screams as I muffle them with killing weeds. I haven't decided yet. All I know is I'm hungry. I'm so very very hungry.

So I dig into some leftover ham quiche because fuck veganism, and while I'm waiting I pop on some of my favourite Discovery Bangisodes.

Josh's words ease the frenzy in my guts with the magic of a snake charmer.

"Hey Bangers! Today we're on H. P. Lovecraft's very own Rhode Island. The master of cosmic horror has helped populate the dark imaginations of children and adults for nearly a hundred years, but although I could spend hours talking eldritch abominations and the Necronomicon with you guys, we're not here for Cthulhu or Nyarlathotep, but to investigate the real-life New England legend of the Glocester Ghoul. Batten your hatches, hold on to your partner—or, if you're lucky like me, your much braver best friend—and join me and my buddy Ty as we fall in holes, scream like children, and possibly, **maybe,** discovery bang-out the truth behind a horror that's plagued New Englanders since before the days of our lord and saviour H. P. And remember, if we nab ourselves a ghoul, Ty promised to do a sexy dance."

Tyler cuts in with a boring joke about how Lovecraft is racist.

I skip ahead.

We're wandering in the woods. It's night. Our

flashlights bounce green off the bark of the trees. Tyler slaps his neck like he's been bitten by a mosquito.

"I was **about** to say, this would be a really nice place to build a cabin and live as a happy old hermit. But fuck, I'm really not into the flies. Aren't they supposed to die down at night? Pretty sure that's a thing."

Josh laughs. "You're just so tasty, man. How can they resist a nice lean cut of grain-fed meat? If I were a mosquito I'd be all up in that shit."

Tyler stares blankly at Josh.

Josh back-peddles. "Not that I—I'm not a mosquito. So I don't want that at all."

Tyler swats another bug. "Just bury me out here, please. Murder me and bury me under a rock. Pick a nice tree though—none of this four-foot shallow grave stuff. I want to be way down there. Deep six. Worm chow. The circle of life."

"I'm **not** burying you out here. This soil's like, really really hard. It'd take a lot of manual labour and I'm still jet-lagged."

"It's cool," says Tyler. "With our audience, you can bet there's a much more **loyal** friend from our viewership out there, who's more than ready to respect my last wishes."

You can bet, Tyler.

You can bet.

you betcha

15

STILLNESS

Echo Island isn't the place to degenerate into a hot fucking mess, but my brain sure disagrees. It doesn't help that the air is a muggy haze.

Crickets chirp from the bank of foxgloves in the ditch and I wipe the sweat off my face on the back of my hand, then reach into my pocket for the photo from Uphill's office.

The pregnant scientist in the image grins at me, clutching the hand of her beau. Could the people standing with Uphill be the founders? Pam said her parents were founders. Logic would suggest the baby the woman's pregnant with is Pam, but . . . yeah, when I flip the photo over, the date reads June 17th, 1976.

This is getting way too science-fiction for me. I'm assuming the photo is a clue because it's the one picture I happened to pick off the wall. The simplest explanation's that these aren't Pam's parents.

Gravel crunches beneath the roll of a car, but the only car I've seen belongs to—

It's Uphill's limo, pulling onto Talbot.

I dive into the bank of foxgloves.

Crushed and bent stalks cushion me. I lie still, staring at the tops of the bluey-purple flowers. Up close, they don't look that much like foxgloves. Must be a wild variety.

As I'm lying there, staring at a blue sky so endless it's oppressive, I'm drawn to the top of what I thought was a streetlight.

But it's not—it's another one of the speakers that lined Uphill's driveway.

Once the car's long gone, I thwack foxgloves out of my face and stand up.

The speakers run the length of the street. I'm betting all the lights I'd assumed were blown out on Allenby were more of these. What exactly does Uphill use them for? When Queen Cee showed up at The Moon for her concert, music was playing outside. Maybe he was using these speakers to do it.

I grab the print and brush dirt from my two-dimensional face. I should toss it in the lake-moat, except it's printed on the kind of plastic that'll never degrade. The whole Earth will be nothing but desert, and my ugly mug'll be sticking out of a sand dune.

My stomach growls as I turn onto Dubrovna. I need to eat something, but first I need to change, need to pack, need to leave a message at White Sails for Josh in case we miss each other and he heads there.

Fuck. Maybe I should wait at the landing pad. Suck up my hunger and take one for the team. In the long—but really kind of short—history of the show, Josh is always the one making small sacrifices: missing time with his family—okay, so that one's not much of a sacrifice—losing out on date nights with his now ex-girlfriend, *losing his girlfriend*, giving up that one role he got as a racist depiction of a store clerk. I mean, there was the one time I guess I couldn't go to Nuit Blanche, but in the grand scheme of things I figure losing your girlfriend is probably worse.

I stroll back toward the cabin. My neck kind of itches—I guess it's the heat, or maybe something stung me in the bushes. I scratch my skin as I amble down the road, breaking out the big motivational gun: guilt.

What I'm saying, *Self*, is that I can stomach—hah—skipping a meal or two for the sake of not being a piece of shit and finally doing something good for Josh.

Wow, this *really* fucking itches. And not just my neck, but my hands kind of—fuck.

My hands are covered in a red rash—one I can only assume covers my neck as well. And my skin's tingling, this weird numbness spreading. Whatever those plants were, they weren't foxglove, and there are a whole lot of really nasty things it could be instead.

I'm not sure I can wait for the cabin shower. What if I'm a heartbeat away from having no heartbeat? What if this rash is only the beginning of melty-face times, cutting prematurely short my movie career before it's even started?

I make a beeline for the lake-moat.

Someone's picturesque little vegetable garden turns to vegetable stew as I kick up carrots and stomp kale—something else to feel guilty about later. I toss the print aside with my phone. I scrabble with the buttons of my long sleeve and haul it off, then make a cannonball leap into the water.

Peaty lake-moat closes over my head, soothing my skin. With the numbness spreading over me, it's the most peaceful I've felt in months. I shut my eyes, hold my breath. Everything is quiet but for the sloshing of the waves above and around me, and as they die down, the stillness catches me, shuts down my thoughts. It's a cool embrace, the first snow of winter, the crunch of an unbroken potato chip.

But I can't breathe underwater, and I explode past the surface, gasping. I slosh water over my arms, my back.

"Kyle?" Tia's voice is only sort of disbelieving. Actually, it's more like a, 'well *of course* Tyler would leap into a muddy lake half-naked after destroying the neighbourhood' voice.

The itching returns under the heatlamp sun and I dip up to my neck. "Hi." I wave.

Tia's holding my weed-covered shirt. She glances at the garden. "Nor's going to kill you."

Guess this is Tia and Nor's place.

"I mean, let's be real. It was bound to happen eventually." I stand up, rub my arms.

Tia bends down, picks up my phone. She points it at the lake. "So, what are you doing in there?"

"Uh." I gaze upstream. "Well, I jumped in some foxgloves and had an allergic reaction. Figured I should wash."

"In the lake."

"I'm a spontaneous person."

She walks to the bank, turning my phone over in her hands. She kneels down. "Let me see."

I raise my eyebrow.

"*Your rash*," Tia clarifies. Before I can turn around, she glances at my shirt, then abruptly tosses it aside. "Kyle, those aren't foxgloves, that's monkshood. It's fucking poisonous."

There goes my promising career as a botanist. "Cool. Well, I had a good run."

"You probably won't die." She grimaces. "Unless you ate it. You didn't, did you?"

"I know I seem like the kind of guy who walks around taking bites out of random weeds, but you shouldn't judge a book by its cover."

"If you'd eaten any, you'd *prooooobably* be dead by now?" Tia says, helpfully. "Sorry to disappoint."

Despite what I said, I'd really rather not die. I duck back underwater, grab handfuls of silty lake-bottom, and scour my arms with dirt. Already the tingling's faded.

I break the surface. "Why are your ditches filled with poisonous plants, and why do you have the same poisonous plant on your jacket?" A third thing clicks, a tiny paperback sandwiched into the sliver of remaining space in my memory bookshelf—hey, some of us can't afford palaces. I snap my finger. "Gene had a drink called the Monkshood Medley on his menu."

Playing poker with Tia would empty my pockets—her face is a mask. "Yeah, because it's bad fucking ass. They grow all over the island."

I float onto my back, spread my arms. A dragonfly zips over-head. "How long do I have to stay in here?"

She snorts. "You're the one who jumped in." She stands up and cocks her head at the road. "Come on, I'll drive you home."

The walk has to be a cumulative total of half a minute, but I'm not giving up the chance to question her, so I wade out. My hands are still red, but it's less angry. I reach for my shirt, but Tia audibly sucks her teeth and I draw my hand back.

"We'll get that for you later," says Tia. "Nor has gardening gloves in the house."

Picturing leather-clad Nor decked out in sunshine-yellow gardening gloves as she pulls carrots brings a smile to my face.

"Sorry about the vegetables," I say, trying to evacuate any residual wackiness from my voice so Tia knows I mean it. I hope she knows I mean it.

"You're forgiven, but only by me and only because I won't have to eat kale soup for a month. *Nor* will skin you alive." She peeks at me over her shoulder and smirks.

The one small window in the side of Tia and Nor's house is occluded by a dark blue curtain, so I'm unable to snoop. A silver moon ornament glitters in front of it, spinning against the windowpane.

"You guys like your moons, huh?" I ask. "Sisters of the Moon, The Thunder Moon, moon earrings, moon wind chimes . . . ."

Tia hops onto her bike and I slide on behind her, awkwardly gripping the print. If she were anyone else I'd feel weird riding shirtless, but I feel completely okay. Tia's one of those people you meet and feel like you've known forever.

"A Thunder Moon is like a Harvest Moon, but in July," Tia explains. "The Dog Days are a big deal here, so I guess Gene chose it 'cause of that." She revs the engine and we chug along.

"This is going to make me sound really ignorant, but what's a Harvest Moon? I mean, I know the expression, I just never thought about it before."

When Tia answers me, she has to yell to be heard over the engine. "It's the full moon in autumn. The Thunder Moon is July. Some people call it the Hay Moon or the Buck Moon. Thunder Moon is a way cooler name for a bar though."

She's not wrong.

"So, I met Pam." We pull into White Sails. I hop off the bike, holding the print.

Tia follows behind me. "Yeah? Pam's cool. Weird but cool." She pauses, and it's like I can feel her worry clogging the air around us. "Weren't you supposed to see Connie today?"

The fact that Tia broached the subject and not me is genuinely shocking. "Yeah. He's a fucking creep. He told me all about the gay conversion camp, made himself seem like some kind of hero. Then Pam let me in on the fact that he murdered her parents. That lovely conversation finished with a trip to the Virgie Kyle Creeper Museum. I'm leaving as soon as I make contact with Josh."

Something's beeping from the cabin. A fire alarm, maybe? My keys jangle as I unlock and push open the door.

Right away, the sound skewers my eardrums, though nothing's actually on fire. I clamp a hand over my ear, drag a chair to the centre of the room. I hit the button and the alarm silences, but while I'm up there I notice a small, black-rimmed lens stuck onto the alarm's side.

Kayla may be 100% of the tech third of Discovery Bang, but I know a fucking camera when I see one. I swallow, hand hovering around the alarm. I want to pull it off and examine it, but that'll let Uphill know *I* know it's there.

Then again, there's no fucking way I'm sleeping here tonight. As soon as Pam's back, we're gone.

Tia steps inside. "What is it?"

Fuck it.

I pull the alarm from the ceiling and jump off the chair. I turn it over in my hand. There's a discretely placed mic on the opposite side to the camera.

I hold it out to her. "Remember I said I had a stalker?"

The Echo Island Diary: Entry 5
Tyler Kyle is a Shit Detective

July 14th, 2019: 3:10 PM

Greetings faithful readers! Greetings, Josh! I never guessed how fun I'd find this new format, but it kind of fits me: archaic, gimmicky, forced.

By now you've probably realized I'm a selfish bastard who deserves to be replaced.

There's a lot of things I don't care about: other people, our viewers, the truth (and the truth is out there, deep in the forest that surrounds Echo Island). ~~It lives in the trees, in the ground, and in the voices of the people trapped here. An island song, if you will.~~

I've also never cared about other people's property, and even less what poor Cathy's going to have to deal with after I've destroyed my cabin.

I do find some of the cameras: one in the bathroom (gross) and another closer to the bed. There's more, but I'm obviously pretty lazy because after an hour I give up.

For some reason, it never occurs to me that there are more cameras outside, that maybe I shouldn't trust Tia so easily, that there's no point running to The Thunder Moon to escape my *big bad stalker*.

I know better *now*, I guess.

At The Moon, Tia shoves me in a booth and forces me to eat. She's got the right idea about putting some meat on those bones. Much harder to starve to death when our body has something to feed off. But that's a problem for later.

It hasn't taken anything at all and I'm a big ball of panic, degrading in real time. I didn't think it'd be so easy to peel back all your layers, for your mind to unravel, but it's like you were only ever a photo in negative.

Are all people this fragile? You seemed so different online, but all that's under my skin is cracked glass. If someone gave my skin a poke, I'd cave in.

At least with the end rising up to meet me I can stop with all the tortured metaphors and neat little phrases. It's so hard to keep it all up, to paint on this facade. If there was ever anything real about Tyler Kyle's soul, it's buried in Conrad Uphill's graveyard. High time for the body to join it.

16

SOMEBODY'S IDEA OF A JOKE

I'm in a fugue state as I eat the burger Tia put in front of me. There's too much going on. I have so many questions to ask the Sisters I can't summon any of them to mind.

While Tia's explaining the cameras to Gene and Nor, Nor sidles over with a beer she sets in front of me. She slides into the booth so we're facing each other and nabs a fry.

"Are you going to sing again," she asks, quietly. It's . . . very weird.

My frown is fifty one shades of grey, and all of those shades are very dark. "I'm not really in the mood."

She shrugs, leaning back in the booth, watching me intently. "Singing helps when I'm feeling down."

I laugh humourlessly. "I'm not *down*; I'm being stalked by Conrad fucking Uphill." I snapped. I'm snapping. Tia and Gene stop talking and turn toward me. "Sorry."

Nor gets up. As she walks to the bar she jabs her finger at the block print, which is sitting on another table. "Hey, why do you have a giant photo of your *face*?"

It feels like a distraction, but maybe not for me. It's like she didn't want Tia and Gene to hear what she was going to say.

"Thought I'd sign it and use it as a bribe for information," I say, voice flat.

Gene gives me a long-suffering look and taps the print. "I hope this doesn't sound weird, but are you really trying to sell this?"

The question catches me unawares—I mean, *I* don't want that fucking thing, so why the hell would anyone else? "Why?" slips out of me, and then I feel guilty, like I'm interrogating the poor guy. Maybe he does have a harmless crush.

Still, none of these people are freaking out as much as they should be, given what we found in my cabin. But I guess they're used to living under the gaze of the panopticon.

Tia sighs. "You said you were on some show, right?" She takes Nor's place across from me. "Gene can add you to his collection of celebrity photos."

I know I joke a lot about being *a celebrity*, but I also know that's not really true, and it should be even less true on Echo Island, where they don't have YouTube.

I shoot Gene an apologetic smile. "I'm really not a big deal. I'm not even a little deal. And that print's grotesquely big compared with any status I have. I promise, you don't want it."

Besides, now my e-mail to Josh is immortalized across the surface—at least when the light hits it right. Not exactly display quality.

Gene strokes his hand over it, as though assessing the roughness of the canvas. "Maybe I'd like something to remember you by. Folks don't usually come back here." He pauses. "I know you don't know us from Adam but having you here's been like a piece of Virgie coming home."

Tia squeezes my hand at the mention of my mom.

For a minute, I let the facade drop, that quipping, deflecting, way-too-confident-to-be-human version of myself that I've been falling back on. "Look, man. You don't want my face on your wall. I talk a big game, but it's part of marketing myself for gigs. I'm not what my mom was." And I'm seriously starting to consider returning to school for air conditioning repair.

"That thing only exists because Uphill's an obsessive creep. I'm nobody."

Tia's hand tightens around mine. "Everybody here is somebody, Tyler."

Gene picks up the print, smiling at it. "And you look like somebody to me."

This is all very after school special, but it feels genuine coming from them. Genuine and me are oil and water. "I look like a goblin."

Tia bumps her shoulder against mine. "Stop that. You're a good egg. I can always tell."

"That anything like a sad sundae?"

She gives me a shove.

Gene is admiring the print like he's looking at Tyson Beckford. "It's missing one thing before it gets a place of honour beside Mr. Nuts."

I can't help but laugh. "No human alive is worth a place of honour next to Mr. Nuts."

Gene lays the print back down. "Then we'll have to kill you." He pats his pants, searching for something "You got a pen?"

He wants me to sign it. "No, sorry. I'm strictly digital." I never even brought one to the island.

"I'll grab one out back." Gene scurries off.

Tia cocks her head at me. "What did you mean, about Connie?"

I nurse my beer, staring into the amber. "What about him?"

"That he's a creep." She rolls her eyes. "I know he's a weirdo, but he's not that bad. You don't know the cameras were his."

I snort. It takes a *long* swig of my beer to disguise my expression. It tastes . . . off, not as good as I remember—maybe I should have gone for the Monkshood Medley, or maybe the real monkshood in my system's fucking with my tastebuds. But then, Nor did choose this for me. She's probably got bad taste.

Once I'm sure I'm not going to laugh or grimace, I turn to Tia, meeting her brown eyes. She doesn't look like she's pretending. "You can't honestly defend him. He lured me here with that video of my mom, knowing she was dead, and I was too late. He made sure I came here alone by denying Josh and Kayla access, he bugged my fucking cabin."

Tia's eyebrows are a peak of incredulity. "Did you ask him if he sent the e-mail?"

"He said he didn't, but he's not going to come right out and tell me, is he?"

Doubt pinches at the corners of Tia's lips. "I don't know, Tyler. Luring someone here—it's not something we do. I know I said some things about Connie the other day, but the video's not his style."

I pause, frowning. I can see her wanting to tell me something, probably the same thing Pam told me this afternoon. "So who the fuck was filming me in my fucking bathroom?"

"Got it!" Gene seems to come out of nowhere. He thrusts a sharpie at me—silver. Gene's a fancy sharpie man, apparently.

I force a very forced smile and hover the pen over the print. It smells like something that'll give me cancer. "Here?"

"Wherever you like," he says.

Gene watches me as I write my signature, like I'm Elvis or Michael Jordan or even Virgie Kyle.

Tia leans toward me. "Nice handwriting, City Boy."

I hand everything back to Gene. "Don't sound so surprised."

Tia steals another fry. "The way you talk, you make it sound like you suck at literally everything."

"Look." I down more of the terrible beer. I stare Tia in her eyes. "Pam told me all about how Uphill's trapped everyone here. About how you all think you can't leave or your heads will explode. But it's not real. I'm leaving, and I'm taking Pam with me. If you guys want in, I'll take you, too, but either way I'm sending the cops back here in a few hours. This hold Uphill has over you is fucking toxic as shit."

Their faces might as well be made of wax, like Mom in the Virgie Kyle Hall of Fame.

"See, that reaction? Not normal," I say.

Nor hops off her barstool and storms outside.

Tia wets her lips, face solemn. "Tyler, there's a lot that's weird about Echo Island, and yeah, Connie's strange, but he looks out for us. He's the reason we're alive." She pauses. When she speaks again her tone's like one you'd use on a belligerent child: a patience so delicate it could be wearing a tutu and doing a pirouette. "Pam has her own reasons not to like him, and I don't blame her."

The phone rings, and I jump. Gene gets up and answers it.

"You're the one who warned me to stay away from Uphill," I remind Tia.

Tia drums her nails against the table. Her white polish is starting to flake. "We really can't leave, Tyler. The founders did something to the island. There's a song it sings to us that traps us here. We can't survive outside it, but we have a supernatural connection with it too. It makes us able to do things you wouldn't believe. So, when Connie and your mom opened the island up to queer kids, they thought they were giving them a gift, making us powerful and creating a home here. But it turned bad. Connie didn't realize how fucked we were until we started dying younger and younger. There are these pills that help, and," she falters. She smiles faintly at me. "Connie's voice, because of whatever the founders were messing with when they built this place."

Connie's voice. Connie's voice and, I'm going to throw this out here for no real reason at all, maybe Virgie Kyle's voice with it.

A chair scrapes the floor as Gene takes a seat nearby, head hung. For a minute, I think he'll pick up where Tia left off, but it's her that continues.

Tia clears her throat. "The singing calms whatever ticking time bomb's inside us, but we only had Connie and your mom." She looks me in my eyes. "Connie's changing, or maybe dying. His voice doesn't work like it used to, and your mom's gone.

The reason I told you to stay away from Uphill is because I knew he might try to keep you here, because whatever your mom had, you have it to."

I was thinking the same thing, but my brain short-circuits as she says it.

"During the karaoke." I hesitate. It sounds like somebody's idea of a joke. "The audience had this look in their eyes while me and Uphill were singing. I thought someone drugged me."

Tia smiles a little. "You drugged yourself. But it's safe. *You're* safe, at least from Connie. He couldn't do that to your mom."

Did Tia talk to Uphill before I did?

I slide the remaining fries on my plate around, caught in the white glaze of the surface like it's a vortex pulling me down. "Mom never brought me here any of the times she visited. She was trying to keep me a secret, wasn't she? Because she knew Uphill would try to persuade her to make me stay."

"I don't know, Tyler. I wasn't around then. I know Connie practically held her hostage for years, and I know it devastated him." Tia shrugs. "That's the Echo Island secret."

That's not all of it. It can't be. Why is Uphill still funneling queer kids here if he knows he's damning them? Her answer appeals to me on some level because it means I'm special, because it satisfies some basic human need for purpose. All holes filled or whatever.

Just because it's seductive, doesn't make it true.

"This is really stupid science," I tell Tia. "Like, really stupid."

She furrows her brow. "*You're* stupid science."

"Apparently. *Tyler Kyle, Stupid Science.* We can put it on t-shirts."

Tia rolls her eyes.

Before she can snark at me, Gene coughs. "That was Connie on the phone. Mary's gone."

17

MIDNIGHT PRETZEL

No one cries. No one tears their hair or throws themselves on the floor. We're all just kind of quiet. There's a cold hardness haunting my chest, the sting of unsaid words and unasked questions. I didn't know Mary, and it would be selfish to claim I care about her as deeply as the people on Echo Island did. But she knew my mom, and for whatever kindly-old-lady reason, she seemed to give a shit about me. No. It wasn't that she seemed like she did, *she did*.

I've never been a big crier, but certain things get me: an unexpected kindness, an undeserved affection, someone else's sadness, reunion scenes in movies.

Mary never had to care, but as soon as I met her she treated me like she'd known me forever. I wish I'd known her the same way she seemed to know me is all. Now she's another empty space sitting right next to the sinkhole that's my mother.

Gene breaks our communal silence, pointing at my ketchup-and-pond- stained chest. "You want a shower? Pam won't be back for another couple hours."

I frown down at myself. "Yeah, that'd be great."

Gene gets up, but I wave him off. "Your apartment's upstairs, right? I saw the staircase when I was back there before. You guys look after each other."

Usually when I'm confronted with serious moments I shut up and walk away. When I do try to say anything, it comes out wrong and I make it worse. Better to run, leave everyone in healthier emotional shape. That typically means leaving a public space to head home, or saying goodbye at someone's house a little early, or your best friend calling you to say his grandma died and all you can think to say is, "That's rough man. I'm sorry," and you can feel the need and disappointment brimming on the other end of the line like a stream during a monsoon, but you *don't know what to say*, and how do some people always know what to say? How do people not run? I'm a coward, really. I always run.

Sometimes, I run away to a weird culty experiment island where it turns out I have magic powers.

Gene waves me off with a reassuring smile.

I grab a fresh t-shirt from my suitcase.

My brain's buzzing as I enter the kitchen. I don't know whether to focus on Mary, or Tia's insane story. Maybe I'm actually dead and this is purgatory and I'm stuck in an endless Discovery Bangisode. It would explain a lot about this place.

The wooden stairs are dark and narrow, creaking as I ascend and opening onto a small landing with a window. Old-timey, white lace curtains create a gauze film over the view of blow-job alley.

My skin's crawling like a million tiny Uphills have climbed inside my pores, cooing at me to sing.

If anything Tia said is real—I'm not gonna say *true*, because she and everyone else believe it's true and so on some level it functionally is because it's keeping them here—but if there's real science behind what's happening, it's something Uphill's orchestrated. He's got animatronics in the woods, explaining the monsters, and special effects, and he's definitely using those pills to get everyone dopey and compliant so they believe in the island song. All that remains is for Josh, Pam, and Kayla to join me so we can rip off his mask and reveal him for the Scooby Doo villain he is.

There's an obvious bathroom at the far end of the upper story, across from the window. Two more doors line the wall on the way—Gene's bedroom and the spare he mentioned, presumably. There's a third tucked into the wall to the right of the bathroom. A blue TV glow flickers beneath it.

"Hello?" I ask. Maybe Nor came back and I didn't notice. She may want to use the bathroom before I lock the door.

Suddenly I'm all about locking doors.

No one answers, but some niggling detail—a tiny gnome taking a pickaxe to my brain—stops me. Maybe it's that there's TV light beaming from behind the door, but no sound. Maybe it's that the technology on the island is so limited that any glimpse of it feels out of place and time.

I turn the nob, half hoping to find it locked so I'll have an excuse not to look, but the knob turns the whole way like it's inviting me in.

Vampires only need an invitation.

I pause. My breath sounds absurdly loud, and even standing frozen in front of the door, the ancient hardwood groans underfoot like I'm the bosun on the *Edmund Fitzgerald*. Wind whistles, rustling the translucent curtains at the other end of the hallway. It was so still before that I didn't notice the open window.

Gene guffaws downstairs. He stomps his foot and I nearly jump out of my skin.

It's just Gene. Just Gene.

I step away from the door. If I'm going to do this—and I'm going to do this—I'd rather not give away that I'm snooping through Gene's things. I slip into the bathroom, turn the shower on, and pull the curtain. When I step out again, I make sure to close the bathroom door loudly.

The door to the spare room creaks when I push it open. I wince, expecting Gene or Tia to run upstairs, but nothing happens. I step through.

Eight TV screens cover the wall directly across from me, each one blasting a different image. Most of the screens show pretty standard security camera stuff: the back alley of the bar where

I, uh, *got comfy* with Queen Cee; Gene and Nor chatting at the table downstairs; the front parking lot with a view of the road; another view of the downstairs, but this time featuring the stage; the kitchen, and then—

My feet move on their own, toward the screens.

Camera six shows a storage freezer. It's lined with shelves full of frozen fare. There's an open hatch in the floor, and a ladder leading down. I've worked in my fair share of fast food joints, and freezers don't generally have hatches with hidden ladders. I can tell it should be hidden, because a shelf that's been divested of its onion rings has been pushed to the side.

What I can only assume is the room at the bottom of those stairs is a swathe of black on screen seven. It's not just that the room is dark, either. It's like the blackness is seething with bugs, bristling with the hair of something too big for the space. Only the corners are empty, glowing an eerie blue like Gene's set up a blacklight.

And then the blackness *moves*.

I bolt all the way to the door, gripping the sides of the frame as what could be a giant-ass cat curves its back against the confines of the wall, like one of Josh's rats moving in its sleep. The shot seems to defy physics—I can't tell if whatever that animal is takes up the whole room, or if the camera is somehow oriented inside a tiny box filming something smaller. I can't tell what's wall and what's ceiling. As the thing settles, I glimpse a nugget of leg or knee. The limb is spindly, scarily narrow for something the animal's size, like a wolf on stilts, like the folded legs of a dead spider.

Something that huge *definitely* didn't climb down the hatch in camera six.

I breathe in, walk slowly toward the cameras again. The thing hunches, something that *might* be a shoulder bobbing under its fur like it's popped right out of the socket. The movement makes it clear how stretched the thing's skin is over its skeleton.

Looking at it is like having worms crawling inside my brain and I avert my gaze. On the wall next to me is a Chippendales calendar and a framed photo of a skinny South Asian man on stage at The Moon. He's wearing Gene's Three Wolf Moon shirt. Must be Gene's dead husband.

The normalcy helps me focus, helps me rationalize the thing trapped under Gene's freezer: the thing that's moving down there *right fucking now*.

Animatronics. Animatronics in the forest, in Gene's . . . basement.

I grip the edge of the desk, force myself to look at camera eight.

This one's totally different, showing a ring of trees in the forest. What look like maybe ten Hallowe'en skeletons—but I'm betting are not—are crucified halfway up the tree trunks. The camera's too far away to see any detail. Deeper into the wood, sunlight shines against metal—the side of that building I saw when I found Mary? The hatch is visible in the distance.

There's a simple machine on the desk that looks like a DVD player. It probably controls the cameras

A door closes, muffled, downstairs. For a second I panic, but then I remember *I'm* the guard in the tower now, and I glance at the screen. It's just Gene in the kitchen, dragging a plastic tub from beneath one of his shiny metal counters. Oil, maybe, for the deep friers? He's dragging it in the direction of the stairs.

In the restaurant, Tia's heading out the door, lighter in hand.

Fuck. Okay. I need to work fast.

The desk is cluttered with crap: paper, an opened box of pens. I empty the wastebasket beside the desk finding financial stuff, some bad drawings, a ton of receipts, some coloured-in placemats like you find at restaurants. There's one handwritten note, crumpled into a loose ball.

I pull it out, flatten it against the desk. It's . . . that scrap of journal I found on the floor two days ago. I flip it over to read the opposite side. The handwriting's practically illegible. I almost throw it to the side, but then I notice something: Josh's name.

It has to be coincidence. Josh is probably in the top ten most common names in North America. But there's that gnome again, chiseling my neurons, and I read. The words are packed tight as pickles.

> *Maybe I've always been a little fixated on myself. I do spend a lot of time staring at myself in the mirror. More than most people do. More than seems normal. But I don't think about me when I'm doing it. That's the truly fucked part. The part you don't admit to other humans, or even yourself. That when I slide my palm over my cheek, my forehead, my eyes, it's Josh I'm dreaming of. It's Josh's face, Josh's skin. Is he as soft as me, is he softer? What would it feel like to wear him like a nice tight Josh onesie?*

There's an explanation. The Josh in the letter isn't my Josh. This means nothing by itself—just garbage from a bar patron. I shove it into my pocket all the same.

I haul open a desk drawer, forgetting at first how loud those things are.

On the cameras, Gene looks toward the stairs, letting go of the tub and wiping his forehead.

Fuckfuckfuck.

"Tyler?" comes Gene's voice from downstairs.

I slip away from the desk, poke my head out and open the bathroom door so it sounds like I'm in there. "Yeah? Everything cool?"

My hands are shaking so hard it seems like my voice should be shaking too. I'm calm. I'm calm. I'm me-in-my-Josh-whispering-voice calm.

"Yeah, just heard something," he calls up.

"I'll be down soon." I pause, trying to remember what my personality is when I'm not freaking the fuck out. "Uh. Sorry about the wasted water."

Gene *pfffts*. "Don't mention it. Relax, towel off."

Towel off like Gene's been watching me do for several days, live and on the big screen.

I wrinkle my nose and back slowly into the office.

The drawer of the desk is still open and I peer inside.

Cameras, mic equipment, all kinds of shit. Some of the cameras look like the ones Tia and I found in my cabin: tiny and round as spiders' eyes. Shoved down the side of the drawer, there's a remote.

Gene's on camera six, hauling the tub toward the hatch.

The paint on the remote buttons has rubbed off from wear, but there's a set that seems like it should change the view on the cameras. I press the one that *should* be six, and yeah, the view switches to the front and I'm watching Gene grimace as he strains. He crouches beside the hatch, mouthing words I can't hear, like he's talking to the thing in the basement. Like he's talking to the black creature folded into a spidery, wolfy, midnight pretzel.

The creature isn't moving.

Sound. I need sound.

There are mic buttons on the remote. I amp up the volume as high as I dare.

Gene is making clucking sounds at the thing in the hatch. He groans to his feet and pops the lid on the tub. Wet meat—no, *offal*—glistens inside. Gene plunges his hand in, grabbing what looks like a liver. It slips in his fingers, fresh. It could be human.

I gag, look away.

"I know you're picky," Gene's saying. "But it's all I got, Ru." He tosses the liver down the hatch. "'least till seven thirty. And I know you hate frozen."

Ru. Tia mentioned a Ru. It has to be Gene's husband. Whatever that thing is, Gene's named it after his husband.

The void on camera seven stirs.

"Here she comes." Gene upends the tub down the hatch.

Camera seven is a blur of motion as the offal slurps onto the creature.

Tia comes back inside. She starts toward the saloon doors leading into the kitchen.

"Gene?" I hear her call from downstairs.

Gene darts a nervous glance over his shoulder. "I'll be out in a sec, Tee!" He's still gripping the tub, pulled by the force of the entrails plummeting out of it.

Tia's on camera five, inside the kitchen, walking toward the freezer.

I won't make it downstairs in time to stop her.

"Tia!" I yell, loud as I can.

She looks up, shakes her head, then walks into view—and audio capture—of camera seven. The freezer.

"What are you doing?" Tia asks, amused, like she thinks she's come upon something funny.

Gene pulls back the empty tub of slop and stands up.

I stumble back, ready to make for the stairs, but the thing on camera seven is really moving now. A low-frequency generator rumble like the one in the woods stops both me and Tia in our tracks. It's the sound of a heavy bookcase dragged across the floor, of stone grinding against stone.

"It's not what it looks like," Gene says.

Tia's clutching her arms round her chest. "*Gene*." She looks disappointed. Not frightened, not confused.

Hand shaking, I hover my thumb over the view button for camera seven. I press it.

The things that might be the creature's eyes are round as headlights, and the light that beams from them obscures the finer details of its face, indeed, even the details of the eyes themselves. I can't see its jaws really, but the light from its eyes glances off the curves of its teeth: sharp and stretching back far enough that it must have a very long mouth.

I want to run. I want to run downstairs after Tia and pull her back and save her and *run*. But its eyes are like binary stars burning into my sight, churning a distant flame. I want to go to it. I want to—

My palm presses against the screen and static needles my skin.

The creature screams, the sound of rutting elks, and it snaps its face away, bowing a long neck draped in a mane of dangling dark fur. Camera seven is blacked out by the creature's body as it feeds.

I never turned the sound on for camera seven.

I pull away, the remote drenched in sweat, slippery as Gene's liver in my hand. A whimper escapes my mouth and I fall to my knees, hurling the remote away. It slides across the floor.

Downstairs, Tia looks up at the ceiling.

"Do you think he heard?" Tia asks. She doesn't seem worried about the creature in the hatch. She's worried about *me*.

Fuck. Nononono. Not Tia.

My shirt lies beside me on the floor and I haul it on, coming face to face with a wall of tapes on a metal shelf to my right. Clamshell DVD cases line the middle shelf, each with a name written in messy cursive on the side. The same cursive that was on that note. *Adam . . . Rudra . . . Tyler*. The *Ru* tapes line most of a whole shelf.

I grab the one with my name and bolt to my feet.

"Tyler?" Tia calls from downstairs.

"I'm fine!" I yell back, but this time I can't smother the panic in my voice as I exit Gene's stalker room.

The stairs creak under someone's weight.

Only the bathroom to my right, and the window . . . The window is open. I make for it, and the footsteps stop as Gene calls Tia back. There's a loud *thud* that must be the hatch closing.

"It's not what it looks like," Gene pleads.

Tia's footsteps retreat.

I reach the window, peer down and scan the alley. The dumpster's directly underneath. Open.

I take a deep breath, clamber onto the windowsill, hang down the wall . . .

and drop.

The Echo Island Diary: Entry 6
Tyler Kyle is Living on Borrowed Time

July, Sometime

When I was fifteen, I decided to kill myself. I know you probably won't ever understand what it's like to have absolutely no one in the world. My parents disappeared so long ago I may as well have sprouted from the soil or fallen to Earth like Kal-El. But I didn't have Jonathan and Martha to wrap me in a bundle and sing to me at night. A village never raised this child. You've been so lucky in so many ways that you don't even realize. Your world was always a wide-open sea of possibility, and I've lived my days in a cage. So to me, you look like the zookeeper patrolling outside the bars, the tender piece of flesh who thinks he's *somebody,* who thinks he's so much better, who whines like he doesn't *notice,* so unaware, so pure. You talk and cry and complain like nobody loves you, but that's so not true. *You're full of shit.* ~~YOU'RE SO FULL OF SHIT.~~ And here you are, beautiful and new, and my tiny, crumpled, paper-bag of a world falls to its knees for you, spreads its legs and begs for more.

When I was fifteen I tried to kill myself. Did you ever do that? Did you ever walk into the woods as deep as you fucking could so no one would find your bloated rotten body because you were so ashamed of yourself that even the thought of your corpse made you shudder with self-hatred?

But you couldn't do it. You cried and cried with what you thought at first was *fear*, but it was *anger*. Did you realize, shaking, that you didn't really want to die at all you wanted to kill. Did it brew inside you for years while you waited for some sign that there was a way out? Did you push it all down so you could try to do what the good Lord said and be kind and good, and all it got you was secondhand love? Did you fall head over heels for the funniest, most handsome man alive and dream that he was the one to come save you from your Hell like the prince in the forest of thorns? And did you almost give up because you knew he'd never come and it was all a dream and you're still asleep, Aurora, deep in the forest

If the princess wants to be saved he has to save himself, and if putting you to sleep and ringing your castle with briars is the only way to do that, so help me

If you're reading this, Josh, I guess I never did get out. But at least I wrote you one last mystery: the Echo Island Diary. Have fun with that. I hope Tyler made you smile one last time. I hope when you find him it's a big one.

What's in the woods, Josh?

What's in the motherfucking woods

18

PHONE A FRIEND

I dangle from the back window of The Moon for barely half a minute before I plummet into the trash.

Black plastic bags choke the dumpster almost to the brim. They're soft beneath me.

My phone's still wedged in my back pocket, and the DVD case is lying next to me. I reach for the gunk-encrusted rim of the dumpster, grimacing.

The lid slams shut.

I snap my hand away in time to avoid becoming Tyler of the Nine Fingers, and darkness overwhelms me.

Darkness, and the smell of stale food.

I wriggle against the trash bags till my back's against the side of the dumpster, trying to get some leverage, and then push up on the lid. It doesn't budge. I give it another shove, then a kick, and nope, it's not that I have absolutely zero upper body strength. This thing's fucking stuck.

"*Fuck*." I kick the lid again for the simple pleasure of smashing something.

My phone rings.

My phone rings.

I scramble for it, but it's already stopped by the time I've pulled it from my back pocket. In the meantime, my ass managed to turn on Joshbot.

"*Tytyty*," it says, all one word, breathless.

"Josh Josh Josh," I say back flatly. I raise the phone to turn the app off, but then I see it:

Call in progress.

That's not Joshbot on the line; it's fucking *Josh*.

"Fuck. Shit. Josh?" I'm too overwhelmed by the day's events, by Josh getting through, that I'm completely incoherent.

The phone statics. "—er, need – lis."

"No, no. Hey, Josh? Josh?" I crank the volume.

Josh may be a burst of stray syllables, but Tia and Gene's voices drift to me wholesale from the side of the building. They're coming closer.

"Probably a raccoon got trapped again," Gene's saying.

Josh's static is still crackling in my ear. "—eed to –t help –ler –out of there –e-mail –aim –off –island."

You're breaking up," I hiss into the phone. "I'm . . . I'm hiding in a dumpster right now. If you can hear me, call the cops. Tell them it was Gene and Tia at The Thunder Moon. Gene's been filming everything I do and he's got *something* in his basement. And Conrad Uphill's drugging everyone on the island and brainwashing them so they think he has magic powers."

"Who cares about the raccoon?" says Tia to Gene, angry. "You're in *so* much shit."

There's a pause. "Please don't tell him, Tee. I need him."

Tia *tsks*.

"I couldn't stand thinking about him all alone," Gene pleads.

"And now he'll have you?" Tia asks, incredulous.

I close my eyes, fumble around the dumpster for something to throw in their faces. My hand closes around a wooden board.

"—Talbot and – Ty? ---ulves – I'm not crazy."

"Shh. For a second." I bite my lip, hoping as Tia and Gene's footsteps stop in front of the dumpster that he doesn't have a taser or a cattle prod or a shotgun ready to take out the trash panda.

"What are we going to do about Tyler?" Tia asks. "He could have heard you."

Metal scrapes against metal as one of them frees the latch.

"I can't hear you, Ty," says Josh, loud and clear. "-eed help. The island's shut down."

Fuck. The connection's better. I need to talk while it's working, but the lid to the dumpster is opening.

I clamber over the side and hit asphalt. I roll away, flailing, wooden board in one hand, phone in the other.

Gene and Tia scream.

I jump to my feet and *thwack* Gene across the face with the board, drop it, and boot it in the direction of the airport.

"Gene!" Tia yells.

I don't look back. "Fuck, Josh, I'm running to the airport to meet Pam and we're flying out of here."

There's silence on the other end of the line as I leap over another ditch full of monkshood and into someone's backyard.

"Also," I tell Josh, panting, "this place is full of monkshood and—"

"No shit," says Josh, like that should be obvious, but his voice is trembling and strained, high-pitched like when we're on an investigation and he's about to beg to hold my hand. "Ty? Did you -ear-thing I sai"

I'm too out of breath to answer. I risk a look behind me. Tia and Gene are nowhere in sight. Maybe the blow to the head's taken Gene out of commission.

From the backs of the houses, Echo Islanders look out at me, and the messes I'm making of their yards.

"I didn't catch most of it," I admit. "Stay on the line."

"—in danger," says Josh. "—need you. —the woods –ih—have to— ---home."

What did Josh learn from all the way off-island that told him I was in danger? "I'm not walking home through those fucking woods, Josh. I," and I draw in a breath, "I saw shit out there, okay? Maybe it's even a fucking Big Foot. Saint Serge's was doing some kind of experiment out here on . . ." I hesitate. Even now, I hesitate. "On gay people."

There's a groan of exasperation on the other end of the line.

"I didn't mean me," I say. Fuck. My breath hitches and I jerk to a stop, wobbling on the edge of the ditch. I take a moment to catch my breath. "I'm not—Whatever. I'm almost at the airport. I'll tell you about it at home."

No one's watching or following me.

I hop over the ditch, avoiding more monkshood. Josh is quiet again, though the call's still active. I have no way to know if he can hear me or not, or if he's talking.

With no obvious and immediate danger, I slow to a brisk walk. If there's any part of me that prays—some stray cell clutching a rosary in the face of its heathen compatriots—it's praying to hear Josh's voice. I'm usually the one calming him down, but in my current state, even his fragmented words are like a towline to a lost sailor.

"If you can hear me," I say, "my mom's dead. I guess it happened a couple years back. Nothing sinister," I choke a laugh, wipe my damp cheek, scowl. "Just an old person being old. She used to sing for people out here." I'm not sure why I leave out the creepy part, but I do. Maybe it's because I don't want to think about her being trapped. It's nicer to picture her glowing on stage before a smiling, cheering audience: loved. "There's even a museum in Uphill's mansion."

No sound on the other line. Josh probably hasn't heard a word I've said, but he's hanging on in case I come back. Classic Josh. The good friend.

I try to be good back, talk like normal, ease his mind. Hearing me panic has to have brought him close to a stroke. "You'd have shit yourself in Uphill's mansion. He had all this crazy-ass taxidermy. Very Ed Gein. And there was this painting—wait. Shit. I'm gonna send it."

I flick open our chat log and attach the blurry photo of the painting. It doesn't look like anything, but who knows with this place. Maybe Josh can even translate the Latin.

I hit send.

"Come on, come on, come on," I murmur, watching my phone contemplate the request.

SENT

Yes. Fucking yes.

And then I get a message back: "king lycaon" and then "WE RESOLVED"

Why the fuck didn't we think of texting? I start typing like a maniac, ignoring the swarm of mosquitoes mobbing my face. Overhead, the sun glows fever-orange with the threat of evening.

"get off island," Josh texts before I've finished.

"I know," I write back. "going with Pam on plane. Stay away. Tia and Gene evil stalkers call cops."

SENDING. SENDING. SENDING.

Call ended.

I punch the phone icon. No signal.

My organs and bones seem to collapse on themselves, like I'm Gene's pet monster trapped in its box. My legs feel so soft I could lie down in the gravel beside the ditch and happily fall asleep. But I keep walking toward the landing pad.

There's no sign of Pam, but there's a parked plane outside the hangar. Whoever Gord was collecting, they've arrived.

19

LET ME DOWN GENTLY

I t's eight o'clock. I've spent hours pacing the grass trying to get through to Josh and Kayla.

What if the reason his call went through was that he's here? What if while I was running, they were checking in at White Sails? What if he saw the fucking note I left him telling him to go to The Moon? What if Gene's already turned him to slurry to feed his monster?

Pam's plane putters in the distance. My heart's in my throat the entire time Pam's taxiing. When she finally approaches me, she has a sheet of printer paper folded in her hands.

"Everything okay?" Her smile fades to a frown.

I was pacing again. I stop. "Long story. Did Josh e-mail back?"

Pam's face is all kinds of pity. She bites her lip and hands me the paper. "I sent it, but this was waiting in your inbox. I . . . kinda read it. Hope you don't mind."

"Better you did." I unfold the paper. I just want to know where Josh is.

> *I got your phone message. Sorry, man. I had no idea you took all that seriously or I wouldn't have joked so much on the show. I always valued your friendship and the last thing I want is to hurt you. I was thinking about views and I should have been paying more attention to how you reacted.*

I assumed you were playing along with the gag but it's obvious now I made you think I liked you, and I don't blame you for thinking that (I even watched some old clips and sometimes I did come off too strong). That's on me. I won't say I've never thought about experimenting with another guy before but it turned out it's not for me, and you've always been like a brother to me. I can't think about you that way. It's really hard, but that's why I think you're right about the show. This really hurts to write, but we should probably take a break from each other, until you sort out your feelings. It's uncomfortable to me knowing what you're thinking. Not that it's gross or there's anything wrong with being gay but like I said I feel like you're a brother, so it's weird because of that. We could probably do one last ep to close out your storyline. If it's okay I want to keep up the show. You probably don't care that much anyway. I know it was always more my thing and I know you're going to knock it out of the park with those auditions. There's tons more roles for gay guys on TV these days.

I also want to say thank you for trusting me to tell me this. It was probably really hard but I want you to know you have nothing to be ashamed of and I know you'll find your people.

I'm not sure there's a word for what I'm feeling because it feels like nothing at all, or like being hit with a bowling ball right in the gut at twenty miles an hour. One of those two things. He's really ticked all the boxes, all the things there's no comeback for, the niceties it would seem heartless to rebuff.

And underneath it all, the words between the lines: I don't want to see you again and I'm not at all cool with this.

The burn of the hot tub is all around me, when Josh kissed me. He did that. To me. But we were both drunk and . . . *fuck*, what if I'm wrong? I was so trashed. Did I initiate it? Is that why he pushed me? Am I what made him realize he didn't like men? His e-mail's not finished but my mind's a swamp. And this is so ridiculous—too ridiculous to care about right now after everything—but fuck. I'm about to get on a plane and go home and this is what's waiting for me.

And Jesus, we're roommates, and I'll have to find a new place, and—and I'm gripping my wrist so hard and bending it at such an intense angle it feels like it could snap.

"Ty?" asks Pam.

I don't want to be reading this in front of her. I shake the paper. "It's nothing. A misunderstanding." I swallow. "I'm fine."

Pam doesn't look convinced. "You read the whole thing?"

I turn back to the printout.

> *You're a really cool guy and I know you'll have grindr dates lining up by the time you read this. You can talk your way into anything.*
>
> *I'm not letting you off the hook yet though. We still need to shoot that last episode and Echo Island seems like the perfect location. I got the greenlight. I'll see you in a few days and I can apologize in person. Kayla's staying behind to work on auditioning a replacement.*

It's dated two days ago. Pam takes a step closer and points at the header.

"He's here." I was right. That's how Josh got through. He's here on the island. I can't leave. He sent me this and I can't even fucking leave.

Pam gestures back at the plane. "I could still fly you to the mainland."

I stare at the e-mail, wishing I was made of stone, but I'm not. "Josh got through to me by phone." Is my voice as raw as it sounds? Pam takes a step back, so yeah, probably.

"What did he say?"

"Couldn't make anything out. I thought he was warning me to get off the island, but," I hold up the paper, "he must be in danger. He said *help* and he talked about the woods."

I furrow my brow, my mind going going going. Fuck Josh and fuck me for fucking it all up and for coming here and dragging him into it. I have to find him. I can't leave him. He asked for my help.

Fuck.

I glance back at the road. "He might be at the cabins, but—look, Tia and Gene are behind everything. They might have him—maybe they're holding him captive in the woods. Gene had this *monster* under his freezer, and he's been filming me in my cabin on these cameras and mics."

Pam laughs. "No way. Gene's nice. A lot of people treated me bad as a kid, but he's a sweetheart."

"He's a *creep*," I say, probably too intensely. I snap my fingers. "Wait! I found something. This weird note where he talks about Josh." I shove my hand into my pocket for the paper but fuck, I lost it. And the DVD case. They're both somewhere between here and The Moon, or inside the dumpster.

Pam lays her hands on my shoulders and gives them a firm squeeze. "Slow down. I'll help you look, but you're exhausted and it's late. If we don't find him right away, we can start tomorrow. You can stay at my place."

"I can't wait till tomorrow," I say. "Tomorrow could be too late."

A sad smile tugs at the corner of her mouth. "Too late for what?" She stands on her toes and kisses my cheek. "That e-mail isn't going to change because you kill yourself playing hero for him. Trust me, I know."

I pull back, and start walking. "The e-mail doesn't matter. He's my best friend and he's in trouble, and I'm the one who brought him here. You go home, lock the door."

Pam jogs up beside me. "I'm not letting you go by yourself." She links her arm with mine, lays her head on my shoulder. "I believe you. Tell me everything."

20

IT'S DANGEROUS TO GO ALONE

J osh isn't at White Sails, but the walk gives me time to catch Pam up and show her Josh's text about the painting.

"What or who is King Lycaon?"

Pam cocks her head at the screen contemplatively, lips pouted like she sucked a lemon. "Oh god, it's killing me. I totally know this one."

I point at the man in the crown at the dining table. "This guy?"

Pam nods, frowns, shakes her head. "No. I think that's a god. King Lycaon was the king of Arcadia. That's why I remembered it."

Arcadia, like Uphill's mansion.

"What does it have to do with the picture?" I point at the man with the monstrous face. "And who's this guy?"

She shrugs.

So basically, this means nothing. "Not much of a clue."

"Why would it be a clue?" Pam asks, the voice of rationality to whatever Echo Island has turned me into. "It's just a picture."

I sigh, put the phone away, start walking down Allenby at brisk pace. "Josh got excited when I sent it. Part of his message was in all caps." Though to be fair, a lot of Josh's messages are in all caps.

Pam grabs my shoulder, stopping me as I march toward the forest. "We should go home."

I shrug her off. "No."

"It'll be dark in less than two hours." Her shoes crunch after me.

"Even more reason to find him. Josh is scared of the dark." And it's only past eight. Plus, there was a small window of time for Josh to have arrived. I would have heard or seen Gord's plane when I was outside, which means he must have landed when I was in The Moon. That's a short enough window that it's worth taking the chance he's still nearby.

The note I left him in the cabin was undisturbed, so it's unlikely Josh went there. But why *wouldn't* he have gone there? It was where he thought I was staying, and where we'd have met up if he'd got permission to come. It suggests someone swooped in before he could. Maybe Uphill seduced him with a visit to the mansion, or maybe that's where Nor sneaked off to. They could have told him anything and he'd have believed it: *Tyler's waiting for you in the woods, Tyler's enjoying a latte at the Virgie Kyle giftshop and cafe, Tyler's trapped in Gene's basement with a demon and they need you to arbitrate their staring contest.*

As we pass Mary's house, I can't stop myself looking at the empty windows, expecting to see someone peering out.

It never stops being weird, someone being there and then suddenly not, like you could step into yesterday and find them walking to the corner store, or if you tilt your head at exactly the right angle you'll see them in your living room watching *The Day the Earth Stood Still.* They pat the seat beside them, like they caught your reflection in the screen, but it was just a shadow, and you snap out of each other's worlds the way we forget even our most vivid dreams in the haze of morning. It feels like they've existed longer than they haven't, though the reverse is true. Sometimes, it happens even with people who are still alive, and the pull inside you when you glimpse a stranger who looks like them, *almost*, until they turn around or speak or crook their elbow all wrong is like a hand clasped and then severed at the wrist.

Reading Josh's e-mail was like the promise of those future moments. A friend turned to a stranger, or maybe turning out to have been one all along. But that's better than him being the dead kind of gone. I should have tried harder to get through to him. I shouldn't have distracted him with my impulsive confession. Maybe if I'd given him a better reason to stay home. Only I didn't know then how fucked this place was. I hadn't met Uphill, or Pam, or visited the museum.

I want this to not be my fault, but it is.

"Slow down, Ty," pleads Pam.

I do, but it's painful. "Look, I'm not trying to be a jerk, but someone's probably taken Josh. If I could, I'd be running into those trees."

"You'd get lost," says Pam. "I grew up walking the forest every day. I can take you wherever you want."

I suck my teeth. She's not fucking wrong, and she's here to help. She's the only person I have here. Maybe the only person I have anywhere. "Gene had a camera near the hatch and the metal building. It could be where he keeps his victims."

Pam rubs her arms. "It's near my parents." She pauses. "But no one can open that hatch. It's been sealed since the founders were killed."

That seems . . . improbable. Even if it's made of adamantium, you should be able to dig underneath or around it. "Gene's freezer dungeon came from somewhere. Maybe it's connected to the hatch underground."

I start walking, and Pam keeps up this time. "You didn't ask about my parents."

She's right, I didn't. "Sorry. My head's not—I'm not thinking straight right now."

She reaches for my hand, laces her fingers in mine. They're soft and gentle. "It's okay. You're worried about your friend."

My friend. My buddy. My bro. Roommate, colleague, former acquaintance. Guy I knew in theatre school. A rope cast into the pit of my mind. "He's . . . special," I finish, insufficient.

"You love him." She squeezes my hand.

"That doesn't matter," I say, as we reach the lake-moat. "What matters is finding him." And I can do that robotically. In fact, it's better if I do, if I turn this into another role. But none of the parts I play are ever heroic and racking my brain for the script that'll help me suppress the fear inside me gets me nothing but a real-life version of the actor's nightmare.

"Then follow me." Pam steps down the slope and wades into the water like she's probably done every day of her life. Her skirt balloons around her like she's Little Miss Muffet.

I stumble after her, noisy where her movements are quiet, disruptive where hers are graceful.

We're both drenched and frigid when we reach the tree line, the cold a perfect distraction from the way her cardigan's clinging to her skin.

The trees are dense and unmoving, straight as matchsticks. Pam weaves between them with a confidence that's baffling, tracing a path visible only to her, like every footfall is a memory.

We pass what remains of the fallen log trap. Someone's cleared most of it away.

"Gene told me these were for bears," I say, mostly to hear her response.

In the distance, the light between the trees has become an angry red glow. We never brought a flashlight.

"You think they're for the monsters, right?" Pam asks.

I chuckle. "Well, there goes my career."

"The real monsters are human beings," says Pam, all seriousness.

Sticks snap underfoot. Pam's led us onto a narrow path.

"*Gene*," she muses. "I still can't believe it."

Partway through the walk I start shouting to Josh, but all I do is startle the birds. By the time we reach the hatch, my voice is sore.

I kneel before the hatch, run my fingers over the writing: Dan. 4.25. Pine needles flood the grooves, and I brush them to the side. "Why do you think they chose this passage?"

Pam's walking toward the small building. She grips the trunk of one of the pines and hangs off it, spinning. "They exiled the people they sent here to the wilderness. They wanted them to find God, like Nebuchadnezzar."

Seems like a vague reason to emboss the reference in metal, but who says the founders couldn't be fanciful? Good guys don't have a monopoly on creativity.

"Josh!" I bang on the hatch, press my ear to its surface. Nothing.

I join Pam at the building: a rectangular metal box with a flat roof and an antenna. It's featureless but for a metal door with a beat-up key-pad next to it. The door is seamless, as though it opens only from inside.

Pam flips the box protecting the pad, revealing a plain black screen about the size of a hand—maybe a palm reader? I press my hand against it and red light flashes from behind the panel.

"Access denied," says a Majel Barrett knock-off from a hidden speaker.

Pam closes the lid. "That's the only way in." She beckons and we walk past the building, toward the grove of skeletons—the ones from Gene's camera. There's a cleanly-cut tree stump in the centre of the circle, a bit like one of Kayla's neo-pagan altars.

Ten corpses ring the grove, each nailed halfway up a tree. Their clothes and flesh have rotted away, but the skeletons remain affixed. The nails hammered into them flash silver in the dying light of the sun.

"The bones fall down all the time," Pam explains, like she could sense the question on my lips. "Last time Uphill used super glue."

She steps inside the circle, reverential, and drags her hand over the rough bark of the trees one by one. She stops at the one directly across from the path that brought us here.

I step inside, but as I do, my gut burns with indigestion and I fold at the waist, clasping my stomach. The wave passes though—maybe it's nausea from the bodies.

Pam faces me, leaning back against the tree like it's a perfectly ordinary pine, entirely crucified-skeleton-free. She reaches behind her, runs her hand down the trunk. It could be sensual, but maybe that's me being off, or the way her bra shows through her wet shirt.

"I know it's weird," she says. She reaches toward her neck like she's reaching for the button of her blouse, but then she pulls out her gold cross. "But this place feels beautiful to me."

I shake my head to clear it. Josh, I need to find Josh. Fuck, my gut aches. Is it the monkshood? Maybe it's the food from The Moon.

"It's peaceful here," Pam continues.

"Because you're closer to your parents. I get it." I sit down on the trunk-altar. My insides are on fire. I need a moment.

In the middle of the grove, it's like the hollow eyes of every skeleton are fixed on me.

Pam lets her arm drop. She's still fiddling with her cross. She stretches her foot out, staring at her toes. "I don't even know which ones *are* my parents. I used to feel ashamed about it, you know? Uphill holds his services here and gives us all these speeches about how oppressive and awful the founders were, about how *dirt lives in the heart*, about how we're free. But *this* is where I belong. Everyone else's disaster was my aster. There must be something wrong with me."

I wince as pain lances up my spine. But the ache vanishes just as quickly. "Grief is weird. When my mom disappeared, it was like a cavern opened up in me. Sometimes I think I'm more hole than person and I'm shoveling shit into all these crevices to try and fill them but it's sand and it spills back out."

Pam laughs. "That's very artistic. I know what you mean though." She pushes off the tree and looks behind her in the direction of Echo Island. "I'm sorry we didn't find him, Ty. We should head back now."

Fuck that. I heave myself up. "We've barely looked."

"It can wait till tomorrow. If Gene wanted him on the island so bad he came up with this convoluted plan, he's going to take his time once he's got him."

Take his time. "Great, I can abandon Josh to get tortured. You go home, I'm staying." My skin's covered in goosebumps. I'm shivering.

Pam shakes her head and walks over to me. She stands right up close—so close it feels like she might kiss me. She reaches for my hand. "He's not here, Ty."

I snatch my hand back. "Then he's at Uphill's or Gene's. I'm not sleeping till he's safe."

Pam swallows, assessing me. "And I'm not sleeping till you take care of yourself. You're no good to your friend if you're dead."

I'm about to tell her she's being dramatic, that I'm nowhere near that level of exhaustion, when pain seers my back, my shoulders, my cheeks. How can *cheeks* hurt? But they do, and I fall to my knees as my nerve endings start shooting like it's the gunfight at the O. K. Corral.

"*Ty!*" Pam falls right beside me, gripping my shoulders.

This time, the pain doesn't go away. This time, it worsens. *This time*, when I stumble to my feet, everything goes black.

21

FREE FROM S(k)IN

When I look down at my hands, they're not mine. I'm standing in someone's living room and from the unevenness of the plaster walls, I can tell it's not a North American home. The furniture is cherry-polished wood, the clothes are simple and old fashioned. My calf-length skirt is peppered with tiny flowers as round as polka dots.

I'm not *me*, but Virgie Kyle.

My parents, my uncle, and the minister are lined up in front of me. My brother and the man they're forcing me to marry stand to either side of me: prison guards, though my would-be husband doesn't know it.

Father coughs, deliberate and cold, and it's then I realize I'm doing that thing again: wringing my hands.

Paul, my husband-to-be, slips his fingers through mine. He's smiling at me—big and bright and reassuring. He's in love with me. He's a good man. It makes it harder because I can't hate him like I want to. I can't love him either, but I'll do my best to make sure he never learns that. My best, Mother always tells me, is never enough.

I'm outside my body, looking at the two lines of people standing across from each other, watching Paul squeeze Virgie's hand, watching my grandparents trap her so they won't have to send her at great expense to Canada.

My mother turns and looks at me as the world blurs around her. Her parents' voices muffle as though smothered with cotton balls. As she always was, Virgie is the centre of attention, drawing eye and ear and heart. She smiles at me. Her hair is no longer brown; her dress is no longer simple. She's wearing her dyed-black movie-star curls. Her dress is soupy starlight scattered on midnight. Her silver songbird earrings glint beneath a spotlight that has no source.

She squeezes Paul's hand, and I feel the pressure on mine. "Everything's going to be all right, baby doll. It's going to be real hard at first, but then it's going to be all right."

This isn't real. It's a dream, and dream-Mom can't possibly know whether anything will be okay. Yet her words are like curling before the fire after a day in the snow, like the waves buoying against your scalp as you float on the surface of the ocean, like what they always say meditation feels like but it never quite does because you're probably doing it wrong.

You could never follow instructions.

We're standing in the dark. At first the darkness is opaque, movie-theatre blackness. Then Mom looks to her right and we're no longer in the black room, but in a blue-patterned elevator. Pam's standing and staring at the corner with her back to me, subtly off-centre. It makes my brain itch.

Her blond hair cascades down her back in waves, pulled neat by a headband. She's wearing the same pink sweater as earlier, the same floral-print skirt. She's straight as a metal beam, unflinching as if she were hypnotized.

"Pam?" I lay my hand on her shoulder. She's loose as a doll.

I tug her round.

There's a hole where her face should be, like someone's taken scissors to a magazine and neatly clipped a void.

I shove my arms one-by-one inside Pam's face. Her cheeks squeeze my chest as though its edges are caving inwards. I slam my hands against the interior wall and it's fleshy, wet, and bumpy beneath my fingers. The walls suck at my hands, swallowing my fingers, my hips, my legs—all in darkness, I flop onto a spongy carpet.

Trying to stand is like trying to balance in a bumpy castle. I try to steady myself as the floor writhes under me, but the walls are sopping wet. The moisture is ropey, but not sticky. It's humid, fetid, and hard to breathe. I stumble forward.

The shape of something white and flat glints before me.

Teeth.

The ground rolls.

I'm standing on a tongue.

The lips part slowly, letting in a ghostly light that feels like a sheet against my skin. It's the light of the monsters in the forest, hypnotic, almost audible in its brightness.

I stare until the image sharpens, until the breeze tickles my skin and I'm not inside the mouth anymore, but on a road watching Nor walk into the forest.

"*Seven thirty, fingers dirty, seven thirty fingers dirty seventhirty—*" Nor whispers. I hear her words as though every tree is whispering along with her.

I'm dreaming. I am. I'm dreaming.

I hold out my arm and pinch my skin. It stings.

Did I sleepwalk? The last thing I remember is being in the woods with Pam.

The air around me is cold and undulating. Nor's isn't the only voice carried on its eddies. It's like everyone on the island's speaking in time with the trees, so softly I can't make out the words. I hear Pam sobbing, I think, Tia's laugh, Gene groaning. I hear Uphill reciting one of those speeches Pam told me about, the same one he likely gave me when I met him in his office. And the buzzing is back—that sound like a million insect wings beating inside my ear: a pulse vibrating up my spine, through my blood, through the soil.

9 kilometers 9 kilometers obey staystay stay 9 kilometers 9 kilometers stay 9999

Something's moving in the woods.

The treetops sway as if jostled by a vast beast. The air rumbles like a generator, and in the distance, the screams of the elk.

Nor walks into the forest uncaring and dreamlike. Just like Mary.

"Nor!"

She doesn't react, and I run for the bank.

I *thud* against an invisible wall between me and the moat.

"Seven thirty, fingers dirty," says a woman behind me.

I swerve round.

Echo Island is dotted with sleepwalkers. Every one of them is speaking asynchronously, reciting the words of what Tia called a poem. They all have the same zonked-out expression.

They all march toward the woods.

"Seven thirty, fingers dirty—"

"—dig into the soil thick—"

"—drink the juice and swallow thunder—"

"Seven thirty—"

"—feed the groundworms with your spit—"

"—pace the forest in its hunger—"

"—burn your anger to the wick—"

"Seven thirty—"

"—swallow thunder—"

"—pomegranate in the vein—"

"—wet the concrete with your lip—"

"—lick the blood and swallow songspell—"

"—whisper to the old wolfsbane—"

"Seven thirty—"

"—fingers dirty—"

"—skin the flesh and sunder shell—"

"*—peel the rind that's turned to jelly—*"

"—heed the night bird's wanton call—"

"Eight and second, that's the catch"

"—cinch the suit and pin the latch—"

"—walk the streets of Echo Island—"

"—bury Summer's naked thatch—"

I can't move, until I do, and when I do, the ground is rough stone under my bare feet. I'm in a dingy square room, standing in front of my mother.

Virgie Kyle recedes into the shadows, revealing a metal chair. Her fingers curl around the chair's corners, red-varnished nails stroking the surface. The chair is dimly lit by a circular light directly above it—like a paper cut-out of a full moon from a Méliès short. Static roars behind me and artificial light reveals dark stains splattered across the seat, wrist and ankle-straps like an electric chair.

Behind me is a wall of analogue TVs haphazardly stacked one on top of another. They're playing dead channels at first, but one by one they click to life. Mine and Josh's faces appear on each one. I'm talking on every screen, the videos all timed so they cut off and switch to a new episode whenever Josh opens his mouth.

"—you do realize H. P. Lovecraft was a racist, right? I mean do we really want to be—"

"—the fact that we have fans for doing *literally* nothing is pretty—"

"—we all know you're the pretty one, so by default I must be the brains of the operation—"

"—later, on our Only Fans—"

"—just bury me out here, please. Murder me and bury me under a rock—"

Hands clamp down on my shoulders, hauling me back. I slap them, but with every one I shake off, two take their place. They pull me into the chair, so strong they don't even need to use the straps to restrain me.

"*Fuck.*" I headbutt behind me, but there's no one to take the blow. "*Let go.*"

The fingers are like spider legs on my skin—Gene's and Tia's fingers, holding me still. I buck against the chair and my bare skin grazes damp, rusted metal.

I wasn't naked before, was I?

Someone tilts my head back, baring my throat, pulling my skin tight. Conrad Uphill's eyes gaze into mine and cold metal presses against my throat. He grins.

I wriggle and a razor prickles my skin. Liquid trickles down my neck. I feel nothing except an intense itch. Then it burns.

I glance down, but with my neck tilted up, I can't see. Something wet—thicker than blood or hair—slaps against my chest.

The next cut I feel.

Unseen hands peel the skin from my throat. The cool air singes like fire against my muscles, my flesh, my bone.

"Please." I'm not above begging. I'll suck his fucking cock all over again.

The hands press against me, all over me, rusty blades clutched greedily: paring knives and peelers. They sink their weapons as tight as they can into my skin, and then they cut.

I'm dreaming. I am. I'm dreaming.

If I wait long enough, this will end. I can stop it. I can clamp my eyes shut and wake up, and wake up and

My skin sloughs off in ribbons. Dimly, I know it should hurt more than it does. Dimly, as my vision blurs, I know the loss of consciousness will be a blessing and a curse.

Familiar footsteps approach from the darkness, and whoever was holding my head lets go. My jaw makes contact with open wound and I bite back a scream.

"Shhh. Shhh." The voice is as familiar as the footsteps.

I hold my head at the right angle to watch a figure appear from the darkness. The TVs behind him light his thin frame, his curly hair, his sneakers.

We're alone together, him and me. Me and me.

Tyler Kyle steps beneath the spotlight with me. He has a pair of scissors in his hand.

Without the hands to hold me I can get away, I can run away, I can slam myself into the fucking bank of TVs and, and . . . .

My attempt to run lands me in a puddle of my own blood.

I crawl. My knees slip and slide.

"No no no," says Tyler Kyle. He bends down, *grabs* me by the neck, and I'm back in the chair again.

I try to scream, but blood and mucus choke my throat, turning it to a cough.

"Shhh. Shhh," Tyler says again. He brushes the hair from my face, gaze drifting from my eyes to my lips, devouring.

Then he jams his thumb against the missing plain of skin in my throat and *pushes*.

I dig my nails into the chair so hard they crack. I can feel his thumb inside me.

In a spike of lucidity, I kick hard at his ankle, but he doesn't budge.

He slides his bloody thumb past my lips, running it along my teeth, pressing out my cheek, creating a space for him to slip the scissors into my mouth. He scrapes the flat of the blades against the side of my tongue.

"No," I manage.

"I told you to be quiet." He wipes my cheek as though I've been crying.

Quiet. I can be quiet. But I'm shaking so much I'm rattling the chair, my breath loud as thunder.

Tyler Kyle pulls the scissors wide, slicing my gums. The lower blade grazes the underside of my tongue. He pulls the blades open, halfway to the back of my throat, my tongue between them. "Cut off the nose to spite the face."

He snaps the scissors shut.

22

CRUSH

Pam's face is bent over me when I wake up. My back is cushioned by one of those beds that's somehow comfier for how ancient its springs are. There's a warm damp cloth on my forehead and I'm . . . well, Pam must have undressed me, because I'm naked under the blankets.

I take in the smallish rectangular room with its mellow yellow walls and its shelves of books and comics. Glenn from *The Walking Dead* is pinned between two *Young Justice* posters. Two small windows with white lace curtains are jarring next to the nerdy décor, looking out on a pitch-black sky.

Pam's smile could melt ice caps. "How do you feel?"

I wet my lips, flick my tongue along my gums to make sure the skin's unbroken, that everything's still there.

It was a nightmare. And it's no surprise, with what I saw today, with Josh out there alone, or with Gene and Tia torturing him.

I clench my jaw. Every part of me wants to move.

"What time is it?" I throw the covers from my chest, sitting up to wrap them round my waist. My shirt and pants are folded on a chair next to the bed.

How long was I out? How much time have I wasted?

Pam scooches to my side and presses her ring and forefinger against my chest, pushing me as if to make me lie back down.

I stay upright.

"*How do you feel?*" she asks again.

"Fine."

Her brow furrows. "You screamed in your sleep."

"Just a nightmare." Vivid, but already fading.

Pam clutches her fists in her lap. "It's three in the morning." She lets out a deep breath. "You collapsed. I had to drag you back here—you had a fever."

I touch my forehead. Sure, it's a little warm, but I could go back out. I *have* to go back out. "I don't have a fever now."

On my way to the chair the room spins, creating a whirligig of Robins and Superboys and Steven Yeuns from the posters plastering the walls.

Pam rushes to my side and eases us both down. She takes my hand and squeezes. "Please wait till morning."

"Where is this?" I ask.

She brightens. "My house." She fans her arm out, indicating the walls. "Well, my spare room. I knew you wouldn't want me taking you to Conrad's clinic."

"You carried me back here on your own."

She bites her lip. "I left you. Just for a second though! So I could steal Nelson's wheelbarrow." She winces. "Sorry about the bruises." Her cheeks glow red. "And the nudity—I needed to check your skin, in case you had a rash from the monkshood? It's poisonous."

I comb my hand through my hair and it . . . sticks. Too late for embarrassment. I snag it free with mild discomfort. "I really don't feel sick anymore."

"You can barely stand." Pam doesn't budge.

Even sitting, the room's not entirely stationary.

The fight goes out of me, and she must sense it, because she takes my hand and places it in her lap, rubbing her thumb along mine, spreading my fingers, playing with them gently. "What happened between you and your friend? You must really care about him."

I swallow. Pam's face is so open, and there's a sadness in her, a need that's painfully familiar. We're both stuck. We're both adult orphans with lingering baggage—hers is perhaps a little more tangible, being nailed to a tree and all. But we're the same in so many ways, and that recognition is unexpected and delightful. The brush of her thumb against mine is kind, almost automatic, like she wants and needs my skin to touch hers. We've barely spent a day together, but I feel like we know each other.

I clear my throat. "Huh. Yeah. Josh and me—he's my best friend. We went to theatre school together, started the cryptid show I mentioned."

Pam's face lights up. "Discovery Bang. I downloaded some episodes for the flight back. It's real cute. I liked it."

I laugh, nervous, and suddenly I'm grinning too. "Really?"

"*Really.*" She locks her fingers with mine. "I get sad a lot and not much makes me smile these days. You made me smile."

Me. Me and Josh.

I scratch the back of my head, laugh again, and *again*, it's nervous. "It's really dumb."

She leans over, kisses my cheek, then pulls back suddenly, retracting her hand. "I-I'm sorry."

"Why?" I look her in her eyes. They're darting back and forth, reading me. I fold my fingers over hers, pulling her forward an inch. She creeps toward me. I want to kiss her, but I wait for an answer, petrified this is another case of me drastically misreading someone's signals.

"Your friend. You need time, right?" She tilts her head. "It must be hard after what he wrote."

It stings, but I brush it off. "It doesn't matter. He's more important to me than whatever happened between us."

Pam bites her lip. "Something happened?"

"Just . . . ." I pull away. I have to get dressed. I have to find him.

But Pam won't let go. She tugs me back down, and my stomach lurches, my ankles threatening to buckle.

"You can't even walk," she says. "Sit with me. Please talk to me." She brushes my hair from my eyes. "Give me the few hours till morning."

She's not wrong about walking. The hard shell I've tried to turn myself into is starting to crack. It feels like failure, so of course, I make a joke. "Are you saying you wouldn't wheelbarrow me to The Thunder Moon if I asked?"

She smiles. "I'd wheelbarrow you to the real moon, pretty boy."

Part of that feels good. I wish the whole thing felt good. The compliment makes me jittery, threatens to turn me to mush, but the idea of wanting Pam, or anyone, only reminds me of Josh, my thoughts jostling between the fact that he's in danger, and the cold truths of his e-mail.

"I'll stay," I say. "For tonight, and then I'm tearing this town apart." Literally, if I have to. I will literally steal a tractor and bulldoze the fuck out of that metal box in the woods.

"That's all I wanted," says Pam, and she takes my hand again. "Both of those things. Fuck Conrad and fuck Gene and Tia." She giggles, covers her mouth. "It feels illegal saying that. *God it feels so good.*"

She leans in and kisses me, climbing half on top of me, one of her legs over mine. She cups my face.

I wasn't expecting it and I draw back. "Wow. I—Sorry, I didn't realize you were . . . wow. I'm sorry."

Pam's eyes are as blue as the underside of an iceberg. She doesn't blush like I'd have expected. She looks blank, shocked. And of course she does. I never did anything to tell her I wouldn't want her to kiss me. I *did* want her to.

She draws her leg from my lap with the grace of a broken supermarket trolley. She fidgets with her hands, knees straight and pressed together. With the pose, the clothes, the face and hair, I'm half expecting her to belt out "Hopelessly Devoted to You."

"Is there something wrong with me?" she asks. "Do you think I'm ugly?"

I need to fix this. "There's nothing wrong with you, I'm just fucked up over Josh." I lean back against the headboard. "It's not just that I'm—that I *was*—in love with him." I am in love with him. "We flirted a lot on the show, like the e-mail said. I interpreted it wrong. I guess." My chest is on fire. Why am I trying to talk about this? I don't want to talk about this. I could be sitting in that rusted chair from my nightmare, peeling off my own skin for how much it hurts. "I fucked his life up. He had this girlfriend, and I made this joke on the show about me and Josh fucking, and she got upset and dumped him."

Pam frowns. "That's a shitty thing to do."

"It wasn't her fault."

"No, I meant it was a shitty thing for you to do," says Pam.

At least she's honest. "Yeah. It was. So, then a few months later Josh and me got trashed. We got handsy with each other in a hot tub."

"Handsy?" Pam's scrutinizing me.

I wriggle my fingers. "You know, with these? And I guess there was a lot of making out."

He climbed on my lap. He grabbed my cock. He pressed his lips against mine. He shoved my hand down his shorts. He told me I tasted like lime and then laughed when I said he tasted like tequila.

Or maybe not. I was too drunk. I'm not remembering right. Was that hunger his, or was I projecting? It should be pretty fucking clear, after the e-mail.

"Tyler?" Pam strokes my knee, drawing circles.

Fuck, I'm crying. *Fuck.*

I laugh, wipe the tears away with the back of my hand. "He, uh. I mean I—I made the same stupid joke, the one she broke up with him for? He pushed me away, told me he didn't want me. We just—we sat there saying nothing until I didn't have a fucking hard-on anymore and I got up and left. Slept on a bench. Didn't ever really talk about it again. Until he started saying *we need to talk about the show*, and I pushed him away. I called him from the cabin and told him I was in love with him, like a dumb-*fucking*-shit, because what exactly was that supposed to fix? I didn't want him to come here. I wanted him to be okay. Why the fuck would he send that e-mail and then come here anyway? I don't want a fucking close-out episode to end my character arc. I'm not a fucking character. How can I have an arc? I'm just fucking me, and he—"

But he wasn't *him*, and that's the part I missed.

Fucking dumbass.

"I'm glad you liked the show. It's real flattering." I avert my gaze, like if I don't look at her she won't see I'm crying. "It's Josh's thing. He made me good—we were good together. If you took him out of the show it'd be nothing, but I—" What the fuck am I doing? What, the ever-loving-fuck. Pam doesn't give a fuck about any of this. She wanted to know why I led her on and chickened out.

"You're not replaceable, Ty." Pam smiles. "It's not your fault. And if that girlfriend really loved him she'd have waited and listened when he explained. Obviously he didn't really want you, so why wouldn't she believe him? That girl had no determination."

It's a unique take. "She was a bit weird," I admit.

"Weird?"

How to put it into words? The effort dries my tears as I scour my memory for all the ways Ashley was strange. Josh is a magnet for strange. "There was this one time, she made us read fanfic—do you know fanfic?"

Pam nods, smiles. "Umm. I *may* write fic actually. *Young Justice* mostly, on Ao3? Artemis x Robin." She laughs nervously, does a little snake wiggle with her head. "Some *Walking Dead.*"

Everything she says and does is charming. She's charming. "Fix-it fic for Glenn?"

She rolls her eyes exaggeratedly. "*How did you know*? He's my number two crush, actually."

"Only number two?"

She winks. "Wouldn't you like to know?" She slides her hand up my leg.

I'm really glad, during all this, that she gave me a thick blanket, and that it's bunched around my waist.

"So—so anyway," I continue. "She thought it'd be funny if we read some fanfiction about the show. It was pretty bad—no offense to the writers. I know fanfiction's an outlet for—"

"You don't have to give me the speech," Pam says, cutting me off.

"Right."

Pam's thumb is still tracing those circles, pressing down hard into my thigh in a way that isn't exactly unpleasant. "So she was weird because she liked fic?"

"No," I say, a little more breathy than is ideal. "I guess it's not a great story."

"People used to call *me* weird." She's staring at me. It's piercing. It's the need I recognized in her earlier, sharpened to a needle's point.

I smile, but it's like I'm skating on a pond that's only partially frozen. "You're weird. But good weird."

She drags her fingers down my leg. It's agonizing. But the way she bites her lip, glances down at herself as she repositions her legs so she's kneeling on the bed with me, as she unbuttons her sweater, as she shrugs it off and starts on the buttons to her dress that *clearly* has no bra underneath—that part is worse.

"You're so neat," Pam says, dreamy. "You're such a really neat guy."

It's the first snow of winter on my skin as she recites Cavale's part from *Cowboy Mouth*. The female lead to my Slim.

"I wish I woulda known you when I was little," she continues. "Not *real* little, but at the age when you start finding out stuff.

When I was cracking rocks apart to find the sparkles inside. The first time I put my fingers inside myself and felt wonderment."

She straddles me, all smiles. She does a little bow, laughs. "I looked you up." She runs her hand through the side of my hair. Unlike mine, her fingers don't get stuck. "I watched some of your scenes online." She nudges the shoulders of her dress down, slides her arms out of them. "Your friend's an idiot not to want you."

Her dress is hanging at her waist and fuck I want to touch her.

I do touch her. I rest my hands on her hips, heart in my throat, and she lowers herself onto me. She reaches down, grabs the blankets between us, and tears them off. My cock brushes against her, and she's not wearing any underwear.

She's not wearing underwear.

"Condom?" I ask.

"I'm on the pill."

Pam buries her mouth in my neck, bites. I put my arm around her, slide my fingers down her spine, enjoying the little jump when I reach her tailbone. I kiss her cheek as her fingers wrap around my cock, her breasts pressed against my chest.

She nips my ear, flicks her tongue against it, then whispers, "I'm a virgin."

Fuck. What?

"I—" I pull back.

Pam blinks. "Don't be all weird about it. I want you to fuck me." She licks my lips. Mine, not hers.

She's right. I'm being weird about it. "Sorry." I kiss her, holding back on asking if she's sure. She's acting sure. She told me that she's sure. She told me what she wants and what she wants is me.

She kisses me back. "I made you go all quiet."

"I can talk," I say. I can do two things at once. Two things at once came naturally with Josh, who I'm not with. I'm not with Josh right now.

"*You taste like lime,*" he says in my head, and I grab Pam round her back and she grabs me. I run my hand over her ass, her thigh. She's wet as my fingers find her, and she moans when I touch her, parts her lips and squeals, eyes closed, when I rub my forefinger up her clit.

"Fuck me from behind."

"What?"

"From behind."

"For your first time?"

"Yeah." She traces her finger along my jawline.

A small part of me, a crazy part of me, wants to stop. I can feel the gravel digging into my knees outside The Moon, Uphill's cock filling my mouth, the shame that rushed in afterwards.

Pam bucks against me and my cock brushes her pussy.

I'll fuck her from behind.

She falls back onto the bed and the creak of the aged springs is electric. She kicks my leg, watching me under bedroom eyelids, teasing her nipples.

I stand up, swallow, and there's this terrible sinking feeling when she flips over and yanks her skirt up and parts her legs.

I mean, I want her. I do. I'm hard as I've ever been in my life. But somehow, it's still like I'm drowning.

"Hands on my hips, pretty boy."

Ugh.

But I do it because I'm horny as fuck and for an instant the pleasure makes the pain subside. And she pants and moans while I fuck her, and tells me to go harder and faster and yadda yadda yadda and why do I feel like I'm in a porno and why does my hindbrain really not care and should I be embarrassed that my hindbrain is pretty trashy as it turns out? I thought I was better than this. No, I never thought I was better than this. I thought I had more willpower than this, and that's different. But why should I even *need* willpower when I like Pam and I want Pam and she's beautiful and kind and most importantly she wants this to be happening. I'm doing exactly what she wants. I want this to be happening.

The bed creaks like it'll collapse, and despite being buried x-inches—ahem—deep in a gorgeous woman as she makes happy sex sounds under me, my gaze wanders and I'm looking at that Steven Yeun poster and . . . *nope* . . . let's stare at the ceiling instead. Better still, let's close our eyes.

"*You taste like lime.*"

My hands are on his hips, and he pulls me back into the water. His back hits it with a smack and he bites my lip, and I don't know if it was on purpose or by accident, but beneath the surface of the over-chlorinated water I catch him, and we're tangled in each other, and we're both laughing and he pulls himself up and drapes his arms over my shoulders, and—

"Fuck me," says Pam.

"Yep, that's currently what I'm doing."

I didn't say it. *I didn't.* I did.

"*Be quiet*," says Pam.

And I do, and we fuck for a while I guess or something and it's super great.

Afterwards, lying on the bed, Pam nuzzles me, head tucked under my chin, wheat-yellow hair pillowed beneath that. She knots her legs in mine, drawing patterns on my chest with her thumb. She pricks the hollow of my bellybutton, then presses inside it. I squirm out from under the touch and she reaches down, for my cock.

It's been like, two minutes, and as Pam herself pointed out, I'm running on empty.

"I, uh. Unless you just want to hold it, sorry." I swallow, close my eyes.

"Seriously?" she asks, flat, incredulous. But I guess she's never fucked anyone before. Still, it's not like we didn't both cum.

"It takes some time for guys, that's all. Sorry."

She snorts, then laughs. She draws her hand back, and why do I feel grateful?

"Sounds like an excuse." She cranes her head back and kisses my chin. "Kidding." But she pauses maybe ten seconds before asking: "So how long?"

Would she believe me if I said ten hours? The fact I'm even having that thought is not normal. I'm not being normal right now. "Half an hour?"

"Okay." She pauses. "I wanna fuck you again so bad, that's all."

I make a face, which she can't see, and because she can't see it, I make another, even worse face, a bit like a weird fish mouth. Fuck, I'm an asshole.

I wrap a strand of her hair round my finger because I dunno, it's what I would do with someone else, and I'm being ungenerous to Pam when I should be nice. Earlier, I wanted to be nice to her.

I kiss the top of her head. "So." I pause. "Why from behind?" It's *very* hard not to laugh. But I don't.

She reaches up and traces her finger along my jawline. "I'm shy."

You know, there have been many occasions so far on which Pam has demonstrated behaviour I would classify as shy, but her practically jumping me after sitting there for what was probably hours with no underwear or bra on as though in preparation and then stripping for me and telling me to fuck her repeatedly is not one of them.

But I have to be nice. And why would she lie? Unless she's embarrassed by her own fantasies, and that's—well, that makes me feel like shit.

"It's okay if that's how you like it," I say.

"Mm. It isn't." She sits up, covers her mouth. "Oh, no, that's not what I meant. You were fine. I mean, I get that you're not feeling 100%, you know? And you never went all the way with your friend, so it's not like either of us is all that experienced. It'll be better next time."

Does she think I'm a virgin? Was I that bad? Fuck. I mean, she made a whole lot of noise. Unless she was faking. She didn't sound like she was. But women do that all the time, don't they, because they feel like they have to, because of assholes and their egos. Maybe that's why she wanted to fuck again so soon.

I edge my hand toward her thigh. I should get her off.

She slaps my hand away. Then she winces. "Just not with you looking at my face, okay?" She kisses my chin again.

"I could go down on you," I say. My insides feel like snakes. "Then it'd be impossible for me to look at your face."

Or, it occurs to me, for her to look at my face. The thought's infectious. Savage.

"We could do that," she says. "But then I want you inside me, okay? I can't get enough."

Dead. I feel dead. But I do it. I do everything she wants, until I can't anymore, and we fall asleep.

This time, if I dream, I forget them by morning.

23

IN DAYLIGHT,
EVERYTHING'S ALL RIGHT

I wake up first, turning over to find Pam sleeping silently with her hair arrayed around her like tongues of sunlight. Her fingers are curled loosely into a fist, resting on her pillow.

Last night seems totally different in the morning. There's nothing wrong with what she said, with what we did. I was out of line, possibly out of my mind. Now I'm lucid again. The weird tone in her voice was all in my head, either that or it was a justifiable response to *my* weird tone. Pam isn't anything but peaceful. I'm just messed up over Josh.

I have to find him.

It'd be a crime to wake Pam when she looks like that, so I inch from the bed and shove my clothes under my arm to change elsewhere. But as soon as I turn my back, sheets rub against sheets, and Pam's groan follows.

"You're not running out on me, are you? After popping my cherry?" There's a smile in her voice, but when I turn and face her, her expression's anything but amused.

I wave my shirt like it'll explain everything. "Just changing."

Pam eyes me, grins. She pulls off the sheets and crawls toward me. "You don't have to wear anything. I don't mind." She takes my hand. "I thought you could fuck me on the table later."

I stare at Pam: her smudged make-up, her only half-open eyes, the way her hair's spiking out in a physically improbable direction that I'm 99% sure is because it's orbiting a nucleus of cum.

"You know. I thought maybe a shower first?"

Pam's face *drops*. She shrugs, let's my hand fall from hers, then hops into a sitting position on the bed.

I don't want to hurt her, but it's just not the most important thing to me right now, you know? "Look, I wasn't running out, but I have to go. Josh needs me, and I feel fine now. See? I'm walking in straight lines and everything."

Pam purses her lips. "Uh uh. We go together or you don't go at all. It's dangerous in the woods, and you need to eat something." She walks up to me and pokes my admittedly skeletal stomach.

"I thought you wanted me to walk around shirtless?"

"Well," Pam says, sing-song-y, like she's properly waking up now. "You know I like you the way you are, but you're not exactly most people's idea of a hot pocket." She winks at me. "Sorry."

"Harsh but fair." She's teasing, I guess. Because otherwise I'm not sure what she's doing. Maybe she watched a bit too much Discovery Bang and she's trying to emulate our banter.

"Josh was always the eye candy," I add.

"I'm starting to get why."

Okay, that's weird. It's a weird thing to say.

But then she winks again. "I'm kidding."

Is she? Yesterday in the graveyard she didn't have that big a sense of humour.

"I'm leaving, sorry." I turn around.

Pam grabs my arm. "*Ty*. You can't keep putting his needs above your own. You need to eat, *we need to shower*, and you're not going to be able to take on Gene, Tia, and Conrad by yourself."

The brightness of the light shining past the windows tells me it's already past eight—what if a bagel is the difference between Josh with thumbs still attached, and Josh without?

But Pam kisses my shoulder. "Please. Take care of yourself. Josh would tell you the same thing."

Josh *would* tell me the same thing, but Josh also wouldn't have got me into the mess I've dragged him into.

Pam wraps her arms around me and squeezes gently.

I breathe in deep, close my eyes. "Fine. But we need to be quick."

My shower's the fastest a human being has ever taken, and then I'm downstairs, working out breakfast so Pam can't insist on making toutons.

By the time Pam appears, blurry-eyed and wrapped in a pink flannel housecoat, I've set a table and am scraping a round of burned pancakes into the garbage. They splatter against a discarded drawing at the bottom of the bin. Whatever it was looked pretty good, and I pull it out, grease stains be damned, as Pam makes toast.

The picture's pen on lined paper, a drawing of a skull with flowers—more monkshood at a guess—filling its mouth. Larvae brim from the eyesockets. I flip the sheet over and there's a picture of a wolf with a dead fox at its feet. The fox's neck is broken and blood pools around it. It'd make a good metal album cover.

The toast pops and she gingerly pinches it between her fingers, flipping it onto two plates. She carries mine over, sucking her thumb and ring finger where she touched the bread. She squints at the drawing.

"Oh god, don't look at that." She tears it from my hand and tosses it back in the trash. "It's garbage."

I pick at my plain toast. "It's badass." I smile. "My tastes run a little morbid."

"Me too." She scrunches her nose. "I knew there was a reason I liked you right away." She stands on her toes and kisses me, wrapping her arms round my neck, nearly knocking my plate from my hand. "That or because you're so pretty."

"I thought I wasn't a hot pocket?" I can banter with Pam. It'll just take some getting used to.

She rubs the tip of her nose against mine. "Fuck me." Before I can lay my breakfast aside she's hauling me backwards toward the table. She hops onto it. Knives and forks clatter to the floor as she plants her legs apart. "We can do it facing each other if you want."

I reach behind her and lay my toast down. "I want to find Josh."

She stares at me, disbelieving. Then, as if someone's flipped a switch, she hops off the table. "Okay. You're right. We should look for him. Just let me get dressed, 'kay?" She plants a kiss on my cheek and hurries upstairs.

24

Calling Shotgun

From Pam's driveway, I have an excellent view of the forest at the back of Arcadia. Fog drifts over the town like seafoam choking the cracks between pebbles. The islanders scurry from their houses, rock spiders fighting the sudden tide.

A gunshot cracks the air. Not a pistol or a handgun, but a rifle blast reverberating across the island from the south.

Pam strolls to my side. "They're shooting the dogs."

The feral dogs. The Dog Days. The whole reason my trip happened when it did. It's all so muddled in my head, wrapped up in the mystery of my mom, and the monsters in the forest, Gene and the stalker, the poem from my dream.

"Seven thirty, fingers dirty," I say. It nags at me, this thing that was there at the beginning and which I've all but forgotten. The words Mary spoke in the woods.

Pam watches me. "You know what it means."

The gears are creaking into place. "Yeah, I do. It's not a time, is it? It's a date. July thirtieth. Tia said you shoot the dogs at the end of the month."

Is this how Josh feels when he pieces together his theories? "When I was in the woods, Mary told me to run toward the feral dogs to escape the monsters. And Conrad keeps the dogs on the island year-round, until you kill them. It's like the dogs are here to keep the monsters away, but for whatever reason, he doesn't need them at the end of July." I snap my fingers. Pam jumps. "And the traps! They said they take the traps away around now."

Another gunshot, then a third coming from a completely different direction. That, or the fog is distorting the sound.

"They take the traps away so we can hunt the dogs," Pam says, like I'm the crazy one.

I shake my head. "No. The monsters have something to do with it. I saw one of them in Gene's basement. They may be robots, or androids, or weapons, but they're real."

More gunshots, and the islanders standing in their driveways head back indoors one by one, or two by two, or three by three—I guess polyamory's a thing here. May as well be an equal opportunity murder island.

"You mentioned the poem." Pam hooks her arm in mine. "It's about how Conrad traps people here. The ground or the water—whatever he infects people with."

The island song.

Pomegranate in the vein . . . monkshood medley. The lyrics from the dream. Could "pomegranate" refer to Conrad's Persephone pills? Monkshood Medley—the cocktail Tia warned me not to drink?

Pam's neighbours emerge from inside their home toting shotguns. It's too early for the Dog Days, so what's everyone doing? Is it a rehearsal for big ol' seven thirty? How did everyone hear the shot and know to come out? As if they'd all received a message.

I glance at the telephone poles. Like everywhere on the island, the speakers are there. I squint. They're crackling. It's as though I can see the sound in the air. There's a drawn out pause, a subtle base tone like when you hit play on a cassette but the music hasn't started yet.

It starts: Queen Cee's "Baby One More Time." Pam's neighbours pump their guns, nearly in time to the piano riff at the beginning of the song.

"Why didn't you tell me about Uphill's magic voice thing?" I ask.

Pam shifts. "I didn't think you'd believe me. You seem like a skeptical guy. And after watching your show, I was right." She kisses my cheek. "Come on, we should head to The Moon. Someone will know what's going on."

And I can look for Josh.

The people on the street are leaving too—not in sync with us, and not exactly following us, but not exactly *not* following us either.

As we turn onto Rivers, I glance at the sign for Pam's road.

"Garou," I say.

"What?" Pam looks at me. "Oh—my street. Yeah. Didn't you have a map?"

Fuck knows where that is now. Even my phone's charging at Pam's. "What's it named after?"

"The streets are named after the founders." She tugs me away from the sign and points down the street. "Tia's outside the bar."

Tia *is* outside the bar. Like the people walking down the street behind us, she's got a gun.

I never thought "Baby One More Time" could be ominous, but it's fucking ominous when an entire island's population is marching toward one road, packing lead.

Pam smiles warmly. "I doubt this has anything to do with you. It's like this when we start the Dog Days. I don't know why it's happening earlier."

Sometimes I forget Pam was born here. All the odd customs, the festivals, Uphill's speeches—they're natural to her. And yet, she has access to knowledge the others don't. She's more worldly than them, but maybe she's also more inculturated with fucked-upness. I think I saw some of that fucked-upness last night.

The islanders have constructed a corral filled with yelping dogs. I can't quite hear them over the music.

"Does everyone attend the festival?"

Two rifle-toting granola lesbians pass us, grinning and laughing.

"Yeah, they do. It's an important time for the island. It brings us together." Pam scoffs. "It's *meant* to. I never bought into Conrad's rituals like everyone else."

"Because of your parents."

She squeezes my arm as we scurry into The Moon's back lot. We press ourselves tight against the wall beside the dumpster. I get Pam to help me with the lid, and dig for the DVD and the note.

Got 'em.

I cram them into my pockets and then it's up onto the dumpster. I lift Pam up on my shoulders—probably should have done this the other way round. But no, after climbing through the window, Pam leans down and grabs my arm. She has no problem pulling me up.

Inside Gene's, I dust myself off. A gentle breeze blows the curtains just like yesterday. The blue screen glow emanates from the room along the landing. I run to the monitors, but when I find the basement camera, the room is completely empty. I jab my finger at it. "That's where Gene keeps the monster."

Pam glares at the screen thoughtfully. "Do you know where this is?"

"Yeah, downstairs."

She heads for the door. I slide my hand into my pocket, hitting the DVD case.

"Wait, we can watch this." I pop it open as Pam comes back. She helps me locate a disc drive and I stick it in.

I'm bracing myself for embarrassment—me taking a dump, me in the shower, me jerking off—but it's none of those things.

The shot's of the interior of The Moon, facing the karaoke stage. I'm crouched, mic in hand, talking to Nor and Tia. Gene's sitting at one of the round tables, back to the camera. I fastforward through the whole show, including the parts where the crowd started acting funny as I supposedly sang us into a stupor.

I toss the remote onto the table. I rub my temples. "Fuck. That's not what I thought it would be."

But there was still the monster in Gene's basement. There were the cameras, and the creepy, crumpled note about Josh.

Pam plucks another DVD off the shelf, one marked "Rudra." She puts it on, and the South Asian man from the photograph on the wall appears on stage at The Moon. He launches into the beginning of a comedy routine: "You ever notice how Nelson never makes it to full moon shows? Starting to think he's a werewolf."

The people filling the tables burst into laughter.

Guess everyone's real invested in Nelson.

"That's Ru, Gene's husband." Pam curls her fingers over the back of the desk chair and bites her lip. "There's nothing suspicious about these, Ty."

I smooth my hair back. "Oh god. Shit. I hit Gene with a—"

"With a fucking *two by four*," yells Tia.

I swerve. She's behind us, leaning against the doorframe. She marches up to me, and there's a look in her eyes like she's about to hit me.

Pam steps between us. "Back off."

There's something unfairly sexy about a petite blonde stepping in front of a blow for you.

Tia stabs her finger at me over Pam's shoulder, eyes red-rimmed. At least she doesn't have her rifle. "You put my best friend in the hospital you skeevy little asshole."

The hospital? She's been crying, and Gene's in the hospital.

"I—I didn't hit him that hard."

"You almost put his eye out with a nail." Tia pulls back, hugging herself. She's a mess. I don't mean emotionally, though she's that too, but she's physically a mess in her sweat and food-stained shirt. "He had to get stitches."

"I'm sorry," I start to say, but *no*, I'm not sorry. "He had a monster in his basement. And a drawer full of cameras." I hold up the DVD case with my name on it and shake it.

"You're a cunt," Tia spits. She sniffs, and tears spring to her eyes. "Get the fuck out of here! I don't want you in here! Get *out*!" She reaches past Pam and grabs my shirt.

Pam punches her smack in the mouth. Blood dribbles from Tia's lip.

Tia stumbles back, eyes wide. "*Bitch.*" She wipes the blood off on her sleeve.

This is too much. I hold up my hands. "I'm sorry about Gene. I'm looking for my friend, Josh. I'm pretty sure Gene's holding him somewhere. Or maybe Nor—"

Tia's staring death at me. "*Nor's dead.*" Her face crumples like a paper bag.

What?

"What happened?" I don't know what else to say. It seems impossible that something happened.

"Motorcycle accident," Tia blurts. She scuffs the floor, staring at her boots.

"Tia—" I step past Pam, reach for Tia, but she snaps away.

"You're not my friend, you dick. My friend's in the hospital. Get out." Her painted nails dig into her leather jacket so hard they must be breaking.

"*Tia.*" I have to do something. I can't do anything. Thinking about Nor being dead makes me think of the same thing happening to Josh and it's like swallowing a tub of nails.

Tia's shaking. "Get. Out."

Pam tugs my arm. "Come on, Ty. There's nothing here."

Tia's here, so it's patently untrue. But Tia also doesn't want *me* here, and Tia still lied. She's right—we're not friends. I've known her for four days and nothing good has come of us spending any of that time together.

I let Pam drag me from the room to the sound of Tia's sobbing.

25

AN ACHE YOU CAN'T AFFORD TO FEEL

Outside the bar, Queen Cee's "Umbrella" has cycled back to "Baby One More Time." Almost the entire town huddles behind the corral, weapons clutched in their hands, while the rest erect a white fence along either side of the street. There's a locked gate in the corral, like they plan to herd the dogs along a racecourse. The dogs snarl and fret against the fence so wildly I'm waiting to hear the crack of a skull.

An image of Nor flashes before me, her brains dashed out on the road, her insides smeared across tarmac.

I force myself to turn from the feral animals as the islanders prep their guns.

Fog blankets the town in an almost imperceptible haze. It's humid, the air electric. Everything is grey.

Conrad Uphill steps from behind the corral to direct the fence builders.

Pam clings to me as we stand in the parking lot.

No one pays us any attention. I shouldn't be thinking about myself, probably, but I'm relieved. It's getting less likely this was arranged for my benefit, and at least Josh isn't locked in Gene's basement. But there *is* a reason this is happening now, and as I watch Mary's wife Colleen slam her hammer into a nail, I start mentally slotting the pieces of the mystery into place.

I turn to Pam. "Nor didn't die in a motorcycle accident."

She hesitates. "No. Probably not. The woods got her, the way they get everyone."

"Because she tried to leave, or because Uphill's music," I wave my hand in the direction of the closest speaker, "isn't working the way it used to?"

Pam smiles. "Nor would never leave Tia. They were a dynamic duo. She'd've cut off her arm first."

"That's what I thought."

Yesterday at lunch, Nor sat with me. She loathed my guts, or at the very least found me tremendously annoying, but she bought me that beer and begged me to sing. She was crying when I sang at karaoke. It's like she knew what was happening to her. She was praying I could save her.

Then we have Mary. She didn't have a stroke right away. She wandered into the forest first, reciting the same line Nor spoke in last night's dream. I *watched* Nor wade across the moat and into the trees, speaking in gibberish like Mary did.

My skin prickles. The fog's thickened, bringing dampness and a chill. My sweater's in my suitcase, and even though I'm right outside The Thunder Moon, there's no way I'm risking Tia's wrath to retrieve it.

What I really need is somewhere to sit and think. Increasingly, I've got this brewing feeling that if I want to find Josh, I'm going to have to solve this mystery. There's more to it than the obvious, or maybe less. Sometimes the simplest answer is the right one. *Often* the simplest answer is the right one.

Pam waves her hand in front of my face. "Tyler?"

"*Ty*," says Pam, waving her hand again. There's a little Josh in the emphasis she places on my name. It's very Josh of her to call me Ty at all.

"*Ty*." She's standing in front of me. "Are you okay?"

"Could we go somewhere quiet?" The hammering, the overeager gunshots, the howling of the dogs, the endless cycle of "Umbrella" and "Baby One More Time," and—oh fuck.

"Razzle Dazzle" is playing. *I'm* playing. Tyler Kyle has entered the Echo Island rotation.

One more reason to flee for the hills.

"Isn't that you?" Pam asks.

Ugh. "Can we check out the forest?"

"If you're sure you want to give up looking for Josh so soon. We haven't checked Conrad's mansion yet."

It feels like a reprimand. Me and Josh, we're not like Tia and Nor. I don't care enough to keep searching, let alone cut off my arm.

"I need to think this through before I'm any help to him." I know from Kayla's *I Survived* obsession, the worst thing you can do is panic. To find Josh, I have to put my thinking cap on. "Besides, he mentioned the woods during our call. Let's go back to the founders."

I start back up Rivers, but Pam tugs my sleeve. "The way we crossed before is easiest. We'll be more hidden."

She has a point.

I follow her across more lawns. My arms are sprinkled with goosebumps. "What happens to people when they start wanting to go out to the woods or whatever?"

The way Pam turns and stares in the direction of the forest feels automatic. "They start having dreams, then the blackouts and the sleepwalking. It's like dementia, until they have a stroke, or get hurt walking in the woods at night."

The stroke comment gets me: Mom, Echo Island got Virgie Kyle like it got Nor and Mary. Out here, she would have been so isolated, easy prey for Uphill to manipulate, and then to top it off, she probably died wandering into the forest and talking to nobody. Was she cold? Was she scared? Did some part of her understand what was happening to her? I can't imagine anything worse than being trapped inside your head, unable to communicate, to move, to do anything but watch your body going through the motions like someone else is in control. My mom hated being alone. It was the worst thing you could do to her.

For a moment, I see my double from the dream disappearing into the trees. *That* sends a shudder through me.

The dream was weird in a way I don't have the gears to process. If I try, and I don't have to try hard, I can conjure the taste of my own fingers in my mouth, the metallic sting of the scissors, the caress of hands over my arms, my neck, my chest—the itch as Echo Island skins me alive.

And Mom telling me everything would be all right. That part of the dream felt like walking inside a memory.

Am I having forest dreams like Nor? What if the method Uphill uses to trap people's already working on me, and what if it's working a little too well? It's probably a drug, and there have been so very many opportunities for people to drug me—endless drinks at The Moon, Uphill when he kissed me. Nor and her funny-tasting beer.

A bucket trips me and I go flying. I just catch myself.

Pam rushes over. "You okay?"

"Yeah, I'm fine. Thanks."

She helps me up and we exit the deadly maze of the islanders' neatly kept gardens for the relative flatness of the road.

"You're a lot clumsier than I thought." Pam laughs, steering me in the direction of the moat. The same place I crossed into the woods both times.

"Than you thought?"

Pam gives me a playful shove. "On stage you were really composed."

"I made an ass out of myself."

"Yeah, but that's its own talent. I could never get up there and try to sing like you did." She laces our fingers together and we stop before the bank. She stares into my eyes like the sun lives behind them. "You have a lot to teach me about how to be shameless and have fun."

It's a compliment, I think? So why are my insides buzzing like I swallowed a hornet's nest. She said *try*. Try to sing. But what does Pam's opinion matter? I mean, she's not right. I was the guy to beat back in school for musical leads, and most people who bothered trying lost the fight.

So why did it dry up so soon after I graduated? Why was The Moon the first time my feet touched a stage—outside the Discovery Bang liveshows—since a bit-part in a local show last fall? And I've auditioned for things—maybe not so many things as I used to with all the flying around hunting owls—but I have auditioned. Do I suck now? Maybe my voice changed. Maybe I lost it. Maybe I peaked in university. Maybe it's my awkward face, or my not-exactly-a-hot-pocket body, or the creeping queerness the casting agents can sense beneath my surface. I'm thirty—the shine of the ingenue waiting to be discovered has worn off.

That doesn't matter. Not right now. And hey, maybe it's all fixable. I'm a project in need of completion. Isn't there some crazy stat like, 90% of actors in Hollywood had some kind of work done? And maybe that's just it—it's a confidence issue and it's affecting my performance, or—

I'm fragmenting, but I need to. I need to not think about Josh.

Pam lets go of my hand and wades into the water. The lake-moat swallows her legs.

"Why has no one built a bridge?" I suck up the bad feeling and wade right into the water. I already know it's fucking cold as shit.

Josh kicked me off the show. Okay, and I helped it along. And I haven't really sat with that. I haven't sat down and reflected on the e-mail, or—yeah, fine—my loneliness. I wish Pam was an answer, but even though she's gorgeous and she likes me, I know in my bones as soon as I've helped her find her feet on the mainland, I don't want to be with her. I should want to, and I don't. Is that how Josh feels?

Pam screams. She vanishes beneath the surface.

"Pam!" I charge toward her, and when that proves difficult in the clogged moat with its snagging, submerged branches, I dive and swim.

My eyes sting as I open them underwater, grit and algae and brown clumps of vaguely organic matter fighting for entry. Pam's snagged on something that's spiking out of the ground. Gold glints on the spike—a buckle on some luggage?

As I reach her, I break the surface. I grab her shoulders and haul her up.

Pam's teeth clack from the cold as her hair does its best Cousin It impression. "S-s-something. Huh-hooked my shoe. There's a b-body down there."

I rub her shoulder, ushering her toward the forest-side of the bank. "It's probably garbage."

"*No.* I saw a body. Don't you believe me?" Her brow furrows, but she lets me guide her.

I sigh. "I'll swim back and check it out. But first you need to dry off. You'll get hypothermia."

Pam nods. "O-Okay." She rubs her arm. "Promise you'll go back?"

"I promise."

She looks up at me, earnest. "You won't laugh if it's not a body?"

"I wouldn't do that."

She smiles. "You do that to your friend all the time."

"That's different. It's part of the show. I won't laugh." I pause. "This island's genuinely fucked up. Maybe it is a body."

She relaxes, like the admission it could be a corpse is more comforting than her being wrong. Maybe there *is* some of Josh in Pam.

I get her to the bank, then swim back.

"Be careful!" Pam shouts from the shore.

Underwater, the flash of gold leads me back to "the body." Even at a distance, I can see why she thought it was one. The branch part looks like somebody's reaching arm. A gold band encircles a twisted, malformed stick that shoots off from the main branch, like a ring around a finger. The finger's even joined with several others like a flattened, shriveled . . .

hand.

It's a hand.

I bolt out of the water and a couple feet back. I'm shivering too now, and not from the cold. "It's a body."

"What's that?" calls Pam, triumphant. "It's a body? I can't hear you."

"Hah," I say, monotone. I shake my hands, steeling myself. "I'm gonna drag it out."

If I think of it as trash, or some branches, or absolutely anything besides what it is, I can do it.

I dip back under.

The remains are mummified, a mess of darkened leathery skin and mushed-together face, boneless as a well-prepared fish. What was maybe an arm has dried at a weird angle, the fingers squished, like an empty glove. The ring is perfect. It shimmers gold in the murk.

I squat, and very carefully, with my stomach in my throat, I slide my hands beneath the shoulders and lift. I drag it up the bank to keep it from sliding into the water, then collapse beside it.

Pam kneels on the ground, staring into the corpse's hollow eyes. Its face looks like it's been torn to pieces and then collapsed together again. How did it keep so well in the water? It's dried out somehow.

Pam shakes as she pulls the ring off the finger.

An animal sob breaks from Pam's mouth as she rubs the ring clean and turns it over in her hand. She holds it out to me. "Tyler."

There ought to be a word for moments like this, when you know without any doubt that one of the worst things you can imagine happening is about to happen, that it was set in motion long ago, and that even though the event itself hasn't quite worked to its finish yet, there's no way for you to stop it.

I take the ring.

Tysha is written on the exterior. A wedding ring. My mom's ring from the photo in the Virgie Kyle Museum.

I lean back against a tree, staring at it so I don't have to stare at the body.

"It can't be her." I swallow. "She's buried in the graveyard."

Pam scoots over to me. She lays a hand on my forearm. "What if she's not?"

It feels like I've swallowed a ball of barbed wire. An ache I can't afford to feel that pulls at me while a choke it down.

On screen, Josh jokes that I'm a robot. I never cry. I don't feel. It's what I grab onto to make these next moments possible.

I stand up. I pocket Mom's ring. I march to the remains and drag them away from the shore. I snap several branches off the smaller trees. I cover her with them like a shroud. I search the forest floor for sticks, for rocks, for anything to hide the body. At some point, Pam starts helping.

When Virginia Kyle is fully covered, I step away. "We're going to Uphill's mansion. We get proof my mom's not buried in Arcadia. We use whatever gear you have to break into those rooms and check for Josh." I breathe in deep. "And whatever we find, we're leaving. We call the cops, bring them back here."

I can't save Josh alone. I can't solve this by myself, or even with Pam's help. It's time to leave.

26

BODYWORLDS

T he lid of my mother's coffin is caved in at the centre, filled with dirt and small stones.

If I open it and she's inside, will she have rotted away completely? Will it be bones? Will there be shreds of the dress they buried her in? Mom was too dramatic not to ask to be buried in a dress. If they'd disobeyed she'd have come back to file a complaint.

I wipe my hands down my black jeans, smearing dirt.

The gown she wore in my dream shimmers before me, only one by one the stars wink out, faded to dull spots against soil-caked velvet.

"Is she in there?" Pam calls from above.

An endless cycle of me and Queen Cee plays distantly behind her. At least there aren't speakers in the graveyard, though the beat to every song still thrums in my head as if I'm standing next to an amplifier. I don't even remember singing some of these tracks.

I suck in a breath, hang my head back. "Give me a second."

Her feet hit the rungs of the ladder. "I'll help you." She bends down beside the cracked coffin lid to pry it off.

I'm not sure what I'm hoping for: the coffin to be empty, or to find Mom's body inside. Would it be better for her to be that dried out mummy I hid beneath the branches, or for her to have decayed underground, starved of sunlight?

Either way doesn't matter. She's not in the body she left behind. She's not anywhere. She's dead and everything is silence.

I balance over the coffin. We lift the broken wood.

Nothing but soil.

I shove my hand inside to be sure, digging a hole in the centre where the dirt's thickest.

Still nothing.

Before coming here, Pam and I retrieved my phone and some of her tech gear from her house. I snap several pictures of the empty coffin. Maybe I should take a selfie or two for the socials while I'm at it. *Hey, Discovery Bangers, look who dug up his mom's grave and found it empty! Caption this for a chance to talk one on one with Tyler Kyle's new therapist.*

My hands are shaking from the digging. It's been hours, with Pam and I working in shifts.

"I know you're exhausted." Pam strokes my back. "But we need to move."

"Yeah." I stumble to my feet, resting my arm on the uneven wall of earth.

How the hell is Pam not tired?

"I already disabled the cameras," says Pam as we march across the lawn. "The external ones anyway, and the alarms."

As we pass the rows of graves, I can't help but wonder if they're as empty as my mother's. And what were they doing with her body that they didn't bury it? Unless she wandered into the woods and was never found. The coffin could be symbolic.

My brain's really struggling to find the moment of calm I need to be able to parse everything that's happened.

I clear my throat. "So, people wander into the woods. They die. At the very least they believe in this magic voice thing enough that it physically affects them." I pause.

There has to be at least something to the voice thing, otherwise how did my own singing affect me so intensely the night of Queen Cee's concert?

"Okay. It *does* affect them. It's a kind of hypnosis that the founders...genetically programmed into Uphill, my mom, and through her, me. I have no idea how to use it, but they *trained* Uphill, so let's assume he could teach the masterclass. He can make people feel things, but not just feel, *think* things—*see* things. He can make people believe or not believe in the creatures in the woods. Maybe he's even got animatronics to help him do it, and he uses his powers to enhance the effects." The more I talk, the more this sounds like the plot of *The Village*. MK Ultra on steroids. "And Persephone, that drug you all take, it eases along whatever he's doing, or maybe it really is to stop some nasty side effects from the hypnosis."

Pam stares at me as I ramble, patient as an angel. "Do you think his hypnosis will wear off once we're free?"

"I don't see why not. Nothing like what I did to myself at karaoke's ever happened to me before, so there must be a combined effect created by the island *and* the voice."

"Ready?" Pam pauses before the door to the lower level of Uphill's mansion. She meets my gaze.

"Ready." I may not understand her, but she's on my side. It's more than I've been able to say in a long time.

It's dark inside the narrow hallway. The place is dead still. Empty.

"Have you been in any of these rooms?" I ask.

"Sure. These are mostly hospital rooms and supply closets. I stayed here when I broke my arm as a kid, and another time I had stitches." Pam walks ahead of me, then stops suddenly. She points at one of the rooms. "*Gene*," she whispers. She holds her finger up to her lips.

When I reach the door, "Patient Room 1" is written on it.

I glance behind me the way we came. What if Josh is being kept unconscious somewhere? A hospital would be the perfect place to do it. I can't break any of the doors open without making a ruckus, but Pam manages to snap the handles on all of them like twigs.

Shelves, cabinets, empty gurneys—no sign of Josh.

"Where *haven't* you been in this building?" I whisper to Pam.

Pam points upwards at the ceiling. "Conrad's house is huge, so there's a lot I haven't seen, but he's always been cagey about the fourth floor. I visited his office twice, but he doesn't even bring many people up there. It's filled with creepy taxidermy."

Metal rattles behind us, followed by a thud like someone very large stepping off a bed.

It's Gene.

"Come on." Pam grabs my hand. She pulls me in the direction of the Virgie Kyle Museum.

"Tyler?" I hear Gene ask past the door somehow, though we're quite far away and moving further. "Come back—I can explain."

His voice is plaintive, apologetic. It tugs at me with near the same force as Pam's hand.

Pam shoves open a door that brings us to a utilitarian stairwell. The stairs only go up. We take them two at a time.

I can still hear Gene's lethargic footfalls in the distance. The wheels of his IV scrape against what sounds like uneven tiling, the liquid in the bag drip-drip-drips—

I slap my ear. There's no way I'm hearing that. I'm dizzy from overexertion. I'm imagining things.

I press my palm to my forehead. It's hot to the touch. "Can we slow down?"

Pam's already a full flight ahead of me. "It'll be the next one."

The mansion's a labyrinth, but I knew that. Based on what I saw yesterday, large chunks of the building would only be accessible from these hidden stairwells—assuming there's more than one.

I pause before the door to floor three, disguising my embarrassing need to catch my breath by waving at the number. "What if Josh is in there somewhere?"

Pam leans over the banister, blond hair hanging like seaweed. "It's more hospital stuff, I think."

But there's a buzzing in the air, one that vibrates along my skin, up every hair on my body. I'm hallucinating, I have to be. And yet. "Uphill has internet here, right?" I try the door and . . . *presto.*

My head is pounding though. It's like everything on the island is chitchatting back and forth. Not every*one*, but everything. The island is singing.

I'm losing it.

Pam pat-pat-pats down the stairs. "Why do you think the modem's in there?"

"Dunno." For now, I'm going to ignore the bizarre and honestly terrifying thought that I can hear the internet. "It's got to be somewhere, right?"

"When he's asked for help with the modem it's been in his office."

"You're Echo Island tech support, huh?" I step through the door into a carpeted hallway. The corridor ends abruptly after thirty feet, with four doors in between here and the end.

"Sometimes," says Pam.

I try the first door. It's locked. "Open the pickle jar?"

Pam rolls her eyes, smiling, then *cracks* the handle.

I . . . don't ever want to be on the receiving end of that.

Pam steps away from the door and stretches her arm out. "Ladies first."

I leave my masculinity in tatters on the floor and step into what looks like an art gallery. It's small and square. The walls are a regal red with gold accents. There's a leather seat in the centre of the room.

"The modem's definitely not in here." Pam twists on her heel.

I grab my phone, check for either a phone signal or internet connection, but there's nothing. "Why don't you check the other rooms?"

"We don't have time to browse Conrad's art collection," Pam cautions. "Come with?"

She jerks her thumb at the hallway. And she's not wrong, but I can't explain it: I need to get a closer look at the paintings. Maybe it's that Josh reacted so intensely to that woodcut of King Lycaon. His brand of crazy feels startlingly applicable.

"I'll only be a second."

Pam purses her lips. "Fine. I'll be quick."

She closes the door, and the room turns claustrophobic. The red walls, the paintings, the veined marble flooring—it's pressing in on me, like if I step on the wrong patch of floor the roof will descend and crush me.

There's a massive mural on the ceiling: at least twenty different arms sprouting from a patch of monkshood, the bodies they belong to invisible. The limbs twist, coil, and beckon. Their nails are sharpened to claws.

Could Persephone be derived from the monkshood that covers the island? The flowers are so pervasive in its iconography that they must mean something.

I snap a photograph in case, then turn my attention to the framed pieces.

The first is another woodcut, this time of a hyena man making the Renaissance equivalent of finger guns while doing a duck walk. There's blood on his fingers.

Next is yet another woodcut, only this one's been badly coloured with inks or maybe watercolour. It shows a wolf walking upright, wrapped in a blue sheet and staring like a zombie as it approaches a blond man in a red outfit. It's all very Little Red Riding Hood. The image is tiny, and there's an even smaller picture within a picture that I can just barely make out. The great round eyes of the wolf in the foreground remind me of the lantern-eyes of the monsters in the woods. This room, these paintings—this is Uphill's inspiration.

A cursory look at the rest of what's in here reveals a coloured medieval drawing of a tonsured monk feeding two dogs and what looks like a Blake watercolour of a dejected-looking man with scraggly hair walking on all fours. "Dan. 4.25" is written underneath—is the man meant to be Nebuchadnezzar in the wilderness? There's a painting of a long-legged wolf suckling Romulus and Remus.

On the pamphlet Cathy gave me, Uphill was dressed in a lupine fursuit.

I shudder, then head for the door. Outside, Pam's opened the remaining rooms. In the last room, she's scanning a wall of electronics—it looks like the circuitry for the building.

"Anything?" I ask.

Pam shakes her head. "Nothing to control the wifi, but I shut down all the electronic locks in the building. We can go wherever we want."

"Pamela Anderson to the rescue."

She blushes. "We should head upstairs."

"He really likes wolves," I say, as we exit onto the floor where I visited Uphill's office. At least the lighting's better here.

"He likes dogs," says Pam.

"So much he shoots them en masse." I scoff.

The first door I try opens easily.

It's full of people.

I leap back into the hallway, heart thumping. "*Jesus fucking Christ.*"

They're wax. At least fifteen life-sized wax figures in the room. Each one displayed on a small stand with a plaque. I walk up to the first—a beautiful young woman in jeans and a peasant blouse. Her blond hair rolls down her back and right to her ass. "Mary Renault" is written underneath.

"Well I've never heard of her." I move on to the next. The pedestal beside Mary is empty but for its plaque.

Colleen Hannigan.

Wait.

I take a step back, squint at Mary the hippie.

"They're us," says Pam, before I can. "Echo Islanders." She hugs her chest.

THE ERSTWHILE TYLER KYLE

"Why would he want wax models of everyone on the island?"
I dart past young Mary and her wife, toward the next cluster. I
don't recognize any of them, until—

Nora Pomeroy. Nor. There's an empty stand next to Nor
with "*Tia Murray*" written beneath.

Everything about this is off, not just because it's unfathomably creepy to keep a private wax museum full of sculptures of everyone in the isolated island community you run like
you're a king and control with hypnosis powers, but because
it's unfathomably creepy to keep a private wax museum full of
sculptures of everyone in the isolated island community you
run like you're a king and control with hypnosis powers with
the intention of expanding that wax museum every time one of
your captive citizens kicks the bucket.

I assume. I mean, I'm just leaning in that direction based on
available facts.

"Did Uphill ever take a mold of you?" I ask Pam.

"No." She sounds utterly terrified. Broken. I turn around and
she's crying. "I don't understand. What *is* this place?" She pokes
one of the sculptures with a trembling finger, then recoils with
a screech.

"What?" I take her hand. She grips my fingers so tight I'm
genuinely worried they'll break.

"It . . . ." She shakes her head as though trying to convince
herself. "It feels *real*, Ty."

"Probably a trick." But my shaking fingers betray me as I
reach for the sculpture. I've never touched a wax figure, but I
can't imagine they feel anything like real human skin. Raybeam
feels like real human skin.

"You don't have a knife, do you?" I ask.

Pam hands me one from her backpack. "You're not really
going to cut it, are you?"

"It's not like they can feel it."

Pam wrinkles her nose. "Are you sure about that?"

"Not really." I press the blade into Raybeam's copper skin. Cotton, not blood or muscle, pops up from inside a detailed plaster mold.

Cotton, like they use in taxidermy.

I make another incision, revealing intricate detail mimicking muscle and bone. I peel the segment of skin back and rub my thumb against the underside. It feels oily yet dry, the same way parchment feels, only thicker.

"It's real." I pull back. "I don't know if it's human, but it's real." I glance at the model of Nor. How did Uphill have time to make it?

"He's killing us, isn't he?" Pam asks. "He killed Nor and Mary. He probably killed your mom. He made us believe all that stuff about going out into the woods, but he was killing anyone who got in his way."

I rub her back. "We don't know that."

She pushes me away, gripping her elbow as she nervously twirls a strand of hair around her finger. "He's keeping us here till we die and adding us to his collection. We're birds in cages to him."

Birds in cages. The Echo Island Nightingale. I picture my mom's wax figure from the museum, and my gorge rises. That one must be wax though, right? Because Virgie Kyle's body is buried under a layer of pine beside the moat.

I reach for Raybeam and *snickt* off a slice of skin for evidence, then breathe in deep. "We can't save Josh alone," I admit. "We can't solve this by ourselves. Once we're out of here, we head for your plane. Get some real investigators on site."

I pull open another few doors—all filled with taxidermied animals and people. Some of them are creative combinations of the two, and now I'm sure the people parts are real.

The last door I try opens onto a room filled with identical models.

They're all of Virgie Kyle.

I try to bring myself down, but I can feel how round my eyes are, and they're not getting smaller.

Pam pulls me back from the entrance. "*Tyler we need to leave.*"

"It's my mom." I try to shove Pam off, but she won't let go.

"They're not your mom. It's a trick. He's made them up to look like her."

The Virginia Kyles are in all sorts of poses, but most of them are singing. Some have their arms outstretched. In one she's pulling back a strand of hair. In another she's blowing a Marilyn Monroe kiss. The worst one holds a small cage with a nightingale inside.

"Fuck." I hobble back. It's too much.

Gunshots pop in the distance.

"It's starting." Pam pulls me down the hallway after her.

27

GOOD ADVICE YOU SHOULD'VE TAKEN

P am yanks my arm, jerking me to a stop in front of Uphill's office door.

I take my sweaty hand back. "We need to leave."

She frowns. "What if Josh is in there? There must be something in Conrad's office."

I want to argue, but Pam's not wrong—we've hardly touched most of Uphill's mansion and there are a million hidden rooms where he could be keeping Josh.

"Okay, but then we hit the airfield."

I hurry around Uphill's desk, try the phone. There's no dial tone. I hold up the handle to Pam as she enters the room. "It's dead."

Pam shrugs, taking in the wall of photos. She stops before the empty frame of the picture I stole yesterday. It's probably back at The Moon with the rest of my stuff.

"Even if it wasn't dead, the phones are only connected to other lines on the island," Pam says.

"But Uphill can talk to people on the mainland. He spoke to me over the phone." And I can hear an electronic buzzing again. So close, though there's not even a monitor on the desk.

Pam abandons the pictures and helps me with the drawers.

Nothing inside but financial reports.

"The government's sending a yearly stipend." I hold the file out to Pam. I rifle through the drawers, piling up more and more reports. The New Ossory government in correspondence with Saint Serge's, the New Ossory government in correspondence with Echo Island. This place was an experiment all right, and by the looks of things, it never ended.

MK Ultra wasn't far off. Partnering with conversion camps and disappearing people no one will miss. Another dirty chapter in the government's history—one they weren't afraid anyone would care enough to unearth. Uphill promises he can eliminate the queer problems of desperate parents, and in one way or another, he delivers. He tells himself what he's doing is better than whatever scheme they were running before, but his charges become trapped here the same way.

Pam frowns over a folder marked "incoming." She hands it to me. "These are the kids they'll be flying in this year."

"Even though, if the voice thing is real, he's killing them." I scan the pages. Most of them mention musical aptitude. I toss the folder on the desk. "Fucking asshole."

The buzzing is louder, accompanied by the sound of gunshots. I stay very still, trying to follow the noise.

Pam taps my shoulder. "Ty?"

"I can hear something."

"It's the gunshots," she says. "And the music from the speakers."

"It's not." I march up to the wall of cabinets behind Uphill's desk and press my ear against the glass, ignoring the taxidermied monstrosities on the opposite side. I pull back. "It's through here."

"Maybe it's another room?" Pam asks. "Want me to check the hallway?"

"No. On the walk here yesterday there was a long gap between the office door and the next one." I turn back to the desk, pat its underside. "Uphill's just theatrical enough to have a secret door."

My hand brushes against a button. I press it.

Pam jumps as the wall behind us groans and splits in two down the middle.

The room beyond the hidden entrance is pitch black. I can hear electronic whirring coming from inside, and a distant theatre boom.

Stars pop to life across a black wall, sliding into place on the ceiling where they orbit a brilliant white moon. I can just make out the size and shape of the space—*big*—and the fact that there's something large, dark, and oddly shaped blocking my view of the far ceiling. "It's another museum, I think."

The further into the room I walk, the brighter the stars and moon glow above, till they shine an aura around the massive shape dividing the room. It's another taxidermied animal, and from the size, it must be an elephant or a grizzly or—

Lantern eyes blink on like headlights on a darkened highway, and the room *thrumms* with the boneshaking base of the monsters in the woods. As my eyes adjust, I get a glimpse of its full size, though the creature's body is too dense a black to look at straight on.

From clawed feet to eartips, it's twenty feet tall. Its back bristles as though with fur, hunched or rounded like a cat's. Its legs . . . its legs are *too long*, too spindly, the joints poking out like the skin is stretched cellophane-thin—like the creature in Gene's basement. Its neck and jaws are long, swooping, so that it could hang its head to the ground if it wanted to. Even though its mouth is closed, I know in my bladder its teeth will be katana-sharp.

"That's what I saw," I tell Pam.

Her footsteps clip behind me. "It's horrible. And beautiful. Like it could swallow the sun and the moon."

The stars above us start rotating round and round, and light shines gold against the base the creature's displayed on. There's a plaque at its feet.

I crouch. "Bella Ridley. S-0."

Pam kneels beside me. "What's that supposed to mean?"

S-0. S zero. "Is it some kind of prototype?" I wonder aloud. "The model for the animatronics."

"*Is it* animatronic?" Pam asks.

I stand up. I have to touch it, but whenever I stare at the impenetrable black of its body, it's like my eyes are being pulled from my skull. Like the creature's got a suit of armour made of black holes.

On Discovery Bang, I'm the asshole who jumps down dark hollows, who skips along narrow footpaths, who wades in first so if one of us is going to get chomped on, it won't be Josh.

I clamp my hand around slick black fur as opaque as a Goth's bedroom walls. The creature is lifeless underneath. The fur *feels* real, but it could be twenty bear skins stitched together.

"Come on." I draw back and walk around the monster toward a door directly behind it. "The noise is past that wall."

The next room is just as dimly lit, but much smaller. There's a desk at the far end with a computer and some radio equipment, and yet another door.

Pam hurries to the computer and hits the power button. "I've got this!" The screen flashes on.

While she's busy, I examine a filing cabinet. The aged manila folders inside are arranged haphazardly.

"*Nightingale* Class." I read aloud, hand hovering over the folder. I swallow, pull it out, flip through. It's mostly jargon out of an academic journal, the impenetrable text broken by charts measuring what look like harmonics.

I tuck the folder under my arm, pull out the top drawer. "Emergency Communications System" is smack in front. Tumbleweeds of dust drift off as I rifle through it. I sneeze.

Pam's typing away in the background. "*Shit.*" More typing.

The file contains diagrams of a base or a lab out in the woods, and emergency protocols in case of a "break."

> *In the event of break, retreat to above ground radio facility located in Arcadia compound. Inform off-island facility of break. If Nightingale Class has not been subdued, access island-wide security sound system and deploy shutdown fail safe. If Nightingale Class has been terminated or subdued, await further instruction. ADAM is not to be accessed without priority clearance. Nightingale Class must be deployed in pairs in order to access ADAM.*

> *In event of break inside Arcadia, retreat to below ground radio facility, Babel. Senior staff or Nightingale Class must accompany junior staff to access above-ground entry point. If neither is available, seek shelter in nearest building. Do not attempt evacuation into forest. Once inside Babel radio facility, inform off-island facility of break. If Nightingale Class has not been subdued—*

I leaf through the document. There are maps of both Arcadia and Babel, along with emergency evacuation routes, protocols for protective gear, and instructions on the use of poisonous gas to incapacitate subjects. The document notes that gas is only to be used when the entire facility is at risk. If staff are at risk of death or injury but there is no immediate threat to the facility itself, gas is prohibited as the safety of the subjects is of greater importance than risk to staff.

Someone needed a union.

I take both folders and walk over to where Pam's swearing at the console.

"Anything?" I ask.

Pam shakes her head. "The communications system's completely down. And Uphill's rewired it so it only services the speakers on the island."

"This is where he plays the music from?" I lean over Pam's shoulder, but the desktop of the monitor only has one icon, and it's for the sound system. The program is playing songs on rotation. It's impressive Pam could figure everything out from this.

"I guess so," says Pam. "If we mess with it, he'll know we're here. We better head to the plane."

I show her the folders. "There's maps for Arcadia and a facility in the woods under that building. And I think Mom and Uphill were something called 'Nightingale Class.' They seemed to have special privileges or something."

Pam smiles at me as she pushes the chair in. She kisses me. "Teamwork."

"Yeah." I don't know what else to say.

She heads for the next door, which opens onto a narrow staircase. As I follow, the boom gets louder and louder. It's the muted sound of music, the distant crack of the gunshots. So when the door at the bottom of the staircase opens onto a theatre, I'm not surprised in the slightest.

"This is the movie theatre." Pam frowns. "We're downstairs in Arcadia."

I crane my head back, taking in the image on the screen. Live video from the Dog Days festival is playing. Uphill stands on a podium next to the corral as gunshots pop off like firecrackers. "Baby One More Time" plays faintly behind him.

"We've lost so very many this year," Uphill's saying in his fake-drawl. "Too many to count, and our pain too deep to quantify with human words. We feel our pain in the pads of our feet, and our nail beds, and our pores. Our skin wears on us like sandpaper. But we remain strong in the face of our loss, and we prepare as we always do, to live our glorious truth in our own wonderful paradise, and dream the sacred dream, and hear the voices of our loved ones once again." Uphill plucks the cowboy hat from his head and holds it to his breast. "And perhaps good fortune will smile on us, as new voices tune their rills and sing across the landscape that undying song."

He steps back. Someone near the corral pulls a rope holding the gate closed and it slams open.

A gun fires into the frenzy of canine bodies. The dogs bolt.

My voice, singing "Ironic," blasts at full volume over shotgun and rifle blasts as blood sprays across the ground and brain and bone splatter onto the road. The dogs race from the corral as the first wave of Echo Islanders marches steadily after them.

Pam steps up beside me. "There's more pens with more dogs along the track. They'll let them out once the march reaches the next one."

It's grotesque. "Who's fucked up idea of a ritual was this?"

Pam shrugs. "They shoot horses, don't they?"

The movie reference isn't buying her points. "Can we leave?"

Like at a normal cinema, a ramp leads down into a concession area. The lobby features cardboard cutouts of Virgie Kyle from *Monster Mayhem*, Lon Cheney Jr., and a woman I don't recognize. Posters line the walls, ringed with lights: *Frankenstein Meets the Wolfman* and *Cat People*.

We exit next to the Virgie Kyle Giftshop and then onto the lawn and driveway.

"We should hurry," says Pam, "if we want to stay ahead of the march."

We're quiet all the way to the plane.

As Pam unlocks the door for me, she directs me to wait while she refuels.

Gord's plane, the one I flew in on, was plain except for a calendar, but Pam's filled every available space with posters: more *Young Justice*, more Steven Yeun, *X-Files*.

I slump into the pilot's chair, spin round, clutching the folders.

Then I see it. I stop the chair with my foot.

Under one of the four passenger seats is a printout of a poster I recognize all too well from threatre school. In it, I'm sitting back-on, naked, clutching my head. *Equus* is printed in large Roman capitals above me while spotlights illuminate me from the front.

I pick it up to confirm I'm not seeing things.

Why does Pam have this?

I turn it over and there's nothing on the other side. The date of the printout at the very bottom is from years ago.

The minutes feel like days. Could I jump out and run? I have nowhere to run *to* at this point, and no real reason to think this is sinister. It could mean anything. It could mean nothing. I wait for Pam, clutching it, debating the relative stupidity of confronting Pam when she returns. When she finally does, her face is sheet-white in contrast to the darkening sky behind her.

"We have a problem." Pam clambers into the plane. "Someone's stolen all the fuel."

I grit my teeth, reading her eyes. She looks normal, not like a stalker, not like she's playing me. She looks terrified and worried and desperate. Probably like I've looked for the last two days.

"What does that mean?" Maybe there's something else we can fill the tank with, or maybe it's a risky but doable trip.

Pam shatters those hopes. "It means we're trapped here."

"Right." I glance at the printed poster, then reach for the Emergency folder instead. I hand it to her. "There's another radio in the facility in the woods. If we got inside, we could get a message out."

"Then we'll go there." She looks behind her. "But not now. It's too dark. We'll have to wait till daybreak."

"I'm not waiting." The words tumble from my mouth.

She looks up at me in confusion. "We don't know how to open it yet. And the woods'll fill with hunters soon. Once they've shot the dogs, they trawl the woods for stragglers. I promise we'll go first thing, but it's *really not safe* now, Ty."

I grit my teeth. I hold out the printout. "What's this?"

Pam takes it, staring at it blankly. She flips it over and hands it back. "A movie poster? Something I printed for someone probably. Why?"

She doesn't look like she's lying. I'm getting paranoid.

"It's me." I run my hand through my hair. "Second year in school."

Pam takes the paper and cocks her head to the side. "Yeah, I can see it now." She returns it. "Probably something your mom asked for. The quality's not great—this was probably scrap."

"Right."

"You sound upset," says Pam.

"I'm not."

Pam snorts. "Don't you like it or something?"

"No. No, it's just. The stalker, remember?" I bite my lip. "You can't remember who requested this?"

"Sorry." She laughs. "You should see how much people ask me for every trip. It's a lot."

"It wasn't Gene, or Uphill?"

Pam lays her hand on my knee and kisses me. "Uphill asks for all kinds of art. Isn't *Equus* one of those pervy plays?"

I hang my head back. I close my eyes.

"Ty?"

"Let's hole up for the night." Assuming I can sleep at all. Assuming there's anywhere we can hide that'll be safe.

28

What a Ratpile Heap a Dog Shit Situation

"Someone's going to see you if you keep staring out the window," Pam tells me from her spare bed, surrounded by files.

I pull back reluctantly. As Pam warned, flashlights dot the woods, panning their beams or whooshing toward the treetops.

"How the fuck are we going to get into Babel?" I face her.

She picks up one of the documents, then tosses it back onto a pile. "It says the Nightingales can open the door. You're one of them."

"Not the way they mean." I walk to the bed. "They programmed that palm reader to read certain people's fingerprints. I wasn't around then." I pause. "We could kidnap Uphill."

Pam guffaws.

"I'm serious."

She shakes her head. "We won't get near him."

I press my forehead between my hands. "We can't do nothing."

"It'd be safer." Pam starts clearing up the folders. "We could wait till the phones reconnect in August."

"That's too long." I start pacing. It's like the characters in Pam's posters are following me with their eyes. "Josh can't wait that long."

He might not be able to wait a night. My mind is a slideshow of Josh racing through the woods, pursued by Uphill. His brains splatter across the trees like one of the feral dogs.

I did this. Me.

When I turn around, Pam's drawn her knees in tight against her chest and is hugging her legs, chin tucked between them.

Was I yelling?

"Something changed last night," Pam says, morose. "I fucked us up, didn't I?"

That's what she's worried about? I throw my hands up. "What does it matter?"

"It matters to *me*. I—" Fuck, she's crying. "I'm sorry about everything that's happening. I'm sorry I tried to impress you. I really like you." She sucks back a sob and wipes her nose.

I feel nothing. I'm fucked up, I guess, or too exhausted and terrified to drum up the concern a normal person would experience right now.

Pam clutches the blankets on the bed and squeezes. "I can feel you going away, like everyone does. I pushed you away and now I don't have anybody." She curls her toes like if she shrinks inwards, she can disappear. She punches her own head. "I'm sorry we didn't get to the plane in time. I'm sorry I'm not Josh."

She moves to punch herself a second time and I catch her hand. I may be a jerk, but I'm not going to stand here watching her crack her skull open.

I crouch at her feet.

Her eyes are red-rimmed and puffy. "I just—I've been alone so long I don't know how to be with people. I thought, if *you* thought I was cool, and sexy, and funny, we could fly off into the sunset." She laughs. "Stupid."

I smile to calm her down. "We can't fly anywhere without a plane, whether or not there's a sunset."

Pam laughs again and wipes her eyes. She snatches her arm back and rubs it.

"I didn't hurt you, did I?" I search her wrist for a bruise.

She bites her lip. "No. It was sweet. I mean good. It was a nice thing to do."

"You shouldn't hurt yourself." While she's drying her tears, I stack the folders on the bedside table and sit beside her. "You didn't ruin things. I'm not in a mental space where I can think about romance, or sex, or dating. Echo Island is home for you. I'm not used to this stuff. It's a lot."

Not everyone is used to human taxidermy mayors and dog massacres and evil government experiments that require contingency plans involving poison gas. I'm just an actor with a crappy comedy YouTube show.

"I know. I wish I could go back in time to before last night." She laughs, taps her head. "That was so silly with the bumping heads, and you spilled my stuff. Like something from a movie. Most of the guys around here aren't as interested in me as they are in the boy next door. And you were so different from anyone I'd met. Bigger, more real. I got carried away. Maybe I imagined you were interested and turned it into a weird fantasy. Some hero come to save me. Sometimes I think it's easier to be trapped the way the others are. When you get to taste the rest of the world, it makes it worse somehow. It's so close, but when I stretch my fingers out to touch it they only graze the surface."

I wanna be where the people are.

I don't say it. I pat her hand.

Her laugh is choked. "That has to be the world's saddest pity handshake."

"It's not pity." And I feel it, the lump forming in my throat. I'm Josh, and Pam is me. I'm treating her like he treated me in his e-mail: insensitive, distancing, cold. "I'm sorry I've been off. It's not you. You freaked me out a little last night." I try to go back in time like Pam wants me to. I liked her as soon as I met her, and so much of how shitty I'm feeling has nothing to do with her. "I'd rather you were yourself." I pause. "When we're out of here, we could try again."

Pam's face lights up, revealing perfect white teeth. "You're not just saying that? It's not a game?"

My phonecall to Josh returns to me. My accusation that he was playing with me. Am I playing with Pam now?

No, I do like her. I did like her. I do like her.

"After what happened, I wouldn't mess around with someone like that." I fold my hand over hers. "I promise."

Her smile is delicate as a snowdrop. "It's going to be impossible to sleep tonight."

I stare at our hands, my skin against hers. "Yeah."

"Maybe I can help." She swings herself over the bed, opens a drawer, and pops out an old laptop. She slides her hand into her pocket, producing a hard drive, then slots it into the computer and lies down on the bed. She pats the pillow beside her. "Sit. I grabbed something on the plane to cheer you up."

I sit cross-legged against the pillow as the computer whirs on. "Is it a message from the prime minister informing us he's about to bomb Echo Island?"

Pam shoots me a look. "*We're* on Echo Island."

"I'm not picky."

Pam boots the flash drive. It's full of Discovery Bang.

"Didn't you just watch these?" My throat's tight.

She clicks one at random and "The Ecstasy of Gold" crackles from her laptop. Abruptly, she hits pause and leaps from the bed. She flicks off the overhead light and sits back down, bed creaking beneath her.

"*For atmosphere.*" She hits play. "Who picked the music?" Her shoulder brushes my outer thigh as she gets cozy again.

"Josh." I should be able to watch this and be fine. It's just the show. Just us. I clear my throat, summon a stony facade. "He's big into Sergio Leone—Spaghetti Westerns, that kind of thing."

Pam snorts. "He'd like Conrad."

"If Conrad wasn't a psycho." Josh'd like him anyway.

Pam strokes my leg and shifts her head so she's leaning against me. I feel like a dork, sitting like this while she lies down. I stretch my legs out, then scooch down so we're parallel.

JOSH: Welcome, Bangers, to Witless Bay, Newfoundland. Today we'll be walking the forests and hillsides of the foggiest place on earth in search of the most deadliest fairies in the world.

TY: And Josh is very happy for the chance to return home, of course. Thanks once again, patrons, for the opportunity to boost Josh's self-esteem by sending him to the only town where he's not the village idiot.

JOSH: Harsh man.

TY: Yeah, sorry. This town's full of smart folks. Didn't mean to put 'em down like that.

Josh gives me a shove, but he's smiling. The shot cuts to us walking downhill toward a rocky strip of beach.

Pam gives me a shove of her own. "You're kind of a jerk."

"Yeah." I wave my hand. "It's just a gag, you know?" Like Josh's flirting.

She kisses me. "You're a pretty jerk though."

"Josh is one of the smartest people I know," I say. "He's gullible, that's all."

"Or open-minded," says Pam.

On screen, Josh trips on a rock and I catch him. He clings to my back, and even though this was two whole years ago, I can feel his shoulder blade under my hand, his fingers gripping my arm.

"My hero," Josh says. He winks at the camera and pulls away, standing on his own. "And that's one for Pornstar Popsicle and the rest of you fanfic writers. Can't wait to see the .gifs."

"Sometimes I think you set these things up on purpose," I say, as we walk downhill, thinking we'll cut the line in editing.

We didn't. He didn't.

"You think I time traveled millions of years into the past and planted that rock so you could catch me like Casanova, all for a joke? I'm flattered you think I'm that committed. And also that I have magical powers." He holds his arms out to the side to keep himself balanced on the rocks dotting the grass.

"Science powers," I correct. "Time travel would be wacky science, not magic. Magic's not real, Josh."

"Not like time travel," he snaps.

"Yeah yeah. Tell that to Nicholas Cage."

"Who is a *vampire*, not a time traveller."

The camera swings to face a little old lady walking down the road next to us. "You young fellas better get out of that field, sure. It's full o' horse shit."

I elbow Josh. "Wow, kind of like you."

"Fuck you," Josh mutters.

"What was that?" The old lady cups her ear.

"It's okay Ma'am," cautions Josh. "We're doing online journalism. We're investigators."

"You know there's a road?" The woman dismisses us with a *tsk*. "Investigating horse shit. Heard it all now. Stunned as me arse."

I turn to Josh. "Why *aren't* we on the road?"

Josh gestures at it. "I didn't see it, okay? I thought this was a path."

"I mean, it's obviously a field." I point at the horse chomping grass seven feet away.

"I saw the road!" Kayla says, distantly.

Despite everything, the exchange does cheer me up. A slice of normal. A reminder I had something, that I'm a person in the world.

"Is that Kayla?" asks Pam.

"Yeah. Sometimes she interjects. Or uses her magic stones to predict where Josh is most likely to find something. So far she has a zero percent accuracy rate for cryptids, but if we wanted to accidentally wander onto private property we'd be golden."

Pam chuckles, but it's oddly cold. "Is she pretty?"

"Yeah, I guess."

"What's she look like?"

Is Pam jealous of my twenty-one-year-old employee?

"Chubby? Brown skin? Big eyes? Has a . . . you know, face. I wish we'd given her more to do. She made the show a hell of a lot better than it had any right to be."

Maybe it's something I could bring up with Josh if we make it home. Maybe he should replace me with Kayla. It'd hurt less.

Pam snuggles against me. "And what's a Popsicle Pornstar?"

Ugh. I'd buried Pornstar Popsicle deep in the garbage dump of my memory.

"It's a *who*," I explain. "This fanfic writer. She—I mean, I assume it's a she, but maybe that's sexist. Anyway, *they* post a lot of fanfic about me and Josh. Josh read it to me so he could watch me squirm. It's full of, uh, sexy descriptions of me. There was all this fandom drama around it that Josh got real invested in for some reason."

Pam nudges me, rubbing against my side. "Oooo. Do tell."

This is too stupid to talk about, but as I watch day change to night on the computer screen, and the setting shift from Newfoundland's rugged coast to a dense, choked forest not all that different from the woods around Echo Island, I could use some stupid.

I breathe deep, absently stroking Pam's shoulder with one finger. "Pornstar Popsicle got into some internet one-up-ping contest with another writer. PP was big into slash and the whole *me and Josh* thing, and there was this anti-slash writer—Artemisia something— who posted terrible stories where I died tragically and Josh got with their self-insert character. Wooden dialogue, adverbs that had adverbs, flowery writing where you needed a hedge and not an arboretum. People were always carding their hands through their hair. The writers fucked with each other in their writing. They're probably both forty-five-year-old men. At least Pornstar Popsicle had solid dialogue and good jokes. She seemed to get the show, I guess."

And admittedly, it's hard not to like somebody who spends entire paragraphs describing you in terms reserved for Olympic swimmers.

"Are you a writer or something?" Pam asks. "It just seems like you have a lot of opinions about what good writing is."

Is Pam insulted? She is a fanfic writer. "No. Never really got into it. When I was a kid my dyslexia made it hard, and I never really cared enough to move past that after the seventh de-motivational speech in elementary school."

"You're dyslexic?" Pam twists so she's propping herself up on my chest, facing me. "Like interchanging letters and stuff?"

"Sort of. Yeah." Not something I want to sit here and explain.

The laptop starts to slide and I *just* manage to grab it before it thuds off the bed. Pam straightens and takes it from me.

"Josh sounds so talented. He can act, and model, and do comedy, and he can write plays and movies." She smiles. "I think I understand a bit better now."

When did Josh become a model? "Understand what? Why I like him?"

Pam flicks her nose against my chin. "To have someone that gifted around you all the time. It's so whelming, but then you're always in their shadow. And he—" she hesitates, shuts the laptop. "He flirted with you all the time, like he did in that episode. But he was laughing at you."

I scratch my ear. "I mean, I don't think he was *laughing* at me."

Pam gives me a pitying look. "What else is the point of a joke like that, Tyler?"

I look away, but it's hard when we're so close. "I don't know—laughing together about it? He thought I was in on it. He didn't realize I was . . . that I like guys. I guess."

Pam's eyes drill a hole in my skull, psychologist sharp. "So he thinks being *queer* is a joke? Which is what you are. Queer. A joke."

"Why are you trying to make me think Josh is a bad guy?" I stare past her at her posters. "He probably thought it was a cute little thing, for the fans or whatever."

"Because *that's* not condescending." Pam's eyeroll is thick in her voice. "So this guy, who's so mega talented, and so beautiful, and so funny, and *so* nice. He thinks it's fine to joke around about his queer, non-traditionally attractive friend who he's constantly upstaging on a show he created, so he can look real good to all the fans and the casting agents by comparison. And it's okay because it's *cute*? I'm sorry, but it makes me so mad. It makes me so mad someone would treat you like that and make you feel like garbage. You're the best person I've met. I was so glad I met you." Emotion floods her voice. "And now I know how he treated you, I'm glad you met me."

"Why? So you can hang around Josh's less talented, not-traditionally-attractive friend?" I'm not sure I've ever felt so shitty in my life. Is it because I know it's the truth, deep down? Is it because I was already hanging by a branch and confronting the me and Josh thing's finally snapped the lifeline?

The cavern in my head is so wide I'm mostly empty space.

"*I* don't think those things." Pam grips my palm, rubbing angry circles in the centre. "That's Josh talking. When did I ever say I thought those things about you? I can't stop telling you how much I like you. It's so bad I thought I was making an idiot out of myself. I can't say it any more than I already have."

She has said kind things about me when she hasn't been trying to imitate Josh. She calls me "pretty" endlessly, and brave, and funny. No one's ever complimented me as much as Pam has.

Well, except Pornstar Popsicle.

She kisses me like she's hoping it'll be a long, slow one. She snakes her hand down, toward the button of my jeans. But I can't. I can't.

I inch away as much as I'm able. "I'm sorry. I'm not feeling sexy right now. Actually, I've never felt so disgusting in my life, so." I shrug against the bed, trying to disguise the way the admission's wrecking me. "I can't. I just can't."

Pam ignores me. Not in a bad way. She kisses me again, all bedroom eyes and reassuring touches. "You're sexy to me. So incredibly sexy." She buries her face in my neck. "I want to be with you for real, not trying to be cool." She strokes my cock and I close my eyes. "And show you how much I want you."

I grip Pam's arms, then abandon them for her hips. She straddles me, slips her cardigan off, looking me in the eyes all the while, nervous and so beautiful. She stretches like a cat across my chest, riding my shirt up, and bends down, kissing my chest.

"How do you want me?" she asks. "I think I can do it with you seeing me, if that's what you need."

I watch her, wary suddenly. She's clever, and she knows things the other islanders don't about the world. It's made me forget about the ways I have power over her. I could so easily be taking advantage of her. I seem wonderful to her because I'm the first man to give her the time of day.

"I want you," she murmurs, and she sits back up again, slides her underwear down her legs, then steps out of them one by one. She unzips her dress and slides that off too. She tosses it all aside and I'm seeing her like I couldn't last night. In the dim mood lighting, her skin is a plain of fire. The purple streetlamp from outside the window casts her blond hair in shades of sunset.

I smile at her. "I want you too."

She bites her lip, giggles. It reaches her eyes, and she reaches for my cock, lowers herself onto me. She moves slowly and I grab her hips, pulling myself upright by my elbows. She threads her fingers through my hair, moans, bites her lip. We go slow like that for a while, and I follow her lead, speeding up as she speeds up. I want this to be better than last time. Like if it is, I can prove to myself this is something good, that Pam and I are good. She feels good. Tight and wet and full of longing.

She smiles at me, hair sliding in front of her eyes as she rides me harder. She laughs, breathless. "Wanna try something kinky?"

She grabs her pillow.

It's on my face before I can tell her no, and she presses down. Hard. She bends over so all her weight is on my chest, and somehow we're still fucking, and she's mashing the pillow into my face one-handed, her other hand like a slab of metal on my ribs. The air is gone so fast.

I try to push her off, but she doesn't budge.

I can't breathe. I can't talk. I can't breathe.

My lungs are on fire, and underneath it, the pleasure, and I hate it, and I'm panicking, and I want it to stop.

I thrash, try to unbalance her. She squeezes her legs tight, shoves both her hands over my face, grips my jaw through the pillow, then my throat. She presses down with one hand, strangles me with the other. Her grip's so tight, so powerful. I can feel my skin bruising.

The inside of my head is an empty tin, my thoughts rattling around inside.

I need to not panic.

I want to puke.

My throat is burning.

My head's burning.

My head's light.

I can't push her off me.

The world is spinning. I'm floating.

I cum inside her, hard, and she lifts the pillow off, and she rolls away from me, and I can hear her laughing as though from the other side of a wall.

I gasp, cough, gasp. I'm hyperventilating. I think. I draw myself up against the headboard.

She's watching me. She's grinning. She reaches for my knee and I snap away.

"That was so wild, baby," she says. She leans over me like she's coming in for a kiss and I can't help it, I start sobbing. Choking and sobbing at the same time. I shove her right in the chest.

"Get away from me." I slide off the bed. My legs are shaking. I can't stand. I do stand. I stumble against a chair in the corner and fall back onto a stuffed bear, then scramble to my feet again. I button my jeans, keeping my gaze trained on her.

"Oh god." Pam covers her mouth, face a mask of horror. "Ty, I'm so sorry. I didn't mean to hurt you." Tears spring to her eyes. "I didn't mean to. I really didn't. I'm sorry. I'm *so* sorry. I thought—I read about that in *Cosmo*. I thought. I didn't know you couldn't breathe. It was an accident. Please."

I swallow, watching her. "Why did you do that? You read about choking people in fucking *Cosmopolitan*? What the fuck."

"*Ty*." She sobs my name, kneeling on the bed. "I didn't. Oh god. I hurt you."

Her shoulders rise and fall, rise and fall. She curls in on herself.

I'm not shaking so bad anymore, but my throat is raw and my skin is on fire. "I'm going to leave." I grab my phone where I left it charging and slide it into my pocket. "I'll come find you tomorrow." Or not. I haven't decided on that part. I can't focus. All I know is I need to be gone.

I make for the door. As I start to leave, Pam's feet thud onto the floor.

"Tyler, it's dangerous. You can't leave—"

I practically fall down the stairs and out the door. I don't stop running till I reach The Moon.

The flashlights in the woods blink on and off. The entrails of the dogs smear the asphalt. People are laughing inside The Moon. I can hear clinking glasses. Bad karaoke thunders from inside. It looks warm and inviting, but it's not. And there's nowhere I can go that someone won't find me. The woods are full of hunters, and Pam knows all the places I might hide, as if there even are any.

The dumpster.

I dart around back. My hands are shaking again. I feel like I'm going to collapse.

Fuck.

Fuck fuck fuck.

I stare at my shoes, willing them to move in a straight line. I don't feel entirely okay.

The smell of cigarette smoke crawls inside my nose. I could use one of those. Or eight. Eight would be perfect.

"Kyle?" Tia peels herself off the wall of The Moon.

I stumble back. "Keep away from me."

She snorts. "Fuck you. *Fuck you*, okay? I tried to help you."

"Everyone here is fucked up." I keep walking backwards, but she follows, stepping from the shadows.

Her cheeks are caked with smeared eyeliner. She points her cigarette at me as if to yell at me, then stops. "Tyler? Are you okay?"

"I'm fine." I glare, try to look frightening instead of frightened. "Get away from me."

"Did someone hurt you?" She drops her cigarette, stomps on it. She starts toward me again. "Your skin is all—" She waves her hand over her face. "Were you in the woods?"

Is Tia strong like Pam? I've seen her do some crazy shit, so I'm pretty sure the answer is yes. I'm pretty sure she could fuck me up. And who knows, maybe she can run real fast and leap over tall buildings. Maybe she's fucking Superman.

"No." I don't know why I say it. It's not meant to be an answer to her question. It's not meant to be anything. "I'm going now."

"Tyler, please come back." She lets out a dramatic sigh that's more of a growl. "I'm sorry about earlier. I wasn't myself. Because of—I just wasn't myself. And you'd put Gene in the hospital. I can see how it looks, but it isn't like you think. I can explain."

I run. First toward Talbot, then away from there because that's where Pam is and—fuck, everyone's so *fucking* sorry. Real big pity party over here on psycho island.

The Ziggy's sign is still on, but there's no movement inside. I walk around back, and there's a dumpster like at The Moon, like where I was going before Tia leered out of the darkness.

I crack it open. It's full, so I pull out a couple bags and set them aside. I crawl in, catch the lid so it doesn't bang, prop it open with a metal bar.

It's cold, but the bags should provide some insulation. If I wasn't all fucked up, if I could control myself, I could sleep. I need to sleep so bad.

And I can't. And I cover myself in the trash from Ziggy's diner. And hidden as best as I can manage, I stare at the light of my phone, at the photos in the gallery. It's all scenery. My thumb flicks past trees and hills and towns. And there's no people in any of them, except Josh and Kayla, scattered here and there like polished glass hidden between beach rocks. There's no one and nothing in the photos. There's no one and nothing in this dumpster.

Morning, July 16th, The Secret Diary of Pamela Matheson

Every time I drink, I watch it. The scene from that documentary. You know the one; you've probably seen it too. It's old now. It's the one where the fox is sitting (no, no longer a fox). There's an animal that was once a fox. And it's panting, and it's surrounded by all these cages with other, soon-to-be-not-foxes all locked up inside them, and the **worst** part, the part that matters, is that even though the fox is still panting, still staring, still turning its unblinking eyes as if in search of something irreparably lost, the fox has no skin. No eyelids.

The reason I think it's not a fox is because if it were a fox, no one could possibly skin it like that, still breathing, able to recognize its loss. The other reason I know it's not a fox is because in what passes for school on Echo Island, I took an English class. In the class we read a story about a fox farm and a teenage girl. The girl tries to set all the foxes on her family's farm free and it's paralleled with the girl's own story (the story of how her family wants to make sure now that she's a teenager that she does all the appropriate girl things she should). I raised my hand and said I thought the end (in which they catch the foxes and the girl and she wears a dress and does as she's told) was about the fact that the fox farmers see the foxes' skin as the only valuable thing about the foxes, and so when they take it they're stealing the most precious thing from the fox, the thing that *makes* the foxes foxes. And in the end, they also take everything that's valuable to about the girl, because they chip and chip and peel away at her until her outside looks the way they want it to. And who knows, maybe she looks the way they want her to inside as well, because it sure seemed like she died at the end of that story.

Back then, I thought I must be the girl, because I was so beaten down by the world, because I knew each and every time the town marched out to that stupid sadistic altar in the woods that the one thing every child has (her parents) had been brutally ripped from me, that I wasn't like the other people on the island and that they saw that as a problem. But I grew up. I grew older (older than you think I am).

I'm not naive. I'm not shy. I'm not nobody. I have more than one thing that defines me. My talents are limitless. There are so many sides to me you didn't even think to ask about. It was just *youy-ouyou* and you didn't see how you were making it so much easier every time you *made* it about you. Never a, "What about you, Pam? What's your favourite movie? What's your favourite song?

What are *you* good at? What do you want to do when you get out of here? What's your favourite fucking book?"

If you'd asked that, I'd've told you my favourite fucking book ever is Exquisite Corpse by Poppy Z. Brite, because it explains so well why some people have **nothing** and others end up with **everything**. It talks all about how some people make themselves into victims. How they really always *were* victims. *"Waifs who wander the world without guile, seeming to offer themselves up to whatever wants them."* They crave the knife. They seek out the killer. And when they do find each other (those perfect partners), the woman holding the blade's really only doing him a favour. '*Even before death*' says the main character '*the victim is more void than substance.*'

So I'm not the girl, and I'm not the fox.

I'm the farmer. And *I'm* holding the knife.

29

THE ECSTASY OF GOLD

I wake up in the dumpster behind Ziggy's. Garbage bags are super-glued to my skin with sweat and static and about a metric ton of dirt. I'm gripping my phone so hard the line between man and machine feels nonexistent.

I slide my thumb across the screen and a photo of an old man giving me the finger while he brandishes a shotgun at Josh and Kayla pops up. Better days, when all we had to worry about was getting our heads blown off.

My nose throbs and I'm thrown back into last night.

I let out a whine I didn't know I was capable of making: small and animal. My hand is shaking. My face and throat hurt, and beneath the generic grime that's become my second skin, the cum I never got to wash off is crusty against my underwear. It feels like I'm a rotting, shambling corpse spilling pus, like a million maggots are squirming under my skin, like I'm the cup in *Two Girls, One Cup*.

Something that shouldn't see the light.

And I know that's normal. My rational brain that never saw something like this happening to me knows the disgust I'm feeling isn't warranted, that I'm directing it in the wrong place. But somehow, my rationality makes it worse. I want to yell my logic down. I want to scream at it till my throat bleeds.

You never think of yourself as *that person*. You think you're way too clever and self-aware not to shut someone down as soon as red flags start popping up like China just won the showjumping gold. And you can see exactly how you got here. You trace each and every cord to its socket and pinpoint all the singular moments when you should have stopped it, walked away, said something. And didn't. Every. Single. Time.

And you hate yourself for *that*, too. You start to wonder, well, if you let it happen, maybe you wanted to be broken. A glass lamp standing an inch over the lip of the table—so hard not to push. Some part of you must've thought you deserved it. You made this happen. You summoned her like Mephistopheles. The Cavale to your Slim.

She didn't even have to hold a .45 to my head.

I bring up the camera on my phone, turn it to self-view and—

I close it. I can't look. That's not me. I don't recognize that person.

But it's just some bruising. It'll heal easy. It'll heal fine.

Bruises like fingerprints ring my throat like a necklace. Like a permanent tattoo.

"Everything is temporary," I say, to convince myself, but also to test my voice. It's scratchy, like my cock against my underwear. Disgusting.

I need to be clean.

The walk from the dumpster to the lake-moat is as fuzzy as an aged furby. By the time I'm standing at the shoreline, the undersides of my ruined shoes are sticky with speckled dog blood.

Warm air slouches against my skin.

What rough beast indeed.

I stumble into the water, propelled by the steepness of the slope rather than my own command of my body. The water drowns my shoes, licks my skin.

My legs motor to where the water is deepest. Just in time, I remember my phone. I make it to the other side of the shore where I leave it, then strip naked, then wade back in.

Eyes closed, I fumble at the bottom of the lake-moat for a flat-edged rock. I scrape it across my skin, *too hard*. I don't want

to miss anything. She's attached to me, and I want every piece
of her gone. If I could right now, I'd scrape myself away with
her. A piece of contaminated flesh that must be excised before
it corrupts the whole body. Only the whole body is the wound.
Just what am I protecting?

I break the surface.

Sucking in air feels like inhaling on an uncut joint.

My clothes are next, and once they're cleanish I put my pants
back on. I take my shirt and socks and leave them to dry against
the bank.

I'm covered in silt but it's better than being covered in her.

Virgie Kyle's balsam tomb is intact. I sit beside it and my back
protests as I hug my knees.

Just can't sleep in a dumpster overnight after getting assault-
ed like I could in my twenties, I guess.

If *it was assault. Pam thought you were into it. She apologized.
She cried. You overreacted because you're stressed. You're not remembering things straight.*

Sometimes my brain isn't on my side.

It strikes me that, sandwiched between my mom's corpse and
my phone, I'm probably the least alone I've been since I arrived.
I can't trust the islanders, can't trust myself. But this dead body?

And Joshbot.

My finger hits the icon before I can shame myself out of it.

"*Tyler, you're an asshole.*"

"Yeah." I don't know what to say. I don't know what to say
to a fake version of my ex-best friend, like deep in its coding it'll
recognize a shitstain when it sees it.

Disgusting. A joke. A brother that wants to fuck you. The
untalented half of a comedy team that only a psychopath who's
never seen another man before wants to touch, and even she'd
rather choke him to death.

I laugh, and yeah, maybe it's not totally laughter. Maybe I
sit there sobbing into my knees waiting for a robot to comfort

me. Or maybe I'm cool and collected. Maybe I pull up my bootstraps and stop feeling sorry for myself and swagger away.

Maybe.

"*What was that*?" asks Joshbot.

Great. It thinks the sound of me crying is a cryptid. I laugh. For real this time.

"Josh, I don't know what's happening to me." I rub my temple. My face crumples, but I swallow the sob I know is coming. I need to get it together. "I don't know what the fuck to do."

The phone is silent while it processes whatever trigger word helps generate its response.

It lets out the mother of all sighs. "*The moment we've all been waiting for ladies and gentlemen. Ty doesn't know something.*" It pauses. "*Wait, that means I need to be frightened, doesn't it?*"

"Yeah, probably." I kick the dirt, watching an ant scurry inside its hole. "You're all I have, man, and you're not even real. The real Josh isn't even real. Just a character."

I'm no better than Pornstar Popsicle, inventing a story around smoke and mirrors.

"*Where's your joy? You have absolutely no magic in your life, Tyler. It must feel awful being you. Seriously.*"

"Real," I say.

"*Where's your joy? You have absolutely no magic in your life, Tyler. It must feel awful being you. Seriously.*"

It's responding to "real." Josh figured I'd say something like "Vampires aren't real" and programmed a response. I'm that predictable.

Or he knows me so well.

Last night, Pam said a lot of bad things about Josh, but he's not bad at all. Me calling him stupid and him pretending he wants me isn't all there is to us. Do I ever think about that? Did I ever tell him? It's not just about being in love with him, it's about loving him. All the small ways he's the most excellent person I've ever known: imaginative, and open, and friendly, and dedicated. As funny as [insert popular comedian here who hopefully hasn't turned out to be problematic]. And yeah, he's beautiful too. And yeah, I could be so lucky to have him feel an inch of what I feel for him, for me.

I have to find him. Nine years of friendship is worth that, at least. He's banked his IOUs.

"*What was that*?" asks Joshbot, and that's how I know I'm crying again.

"Nothing," I say.

"*Pretty sure* nothing *doesn't make a sound like that, Ty. Pretty sure nothing doesn't make a sound at all. That's kind of the point.*"

I hesitate. Even admitting it to a program's almost impossible. "I'm not okay, Josh." I pause. "I really fucked this one up. And I need you to fix it, but it's you I'm supposed to help." My foot *tap tap taps* against the ground. The phone is silent, like I've overloaded it talking too much. "This is probably the first time in your life you've genuinely needed me, and I'm fucking useless as shit. And all I can think is that I need you to know I love you, but not even *like that*—okay, maybe like that. And it's selfish, but it's not meant to be." I breathe out, clear my mind. "I just fucking love you, man. And I miss you. And I'm gonna miss you when you find someone else for your show."

The engines in my brain feel like they're chugging along with Joshbot's as it searches for its keyword.

"*Whoa—whoa man. That's big—*"

I punch it off. I can't. I can't right now. I can't listen to pre-programmed Josh verbally eviscerate me like the real one did two nights ago via e-mail. I know it all already. I hate myself enough already.

Just pretend like he said, "I love you too, man. You too," like we're bro-ing around, like we've done before. Pretending should be easier for an actor. "I'm going to find you."

The sun glints off Mom's ring where her outstretched arm erupts from beneath her shroud.

Her ring. Her arm. Her *hand*. Partially preserved, handprint and all.

I don't waste time.

Josh, I'm coming.

30

THE ERSTWHILE TYLER KYLE

Virgie Kyle's severed hand doesn't want to lay flat against Babel's palm reader, but with some filially blasphemous bending and finger-snapping, I manage.

"Sorry, Mom," I say.

"Access denied."

Majel Barret. You're supposed to be on my side.

I try again. And again. And again. I try over and over and then I kick the fucking wall.

"Access denied. Access denied. Access den—"

"Urrrrrrrggggggh." I turn Mom's palm over. The skin's too marred by wrinkles of collapsed flesh.

A stick snaps to my right and I swerve.

Pam's standing fifteen feet away, holding what looks like a fresh arm, severed at the wrist.

I almost throw Virgie Kyle's hand at her in super-effective self-defense, but then I realize: the wrist's not dripping blood. It's from one of Uphill's models.

Pam raises the hand and wiggles it like it's waving. "Peace offering?"

I stand my ground. "Stay back."

Pam lowers the arm, holds it in front of her. "I'm sorry, Ty. It was an accident." She pauses. "We don't have to fuck anymore. I'm not going to hit on you or justify my actions. I only want off the island." She shakes her head. "We don't even have to talk once we're on the mainland. We can part ways." She holds up the hand again, lays it on the ground, then backs away several feet, palms up. "Or you can go alone. Once you radio the authorities, we won't even have to ride in the same aircraft."

I swallow. It sounds reasonable. It could be the honest fucking truth. Still, Pam could have been working with Uphill all along.

But 100 bucks says Josh is in that lab.

I walk toward her slowly, bend, *and snap*. Mom's "wax" hand feels like one of those plastic-preserved organs they show sometimes on school trips.

"I checked all the models and the palm prints all looked identical," she says. "So if the original mold was made from your mom, this should match."

My heart's in my throat as I raise Virgie Kyle's palm to the reader, trying to keep Pam in my sight.

"Access granted." The reader flashes green. There's a click beyond the door. The metal slides soundlessly to the left, revealing a plain cement room. There's a hole with a descending ladder at the far end.

I glance at Pam, then back at the room. I step inside.

"Welcome, Virginia Kyle," says Majel.

I inch toward the opening. No light shines from below. It's all darkness. Rust or faded bloodstains smear the handholds.

"You first." I point to the hole with Mom's hand and lay the mummified one down.

Pam curtsies. "What a gentleman."

"Chivalry's just misogyny with a smile. You first." I point again. This time, Pam descends the ladder.

I lean over, watching. Waiting.

Natural light flares to life below.

"Whoa! Ty—this place is nuts." Pam's footsteps recede.

Even with the light on, that opening is dark as a black hole.

Josh. Think of Josh.

I follow Pam down.

The ladder opens into a long, hospital-white hallway. Huge windows filled with blinding, faux-natural light line one side, and identical white doors the opposite. Blood splatters the walls in abstract patterns. They're bigger than what I'd assume you'd get from a gunshot, like the victims exploded from the inside.

Pam's already halfway down the hallway. In her cardigan and poofy skirt she looks like Alice down the antiseptic rabbit hole.

As I pass the windows, I rap my knuckles against the glass. It feels thick.

"Josh!?" I call out.

Pam jumps and screeches. "You scared me."

"Colour me not sorry."

She scowls. "You don't have to be a dick."

I try one of the door handles, then follow Pam as she walks down the corridor. "Actually, I do. It's in my contract."

She snorts. "Like you have a contract. You don't even have an agent."

Why do I feel like this is the real Pam, mask off? "It was a joke."

"Not a funny one. Hey, tell me, is being unfunny in your contract too?" She reaches behind her, grabs her backpack, un-zips it.

I stop, ready to run at the first glimpse of a gun, but she pulls out the folders I stole from Arcadia. She rifles through them. "Comms room is down three levels." She glances right, then down the hallway. "The stairs are the last door on the right."

"Lead on." No way I'm letting her walk behind me.

"On the show, you always play the big strong man. Was that an act too?" She heads off, faster now that we have a goal.

"I only leap in front of Ogopogos for Josh, sorry." As I follow, it's hard not to get distracted by the blood. Could it be the founders' blood? Pam's parents' blood. She doesn't even look at it though.

Pam sighs as she opens the stairwell door. "No, I'm sorry. You're the one *I* hurt. I'm being a complete bitch."

"Keep going." I point at the door.

She enters and I listen as her footsteps descend. When I reach the stairwell, there's a door at the end of the hallway. An arrow on the wall points toward it along with "Nightingale Project."

I hesitate, but Pam's already halfway to the next floor. I can't let her disappear with the maps. I should have taken them.

Inside the stairwell, there's one more level above the current one. It doesn't seem to make sense, given that there's nothing above this floor but forest.

The steps are disgusting, tiles littered with dust and dead insects. Wherever I press my foot, there's a crunch. A door opens and closes ahead of me.

"Pam?" I hurry down the next couple levels to an open door marked B2. A faint orange glow emanates from inside.

I march through the door, finding a dark, dingy corridor lit by orange emergency lights. Where the light shines, the walls are ochre and every few feet, in between each pair of lights, a gold crucifix shines biblically.

"How far?" I ask.

Papers crinkle. "Not much. It's through another hallway on the left." She pauses. "I want you to know, Ty, I meant everything I said before. Being with you's been life changing. I was so shy before, and you helped me break out of my shell."

"Uh huh."

Wood creaks as she opens a door to her left and goes through.

"Wait!" I rush after her, find another hallway.

The walls inside are white, the ceiling high. It's lit by flickering fluorescent lights. Human-sized cages line the room. Withered, contorted human remains crouch inside them, brown and leathery. There's a *huge* bloodstain in the centre of the floor. An arrow marked "processing" points in the direction we're walking.

"Pam, mind handing me the map? There's directions on the walls—maybe those blueprints aren't right." And who puts a comms facility *further* underground?

Pam ignores me, keeps walking. I stop. This isn't right.

"But you weren't the nicest to me either," Pam's saying, like I didn't speak at all. "You never asked me about myself, never checked in. At first, I was so totally whelmed . . . ."

She disappears into another room. She's got the maps, but I'm positive I can make it back upstairs without them. The comms room has to be on the top floor. I turn around, heading back.

". . . . so, totally *traught*."

My heart stops beating. I stop moving.

Move move move.

"When you showed up in the graveyard, I really wasn't expecting that. It was serendipity. You took my breath away—like a cartoon character had come to life and strolled into my living room. In that second, for a moment, you were beautiful. It didn't last."

The promo picture from *Equus*. The e-mails from Traught-Dog01 when I only know of three fucking people with e-mail access on the island. Pam's fascination with me, *with Josh*. Pam's a tech nut. She can break into electronic locks. She can tap cameras. She probably made all those tapes for Gene. I *watched* her hack the lock to the Virgie Kyle museum, and then not even half an hour later Uphill mentioned a break-in. Did she steal my mom's ring? Was that body Pam "found" even Virgie Kyle?

And if it wasn't, who did it belong to?

The bodies in the cages against the walls look like they're watching me, mouths and eye sockets screaming.

I tear back down the hallway, clutching my mom's hand like a talisman.

My own voice sputters to life from speakers in the corners of the hallway. "—ust bury me out here, please. Murder me and bury me under a rock. Pick a nice tree though—none of this four-foot shallow grave stuff. I want to be way down there. Deep six. Worm chow. The circle of life. Just bury me out here, please. Murder me and bury me—"

Doors flash by. Subject 15, Subject 14, Subject 13 . . . .

"—the circle of life. Just bury me—"

I reach the stairs, and it's Josh, not me, who's playing. "Welcome, Bangers, to another episode of Discovery Bang. I'm here with my co-host, the erstwhile Tyler Ky—

"Erstwhile?" I cut in.

I leap back up the stairs.

"Yeah, you know. You're an erstwhile kind of guy," says Josh. The audio skips ahead. "Guys, if you're as interested in replacing Ty as *I* am, get your audition tapes ready and sound off in the comments."

It repeats and repeats and repeats, and then several recordings start playing one over the other. It's like the dream. Fuck it's just like the dream.

Do I run up that last flight of stairs for the radio, or head for the door? I need to get out. Everything else can wait. I dart into the entrance hallway.

The speakers go silent, then crackle.

"Ty?" It's Josh. He sounds terrified. "Tyler, it's so fucking dark, man. I need you. I can't handle this."

It *sounds* like Josh. It does. But that audio could be from over half our episodes. He didn't mention anything specific—not a woman, not Pam, not Babel or Echo Island.

"Ty? Please. God. Please."

The pull on my insides is what I imagine happens when you hear your child's frightened cry. I'm panting, standing in the hallway. I'm only twenty feet from freedom.

I need a weapon.

I *slam* against the door to my left, and when it doesn't break I kick the handle hard. Adrenaline and need are powerful poisons.

The room's just an office. Just an office with pieces of desiccated corpse strewn across the floor. Whoever this person was, their killer tore their limbs off one by one. One of those limbs is clutching a handgun.

I grab it. I hurry back into the hallway.

"*Tyler?*" pleads the speakers.

Pam doesn't seem bothered that I have a gun. Maybe she can sense I have no fucking idea what I'm doing. I can't tell if it's busted, if it's loaded, if the safety's on . . . .

"That's not Josh," I say, trying to flush out the truth.

"It's not?" asks Pam, amused. "I think I know Josh when I hear him. I've watched every single episode at least twenty times. *At least*. He's my number one crush."

She steps toward me. I back up. She steps toward me. I back up. She reaches for her backpack—

I fire.

A bullet *zings* against the wall.

Pam draws something small and black from her bag.

I fire again, and this one grazes her arm.

"Ahh!" She squeezes her eyes shut, shakes her arm out. "Dammit. I was planning to go sleeveless at the Dog Dance."

She presses a button on the black square and something thuds shut behind me. The lights go out.

I fire.

Footsteps scuffle toward me.

I fire. I fire. I fire.

Pam laughs next to my ear.

The gun clicks empty.

She grabs my arm and throws me against the wall—not a small throw, but a fucking toss, enough to knock the breath from me.

The gun, empty, slides across the ground.

"You're a real pal, Ty," says Josh, and from his casual tone, I now know it's from Discovery Bang. "Leaving your BFF in the woods to get ripped apart by rabid Squatchi."

I pull myself onto all fours, back throbbing.

Pam kicks me in the gut and I fall. She latches onto my hair, flips me onto my back. She drags me by my shirt collar.

I try to dig my heels into the ground, try to grab the door jamb and wedge myself inside the entrance of the stairwell as she pulls me down. As I bump down every step, I try to punch her, I try to force her to let go by digging my non-existent nails into her hand. I try everything.

It's pitch black. I still can't breathe properly.

She drags me to where I abandoned her, then another hallway. Through one of the doors lining the hall, I glimpse the flash of TV screens—Pam's monitoring room? She wanted me to follow her down this hallway. She wanted me to see everything.

"You don't have to do this." Fuck, I'm that person.

Pam doesn't speak.

"I'll stay with you," I plead. "J-just like it was before. Remember? We bumped heads?"

On this one episode of *I Survived* I watched with Kayla, this woman got away from a serial killer by convincing him she wanted to be there, by spinning a story about how he'd rescued her, by seducing him. If I can bring myself to try a little, me and Josh, wherever she's got him, can still get out of this.

"This is really great," I stutter. I force a laugh. "It's so fun. Me and you, playing this game. I can't—I can't wait to kiss you again. You're beautiful, Pam. A real goddess."

My leg bangs a door as she pulls me through. There's a light ahead of us. I twist so I can see.

"The Hole" is scrawled in red paint at the centre of a rounded spotlight. A spray-painted arrow points down.

I can't do this. I can't. I'm not convincing. I reach for the wall, but my nails only scrape against it.

"I'll be with you forever. I'll take Uphill's drug if that's what you want. Just. Josh. Let Josh go. He's not like me. He's got people. He'll be missed. They'll come looking and catch you."

Pam laughs, slowing. "It's cute you think Josh was ever on the island."

She may as well have kicked me again. I can't distinguish whether what I'm feeling is relief, or my hope finally dying.

She pulls me to the edge of something.

The Hole.

I have to keep her talking. "The e-mail—"

She clucks. "Aww, Tyler. *Sweetie. I* wrote that last paragraph. What kind of guy tells you he never wants to see you again, then shows up for seconds?"

She lets go of my shirt and my head falls. It's hanging over the lip of the hole. I scrabble to get up and she punches me in the stomach. "Turns out I have some writing talent after all."

I scream. The pain's white-hot in my back, in my chest, behind my eyes. It pulses, and as the pulse dims, I fumble for Pam's hand, for her fingers. I lace mine in hers.

"The erstwhile Tyler Kyle," she says, flat. "Josh doesn't want you. And neither do I."

She shoves me into the darkness.

31

A HOLE SHAPED LIKE A PERSON

Water spills out of my lips and dribbles down my chin. I cough and it tastes of blood.

I'm sitting upright in a chair. Everything aches.

Pam's standing in front of me, holding a cup, face lit from above by a bright white light. Her pale skin and blond hair seem to merge with the spotlight, an effect that would transform her into an angel on stage. Underground, she's the bleached white of a corpse.

The spotlight is the only illumination in the dingy room, granting only a glimpse of plain cement walls.

I part my cracked lips, flick my tongue over them. It brushes a deep cut and I suck in a sharp breath.

"Careful, Ty," Pam says, soothing. "You hurt yourself in that fall. I think you hit your head."

"Not . . . ." I wet my lips, swallow. The words come hard. Thoughts come hard. Did she drug me?

The last thing I remember is Pam turning out the lights. After that, I passed out from pain or exhaustion or stress.

"You pushed me," I spit out.

She raises her hand to my face.

I flinch.

"That's right." She brushes a curl out of my eyes, strokes my cheek. "But everything's as it should be now. You don't have to try anymore." She runs her thumb over my lips. When she finds the cut, she presses down.

I scream, heart pumping. My bladder lets go.

"Oh god Christ." I tilt my head back, away from her.

"Didn't think I'd make you a believer so soon," says Pam.

I wriggle my fingers. My arms feel heavy. *I* feel heavy. But my hands aren't bound.

I lumber out of the chair and throw myself at her. She steps out of the way easily and I hit the ground like a sack of potatoes. I roll onto my side.

"This'll go better for you if you lose the attitude. You've never been the most coordinated, and the pain meds in your system aren't going to improve that. Leave the antics for the living." She bends down, lifts me easily, and slumps me in the chair. "Because you know what you are, Tyler?" She pauses, hooks my eyes with hers, grins. "*The walking dead*."

Laughter explodes from me, and it's fucking painful. "You're. You're fucking nuts. So fucking—" There's tears in my eyes. My mouth is a rictus. I let out a drawn-out noise halfway between a groan and a sigh, nearly monotone. "Ha. Ha. Hah. Nuts. *Nuts*. Like Mr. Nuts. Should've recognized the resemblance. Fucked him instead."

For some reason, comparing Pam to a dead squirrel's taxidermied ballsack doesn't improve her mood. She reaches behind her.

Small wheels rumble over the cement floor. I picture dentist's tools, sharpened knives, instruments from *Saw*. But it's not that. It's a trolley filled with lidded test tubes suspended in a small rack. The tubes have labels, but the words are turned away from me.

I jerk back, aiming to upend the chair, but Pam catches it like she's Spider-Man. As she holds me one-handed, she turns one of the tubes round so I can read the label.

Sperm sample. It says sperm sample.

Pam replaces it in the rack with at least eleven more samples. Some of the fluids are dark as blood.

"Is this where you reveal your evil plan to complete your parents' mad Christian science experiment?"

She pulls the chair upright. She straddles me. She leans in as if for a kiss, then veers left and licks her flattened tongue up the side of my face. I can't possibly taste nice.

"Mmm," she moans. "Why would I tell you anything, Tyler?"

"The satisfaction of an audience?"

She drags her tongue beneath my eye, probing, and I squeeze my lid shut before she can lick my eyeball. She twists her tongue inside the corner of my lid, worrying at the build-up of crusty sleep. I feel it come free, sense her eat it up.

I try not to shake. It's not working.

"Some of us don't *need* an audience, Tyler," she mews. "Some of us aren't attention-seeking whores."

"I prefer attention-*stealing*, actually."

"Oh baby, it doesn't matter what you prefer." She flicks her tongue across the bridge of my nose, scrapes her teeth over my skin. Maybe if I'm lucky she'll get beaver fever from the layers of lake water.

She bends in close to my ear. "I'm gonna devour you."

I lean my head back, squint under the brightness of the spotlight shining from above. There's a short rope ladder hanging inside the hole.

Pam wiggles her tongue inside my ear, and I squirm involuntarily. Her smile, flush against my skin, is wet and toothy.

If I get away from her. If I jump. If I grab that ladder and *climb climb climb*, I can get out of this. I'll be above her. I'll have the upper foot. I'll kick her down if she comes after me. I'll pull the ladder up so she's stuck.

Pam looks me dead in the eyes. She plunges her tongue up my nose and *fuck it hurts*.

I slam my foot against the ground. The sudden movement tilts the chair and we're falling backwards.

The chair takes the brunt of the impact. Pam catches herself, gasping like she hurt her wrist. She curls her hand into a fist, draws her arm back. I bring up my hands to block the blow.

She punches the cement beside me, and I swear it fucking cracks.

I swallow, staring into her eyes. Eyes round as full moons. She draws her lips back in a snarl.

"*Fuck you!*" She *whacks* her hand into the floor, pulls it back. Cement dust scatters across my face. She slams her fist down again. And again. And again. "*Fuckyoufuckyoufuckyou.*"

I spit out tiny stones, wipe the debris from my eyes. I want to be defiant. I want to be strong.

Pam just punched a hole through the motherfucking floor.

"I'm sorry," I say.

Pam slides, sinuous, to her feet. "Not sorry enough." She steps around me. Kicks my leg. "Get up."

I move, but it must be too slow for her because she kicks me in the side of my knee.

"*Get up!*"

I move faster, sneaking a glance at the rope ladder while her back's to me. The rope's taunting me. It's Pam throwing her balls around because she knows if I leap for it, she can pull my fucking leg off and club me to death with it.

Pam trails her fingers over the test tubes. She slides a sperm sample out of its slot and pops the lid. She tosses it back like a Jäger shot.

I cringe. "You know, I hear it works better from the other end." Oh god. Oh no. I didn't.

I did.

Pam smashes the tube against a wall. I take some *very* quick steps back.

"We need to set up some ground rules." She strolls toward me, casual, but her eyes are made of knives.

I run to my left along the wall, searching the perimeter. This room isn't any bigger than 15 x 15. The walls are immaculate.

No doors, no footholds. Speakers leer at me from the corners like giant triangular mouths.

Pam stands in the centre. She covers her laugh with a dainty hand. "Sometimes you're so cute," she muses, while I pat down bare cement. "Your mom used to tell me all about you."

Mom.

Ignore Pam. Ignore her. Ignore Pam.

I hunch against a corner, into the darkness. There's nothing in this room I can use, only me and Pam, the chair, the trolley with the tubes.

The tubes. There's glass somewhere from the one she shattered. However strong Pam is, her skin's not metal, and she shouldn't be able to see the details of what I'm doing. I walk back along the wall. My toe brushes a small, jagged piece of tube. I pick it up. It's still sticky with spunk.

"Did you spend a lot of time with my mom?" I ask Pam, conversational, like she's got answers I want. I don't want anything she could give me.

Pam rolls a kink out of her shoulder. She rights the chair, shrugs off her cardigan and drapes it over the plastic back. "She's how I learned about Discovery Bang. Cool, right? She wanted me to look up her precious boy and see what he'd made of himself." Pam's staring into space, like she's remembering. Her nose twitches. I tighten my grip on the shard of glass. "She told me *a lot* about you. Old people are easy to butter up. You don't even have to compliment them. Just sit there and listen." Pam scuffs the floor with her shoe. "And she was nice. At first. It was surreal the way she made people love her, even people whose parents she murdered in the most horrendous way imaginable." She trills a laugh. "Real charisma, that's what she had. She treated me almost like a daughter, from the moment she came back. I thought she wanted to make amends. It would have been the *Christian* thing to do. And I wanted to forgive her *so bad*. She was so pretty, and vibrant, and talented. She's what I always dreamed Angela Matheson was like."

Angela Matheson. The woman from Uphill's photo.

My mouth is cotton. "Did you kill my mother?"

Pam laughs. "The *island* killed your mother, same as it kills everyone. No, I didn't kill the glamorous *Virgie Kyle*. She killed me though—that other me. The innocent me. The me who had *hope*. I asked her one day, after months of building up the courage, if she'd be *my* mom. She'd lost a son; I'd had my parents taken from me. She just shook her head and laughed. And you know what she said? What did she say, Tyler?"

"I—have no idea."

Pam clenches her jaw. "Rhetorical question, *Tyler*. She told me *she never wanted kids*. She *told* me she didn't even want the first one. She *told* me she banged some rando 'cause she thought a baby Nightingale was her ticket to freedom." She waves her hand at me, face contorted into a grimace. "Like you're made of fucking magic juice or something." She snorts. "Didn't work, obviously. Not for Virgie anyway."

Seems like Mom. "It did work for a while. I assume."

Pam bites her lip. "You say that like it's good for you." She shakes her finger. "It's not Tyler. Not good at all. Because I have more information than your mom ever found, and I had her as a living experiment."

She pats the seat beside her. I slip the broken vial into my jeans pocket and inch toward her.

"That's it. Don't get shy on me."

"We could work together." I sit down. "I could still help you get out of here. *All* of you."

"I don't care about *all of us*." Pam's face is stone. "Those assholes can rot. You saw the bodies, right?"

"Uphill's models? We were both there, Pam." On *I Survived*, you're supposed to say the killer's name. It helps build a rapport. Or something. Unless that's from a movie.

The spotlight flickers, and the dying and rising light in Pam's eyes reminds me of the monsters in the forest. "No. I don't mean the models. That's Uphill's game. Sick fuck. You'll have to ask him about it, and *oh no* you're never gonna fucking get to."

I breathe in slowly. My arm's starting to ache, like I twisted it while I was running, or maybe when we fell. At least my thoughts are coming easier as the drugs wear off. "So the bodies upstairs."

She's silent. Her pupils are dilated, despite the light. She hardly looks human. "*Your mother* locked them up. Shut the door and threw away the fucking key. They starved to death. It's not a good way to go." She clutches the neck of my t-shirt and pulls me toward her, our faces so close the tips of our noses touch. "I thought about *a lot* of ways to kill you, Tyler. Murdered you on the page so many times in so many ways. But starvation—that's the most poetic, I think. Down here, in the dark. Alone. Just like your mom left you alone in your apartment eighteen years ago." She kisses my lips. "And I'm going to replace you. I'll make sure and give Josh a kiss—"

I stab the broken vial into her neck.

Pam screeches and stumbles back.

I don't waste time: I jump. My fingers close around the rope. I heave with all my non-existent abs, ignoring the burn in my right shoulder. I pull myself up one rung, then the next.

Pam grabs my sneaker. I kick and the shoe comes off in her hands. I tuck my knees in, groaning. She slaps at me.

Then she jumps.

Her whole body weight *smacks* me. The ladder sways. I don't know what she's tied the rope to, but I hope it's reinforced.

"Come on, Tyler," Pam coos. "This thing falls, we're playing house till one of us croaks."

"I'm down if you are. Seems like the same deal for me either way." I reach for the next rung, hauling both our weight. I have to get to the next floor. If I don't, I'm dead.

Pam's elbow hooks around my neck and she lets her entire body drop.

I choke. I let go.

Dead dead dead.

Pam cushions my fall. I roll off her, but she's already on her feet, kicking me in the back. She pulls me up then slams me down.

I'm in the chair. The world is spinning.

Pam reaches for something on the trolley. "I didn't want to have to hurt you, but you make it hard."

Whatever she's holding is too small for me to focus on. She draws it up to my left eye.

It's a thumbtack.

"No, *nonono*." I try to pull back.

Pam holds me. She pushes the tack into the centre of my eye.

32

PHILOMEL

It's been days.

She left me a bowl of water and an apple. I force myself to make it last, but only after I've rinsed my eye.

It's pitch black except when I use my phone's flashlight. The vision in my left eye is blurry, like being underwater. Clear liquid dripped out when Pam pulled the tack free, so she punctured something. I don't fucking know what it was. I don't know about eyes. I only know it hurts, even days later, and that neither of my eyes will stop watering.

The room is impenetrable. There are speakers in the upper corners, like everywhere on the island, but I can't reach them, and don't know what use they'd be if I did. I find scratches in the walls—what feel like people's names when I trace the patterns with my fingertips. I think about using my phone to read them, but I don't want to waste the battery. I mouth the messages to myself anyway.

Jake + Andy. Sarah. Conrad.

Pam was never working with Uphill. I go over that in my mind relentlessly. I examine every clue, every moment I made the worst choice I possibly could. I try my phone, thinking I can call Arcadia, but there's no signal. Even if I did reach Uphill, there's no guarantee he'd help me. He and Pam are both monsters.

The only other things in the room are the holes Pam busted in the cement floor. There's soil underneath, but it's hard. I dig till my nails bleed anyway, piling the dirt into a corner I've designated as the toilet. After a while, I stop needing to use it. I piss into the depleting water bowl. Eventually I'll run out of water, and you can drink your own urine at least a couple times.

Then there's the cramps—the same ones I experienced in the woods before I collapsed. And I *do* collapse a few times. I pass out as pain strikes a match and cooks my nerves alive. Every time I wake up, I think Pam'll be there, and every time I'm disgusted to realize I wish she was.

It's lonely in the dark.

My hand hovers over Joshbot more times than I want to admit. I resist. There's still a chance someone'll get through if I can make the battery last.

I start singing instead—whatever comes to mind. And I talk to myself to keep me sane, reciting lines from shows, telling myself stories.

Then Pam comes.

Light spills into the hole, and I'm pretty sure the only reason it doesn't blind me is because I've been using the phone occasionally. I hide it under the cement floor in case it was an accident Pam missed it the first time.

The ladder flips over the lip of the hole and I back away.

She tosses down a small basket of apples. They spill across the floor.

I grab one, bite. It's soft and rotten and it's the most glorious thing I've ever tasted. I watch her descend, thinking about grabbing her. I can feel her hair in my fingers, the *pull* and the rip as I whip her against the wall and smash her brains out. But I don't move. I clutch my apple and eat.

She turns to face me, platinum in the light. Beautiful. She smiles.

"Done something new with your hair," I say between bites. It's true. She's pulled it back in a ponytail, and straightened it so it's sharp and flat, like that pop star with the bunny ears.

"Glad to see you're not insane. Or maybe you are." She pats her ponytail. "But thanks. Sometimes you've got to change it up."

"It doesn't suit you."

"*Tch.*" Pam wags her finger. "Oh you."

She's in a good mood. I don't know what to think about that.

I swallow the last of the apple, then lay the core down for later. And hey, maybe if this gets real bad, I can mash the seeds up and poison myself with cyanide.

"Thanks for the apples," I say.

"Well I don't want you to die yet," says Pam.

"Mm."

She peers at the bowl of piss-water, gives it a light kick. Water sloshes onto the floor and I have to hold back from running toward her, heart in my throat. How many days are those drops worth? How many hours?

"Smart thinking. I'm surprised." She surveys the mess on the floor where I've dug a stupidly shallow hole. She chuckles. "Maybe if you had a shovel."

I smile weakly as she walks the perimeter. She checks out the dirt toilet in the corner. "Love what you've done with the place. *Tres chic.* That's right, isn't it? Chic? You like your French words."

"Mm."

She walks right up to me. I shrink away but she grabs my arms, firm but gentle. She rubs her hands under my shirt, pinches my side. There's nothing to pinch, and I jump at the pain.

She giggles and reaches for my mouth, gazing into my eyes. "You look like shit."

"Mm."

She shoves her thumb past my lips, runs it along my teeth. She tastes of clean.

Bite her bite her bite her.

I don't. I can't beat her in a physical contest. She'll just stick another pin in my eye.

She presses her thumb against my tongue so it's flat against the base of my mouth. "You're losing your voice, little bird." She draws her thumb out, searches my eyes. "Where's that magic?"

It's so hard to tell when she wants an answer and when she doesn't. "There's no such thing as magic."

She bats her eyes. "*Oh?* You really haven't learned anything, have you? There is magic, and I've stolen yours all away. Can't you see I'm glowing?"

Literally, in the sense that she's lit by a bright light she put there herself and she's blond, so.

"You're mesmeric," I say, flatly. I pause though. I could try something else. "I mean that. From the moment we met I sensed there was something different about you. We've both lost people. We've both been abandoned. We're outsiders."

The room is still. Pam's still. She's staring. She's not *glowing* in the way she means it, but she looks . . . bestial somehow. Feral. She sits down, folds her hands in her lap. "Go on."

"I wanted you so bad," I continue. "Right from the start. I wanted to run away together. Be the . . . Glenn to your Maggie."

"The Robin to my Artemis," Pam adds, soft.

I grin, wave my hands. "Yeah yeah. Like Robin and Artemis." I have no idea who Artemis is, only it's an awful lot like the name of that fanfic writer.

The realization must show on my face because Pam bends over, laughing. Her ponytail sails over her head. "You must think I'm a fucking dumbass. If you'd read any of my work, Ty, you'd know you never make it out alive. But go on, why don't you do a little dance. A striptease. Didn't you promise the viewers you'd do a sexy dance if you bagged a cryptid?" She leans back. "Well, cryptid *and* audience here, and I'd like my dance."

"You're not a cryptid, you're a science experiment."

"Keep telling yourself that." Pam smiles. "Josh will be impressed."

I clench my jaw. I'm not gonna dance, no, but I'll do her one better.

I sing.

The first words of Radiohead's "Creep" make it past my lips before Pam jumps me and rams her fingers into my mouth. She pins me against the wall, and I can't breathe—I can't move.

She draws a knife, pulls her fist out of my mouth, and slams my neck against the wall with her right forearm.

She turns the knife over. "You shouldn't have tried that. Getting all mouthy." She sounds almost sad. "Now you know what I have to do. You know the story of Philomela, right? Ovid says it's where nightingales come from. This beautiful princess has everything, but she can't keep her trap shut, so someone shuts it for her. When she escapes, she turns into a nightingale. That part never made sense to me, because even after she's changed, Philomela still can't sing. While nightingales . . . ."

Pam holds the knife up, nudges it against my lips. I keep my jaws clamped shut. The tip of the blade clinks against a tooth.

I moan, feel tears sliding down my face. I can barely see out of my right eye anymore. I shake my head.

"*Now* you're quiet. Why is that?" She increases the pressure on my throat.

My teeth are chattering. Fuck. I—I'm hyperventilating.

"If you don't open up, I'll give you a Chelsea smile. You won't like that much."

I plead with my eyes, with everything I have. All the pathos I can summon. And it's not an act. It's real. It's real.

Pam slices half an inch into the right corner of my lip. It hurts it hurtsithurts. My skin feels *loose* in a way that's not good. It's no good.

"*Please.*" Speaking hurts, but the word spills from me, liquid to blend with my tears. I clamp my eyes closed. I can't look. "Please. Please don't. Don't." Every word is a stutter, my teeth clacking together, my chest heaving.

"Hold still, baby." She pushes it inside me, cutting my cheek like that other Tyler did in the dream. She pins me hard against the wall, forearm nudging my chin up to control the movement of my head.

She sighs. "This isn't going to work."

She lets me go.

I fall in a heap at her feet. "Please."

"Get in the chair."

I don't. I can't. I crawl toward it. If I don't stop her she's going to cut my fucking tongue out like in the dream. I have to try. I open my mouth, start to sing—

Pam kicks me. I land on my back. I punch and kick but she's on me again. She pins my arms with her knees, reaches for my jaw. She squeezes so hard it's like she's going to break it, and I can't stop myself from opening my mouth, and she pulls my tongue out, and she—

Blood pours down onto my face. The pain is excruciating. Then I start to choke.

Pam gets off me. I roll onto all fours, choking out blood, spitting blood. I'm bleeding to death. I'm bleeding.

"Look at this thing. This is what everyone's wetting their panties over?" Pam laughs. "Think I'll fry it with some fava beans and a nice chianti. Hope you appreciate the reference. I *did* think about eating your brains like he does in that one movie, but you're not very smart, Tyler."

I need to staunch the bleeding. I haul off my shirt, and I open my mouth and it *hurts* but I shove in the fabric, press it hard against the wound.

The wound. The wound. An absence. Right at the back of my mouth. Empty.

"Oh don't go into shock." Pam's walking toward me. I crawl away. "Let me help."

I hear a match strike. She steps around me, holding the knife again.

"Get that shirt out," she says, and she tugs it loose. Blood seeps from the stub of my tongue again. I close my eyes, but I let her hold her heated knife out and press the flat of it against the injury.

Something like a scream, like a whimper, slips out of me.

I pass out.

33

EXQUISITE CORPSE

Several days in, I give up on a phone signal. I think it's several days anyway.

Pam came once more to treat my wounds, but said nothing, and I tried nothing. The last time she came, all she did was throw an apple into the hole and leave.

I tried counting, but it's impossible to measure the passage of time in the dark. Still, I think it's been eight days. Eight days on barely any water. Eight days on food I can hardly chew now that—

So I'm staring at the phone, curled around it, very aware of the battery ticking down. My finger hovers over Joshbot and it's not the first time I've turned it on. On off, on off, on off again just to hear someone speak. To hear Josh speak.

The last thing I'll ever hear, except in dreams.

The dreams are vivid. I slip in and out of them, unsure anymore when I'm awake or asleep. In one of them, Tia danced under a purple spotlight, her silver moon earrings like violet stars. She was crying and I knew it was for Nor.

In most of the dreams I see islanders wading across the lake and into the woods. When that happens, I sense others with me, and it's like that first weird dream, when Nor marched into the forest and the whole town stood on the streets watching her do it.

I've tried talking to people in the dreams. No one answers, like I'm invisible.

As of yesterday, the food is gone. The piss is gone. I dug up a worm from the hole and ate it. It took everything in me to keep it down.

"*Tyler, you're an asshole.*"

And still, I'm dying. I keep fading in and out, and my skin feels . . . *brittle*. That can't be a good sign.

I hold my finger over Joshbot. *I just want to hear him talk. I just want to hear him.* I'd give up another eye to talk to it.

"*What was that?*" asks Joshbot. It waits. "*Ty? Say something. It can be anything. Tyler I can't hear you.*"

I suck in a whine, long and pained, and I hold the phone close like it's a person, and I run my own hands over my arms and the too-prominent bones beneath, and I'm alone, and I'm dying, and what does it matter if I think shameful, stupid things when I'm dying? So I pretend they're Josh's hands. I pretend I'm not alone. He folds his fingers over mine and strokes his ring finger over my ring finger.

I close my eyes.

We're dancing, surrounded by people. We're at the hotel. Josh is waving a half-empty bottle of tequila in the air. We're close enough to touch, except we don't. We're smiling, grinning.

Happy, I think. I know *I* was happy. No. He was happy too. In my fantasy, why not let him be happy too?

"Wanna hit the hot tub?" I ask, and he lays the tequila on the floor against the wall. That should be the first sign we're both too wasted to go near water, but he grabs my hand and pulls me along and I'm too drunk to protest, and his fingers around mine are tight and unyielding and it's like I can feel desire in them, and yeah, love too. And it's my dream and I'm dying so maybe that's true. It can be true for now, can't it?

"*What was that?*"

Light flashes behind my eyes, and the dark edges in again. I'm falling asleep, I think. But I can't sleep, because—

We're in the tub. We had to help each other undress to get in here, and now that we are in here, we can't seem to let go.

My hands hold his back, his hand is on my neck. He traces his fingers down to the space between my shoulders. Our fingers are trembling.

"It's so bullshit we lost *Best Unscripted* to *Russian Housewives Eat Oreos for the First Time*. I bet if you went to Russia, there'd be fucking Oreos all over the place. Anyway. I mean. It's a lie. You worked hard." I swallow. I'm giving him an out. A chance to let go.

He kisses me.

"*Ty? Say something. It can be anything. Tyler I can't hear you.*"

We fall into each other. When he pulls back he says I taste like lime, and minutes later, when the stupid me, when the me who doesn't know when to shut up made my stupid joke, I don't. I can't. I can't talk anymore. And Josh talks for both of us. And what he says is, "I want you, Tyler Kyle. I've always wanted you. And I love you. You've never been alone."

I'm so fucking stupid.

"*Type for text option. Just know I couldn't pre-program for all your dyslexic shit, so you get what you get. PEACE.*"

I stare at the screen. At Joshbot. "Battery low," pops up on the phone. It's at 2%.

Me too phone. Me too.

A text option. At 2%.

My vision's swimming. Everything's dark. I'm so so tired.

There's only one thing worth saying, same as there ever was.

INTERMISSION

Whoa—whoa man. That's big. [Pause][Sigh] Ty, I'll be straight with you. I don't know why I'm recording this. I don't know why I made this app. [Pause] That's a lie. I made it because of this. Because you're never gonna listen to this thing and I'm too scared to do it any other way. I'd be surprised if you turned it on after the Christmas party. Oh no—don't give it to Christmas party people. They might trigger this message and that's not—well, maybe that'd be okay. Yeah. It's okay. Suck it up, man. You're cool. You're calm. [Clears throat] If you know me, you'll know that was a lie (not the cool part. I am pretty cool). So, uh, first thing first, I guess. You probably said that as a joke, or, uh, as a platonic thing. Thing is, I love you. [Pause] That space is so you can make a joke, 'cause I know you'll want to. You don't do big moments well. This recording's probably evidence that I don't either. But I, uh. This is my big moment. My, "I love you" moment. Like love love. Please don't hate me for it. It's just [sigh] I don't know how long I can do this. All my life, I've had these feelings. I've wanted things I knew I shouldn't want. [Crying] In this moment, right now, I'm feeling brave. So I want to tell you. [Pause] [Sniff] There's this girl, Ashley, and she's real into me and she's great, but she's not you, Ty. And I'm gay, but it's hard with parents like mine not to try not to be, and I don't know what to do I just wanted you to know and I'm too scared of what it'll mean to tell you. You don't deserve that. You're probably not even into dudes. Crap, man. Why did I think this was a good idea?

[Pause] *I'll start at the beginning. When I saw you for the first time I'd just got my acceptance letter. Mom and Dad insisted we see all the end of year shows so they could check out the school. When they saw* Equus *was playing, we went as protesters. I had to beg them to let me enroll. They only paid my tuition when I promised to start a campus crusade against pornographic thespian material.* [Laughs] *I went back to see* Equus *though. I came back for every performance. Every. Single. One. Your back is what I remember most. It was on the poster and you remember Ava did that killer lighting? I wanted to touch you. I wanted to meet you. Every performance, Ty. Every performance. It moved something in me no one had moved since this time in junior high—Never mind. The point is, that's why we met. I loved that show so much I snuck into the cast party. I thought you'd be orbited by other actors, or coolly aloof and sipping wine while chatting with profs, but you were alone. You were a wallflower, and not the cool kind. That shirt—you remember the red shirt with the green dots? It was hideous. I was really disappointed, but I walked up to you. You smiled, and then you talked.* A lot. *You weren't anything like what I thought you'd be. A month later we were finishing each other's sentences.* [Inhales] *No one works together like us. I'm telling you this because I need to get it out before I shut myself back up again. You probably don't feel the same. Just in case though—*

BATTERY LOW

—I'll leave with a line I wrote about you. [Sighs] *See, that's a whole other confession. About Pornstar Popsicle—*

ACT 2

1

THE INDOMITABLE JOSH
LIKENS

E veryone knows gay people can turn into wolves. Everyone
except Tyler Kyle, my best friend.

As me and Kayla and a pilot named Pam fly over trees and
trees and trees all the way to the horizon. I turn to Kayla who's
sitting in the seat across the aisle from me. Her recording gear's
piled on the seat beside her, along with some Wiccan staples.

I grab my pen and notebook, start doodling circles. "I've
been brainstorming locations for next season. There's this place
called Peckham's Point." I swallow, then laugh. "It's tiny and in
the middle of nowhere. Ty's going to love it."

"Josh," Kayla says softly. It's a warning. "We don't know if
Tyler's okay."

Of course he's okay. He has to be okay. "He's fine. He's
always fine, Kayla. You know that. And I'm coming after him.
He wouldn't die without me. We're supposed to die together on
screen being swallowed by anaconda." We're Scully and Mulder,
the jokers in a deck of cards.

A set. A pair.

It'd be equal parts terrifying and painful to dwell, so I think
about a future so distant it feels safe. My pen spirals against the
pad. "So Peckham's Point. Next season. There's this weird ghost
kid only other children can see. Creepy shit, right?"

"Uh huh." Kayla nods as she readies one of her handheld
cameras.

"And Tyler hates spooky children. I can already imagine what he's going to say when—"

Shhkrrrrck. Paper rips and my pen veers off the notepad and onto the tray table. There's a hole several layers deep in the paper.

"It's just." I lay the pen down, start picking at my nails. When my therapist told me I should find physical outlets for my stress, I don't think this was what she meant. "Every time I try to talk to him about next season he acts like he doesn't want to be there."

Kayla pulls the camera from her eye. Was she already recording? "Well," Kayla starts, gentle. "You've been doing this a long time. Maybe he wants to move on and doesn't know how to tell you."

Ty would tell me. Wouldn't he? We tell each other everything. *Used to.* It's been different since the awards.

"It's more than that." I tear the nail too deep and blood wells at the cuticle. "It's because of me."

"Is this about you trying to date him? Because I told you to tell him. You can't keep making him sexy vegan dinners and hoping he gets the message."

I flick my ripped-off nail away. "*Seductive* vegan dinners. The video said *Most Seductive Vegan Meal Ever.* All he did was eat it."

Kayla squints. "What did you think he was going to do? Stick his dick in it?"

"It was risotto. It took a long time."

"So that's a yes."

I grab the pad and start drawing squares. "I wanted him to stick it somewhere." Blood rushes to my cheeks. "Oh my god." I bury my face in my palm. "Anyway, it's not 'cause of that. It's because of the hot tub. We were really going, and then he made this joke and I told him I didn't want him and pushed him away."

I'm a coward and a liar. I'm a man-shaped worm.

Kayla whistles. "I did *not* know that happened. That was after Ashley, I hope?"

I nod. "Yeah. Ashley figured out about me during this three-some thing, it's ancient history. We're cool now."

Kayla looks skeptical (it's justified). "Josh, I mean this in the nicest way possible, but you're a grown-ass man asking advice from your twenty-two-year-old employee. You need to tell him how you feel to his face."

I fall back onto the window seat, legs hanging into the aisle. "But that's so hard. Why can't I steal his stapler like in Grade 5?"

"Maybe that would have worked a year ago. Tyler's weird. But you can't tell someone you don't want to be with them, then act surprised they didn't toss your risotto." She pauses and kicks my boot. "He's acting all funny 'cause you broke his heart."

There's a nail in my stomach. It's been rusting since my parents put it there, and when I think about that moment pieces of it flake into my blood stream. It's my doom, a ticking time bomb. One day it'll kill me, assuming it hasn't already. Me or Ty.

Pam shifts in the cockpit. She slams a cabinet. I hope she didn't hear all that. It'd be embarrassing.

Embarrassing. I laugh. "There was this one time—okay, get this, Kay. We're sleeping in the woods, right? I don't remember what we were hunting that night, but it was August definitely because it was so hot we didn't get in the sleeping bags. He was lying there, and I didn't know if he was awake, but I reached out and touched his back—people don't talk enough about how important sexy backs are. Anyway, he *rolls* over and I'm thinking: this is it, he's going to clock me, and we'll hash it out or he'll kiss me or *something*. But when he looks at me I can't do it, so I tell him there was this spider on him? And he asks how big and like, I made it up so I say eight inches and he freaks and he's all 'there aren't any eight inch spiders what the fuck was it,' and he starts tossing his bag over, and he makes me help him, and then *I'm* freaked out because what if there was a spider and it's on me and—"

"You need couples counseling." Kayla sighs. "Get up. We're done talking about this. We need to prep."

I sit up, lean over the seat, and call to Pam. "Are we there yet?"

She doesn't answer immediately. Eventually she barks back: "One hour."

I slide into my seat and bring up Ty's e-mail for the millionth time.

> *Josh I nede you. Something bathsit's going down on the ilsand. A bar owner named Gene's stakling me with these bicker girls called Nor and Tia. They're behind the RtaughtDog10 account, but I'm not sure yet if they're working for Cornad Uphill. Cornad's behind an animartonic monster that scars everyone into staying here. I've hooked up with the local pilot, Pam Matheson. I cc'ed her on this so she can sneak you onto the ilsand. She's the only one not under Cornad's spell. If you don't hear from me, come looking.*
>
> *P.S. So you know this is real: "I don't want you."*

The e-mail is dated July 29th. Yesterday morning. He'd cc'ed Kayla and Pam. It was Pam who offered us an illegal flight onto the island, saving me from almost certain death by bear.

Kayla's seat creaks as she adjusts the camera. "Are you reading the e-mail again?"

"Yeah," I admit.

"What do you think you're going to find?" She's asking the question for the viewers, for when we build the narrative in editing.

Pam starts humming. A mechanism beeps, and "Start Me Up," plays. Pam sings along for a few bars. Her voice is jaunty and cheerful. "Hey, Josh! You like the Stones, right? Ty told me they were your favourite."

"Yeah," I yell back. The engine's so loud it's hard to hear. "Kay's not a big fan of Jagger though. You got any Fleetwood Mac?"

Kay peeks out from behind the camera lens. Her witchy liner's smudged. "*What doooo youuu think you're going toooo find?*" she repeats.

"A clue to who wrote it?" I wave the phone at the camera. "It wasn't Ty."

"What about that P. S?

I shrug. "Torture exists."

My chest aches when I look at it. The person who wrote this did something to my best friend.

I'm ride or die for Tyler. He knows all he'd have to do to conjure me into being is vaguely suggest he may not be okay, or protest too much that he's fine on his own. He'd never ask for help like this, especially not if he thought it'd endanger me. He'd just tell me to do something useless like call the cops—*which I did*. They clammed up a few days after my call, saying it wasn't their jurisdiction, and Sundar investigations—the PI I hired based on a fan's recommendation "accidentally" dropped my call. If this isn't a government cover-up, then I'm not an ace detective cryptid investigator.

"How do you know it wasn't Ty?" Kayla asks.

I grip the phone and stare into the empty spaces between the letters. My fingers clench around the cracked black case. "This ableist asshole either thinks Ty's an idiot or that I am. He's taunting us." I look directly into the camera. "It *does* tell me he's in danger. And according to the IP address, this e-mail came from the island."

Not like the TraughtDog01 e-mails. Those came from off-island. It's what I was trying to tell Ty during our phonecall. That, and about the werewolves. *King Lycaon, Ty, really?* Debatably the first recorded werewolf ever (him or Nebuchadnezzar). The whole reason lycanthropes are called lycanthropes. It's like he's learned nothing from the show at all.

From the cockpit, Pam sings along with Stevie Nicks.

Kayla eyes her, frowning. She puts her camera down, then cups her hands over her mouth. "I don't trust her. What has she really told us?"

"She thought the e-mail was suspicious too."

"Yeah, *after you called it out.*" Kayla closes her eyes as if praying to Diana for patience (it's because she *is* praying for patience, which I know from experience is specifically directed at me). "Pamela never looks me in the eyes. It's like I'm not there. But *you* she watches. That's a girl who's seriously crushing, trust me. And bitch please, she was friendly with Ty?"

Up front, Pam drums her hands on the console, bouncing along to the beat. Her sleek ponytail bobs up and down as she jams.

"She's not exactly broken up about his disappearance," Kayla continues.

Kayla is wise beyond her years. She takes my hands in hers, stares me in the eyes, and that's how I *know* things are about to get serious.

"Let's bring out the big guns," I say.

Kayla nods decisively. She reaches behind her for one of the rucksacks and pulls out her purple velvet drawstring purse with gold moons and stars. The purse contains the stone she uses to contact her spirit guide, Lazaria Crystalis. Lazaria's gotten us out of many a deadly situation. She predicted a field full of nursing Tatzelwurms, so naturally we avoided that area entirely. It was real tense out there for a hot minute, but me and Kayla decided the evidence wasn't worth risking our lives.

This is different. This is special. We're not playing games here.

She slides out her Auralite-23. The twenty-three separate minerals contained in its pressurized core gleam red and orange and white, united in a harmony Kayla tells me is like a spiritual defibrillator.

Tyler says it's plastic and a knock-off, but Tyler's not here, so we're going to save him with crystals.

Kayla stands up, wobbling as the plane tilts slightly. She sticks the auralite in the pocket of her overalls and adjusts her glasses. "Give me ten minutes to set up." She grabs her rucksack and lays it on the floor to work on her circle.

"Everything okay back there?" calls Pam. "Why don't you come up here and we can talk Echo Island. You've got questions, right? I can give you the run-down."

I have a million questions, even though Pam already answered some of them. She told me all about this weird journal Ty left in his cabin, that he was acting paranoid, that he'd disappeared without a word (other than his cryptic e-mail). None of it sounds like the Tyler I know. He's probably chilling in the woods roasting veggie dogs and drinking beer.

I walk toward her, balancing myself against the walls.

"So werewolves," I say. "How does that work?"

Pam's smile fades. "You know about the werewolves?" She presses her palms against the console. "I *tried* to tell Tyler, but he said I was making it up. You'd think he'd trust his own girlfriend."

"Girlfriend?" It's a gut punch. Ty with this leather-clad bombshell. The lizard king and queen. I'm too late. At least I don't have to be gay now. That's how it works, right?

"Oh yeah." She lights up. "We got pretty hot and heavy. That was after Conrad and Gene though."

I slump into the chair across from her. "Conrad Uphill? Isn't he eighty?"

Pam crosses her legs, lean and angular in her tight leather pants. "The *first* time I saw Tyler Kyle he was wasted on stage making out with Conrad at a drag show. The *second* time I saw him, ten minutes later, he was on his knees with Conrad's dick in his mouth. The Gene blowjob was before that. He said he traded it for a coffee."

I blink, trying to reconcile my Ty with the image Pam's conjured. There's no way he'd do that. Not that it'd be wrong if he did, but he wouldn't. "He's a kidder." I grin and Pam smiles back, narrowing her eyes like I'm hopelessly naive.

I slap my knees. "Werewolves, werewolves . . . where were we with werewolves?"

She winks. "Why don't you tell me what you know, sailor?"

For a person, Pam's . . . *odd*. I should know because I'm odd and so is the man I spend ninety percent of my time with. The fact that Pam's oddness is notable to me is therefore not a compliment. *Gross*, that's what I'm looking for. Pam is gross. It's not 'cause Tyler fucked her either. This is a distinctly separate issue.

I clear my throat, use my serious business voice like we're recording. A waste really. "The street names—they're all famous movie werewolves. Except Garou, that's just werewolf in French. It's usually Loup Garou, so I've got to assume Tyler blanked on that—"

"He's stupid, Josh, you can say it." She chuckles. "We're all thinking it."

Gross. "Why would you date someone you think is stupid?" I frown, avoiding eye contact. I pick at my nails. "My best friend and co-host and fellow cryptid hunter is *not* stupid."

Pam pats my leg. "Relax, it's a joke. I found it endearing. He called you stupid all the time on the episodes he showed me."

"Werewolves." I glance around the cockpit at Pam's posters. One of them's of *Young Justice* and it reminds me of Artemisia Grayson. Of course I hate Pam: she's like my nemesis.

I start counting off the obvious clues—ones I'd have pinned on my conspiracy board if I'd had time. "The streets, Lycaon the first werewolf who's king of Arcadia, the wolfsbane that's everywhere, the fact that half the businesses have full moons in their names or logos, the 'Dog Days' thing."

Pam nods along. "I can't believe you put that together so fast. Have you ever taken one of those MENSA exams?"

"Yep, that's me. Joshua Likens, genius." It's just some pop culture knowledge, lady. "Now you go. How does the werewolf thing work?"

Pam cocks her head at me, keeping her eyes focused on the sky. "You already know about the gay people, right?"

I nod, watching the trees below us. Narrow rivers wind over scrub, emptying into marshland. "Conrad Uphill's converting queer people."

My guts churn as my parents' voices echo in my head. I'm in a circle surrounded by other troubled kids and we're spilling our confessions out for a man in a perfect grey suit who never stops smiling except to tell you he's disappointed. He'd clap his hands. I'll never forget the clap. It was a clap and then a rub, and he'd say "let's get started." He made it sound like a buffet.

He'd give us homework. Most of the time that meant writing something and sharing it with the group, but there was another trick he taught us, one I kept doing even after the sessions ended. Ritual was important, he told us. Breakfast is the most important meal of the day, so what does that tell us about starting our day right by God? So each morning I'd walk to the bathroom before I did anything else and stare at myself in the mirror. I'd look myself in the eyes and I'd tell the Josh on the other side of the glass that he wasn't gay. It was then I'd know everything was going to be okay.

The first morning I didn't do it was nine months ago, and every day's a struggle not to talk to my mirror and feel the rush of relief when Joshua Likens looks me in the eyes and tells me I'm normal. I did it this morning, and I can't promise I won't do it again tomorrow. If Ty does feel the same way, and if he'll forgive me, I can't promise him I won't spend half our time together wishing I wasn't. That's not fair. He deserves a real partner. What if I tell him the truth and he tells me he loves me and I hurt him again? I'm not brave like he is.

A mist rolls over the trees—or is that cloud cover? Did Pam change altitude? I face her so my vision's not a ghostly sheet of white.

"Are you listening?" asks Pam.

"I am, sorry. My mind drifted." I laugh. "I was thinking about Tyler."

Pam's fingers tense on the controls. "Conrad's not converting anyone. A long time ago the government started a research program out here. They were trying to build an army, and they needed human subjects to do it."

I nod. "Classic Cold War."

"Exactly." Pam rattles off a bunch of facts about the Echo Island Experiment: that the government partnered with faith camps across the country to take on "incurables." That instead of curing anything, they turned their subjects into something new. That some of their victims were called Nightingales and had special powers that helped control all the others—people like Tyler's mom and Conrad Uphill. That Virgie and Conrad rebelled and killed the founders.

"This is where it gets weird," she says.

It's like the light drops several levels. I can hear my heart in my ears. "I'm ready." I've been ready all my life. I just wish Kayla wasn't busy so we could film it. I'll have to make Pam recount it again once we've landed. No way I'm catching my first cryptid without documentation.

Pam waves at the landscape ahead of us, to Echo Island, unseen in the distance. "Every subject was programmed not to be able to leave the grounds of the experiment: Echo Island and the surrounding forest. If we did, we'd suffer *enormous* pain, then death. The Nightingales could trigger the pain too, or stop it, or make us transform. One day the founders would have made it so they could force the change at will, but for the time being it was set on a clock. 7/30. July 30th. Every summer we go wolfy at night for just shy of two weeks."

"The Dog Days."

Pam smiles nervously. Her eyes dart in her sockets as she looks from me to the windshield. "We turn back. *Most* of the time. But we're an unfinished experiment. When they slaughtered the scientists, they killed any real chance we had of being finished." She swallows. "After a while, the transformation becomes permanent. When someone's going to change, they lose their sense of self. They'd rip through walls to get to the forest. Half the island's population lives in the woods year-round as monsters. The Nightingale's voice keeps us human longer, but Conrad's powers are fading. We're trapped here and we're dying. We lost ten people to the woods this month. A long time ago, Tyler's mom figured out how to leave, but she never told anyone how she did it. Conrad keeps bringing more people to the island. He says it's to give them a chance to live free, but it's so he can make another Nightingale to replace him."

Fleetwood's still playing, but all I can hear is Tyler's voice. "Did Conrad lure Tyler here so he could make him like you?"

Pam purses her lips. "They wouldn't have told me because I'm an outsider. I was . . . I *am* the daughter of two of the founders. Ty was okay with the Nightingale part. He believed me about that. When I told him Conrad wanted to turn him into a werewolf it didn't go well."

I wet my dry lips with my tongue. "Conrad didn't succeed though. Right?"

"I don't know, Josh. Tyler disappeared two weeks ago."

Two weeks? His e-mail was dated yesterday. Ty's been gone for two weeks. I rake my fingers along the underside of the hand rest. Two weeks is a long time for someone to be gone. They say after the first 48 hours, chances are slim that—

But it's Ty. Ty's fine. He's hiding out, playing it cool. Maybe the e-mail's a prank. It could be his way of getting even for the hot tub.

Except Ty knows what the worry would do to me. He'd never hurt me.

I'm bug-eyed, and I blink to stop my eyes shriveling to raisins.

"Two weeks." What the fuck was Pam doing for two weeks while her boyfriend was missing?

"Conrad could have done a lot of things in that time," she says. "If he didn't get what he wanted from Tyler, he might've killed him. Tyler wasn't the most cooperative with people. He annoyed a lot of islanders. Some people never learn when to shut up, you know?"

I *don't* know. But the comment reminds me of the awkward dinners with my parents, the way they talked about him when he wasn't around, and how I tried to stop it by turning it into a game. Instead of asking my parents to change, I asked Tyler. "Still. That's no reason to kill somebody."

And he's not dead. He's not.

Pam shrugs. "They shoot horses, don't they? No one keeps songless birds."

Kayla's right about Pam: she's creepy, and she isn't acting like someone who lost a friend, let alone a boyfriend. It's like she thinks I shouldn't care either.

I hide my disgust with a half-smile. "How does Conrad turn people into werewolves?"

She wrinkles her nose. "Haven't you heard the poem? *Seven thirty, fingers dirty.* There's a lot of different steps. It's only a little like the movies. Getting bitten or scratched, or otherwise ingesting part of someone who's already a wolf. The wolfsbane too—or a couple doses of the pills Conrad makes from it. Soil from Echo Island. And a special tonic—that part's key, and it's also controlled, so there's no way someone could turn by accident."

"Sounds like a witches brew," I say. "Then what happens?"

"Depends on the wolf. Most won't change for the first time till 7/30. There's a lot of pain, and your senses get more acute. We're really strong, though that comes later. But the weirdest part is that Islanders can share each other's dreams. We don't choose who we see most of the time, but we catch glimpses of what's going on in their heads. *OH.* And when we shed—when we turn, I mean—we lose our skin, so when our human forms grow back, we don't age always. Like, I'm a *little* older than I seem. Not by a bad amount or anything."

What's a *bad* amount? I'm not rude enough to ask a lady her age, but I wonder if Tyler knew.

It's nothing like most of the werewolf stories I know, but then, these are science werewolves. "That's pretty great. Apart from being trapped on a death island and everything." I need to stay on her good side. "So 7/30."

"Yeah," says Pam. "That's tonight."

She smiles, but it disappears as Kayla enters in the cockpit.

"What did the crystals say?" I ask.

Kayla's stare is dead cold. "Outlook not good."

2

MR. LIKENS

A man Pam identifies as Conrad Uphill is waiting for us outside the airstrip, surrounded by cops and framed by a black limo. He nods at me, Pam, and Kayla each in turn.

I wish my first thought was something cooler than, *I want to steal his cowboy hat* (followed immediately by *he fucked Ty*, and then, *he kidnapped Ty*). Please don't think that's in order of importance.

"We know about the werewolves," I assert, to unbalance Conrad. He doesn't flinch, as though he's sticking to a script.

"Ms. Matheson," Conrad says with a southern drawl. He smiles at me. "You must be the handsome Mr. Likens, I presume?" He raises his hand, twirls his finger in the air indicating Kayla. "And you are?"

"*Not* part of this," says Kayla.

"That was what we call a courtesy, Ms. Hernandez. I'm well aware of your name." Conrad reaches behind him, and one of the cops (who, now that I'm looking, are dressed like strippers), hands him a tablet. "You're all very busy people, so I'll make this quick." He taps the screen, laser-focused. "In the absence of one Tyler Likens—"

My heart jumps. "That's *Kyle*. We are, uh, *not married*, contrary to popular internet opinion. I'm, uh. I'm straight."

Conrad gives me a grin that I *don't* appreciate. "Of course, my apologies. I do believe Mr. Kyle *also* disabused me of that notion."

My heart shrinks. Did he? Of course he did, because I convinced him it was true. And it *is* true. Because otherwise we're going to Hell, and I can barely make it through a cold without complaining, let alone an eternity's worth of pokers up my asshole.

"Good." I glare and lower my voice. "What have you done with him? Is he in your big torture mansion? I know you're turning people into werewolves."

The look he shoots Pam is so fleeting anyone else would have missed it, but I'm the internet's own Josh Likens, and I'm extremely fucking perceptive (read: paranoid, or, as Ty would put it, excellent at spinning insignificant details into massive conspiracies that a normal person would immediately dismiss). It's an admission that everything I suspected, everything Pam's revealed to me, is true.

Werewolves are real and eight of them are standing in front of me.

"I'm not here to talk about Mr. Kyle's disappearance," says Conrad. "Though I can reassure you that it has nothing to do with me. What I am here to discuss is his erratic and occasionally violent behaviour leading *up to* his disappearance. Behaviour that resulted in damage to my property." He glances at Pam, "*Ms. Matheson*. As well as significant injury to the citizens of Echo Island. As I've been unable to locate Mr. Kyle, I'm holding you financially responsible for the damages sustained during his time on the island."

I laugh. "Ty is *not* erratic. Trust me, he's, like, completely unshakeable. Guy barely breaks a sweat." But as I say it, I remember the phone call. I only heard some of what Tyler said, but he sounded panicked. *Scared*. And Pam said he'd been acting weird.

No. Not Ty. Not *my* Ty. Man doesn't crack. He's cool. He's calm. *I'm* the bundle of nerves, the one he has to talk down from a panic attack almost every trip we take (okay, *every* trip we take).

Conrad clears his throat. He taps his tablet, then hands it to me.

The screens's filled with camera footage of Ty from six different locations: Tyler running, Tyler pulling a picture off the wall and sticking it in his pocket, Tyler jumping in dumpsters, Tyler jumping into a dumpster from a *window* and—oh god he hit that man in the face, Tyler puking, Tyler tearing a painting off the wall and falling on the floor while Pam and Conrad look on, Tyler breaking open doors, Tyler jumping into a ditch full of monkshood (aka wolfsbane), Tyler stripping and leaping into a river, Tyler *digging up a grave?*—wtf Ty—Tyler stealing files from a cabinet, Tyler destroying people's lawns, Tyler cutting skin off a wax sculpture, Tyler—I'm done.

I hand the tablet back to Conrad. I swallow. We *do not* have the money to cover whatever he's going to ask and I *do not* do well with stress.

"Please," I start to say, but I stop. I rub my face. "No. I'm sorry. That's not how he normally is. We don't have a lot of money, but I'll make sure whatever he broke gets fixed, but please—" I can't. That's not Ty. *It's not*. What happened to him? I'm getting choked up. "Please help me find my best friend. Something bad happened to him. If you—if you have him, please give him back. I know you think he's magic, but I promise if he could help you he'd try. He's good like that. I know you think you need him, but I need him too. He's got people who care about him. I care about him." I clench my fists. "I'm not leaving without him, and if you think Ty fucked up your town, then just wait till hurricane Likens comes through."

Conrad looks tired, the heavy lines on his face growing deeper and longer. "I have no idea what happened to Mr. Kyle. We barely interacted—despite the many times he broke into my home and robbed me."

I grit my teeth. "He gave you a blowjob, didn't he? Seems like a lot of contact to me."

Conrad holds a hand to his chest as if offended. "I don't appreciate lewdness, Mr. Likens, especially when it concerns a third party and his private choices."

He did. Tyler gave this old man a blowjob.

I comb my hand through my hair. I swallow a stupid scream I have no right to make. It's time to set aside my personal feelings and become Discovery Bang Josh. The one who leaves no stone untouched, no clue unmolested. "What's the last footage you have of him?"

Conrad taps the pad again. He hands it to me. "That would be the morning of the sixteenth. He was filmed leaving the dumpster of a local diner early that morning and heading for the lake. We have no footage of Tyler returning." He sighs. "I'm sorry to tell you this, Mr. Likens, but it's unlikely Tyler survived the woods, and it's equally unlikely you'll find any trace of his body. These forests are full of bears, and hikers have been known to disappear."

I watch the footage. Kayla creeps up behind me.

Tyler moves like a zombie, loosely hugging his chest. His footsteps are wobbly. At one point he takes out his phone, gripping it tightly.

Conrad reaches over and tabs to another camera. Onscreen, Tyler walks right down the middle of the road, past some seriously concerning pavement stains. He's walking toward the forest all right.

"If your monsters killed Ty," I tell Conrad, meeting his eyes. "I'm going to rip your spine out and shove it down your throat."

3

SITTING AT BUS STOPS
WITH BOYS

A couple years ago, Ty and I were waiting for a bus. I was depressed that day. I guess I get depressed a lot.

Nothing had happened to me that week, nothing I could point to and say, "Hey, look, this terrible thing went down and it made my neurons stop working right." I was in a happy relationship (or as happy as my relationships get). Views and sponsorships were up. We were closing out a solid season and I'd already prepped for our next few locations. Global news was bad, but isn't it always? People getting killed somewhere over bullshit they don't deserve.

That's not the point though.

The point is I turned to Tyler and said, "This world is too sad to live in."

He stared at me, not saying anything right away. Then he smiled—not obnoxiously, or meanly. He smiled carefully. "Sometimes. But it's beautiful too. There's good things in the world."

I knew that, and somehow it didn't make a difference because it's not about knowing, it's about feeling. So I asked him "Like what?" even though I knew, because I wanted to hear him describe it, because when he feels happiness he glows, and I needed to sit inside his heat.

And he smiled again, one that reached his eyes. "Like the warmth of a steaming bath after a cold day, or a cool plunge into a pond on a hot one. The first sip of beer after a toast, and waking up to birdsong. Taking the bus with a friend." And he bit his lip as he looked in my eyes, like he'd stopped himself short of saying something. The thing I didn't want to want him to say. The thing I needed.

So I spoke instead of living inside that possibility, before he could turn it into something real and in the world. "I want to shoot the bird that wakes me up," I said, and he said, "You'd miss it if it were gone."

I can't stop thinking about that as I walk away from Conrad's limo. That I'd miss it if it were gone. It's stupid, but in my head the bird is Tyler and I pushed him away, and he's gone now, and I do miss him. I miss him so bad. And I'm not like him. I can't put a mask on and pretend. I was never a great actor. My heart's sewn into the sleeve of every shirt I own and it always has been. So as I walk, I wipe my eyes dry, and I imagine he's next to me and—oh my God, that's worse. Who cares. The viewers know me, they know I cry sometimes. We've blasted way past toxic masculinity already.

I suck back humid air that (apart from weird science were-wolf poison I assume we're breathing in) is probably undoing a decade's worth of carcinogens. I read once that Russia sent sick kids to Newfoundland to recuperate because the air was so pure. We're not that far from there—the ass end of nowhere. Nowhere, it turns out, is beautiful.

I promised Conrad we'll pay whatever he wants, once Tyler's safe and sound. He didn't seem convinced we'd find him, which only goes to show he hasn't watched enough Discovery Bang.

"Where are we headed?" Kayla asks, and the three of us stop, forming a circle in the street.

Some distance away, a motor rumbles to life, and the black limousine drifts away like an alligator gliding through swamp water.

Discovery Bang Josh takes over. "Tyler was last spotted wandering into the woods. Pam, do you know where he could've gone? Did he mention anywhere specific?"

Pam stares at me wide-eyed for a solid five seconds. She shrugs dramatically. "It could have been anywhere. He was probably trying to hike to the mainland. I told you, he didn't believe me about the werewolves, so he thought it was safe."

She hesitated. She's lying.

"We need to go to the woods." I push past the fear that washes over me at the prospect of going anywhere near a werewolf-infested forest. "Which means we need supplies. We don't know which direction he went. Whistles would be good, or a loudspeaker if you have that."

How far can you walk in two weeks? Ty didn't look like he had food or water with him.

Kayla screws up her face. "We should hire a guide."

"Or look for more clues," Pam suggests, perking up. "Maybe Tyler left a message in his journal." She jerks her thumb toward the centre of town. "My house isn't far."

Whatever we do, it can't be what Pam wants.

"The e-mail mentioned some suspects," says Kayla. "Gene, Tia, Nor—maybe we should start with them."

Tyler warned me about them on the phone as well, which means either they really are guilty, or someone wanted him to think so.

"Tia lives straight down this road," Pam offers. "She'll be at The Moon helping Gene right now, so if we want to break in, it's the perfect time."

Why does Pam want us to go to Tia's? I turn and face her. "Do you think she might have Ty?"

She tilts her head dramatically, ponytail dangling. "If anyone has Tyler held somewhere, it's Conrad, and his house is *massive*. If we go there, I can get you all the evidence you want about werewolves."

She's herding us, pointing us toward clues. My guess, and it is a guess, is that any clues we found in Conrad's house will have been planted.

"Let's try White Sails first," I say. "Conrad's probably heading home, so we should wait till we're sure he's gone. If worst comes to worst, we wait till nightfall when he's wolfy and sneak in."

Pam smiles weakly. "That's a great plan, Josh. Should we get a shot of us talking that out? I could be your Tyler for this one."

This manic pixie murderer is *not* the Tyler for this one.

"Let's just head out?" I walk away so she can't see my rage.

If Pam turns out to be a sweetie pie I'm going to seem like a terrible person, but I watch a pathological amount of serial killer documentaries, so I'm confident.

Kayla *does* film us and Pam's attention wanders to the camera, like she's addressing the audience. "Hey, Bangers! It's me, Pam. Josh is here to help rescue me from werewolf island. Unlike Tyler, I *know* cryptids are real. Because I am one. So whelmed to be here!" She grins, then turns to me. "Was that good?"

"Yeah, great job, Pam," I say. Pissing her off seems like a bad idea. "Soon you'll be canon."

Her cheeks beam a brilliant red and she tucks a loose strand of hair behind her ear. "I've never been on TV before."

"You're a natural," says Kayla.

As we're heading down the road, Pam suddenly turns and smiles at us. "Why don't we split up—I have to feed my cat. She's on these timed pills that—"

Kayla cuts her off. "Cool! Where and what time?"

Pam's smile is tight. "Okay, then. You won't be long, right? How about an hour? My place?"

Every second of every acting class I took is replaying in my head, every role and every warm-up exercise. "Gee, Pam. Sounds perfect for me. Um, as long as you'll be safe on your own?"

"Yeah," Kayla adds. "Are you sure you don't want Josh to come with you at least?"

Please say no, please say no, please say no. I'm not going *anywhere* on this island without Kayla.

Pam's face looks heavy. Then she snaps back, twists her ponytail around her finger. She reaches for a little cross at her neck. "I can take care of myself. Promise. How about two hours instead, that way if you get lost, you have time to find me."

Actually, that is a good point. We have no idea how to get around the island. "Do you have a map?"

"Mmm. No, sorry. You got something to write on?"

Kayla hands her a notepad and she draws a simple map. There's nothing on it but her house and the road names. She *really* doesn't want us exploring.

My heart thumps the whole time Pam's leaving, and me and Kayla watch her until she disappears. We turn and look at each other.

"She's . . . ." I start.

"Yeah," says Kayla.

On the way to White Sails Cabins and Resort, I explain werewolf science to Kayla.

"Can we believe her?" Kayla asks.

As we approach the resort, a parked motorcycle comes into view. I slow, recalling the e-mail's characterization of Tia and Nor as "bicker girls." Unless there's a larger werewolf motorcyclist contingent, one of them is inside the cabins.

"Don't know," I say to Kayla. "Maybe? Pam wants us to help her get off the island, and Conrad seemed reluctant to confirm or deny her claims, which is a point in her favour. But it *could* be a double-bluff."

"Lazaria said we couldn't trust her," Kayla reminds me. "She said Pam's aura's black."

Gravel crunches beneath my feet as we step onto the grounds of White Sails. "Doesn't black also mean protection?"

Kayla snorts. "In this case, it means we need protection *from*."

THE ERSTWHILE TYLER KYLE

The door to what's clearly the registry office opens and a Black woman in leather walks out.

Me and Kayla back away.

The woman holds her hands up, palms out. A set of keys jangles in her fingers. "You're John and Kayla, aren't you? You're looking for Tyler?"

I stop, motioning for Kayla to stop with me. "Josh and Kayla. How do you know that?"

The woman snickers. "Small island, and word travels fast. I'm Tia. I figured you'd come here." She pauses, and her expression melts to something more human. "I think Tyler's in real trouble. At first I thought he'd just, you know, fucked off?" She shrugs, flicking chipped polish off her nails. "But I dreamed about him. About five days ago. Someone was hurting him. So I looked around, but turned out no one'd seen him since the night I did."

A dream about Ty. Then the second thing settles like a stone in my belly: someone hurting him.

"We know about the werewolves," I open. "So, no bullshit, all right? Pam told us everything."

Tia shoves her hands in her pockets. "Are you *filming* this?"

Kayla lowers the camera. "You got a problem with that?"

She kicks some rocks. "Fuck it." She walks to her bike and beckons us over. "Roll the cameras if you want. I'm tired of keeping Connie's secrets and watching people I care about die."

I follow slowly. "People like Tyler?"

She glances at me. "I really hope not, but there's stuff you should see. He left his suitcase back at The Thunder Moon. And the last time I saw him he was all beat up. Like, *real bad*. I tried to help him, but he ran away."

Conrad showed us that footage, only the camera was too high up to see any detail. Her story at least fits available evidence. "He called me from the island. He said you and Nor and Gene were up to something. That you were filming him in his cabin."

Tia rubs her arm. "Nor is . . . Nor's gone."

The pain in her voice is impossible to misinterpret: grief over a lost loved one. "I'm sorry." I pause, thinking about what Pam said. "Dead gone, or werewolf gone?" I trot my fingers like they're walking toward the forest.

"The second," Tia hangs her head back, leaning against her bike. "Me and Tyler found these cameras in his cabin, so he moved all his stuff to my friend Gene's bar. He left us downstairs to get a shower and accidentally saw Gene feeding—"

"His cocaine habit?" I offer.

"Oh my god you're just like Tyler," says Tia, in a voice that suggests long hours of suffering.

"Yeah, I know," Kayla commiserates.

I should probably be insulted for both of us. "*Hey*. But also fair. Anyway, you were saying Gene was feeding what?"

Tia shoots me an under-the-eyebrows look. "He was illegally holding his husband who, uh, turned for good. He was keeping him in his basement and feeding him guts and shit."

What does *legally* doing that look like? "So Ty saw that, and . . . ?"

"He jumped out the window and hit Gene with a plank. He thought we were the stalker who lured you guys to the island. He thought *you* were here too, because of an e-mail he got saying you were coming."

I share a look with Kayla and the camera. "I *never* sent an e-mail," I tell the viewers. I turn back to Tia. "We're the ones who got e-mails telling us to come here."

Tia shakes her head. "*No way*. Keeping you away from here was literally all he talked about. Someone's got him for sure." She stares into the distance, toward the woods. "My dream—did Pam tell you about the dreams?"

I nod. "You share them, right?"

"Bingo." She shivers, but it's sweltering out. "Let's walk and talk, okay? It's not far to The Moon, and we don't have long before sundown. And I think, after what I saw, Tyler may not have that long."

We follow, and only two seconds into the walk I could strangle Tia for not coming out and saying what she saw. I'm a big boy; I can take it.

Tia pulls out a cigarette and lights it.

She offers me one and I wave it off. "Thanks but no thanks on the cancer."

She rolls her eyes. "I dreamed about someone hurting him, like I said. He was in this dark basement, but most of the buildings around here don't have basements. He looked *wrong*, all crumpled up like dead bugs get." She puffs her cigarette several times in quick succession. "He didn't look right."

"What does *not right* mean?" I'm trying not to scream.

"Like . . . skeletal. Dried out. Like he was dead—fuck, *I don't know* it wasn't my dream. But he wasn't dead, 'cause someone kicked him and he moved. His face was covered in blood." Tia turns to us, glances warily at the camera as if it might bite her. "I went looking."

"Did you look at Pam?" I snap.

Tia breaks our gaze. "Yeah. After he showed up all," she waves her hand over her face, "*bruised.* He was hanging with her pretty exclusively after the incident with Gene. I never thought Pam would do something like that—she's so chill. She was always a loner, but she gets people stuff off the island all the time, stuff Connie won't bring in for us." She raises her cigarette as an example. "She makes a lot of money that way."

"Money for fancy cameras?" I ask.

Tia shrugs. "Maybe. I thought she spent it all on nerd stuff. I went to her house once and her walls are covered with Robin and this green chick called Arrow Girl. She writes bad stories about them."

I stop. Kayla bumps into me, whacking the back of my head with the camera. "Artemis. *Artemisia Grayson.*" I twist round, grab Kayla by the shoulders and shake. "She's my nemesis, Kay."

And she's going to fucking kill Tyler. She's going to kill Tyler so Josh Likens of Discovery Bang semi-fame can marry his new co-host, a beautiful blonde Artemisia calls Brenda (Bren for short, Bren-Bren to ficJosh).

"Quick, Kayla, what happens in Bren's stories?" I give her another shake.

"Who's Bren?" asks Tia.

Kayla bites her lip. "I mostly don't read them, Josh. Sorry. It's not healthy that *you* do."

I wave her concern away. "Forget health. Bren and Josh help each other look for Tyler, or try to save Tyler—"

"Who's *Bren*?" Tia asks again.

"—and they find Tyler dead. Or they find him alive but they're too late. But Pam can't let him live, because he *knows* it was her. And I'd never date Bren if I knew Bren was Jeffrey Dahmer."

"*Who are all these people*?" Tia yells.

Kayla points her camera down, holds up her hands. "Okay. *So*. Pam is a fanfiction writer who writes self-insert fanfic about Discovery Bang, and her self insert character is called Brenda, who in the stories gets with Josh, but only after Tyler tragically dies so she can comfort Josh about it, except in *real life*, Josh is secretly a fanfic writer *too*, and he's in a feud with Pam—who writes under the pseud Artemisia Grayson—where he writes stories about Tyler railing—"

I hold my hand over Kay's face. "That's enough. Point is, Pam is evil. She's psychotic. She's a demon. We have to kill her."

Tia holds up her hands. "Whoa—*kill*?"

"If I have to. I can't promise what these hands will do when I see her again." I grit my teeth. "We have to look for her. Fuck The Moon."

Kayla grabs my shoulder and stops me. "Calm down, Josh. Let's check out Ty's stuff first, okay? We have literally no idea where Pam is, but Tyler could've left clues with his stuff."

I try not to look at her, because I know what she's do-ing—she's trying to snag me with her soulful brown eyes, like

Ty does. I don't want to be snagged. I want to smash Pam's face into the pavement.

"*Josh*." Kayla's done it. She's snagged me. "We can't run around like a crazy person jumping in people's gardens like Ty did. That's what gets you kidnapped by internet creepers."

Tia snorts.

"Fine." I grimace, imagining I'm stabbing Pam, because if my imagination's stabbing Pam, it's not finding Tyler cut up in pieces and put in little gift-wrapped boxes under a Christmas tree (Artemisia's holiday special), or hidden inside hollow chocolate bunnies (the Easter special), or cut to ribbons by shamrock shuriken (the St. Patrick's Day extravaganza/ninja leprechaun crossover).

We walk in silence most of the way to The Thunder Moon, which turns out to be a dive—the fun kind of dive, if my fear hadn't coated me in a layer of sweat thick enough to drown in and my heart wasn't torn up at my feet.

Tyler's suitcase is leaning against a wall. I run to it, unzip it, then collapse to the floor, rifling through his boring-ass clothes looking for clues. I find his laptop and hand it to Kay. There's a brochure for the island, as well as a folded photograph of a pregnant couple with 1976 written on the back.

While I'm on my knees, a fat ginger steps up to the bar from behind a door. "You must be Josh."

I don't even look up. "Yeah hi."

He chuckles. Glasses clink. "And you little miss?"

"Kayla Hernandez. I'm the camera girl."

There's fucking nothing in the bag. *Nothing*. TYLER WHY DO YOU HATE ME. I hurl one of his shirts at a stool.

I look up at a meaty hand placing a tall beer on the bar.

"You need a cold one," says Gene.

"Did Tyler give you a blow job in exchange for a coffee?" I wail at him.

Gene's already ruddy complexion turns the colour of the communist manifesto. "Uh uh." He averts his gaze. "Those are a dollar."

Tia chuckles. "Gene's a *cheap* whore."

"I meant the coffee, Tee." Gene turns his back on us, muttering as he pretends to fix the menu hanging behind him.

"Umbrella" but sung by a man comes on the bar speakers.

I hug my knees.

Kayla kneels beside me. "Josh, it's okay." She puts her arms around me and squeezes.

I look up at her, tears brimming at my eyes, nose running. I feel ridiculous. "It's not okay. He should be here and he's not. He's fucking dead and I wasn't with him."

A new song starts and Kay walks me to a barstool. Gene slides my beer toward me.

"On the house." He smiles warmly. "I see why he likes you."

I'm disgusting and covered in mucus. "I wish I did."

"Ironic" continues to play in the background, and only after several seconds do I recognize the vocalist. It's Ty, singing his fucking heart out. The audio *zings* through me. It's magic, it's electric. It's werewolf fucking science. "Ty recorded a song here?"

Gene's all smiles. Kayla sits down beside me and Tia shimmies behind the bar. She hip-bumps Gene out of the way and pours another couple beers. She slides one over to Kayla.

"Oh, no. I don't drink," Kayla says. "B-but thank you."

I've never heard Kay stutter before. It forces a smile out of me.

"No, I'm sorry, I shouldn't have assumed," Tia stumbles. "More for me, right?"

Gene steals the second beer before Tia can. We toast, all four of us, and I think back on what Ty said at that bus stop as I down my first sip. I think about the fact that I'm not going to let this be some dumb fucking moment where I reflect on all he's meant to me and how he brought all four of us together so I can move on. Josh Likens doesn't move on. He digs in his heels, pulls up his anxiety bootstraps, and forces himself to keep performing a task well past the threshold of sunk fallacies.

I chug the beer.

"Tyler sung a ton of songs the night of Queen Cee's concert." Gene shoves his thumb behind him. "Wanna see the tapes?"

4

TAPES

Gene sets up a projector and we watch the footage from a table. Ty's on stage at The Moon: magnetic, vital. I haven't seen him come alive like that since before Discovery Bang. He looks the way he did in university, the way he looked when I fell in lust with a man I'd never spoken to, before falling in love with him when I discovered he wasn't anything like his performance but a whole different kind of special. He sings like I haven't given him time to for too many years. Kayla probably didn't mean to be right, but she was: I killed Tyler Kyle's big bright career the moment I asked him to be my stupid sidekick on my stupid channel.

It's terribly hard and horribly easy, but I tear my gaze from the film and stare into my beer. I swish it round in the glass.

On screen, the crowd cramped into The Moon screams with delight, with desire, with need. It's not natural, but I understand it completely. Whatever these Nightingale powers are, they're working on me too.

"He skips all the love songs. The tune starts playing and he skips them." I want to ask why, but Kay and I both know the answer.

He skips them all, till he gets really out of it, and then he sings whatever comes along, gripped by the tide of the music. When he starts on "Magnet and Steel," it's like he's singing to me.

"Turn it off." I stand up and push my chair away from the table.

"Are you okay?" Kayla asks.

"No." I suck back a breath. "We're not learning anything here. Blah blah blah, Ty's good at singing and the island loves him."

The sound cuts off and I hear the other chairs scraping behind me as everyone gets up.

"Conrad played his songs *constantly* on the alert system during the parade," says Tia. "I almost shot *myself*. Hypnosis only goes so far."

"Alert system?" Kayla asks.

Gene burps. "You seen those speakers 'round town? Back in the old days the founders used them to send alerts or play Nightingale audio for their experiments. Conrad uses them for all kinds of things now—mostly music."

"To stop us changing," Tia adds. "They know we're werewolves."

Gene sighs. "Now who's breaking Connie's rules? Tee, you *know* better than that."

"It wasn't *me*," says Tia, "It was fucking Pam. And Pam kidnapped Tyler apparently. She's hiding him somewhere. You remember that dream I told you about?"

I'm staring at Ty's suitcase as their words tumble around me. There's a picture of Tyler on the wall, blown-up from one of our episodes. There's writing on it—the impression of words when the lighting hits it. "Hey, Gene. Where'd you get that?"

"Oh, uh. Tyler had it with him. I asked if he'd sign it." I can hear the grin in his voice as I walk toward it and unhook it. "The Echo Island hall of fame."

I trace my finger over the impressions in the print. They're letters all right. "Paper and pencil, Kay?"

She unzips one of our bags and pulls out the necessary equipment. "There's a message?"

I sink into the booth in front of the window and start scribbling graphite over the paper on top of the print.

"It's an e-mail from Ty." I swallow. "And this one's real."

I'm leaving the island ASAP. ~~DO NOT COME.~~
*Don't come. The mayor is a crazy cult leader who's
convinced the townspeople they can't leave or they'll
die.* ~~There's a weird hatch and animatronics in the
woods and~~ *I'm getting off the island and going to
the cops but I need to know you won't come. There's
no monsters. It's not Big Foot or vampires or the
chupacabra. It's just evil weird humans and they
will kill you. There's no internet or phones, so a
pilot named Pam is sending this for me. I've cc'ed
Kayla so listen to her please when she tells you NOT
TO COME. Remember, she's smarter than you.*

- Ty

P. S. You taste like lime.

You taste like lime.

I hold the paper up to Kayla. "It's the e-mail Ty wanted Pam
to send us. He gave her his password. He gave her our e-mails.
She did it, Kay, she one hundred percent did it."

Kayla takes it from me. She snorts. "I *am* smarter. Thanks,
Ty."

"Is that really important?" I ask.

"It is to me. And hey, Josh? While I'm being smarter than
you, you see where he mentions a hatch?"

Gene walks over and stabs his finger at the print. "The hatch
is near the old lab, but it's a maze in there—you'll have a hard
time finding anything. Is that like something you two would've
investigated?"

Fuck yes. "One hundred fucking percent, man. Does it have a
basement?"

Kayla locks eyes with me. She's grinning. "And does it have speakers?"

5

THE ECHO ISLAND DIARY

We don't want Pam to freak out, so we walk to her house alone while Tia and Gene head for the woods.

According to Gene, no one's been able to open Babel since before Ty's mom left. Conrad used to have access, but someone changed the palm reader so it wouldn't recognize him. It's one reason no one's been able to do more research on werewolf science.

No one but Pam.

It's been over two hours. The sun bakes our backs as we head up the road, but it's starting to set.

Tia warned us wolfing hour was around sundown. We don't want to be caught with Pam when that happens. Even if she wants me alive, Tia told us, they can't control themselves most of the time. She could kill me without even meaning to.

Pam's waiting for us on her step. She leaps to her feet.

I force a grin and wave. "Hey, sorry we're late. We got lost. I'm terrible at maps."

She cracks open her door. "Come in. I found some stuff while I was waiting. Ty left all these blueprints for the lab in the woods inside his journal."

Shit. If Pam's directing us to the lab, it could mean a lot of really bad things.

"Awesome," I say. "Let's go there."

"Hold on," says Pam. "No one's been inside for decades. We'll have to see if Conrad can help us. And I've got this old map of Tyler's, and his mom's journal. We could decode it together."

Tyler can't wait for us to play this stupid game, but I follow Pam inside. Her house is . . . normal? But serial killer lairs usually are. It's the basements you have to worry about, and Pam's got a whole underground lab as hers.

Snacks in bowls cover a coffee table in front of Pam's couch, accompanied by two glasses of wine. Craft supplies, including a massive poster-board, lean against the wall.

Pam pats the couch. "Sit. Relax. I've got the Echo Island Diary here for you ready. I thought we could make a conspiracy board?"

It's cute that she thinks her laughably simple murder plot requires a whole board to unravel. Lazaria had her sussed in ten minutes.

Pam grins, looking only at me. Kayla's right: it's like she's not even here.

I hesitate. Pam wants me to read the diary. From the massive stack of glued-together construction paper sitting in front of her, she spent a lot of time on it.

"Sure." I sit beside her and my ass sinks into well-loved cushions. Did she fuck Ty on this couch?

I'm sure she can see all my hairs standing on end, can hear the hitch in my breathing, can read my mind as it tells me to *run*. But all she does is bite her lip and smile, fucking me with her eyes. I glance past her, hoping she'll interpret it as shyness, but my gaze settles on a Steven Yeun poster—the actor fans constantly tell me I look like.

I wriggle my upper lip into something that's intended as a smile. From where I sit, it feels more like a Frankenstein impression.

Pam nudges a plate toward me. It's some kind of braised meat with fancy leaves on top. "Tongue? It's leftovers, but I fancied it up for you."

I rub my belly. "Watching my figure."

"Hmm." Pam stares at me. I can see her digesting my jawline, my lips, my throat. "You're handsome." She strokes my arm. "Have you ever modeled?"

I tense under her touch. "Too short, you know?"

Kayla's in the kitchen. I try to watch her instead of Pam, but the way Pam's probing my bicep with her thumb is making that very difficult, and not in a sexy way.

Kayla holds up a book she's uncovered on Pam's kitchen counter. "You like to read?"

Pam grips my arm a little hard. It's better than being stroked. "*Exquisite Corpse.* It's my favourite." She squints at Kayla, then me. "Where's all your gear? Your camera and stuff? I thought you'd want to film this?"

"We left it at White Sails," I blurt. "It was too heavy lugging all that around."

Pam tilts her head, beams. "It *so* was, wasn't it?" She bats her lashes. SHE BATS. HER LASHES. "SO, you're Christian, right?" She fingers her cross. "I can't believe we have that in common—it's pretty rare out here. Actually, I'm the only one."

"Like a unicorn," says Kay from the kitchen. She leafs through the book.

"Ty made fun of me the whole time," Pam says, soft, like she's sad, ignoring Kayla completely, which is for the best because Kayla's not good at pretending. "I thought I must be stupid, or a fool, just for believing in something. Am I a fool, Josh? For believing?"

This is a *key* moment in every Brosh (Brenda x Josh) fic, except usually it's ficJosh who makes the confession: boohoo, I'm so sad Tyler makes fun of me, what a dick, did he ever really care? And then Brenda breaks in to tell him how *she* believes him, and they make out next to Tyler's severed head, or hand, or melting, acid-covered sludge-corpse.

"Of course not." I take her hand, like I do in her fics. I gaze into her eyes. "I'm sorry Ty hurt you. He probably didn't mean it. He doesn't mean it when he makes cracks at me."

Pam cups the side of my face, her brow furrowed with deep concern. "Oh, Josh. It's okay, honey. You can be honest with me. He hurt you with those *mean* words. It's time to let it all go."

I'm not going to burst into the song from *Frozen*, but Artemisia does occasionally include the lyrics.

"You're so sweet—" I stop myself from calling her Brenda just in time. "Honey. Gosh, did I say that?" *Teehee*. I want to stick my head in a blender. Pam can't really be buying this Stepford boyfriend act.

But her face looks tragically sincere. If she wasn't basically Satan, I'd feel bad.

I pull away to spy on what Kayla's doing. She's still skimming Pam's book. Her eyes widen.

I bend over the hideous fake journal Pam's set on the table. "Let's do some digging. You must really want Tyler back."

Pam twists her hair around her finger. "He was my first, you know? I wonder if I was his."

Across the kitchen, Kayla cackles. "Oh my god."

Kayla. Really?

"Something funny?" Pam snaps.

I turn the cover of the Echo Island Diary (a title I'm supposed to believe Ty cut into bubble letters and bejazzled with gold glitter). The inside is a mess of hot glue, more glitter, impossible-to-read handwriting, and poorly inserted spelling mistakes that I'm guessing are representative of Ty's "dyslexia." The messy handwriting is the same as on Pam's map. It's like she doesn't even care how obvious she is, or like she thought it was impossible for us to catch her.

Kayla holds up *Exquisite Corpse*. "Just laughing at the book. Also Ty's a slut, but mostly it was the book." She pauses. "It seems kind of dark for you. What do you like about it?"

Pam watches my fingers as I flip the pages, like I'm skimming too fast through her life's work. I slow down. When I dart a look at Kayla, she quickly holds up a second book—*A Case of Conscience*. It's the book from the video.

"I like murder books where the killers have a moral imperative," Pam explains. "People learn, like, a valuable lesson."

"As they get sawed in half," Kayla adds.

Pam grins. "Exactly. Like the *Saw* movies, or *Se7en*."

She thinks that's what *Se7en* was about? We did not watch the same movie.

I shrug. "I don't know. I read *Exquisite Corpse* when I was thirteen, and even then I thought it was edgy teenage fanwank." Probably shouldn't have said that.

Pam adjusts herself on the couch. "Yeah," she says, voice high and pinched. "Agree to disagree." She points at the journal, where "Ty" has written a screed about how much he wants to fuck Pam. I sense I'm being baited, but I scan the page. It starts off reasonably normal, for the journal entry of a stalker. Then she brings in a whole lot of Greek mythology BS. It gets violent.

My throat knots into a ball. Kayla needs to hear this so when we're alone again she can tell me I'm imagining things, that what's written on the page isn't Pam's fucked-up fantasy about Tyler.

"I want to wrap razor wire round her neck and pull and pull and pull till it slices right through and his pretty head," I hesitate. *His* head. Ty's pretty head. I clear my throat. " . . . comes off. And then I want to bury it and watch it rot and take it out to look at; watch the worms impregnate his eyes until they finally burst and his ichor runs out like punctured egg yolks and I can drink it up and see what she sees and dream what she dreams. Her liquefying body will taste like Josh."

Pam runs her finger over the page. "It's about me. It's terrifying, knowing he wanted to hurt me like that. Knowing he could have done it at any time and I wouldn't have seen it coming. I'm such a stupid little ditz."

"He switched pronouns," says Kayla. "Did you notice?"

"Huh," says Pam. "I guess he was talking about you at the end there. *So gross*, right?"

I feel dirty touching the diary, but I flip to the next entry. The room is deathly still suddenly. Does Pam suspect us? We were so careful. I'm playing the good boy like she wants. I need to take it easy, but something's off in a way it wasn't when I first sat down.

It's there in the next entry. Pam describes Ty and Tia tossing his room at White Sails. When they leave, she mentions cameras at The Moon, cameras on the roads. Pam's completely plugged in. She's probably heard every word we've spoken since we separated at Tia's house.

"What's the matter, Josh? Aren't you going to read that one to Kayla?" Pam's voice is a controlled purr. She touches my hair and her fingers are so soft I barely feel them.

This is it. The end. "Kayla, run."

Pam pins my neck to the couch and I gasp. I grab her cross and twist it. The necklace breaks off in my hands. I'm seeing stars. She's going to crack my neck. I punch her and her head whips back, but she doesn't let go.

"You like that?" Pam's grinning. Her mouth is blood red, but it's just lipstick. Just lipstick. "Ty liked it. He came inside me with my hand around his throat and a pillow over his eyes." She climbs on top of me. "I rode him like this. Is that how you wanted to do it? Tell me all the details, *Mr. Pornstar*. I want to know how to pose you when I stuff your corpse and shove it in a hole with his."

Ty. Dead. Ty's dead.

I grab her earring and yank it through her lobe. She screeches, blood dripping onto her shoulder. She lets go briefly, but then she slams her fist into my jaw. It's like being hit by a sackful of bricks.

She clucks. "You were supposed to stay pretty." She laughs. "But pretty's relative." She wraps her hands around my throat again and squeezes. "You want to know how Tyler died? Down a deep dark well, with nothing to eat and nothing to drink, and an e-mail from Josh Likens calling him a fucking fag."

Someone pulls Pam off me.

Kayla. No.

I gasp for breath, reaching toward Pam and Kayla, but the world is blurry and I can't move. I watch, helpless, as Pam elbows Kayla in the shoulder.

"Breeder bitch," Pam spits. She faces Kayla, grabs her hair, ready to slam her face through the glass top of the coffee table.

I try to throw myself between Kay and the glass, but pain shoots along my jaw and I fall short of the table, looking up at them helplessly.

In her left hand, Kayla's holding her purple purse with the moons and stars. She pulls out the Auralite-23, pulls her arm waaaay back, and—"I'M A BISEXUAL," Kayla screams.

Crack. The Auralite-23 brains Pam in the side of her head. She thuds onto the carpet, convulsing.

Kayla pants over the body as blood spurts from the gory head wound into the carpet. Pam's perfect ponytail is dyed a sickly red. Her eye is mush, partially popped out of its socket. Kayla's own hair is a bird's nest, and there's a clump missing that I'm sure is clutched in Pam's hand.

Kayla roars, guttural, at what I pray to God is Pam's dead body.

Then she throws up on Pam's face. She heaves, clutching her knees, mouth fixed in a grimace. She grabs a napkin from between the chip bowls and cleans off.

"I told you to run." I rub my throat—it hurts, but already the pain is dimming.

She shrugs, staring into space. "If you die, who's going to pay me? I have student loans."

I stand up and Kayla hurries to support me. I wave her off. "I'm okay. But we need to get to the lab. Tyler's . . . ."

Kayla gives my shoulder a comforting squeeze. She kicks Pam with her foot. "Gene and Tia said we needed a palm for the palm reader."

Aw, shit.

6

FROM NOW UNTIL THE END

I don't recommend severing a dead woman's hand as an employee bonding activity, but as far as dismemberments go, I don't feel as guilty as I expected. Mom and Dad wouldn't like it, but Mom and Dad believe a Jewish-Muslim coalition is responsible for a global conspiracy to ruin Alberta's economy, so maybe who cares what they think.

I wipe the sweat off my forehead, smearing blood across my skin.

Kayla pops Pam's hand into her drawstring purse.

Conrad's limo is parked outside. He's alone this time, and he leans against his car, assessing us as we leave.

I glance at my bloody white t-shirt, at Kay's splattered face.

"Now where would you be going this late at night, Mr. Likens? Ms. Hernandez?" He arches his eyebrow. "Don't you know it's dangerous in the dark?"

I grab his cowboy hat and *go*. "Kayla, run!!!!" I call back, already ten feet away. I squash the hat onto my head.

"*Josh, I'm shorter than you,*" Kayla yells back, but her feet pad along behind mine and I'm laughing. I'm sucking back air. I'm winning. We're going to win this.

The river stops us. Kayla slams to a halt beside me. I look behind us, but Conrad didn't follow.

Kayla grips her knees. "You have your phone?"

"Would I forget it? Original flavour Josh Likens is back in action." I grin and slap Kayla's back. I feel high.

"What does that even mean?"

"No idea." But Tyler would love it. I stare at the woods. They're dark and foreboding, and I know I'd be lucky to meet something half as friendly as a bear in these trees, but Ty's in there. So I'm going too. It's how we roll.

We wade across the river with minimal screams and only one visit from a concerned lesbian, and then it's the woods.

My favourite place.

The woods grow thick before thinning out again, revealing a small grove. Piñatas hang from the trees. "Hey weird." I flash my light over the decorations.

They're skeletons.

"Holy shit. Kay, this place is cursed."

Kayla hangs back, but it's too late for me—I'm already halfway into the glade. I dash the rest of the way, trying to let as little of my feet as possible touch the haunted moss underfoot. "I'm going to need a cleansing ritual later."

There's something ahead of us in the woods. A twig snaps and I freeze.

"Tia?" Kayla calls out. "Gene? We're alone, it's okay."

Two lights flash ahead of us and Gene calls out.

I wave my phone. "If we *witness* an actual cryptid tonight, and we don't catch definitive proof, I'm going to kill someone. It'll probably be Ty."

A branch scratches my skin and I yelp. I feel Pam's nails digging into my neck, hear her taunts in my ears. She left Tyler to die of thirst. It's been two weeks.

I swallow a sob and speed up—oh who am I kidding? I start crying, silently.

Kayla grabs my hand.

We reach Tia and Gene, who are standing outside a plain concrete building. "We have to hurry. She left him in there to die."

Tia frowns, lit from the side by her torch. "How're we getting in?"

Kayla triumphantly pulls a bleeding hand from her purse. "Presto magico." She presses it against the palm reader and the door slides open.

We're through.

"Welcome, Artemisia Likens," says a computerized voice from invisible speakers. Electric lights flicker on.

Everyone's polite enough to keep quiet about the name.

"It's getting late." Gene nods at the door as we approach a bloodstained ladder. "I have to head back—I change early some nights. I'll stick myself in Ru's tunnel just in case." He cocks his head at Tia. "Come on, Tee."

Tia faces us, worried. "Bring him back, okay? And if you hear strange sounds in the woods, lock yourselves in here. And don't look in their eyes. That's how they get you."

I swallow. I can't think about the werewolf-infested forest now. "Promise."

At the bottom of the ladder fake daylight shines blindingly from windows, glancing off the metal handles of the doors lining the opposite wall. Only one is open. I pummel the closed ones as me and Kay call Ty's name.

There's a gun on the floor. I pick it up—it's empty.

As I'm laying it down, Kayla turns to me. "Gene said this place was a maze. Did you get those blueprints Pam had?"

Shit, that would have been smart. "Nope. That's the kind of thinking I rely on you and Ty for."

"The kind that uses your brain?"

We continue down the hallway, leaving fist-shaped stains in Pam's blood on each door. With every echoing silence that greets us, my heart plunges into a new abyss. In one of the rooms, a browned, desiccated corpse with a missing hand is crouched in a corner, its face frozen in a scream.

For a second, I think it's Tyler. But it's too old. It can't be.

Ty's dead. He's dead. He's dead. He died down here five days ago, alone, hungry, thinking you hated him.

I shake my head. I try to think the way Tyler would: Pam lied about so much. She was a twisted creep and she wanted me to suffer. She probably made up the e-mail. She might have made up that Tyler was dead.

Nightingale Project is painted on the wall. Kayla rattles the door but this one's locked too.

"We have to break in," I say.

Kay grabs me, drags me to a door marked *stairs*. "Josh, think about it. Pam had no reason to think anyone would come after her. Why would she lock a door she needed to use?" She pushes the stairwell door. It bobs open. "See? And we need the control room, for the sound and the cameras. It's the fastest way."

I follow her through. She starts down, but I stop. "Wouldn't an alert system be near the surface?"

Kayla marches back up after me. The stairs end on the next level. There's one door: Communications Room.

I slam my full weight against it, expecting it to be closed, but it swings open wildly. The room's filled with surveillance screens and audio equipment. Most of the cameras are pitch-black. I start hitting buttons, holding my breath as screens flicker to life.

Bodies fill so many of them: bodies in cages, bodies huddled in corners, dismembered bodies strewn across brown and red-stained floors.

Kayla's messing with the audio controls. She holds out her hand. "Phone?" she says, like she's asking for a scalpel.

I scroll to the track we agreed on earlier, then hand the device to Kayla.

Click. Click. Click. I cycle through endless footage of crumpled, unmoving bodies. How many people did Conrad and Virginia kill?

The glow of the screens slicks over a glossy image to my left. I make the mistake of looking.

At least fifteen photographs are tacked to the wall. Most of them were taken from above a hole in the floor, showing Tyler below. Some are close-ups. He looks like he's sleeping or dead, his face swollen in some, bloody, then thin. So thin. Skin stretched over bone.

A machine clicks to my right as Kayla connects my phone to the audio system.

The first notes of "The Ecstasy of Gold" hum from the speakers in the control room.

I have to watch the cameras. I click through, but nothing's moving. My eyes are drawn to the photos, the ones where Ty is dead. He looks fucking dead as shit.

"Turn it up, Kay."

Kayla flicks more switches, hits the volume. It's deafening in the small room. "It's playing all over the island. If he doesn't hear this, he's not going to."

We hold our hands over our ears.

And I pray.

Dear God, if you make this not be real, if you make this not happen, then I'll try harder not to be . . . .

"THERE!" Kayla stabs one of the screens as it's changing, and I flash it back.

At first I don't see anything. The room's lit only by a spotlight shining from above. There's something small turning over on the floor, just inside the light's range.

A shoe.

"WHERE IS IT?" I check the corner of the image for a floor number, and I'm *gone*. I swing round the banister, nearly tripping. The *thud* of my sneakers on the floor reverberates up my leg.

Drums rumble from the speakers, so loud my head swims. The floors spin beneath me, an Escher drawing. There can't be as many levels as it seems.

I ram through the door with my shoulder and tumble into a green hallway. The wallpaper's peeling, and beneath the eerie glow of orange floodlights, it's like the wall is melting. Crucifixes cover the walls—I want to think they're on my side (I prayed, didn't I?), but my heart's in limbo, and that's not where you want to be.

I shove open door after door. Most of them are offices or small quarters with bunks against the walls. Some of the bunks have chains and collars attached to them.

"Ty!" I have to scream to compete with the swell of the music. I open doors, call his name, wait, pull the next door. One of them opens into a big white room. No one answers me, but as I turn to leave I hear a dim thud beneath the rumble of the strings and the wailing soprano. A thud, and a scrape.

"I'm coming!" Corpses trapped in metal cages line the walls, but I run past them and into the next hallway. Ty's not with them. He's not with them, because he's not dead. He's not dead, because I say so.

I follow the steady thumps.

I stop.

At the end of the hallway are two hand-painted words: "The Hole" and a downward-pointing arrow. A spotlight shines from above. There's a rope ladder and a chair sitting next to the hole along with a basket of liquefying fruit.

I throw the rope over the edge.

7

THE BODY

"Ty?" It's impossible to see while under the spotlight.

As I reach the last few rungs I leap onto the floor. It smells of death.

There's something black and rectangular—a phone case—tied with strips of shirt, and a shoe and—someone in the shadows is flinging it, so it scrapes the floor.

"Ty?" I swallow my fear and walk toward it.

But the thing in the corner doesn't look like Ty. The swelling in Pam's photos has gone down, but it's not Ty. Is it Ty? Its eye is shut, and that looks bad. It's more skeleton than body. It could be anyone. It's anyone but Tyler. I don't recognize Tyler in that face. Its hair is limp and dirty and the colour's impossible to discern.

"Ty." I want him to say something, but he doesn't. He looks at me. He blinks his one eye, and it's like he doesn't quite see me.

I kneel beside him and pull his shirt from hands that are more like claws. I hold him gently, and he drapes his arms over my shoulder and lays his head flat against my back like it's too heavy to hold upright.

The bells thunder around us as the music plays, and I tie him to my back as tight as I dare. He shouldn't be so easy to carry.

I wish he'd talk, but he needs water. His throat must be raw.

I take one rung, another. I go slow. Are you supposed to give a dehydrated person water right away? Will he puke it up? Would that kill him? It looks like breathing should kill him.

"I've got you, Ty." My voice cracks as my vision clouds with tears. I try to steady myself, but my shoulders only heave more. I wish I were strong enough not to cry. I should be comforting him, but I'm the one who's breaking. "Me and Kay. We're here. Pam's dead and we're going home. Everything's going to be fine."

His grip on my shoulder tightens.

I pull us onto the floor above the hole, sitting on hands and knees. Kayla's racing toward us.

"We have to hurry," she rasps between ragged breaths. "It'll be dark soon." She stops four feet away, staring at Ty like she's trying to discern if I'm carrying his corpse.

"He needs water. Food too, but water first," I say. "And electrolytes, right? Like Gatorade." I remember that from some survival show.

Kayla nods. "There's a sink back there. Talk to him, try to keep him conscious."

If the music doesn't do that on its own, it's probably too late, but I talk anyway, more for me than him. Now that I'm here, now that I've got him, I'm not sure everything will be okay. He doesn't look like someone who can be fixed.

"You missed so much about the island," I tell him. "The fact that everyone's werewolves is a pretty big deal. How did you not catch King Lycaon?"

His hand moves, and for an instant, my heart moves with it, because it felt like a slide and not a deliberate motion. But then he drags it back into place. He clasps his hands over my chest, around my neck.

"King Lycaon was this Greek king who tried to trick Zeus into eating human meat, so Zeus cursed him with lycanthropy—it's where the name comes from. But not all werewolves are bad. Tia and Gene helped me find you. Tia was worried—she had a dream about you and everything. Not a sex dream, a regular dream."

We stop at the sink. Kayla runs the tap. It sputters and glugs, but clear water pours out. It looks safe.

Tyler perks up, reaching, and I stop him. He's got to be way out of it. So out of it he hasn't even argued with me yet.

Kayla quickly searches the room, finds a clean beaker in a cabinet. She fills it a little. Ty practically snatches it from her, but she pulls back. "Slow, okay? I'm the smart one, remember?"

Ty chokes on the water. He spits it over my bloody shirt, adding more red.

Don't think about that.

Kayla fills the beaker again and holds it to his lips. This time he keeps it down. She fills it again, but she doesn't give it to him. "We should go. We can get more at The Moon."

Tyler spasms against my back. A broken scream rips out of him. I kneel down, ready to lay him out and check for injuries, but Kayla shakes her head. Her eyes say it all: if we don't get him help, he's not making it out alive.

My knee screams as I rise and my shoe slips on the floor. Kay grabs my elbow and helps me up.

"Why not let me—"

"*No.*" I start walking. "Sorry. I just—I can't, okay. I mean I can. I can do this. But I'm not letting him go."

Kayla follows behind. "If you fall, it's not you who's going to snap in two."

"I can do it." The pain's fading already, drowned out by "The Ecstasy of Gold."

I ignore Kayla and try to follow its rhythm. As we pass the crucifixes, Jesus watches us from twenty sets of eyes.

"So I stole Conrad's cowboy hat," I tell Ty. I reach for it and pull it off, then tug it onto his head. He doesn't resist. "But you can have it, because you're stupid and I missed you." I swallow. "And I need a solid bribe to lure you back to Discovery Bang."

We're almost to the stairwell. We speed up. What if I go too fast and he falls? What if I go too slow and he never sees the sun again?

"You're not saying anything," I mutter. I glance behind me, catch Kayla's eyes. "Why isn't he saying anything?"

Something's wrong, besides the obvious things. He heaves against me, and for a second I think he's seizing, but he's not. He's crying, dry-eyed, face buried in my shoulder, arms hooked limply round me.

Kayla walks beside us. She takes out her phone and shines it on Ty, nearly blinding my right eye. He flinches away from the light, unbalancing me.

Kayla whimpers and covers her mouth, pulling the light away.

"What is it?" I ask.

Ty shakes his head against my back.

"His mouth is bloody." Kayla sounds like she might be sick again. "I think she cut out his tongue."

I hear the scrape of glass on glass as Pam slides a dish across her coffee table: meat dressed with leaves. She tells me on the plane ride how no one keeps a songless bird. It doesn't appear to be an answer to the question I asked, the question of why someone would kill Tyler. But it was. Pam took what she wanted and discarded the rest.

I rub Ty's arm. I don't have anything to say that'll make it better. There's no wisecrack that'll give him back the parts of him Pam's taken away. Me and Kay beat her, and she still managed to twist the knife.

"I missed you, Ty." It's all I can think of. "Both me and Kay did."

Kayla laughs hollowly. "Yeah, feels a lot longer than three weeks." She looks at me over Ty's head. "Why don't you tell him about that location you found—the one with the creepy cryptid kid?"

"Yeah, yeah. Peckam's Point. You and me and Kayla . . . *and Lazaria.* Oh, that's right—we saved you with crystals." I grin a little at that. I feel the bones in his hands shift against my chest, his hands gripping his hands. I pry what could be skinless bones apart and slide my fingers between his. "Stay awake, okay? If you don't, who's going to tell me not to be scared of the dark?"

He shudders again in a way that feels involuntary, moaning in an unfamiliar, gravelly way.

For an instant I teeter on the steps, but I cling to the railing and wait for it to subside.

He needs fresh air. Fresh air, first aid, and something to eat and drink.

The stairs fly by like my shoes have wings. We slam open the doors that lead to the white hallway. The ladder back to the surface is so close—why can't we just be there? Why can't we be safe inside The Moon where Gene must have first aid supplies?

Tyler screams, convulsing. His fingers squeeze mine so hard my knuckles feel like they're breaking, and a mangled word tumbles out of him, something that might be my name. He's breathing very hard against my back. I feel his every inhale and exhale closely enough that they may as well be mine.

"We're close, Ty. So close. Hold on." I sob. "*Please.*"

Kayla strokes Ty's back as he twitches. "Is it hunger cramps?"

"Has to be." It's not though. It's not. It's death throes, or poison, or an infection that's reached his spine or his brain . . . .

We're at the ladder. I don't go slow this time, and I don't stop when we make the top. I run into the deep dark woods, where for the first time in my life I'm one hundred percent positive there are monsters ready to tear me apart. My only regret is we have no camera to film it.

Kayla bursts into the trees next to me. Morricone's still playing in the background, but it's far away now, pulsing from the speakers on Echo Island.

A low rumble thrums to life deeper in the forest. Unless it's *not* deeper and I'm disoriented. Could the island be in the opposite direction? I start toward the noise, and Kayla pulls me back by my sleeve.

She flashes her phone in the opposite direction, and the skeletons nailed to the trees in the grove shine chalk-white. "It's this way. Try and be quiet."

I follow her, stroking Ty's hand. He gently scrapes his thumbnail across my skin. He's shivering, teeth clacking, but the small movement is soothing. His heart's beating fast against my back. As long as it keeps beating, we're cool.

Kayla swerves round suddenly. Her flashlight pans over my face. "Did you hear that? Like a pulse?"

Something screams in the forest. It's even worse than all the cryptids we've almost run afoul of in the past and which Ty pretends are owls to make me feel better.

Ty kicks my leg—not hard, but the equivalent of hard for an emaciated, dehydrated trauma victim. That's all the encouragement I need.

"Run!" I scream and charge ahead. The lights of Echo Island gleam like gemstones past the trees. When we reach the river, I grip Tyler tight. "Hold on, okay?" He does.

A discordant chorus of screams bursts from the trees as though the monsters are all throwing their necks back and, well, howling at the sky.

I let the incline propel me into the water. "Is Kay following?"

But Ty doesn't move. When I rub his hand, he doesn't rub back. He's not even shivering.

Water ripples against my back. I turn around and Kayla's caught up.

"He's not moving," I stutter.

Kay puts her arm around both of us and we march to the shore. I can see The Moon from here. In my imagination, if we make it through the door of the bar, Ty will be fine.

The roads are filled with bodies. Red streetlights form crimson halos around humps of shed flesh. We keep our distance and I pretend they're Hallowe'en costumes.

As we speedwalk down the street, Kayla rubs Tyler's back. "Maybe he's cold. We don't know what the temperature was like in that hole most of the time, and the water might've shocked him."

He thrashes backward, so strong that he rips free from the binding strapping him to me. His phone clunks against the pavement. He arches his back the way strychnine victims do, clawing the asphalt. Blood spurts from his mouth.

Outside of anime, that only happens when something is badly broken inside you.

"C-Come on." Kayla bends to lift him, but I'm stuck in place.

The cowboy hat I secured on his head rolls onto the road.

"*Josh!*" Kayla yells at me. "*Come here and help me or your boyfriend's going to die before you get a first date.*"

The stupid ultimatum snaps me out of it. I grab him. Kayla helps me get him onto my back again. We're about to start running when a rifle blast cuts the night, followed by the sound of a bullet casing hitting the pavement.

I turn around.

Tia's holding a hunting rifle. It's aimed right at us. "Put him down."

8
7/30

"T ia?" I turn so Ty isn't facing the gun.

Kayla raises her hands. "Please don't shoot."

Tia takes a step toward us. "Put. Him. Down."

Ty stops thrashing. He whine-screams.

I pull his arms around my neck and hold him tight. "Fuck off."

Tia fires another round into the air and reloads. She starts to speak, but then pitches forward, screaming, nearly dropping the gun.

"Quick, Kay, grab it!" But Tia's already righted her weapon by the time I yell it.

"*No*," Kay says, also belated. "Tia, what's happening? Are you wolfing out?"

Tia digs her nails into her shorts and groans. "Yeah, and so's he. Get the fuck out of here." She grabs something from her pocket. She tosses it over and it rattles.

Keys.

Kayla bends down and takes them. "Josh, do what Tia says."

No. I shake my head. "He's real hurt, Tia. If I leave him, he'll die."

Tia lifts the gun between involuntary jerks and throws it away from herself. Then she stumbles toward the river.

Kayla pulls at the straps holding Ty up.

I slap her away. "*No!*"

Tyler rears back, kicking the backs of my legs so I tumble over. He tears himself from the restraints and crawls over the concrete, screaming.

"Josh, you have to leave him. Now. We're going to lock ourselves inside that bar and we're going to light some candles and we're going to pray to Jesus and Mohammad and Vampira that we don't get eaten by werewolves. But we have to go. You can't help him."

Something moves under Ty's skin.

Me and Kayla freeze.

A rip runs up the underside of his arm from wrist to shoulder. Inside his skin, his flesh is squirming, reforming itself from tendons and veins. His arm stretches length-wise, fingers pushing several feet from where they should be. At his elbow, his skin snaps. Then his neck starts to stretch, like his head's trying to dislodge itself from the spine, but it's the spine that's growing, pushing everything outwards.

His chest bursts open.

Kayla grabs me and hauls me away. I'm still screaming when she throws me against the wall of The Thunder Moon and starts fumbling with the keys. Her hands are shaking so much they sound like sleigh bells.

The thing inside Tyler is over ten feet tall and the rest of his skin slumps away from it as it thrashes its neck, squirming in the blood as its joints snap into place. It rolls over, the movement like a dog rolling back onto its belly. Its neck hangs low, hunched, its legs peak like spider legs over its resting back. It screams like the monsters in the woods, but the sound is strangled, *off*. It flexes its fingers against the concrete—hands that are too like human hands but dusted with the same dark fur that covers the rest of it.

"Got it got it got it," says Kayla, jamming the key in the lock and turning.

The creature opens its eye, round and yellow like a cartoon spotlight.

It's beautiful. Inside the light, everything is warm and whole. All my fears strip away from me. If I curl inside it, I'll find Tyler there, and he'll hold my hand and tell me I'm beautiful and everything

will

be

"*Josh!*" Kayla slaps me and pushes me inside the building. The warmth snaps away and I'm so cold I could scream.

"I think he *hypnotized* me." I stroke my hand down my face, the stink of dried blood strong as my still-wet hand smears Pam's bloodstains over my swollen cheek.

Kayla locks and bolts the door. Together, we stare out the window as the thing that was Tyler stutters to its long long *long* legs and wobbles toward the river. The beam of its eye winks on-off as it swings its also-long neck around, taking in the trees beyond the water.

Near the edge of the ditch, he trips, losing his balance and falling in a ball of leg and hair into the river.

"Awww," says Kayla.

Things like that reaction are why we're friends.

Except Ty struggles to stand. I can't see the water, but I can see the edges of his shoulders and back dipping up and down, failing to support itself. I press my palm to the glass.

He's sort of . . . crawling up the bank. He doesn't look well.

Kayla rests her hand on my shoulder. "Tia's out there. She'll take care of him."

I shrug her off. "*How?* Is she going to do werewolf first aid? He needs electrolytes."

And me. *He needs me.*

I start to unbolt the door. Kayla punches my fingers away. "What are you doing???"

Tyler's motionless on the bank. His eye blinks open, closed, open. Slower.

"He needs help, Kay. I'm going to help him." I lift the bolt.

"Josh, he's going to eat you." Kayla whips me round. I haven't looked at her properly since before Pam. Her face is scratched and bloody. Her eyes are buggy. She's been the best camera girl a small-time cryptid hunter could ask for and so much more.

I pull her phone from her pocket and press it against her chest. "Probably, but if he does, do me a solid and film it?"

"Josh . . . ." Tears brim in her eyes. She hugs me. I hug her back and kiss the top of her head.

"It'll be okay."

She pulls away, sniffling. "At least grab Tia's gun."

"Guns don't have electrolytes," I joke, and Kay rolls her eyes. "Okay. I'll take it."

When I turn back to the window, Tyler's half-dragging himself into the trees.

Kayla taps my shoulder. She's holding a pair of black shades circa 1992. "They were on the bar."

I slide them into place. Whether or not they work against hypno-wolves, I'll look cool as Hell when Ty chows down.

Now or never.

I shove open the door and step into the night. The bolt clicks into place behind me, muffled under the barrage of Morricone and the thrum of the wolves.

I run across the parking lot, grab Tia's rifle, and break for the forest.

All my life I've made fun of idiots in zombie movies who, as soon as they see a zombified family member, lose all ability to comprehend the concept of zombies and get tragically eaten to the screams of their companions.

Well, Bangers, it turns out I'm that idiot.

It takes everything in me not to scream as I race through the water and up the bank. Screaming is my outlet, and without it, my anxiety is in the danger zone.

"Ty?" I whistle. "*Phw, phw, phw.* Here boy?" Maybe that's culturally insensitive.

I'm walking too slow, or Ty picked up speed. If he did, I might be killing myself for nothing. I step nimbly over the sticks and roots crowding the forest floor, swiping away spiderwebs that normally would have made me run.

Tyler better toss my seductive vegan risotto after this.

From far away, there's a rumble and a screech.

I still myself, rocking back and forth. "Oh boy. Oh boy oh boy." I make my feet move toward the sounds.

How am I even going to help if I find him?

A huge branch *snaps* to my right and I jump away. He's there, standing tall.

The shades help protect from Tyler's one pulsing eye, but it's still so hard not to look at. It's so beautiful, and—

I force myself away, watching him sideways.

He's huge—waaaay over ten feet tall, probably more like fifteen or sixteen. He doesn't look too injured anymore, but he's limping real hard on his front hand-paw. The air rumbles with a basal groan that vibrates my skeleton. There's a very faint light inside his other socket, like the eye's mending itself.

He hobbles toward me. It's his right paw for sure. It's broken or sprained, injured in the tumble into the river.

I step back, hold my hands out. The rifle slung over my back suddenly doesn't feel so terrible a thing to have. "Ty, it's Josh. I came to help. I can see that you don't need my help now, so I'm going to leave and wash the shit out of my pants instead."

He doesn't stop.

He opens his mouth, ten feet from me. His teeth are sharp and dripping, his tongue coils outward like a snake swimming in the air.

Ty doesn't have a tongue.

But there's another werewolf with only one eye. Another werewolf whose hand we severed and who I thought Kay bludgconed to death in her living room.

That's not Ty. It's Pam.

I turn and run. I leap over root networks and smack past trees, but Pam's *big*, and fast, and she catches up easily, knocking down every small tree that doesn't bend before her. As she reaches me, she *whips* her neck and I fly legs over head through the air and slam against a tree trunk.

The world blinks on and off. One second, Pam's stalking to my left like a mountain lion, the next she's crouched in front of me, jaws open, belly rumbling.

I reach underneath me for the rifle.

Pam rises above me. Her lantern-eye so bright, so bright . . . my glasses are gone. She's so bright. Her jaw stretches, eclipsing the light, eclipsing everything.

I'm too far from Kayla for her to record this.

Something fast and huge hits Pam in the side. Two were-wolves roll over each other, coming to a stop at the base of a tree, the massive jaws of the smaller one buried in Pam's side. Its eye beams bright over her, and for a moment, she stills, but then she shakes her neck and screams at it, clamping her mouth closed over its face. The smaller one—the smaller one that must be Ty—kicks her stomach with all four of its clawed hands, then scrambles away.

I try to crawl toward him, but I can't. I can barely raise my arm. My back's broken—no, it can't be, because I can feel it. I force myself to move and it hurts in ways I didn't think possible, but I *can* move.

Pam and Ty are knocking down every tree in the vicinity. If I try and help, they'll crush me. And there's no way Ty recognizes me, is there? There's no way either of them did, but what I felt from Pam was more hatred than hunger. And Ty saved me. He saved me, and Pam's crushing him.

He's lying on his side, kicking his legs to keep her at bay, but she's leaping down at him from all directions, striking him with her claws, biting his joints and the side of his head. A light sputters in his face like a lightbulb coming to life. It dies for an instant, but then it's back—two beams shining. He screams at her and she shrinks back briefly.

"Ty, come on." I whisper it into the air. If his senses are as acute as Pam's, he'll hear it. "Tear her throat out."

Not even a werewolf could come back from that.

Pam beelines for me.

I have just enough time to throw up my arms and curl my legs to my chest. Downy, blood-caked fur pushes against me—the smell's something like horse, something like death.

Werewolf screams threaten to deafen me, and one of them rumbles low and intense, a sound that should be heard for miles.

The woods burst to life with distant cries, like the trees are talking.

I open my eyes and it's Ty in front of me, his back up against me. Protecting me.

Pam screams and plunges her jaws into his stomach.

I know from the noise Tyler makes that the bite's deep.

There's a nauseating squish and a tear. Her jaws pull back, dragging entrails like jellyfish tendrils, dropping meat and fur from her mouth. She *rips*, pulling, shaking her mouth from side to side, spewing viscera.

Ty wails a broken werewolf scream. His claws rake her face and she steps back only to lunge and take a second bite.

I can't do anything, wedged between Ty and the tree, and she's digging, digging, digging into him to get to me, burrowing a hole.

Ty slumps. His body's just a heavy lump in her way.

I fold my hand over a wisp of fur, touching Ty's skin. I let out a breath I knew I was holding. I close my eyes.

Pam's not an anaconda, but she'll do.

Everything goes quiet, except for the rumble. From behind me, a werewolf whines.

I open my eyes and the trees are filled with lights like full moons. They ring the flattened patch of forest where Pam and

Ty were fighting, and from the multi-directional nature of their rumbling, the wolves are behind me, too. Behind *us*.

They sit, or stand, invisible but for their unblinking eyes, all of them watching Pam.

Then one of them walks forward, and I can't place what it is about its gait, but I know it's Conrad. Pam shrinks toward the edge of the circle, though the Conrad wolf is smaller than she is. He walks toward her, opens his mouth, sinks his teeth into her leg where it becomes her shoulder, and *pulls*. I feel the pop of her leg as it's dislocated.

The werewolves tear into her, ripping off skin, an ear, scouring her face with their teeth. They pick her apart, and not a moment of it feels sweet at all, because Ty's completely still on top of me. His chest doesn't rise and fall, and when I crawl further underneath him to hide in his steaming entrails, I feel nothing like a heartbeat.

ACT 3

1

A HOSPITAL BED

I wake to Josh. He's asleep next to me in a rocking chair, his hand stretched across my hospital bed and breaking a ring of polished gemstones that Kayla must have arranged. He's drooling and snoring at the same time, and he's the most beautiful thing I've ever seen.

Disrupting him feels like a violence, so I watch him quietly—what other way is there anymore? Except, there is something in my mouth, not quite a tongue, but something, and my vision's not perfect, but it's better than it was. And I remember my sight improving, though the memory doesn't make sense. My brain wants to push it out like an immune system forcing out an infection through sneezes.

I was a monster.

I glance at my chest and there's a swathe of bandage over my stomach. Even looking at it's painful. I can feel Pam sinking her teeth into me, the rush of panic as parts of me that should be inside are pulled outside. I grab my left wrist to calm myself.

My skin feels . . . better. It *looks* better, not dried out. It doesn't look like I was trapped in a hole for weeks. And all of me feels clean and new. This skin isn't the one Pam's fingers touched.

Josh stirs and my chest bursts to life like a busted anthill. If he wakes, it'll be the first time we've talked—really talked—since before the e-mail. I remember him saving me, I remember immense pain—though that's mostly fog—and I remember being in the forest and getting attacked by Pam and calling out for the others instinctively.

Then nothing. Then here.

Josh's eyes blink open, and embarrassingly, I'm already staring into them.

"Ty."

I try not to cry for half a minute, then give up. I hang my head back and close my eyes and waste so much water that past me would be rolling in his hole-shaped tomb.

Josh stands, and when I open my eyes I can tell he wants to hug me and is thinking real hard about whether the force will squeeze out my internal organs like a freezie. So I smile at him, and I reach for his hand, and I take it, and we're quiet like that for what feels like years and is probably ten seconds.

An array of polished-smooth amethysts, quartzes, and sapphires clatter onto the floor from my bed.

I part my lips. There's so much I want to say.

Josh lets go of me and reaches behind himself excitedly. In his hand, he holds my cellphone. The sight of it almost sets me off again, but I hold it in.

I take it from him with the reverence of a trophy and smooth my thumb over the screen.

"I miss your voice." His face crinkles and he starts to cry. He points at the phone. "But you can talk on that, before—" He jumps, sucks back some snot. "Right—it'll grow back, because of werewolf science. Conrad thinks it'll only be a few nights max. And he's got a special werewolf hospital room, so he'll keep you under when you change, until you're better."

What.

"*Werewolf science*?" I type. I *dimly* remember Josh rambling about werewolves back in Babel. But I'm not a werewolf. That would be very stupid.

I breathe in hard.

Josh paces, pointing at the air like he's tracing theories and clues across his conspiracy wall. He's invested in this. "You're a werewolf Ty. Everyone on the island is a werewolf."

"*How?*"

He throws up his arms. "Science! And the Cold War. Everyone was doing strange things during the Cold War. Come on, I know you read books."

Not the books Josh is reading, clearly. "*I know I changed into something. It wasn't a werewolf.*"

He settles back in the chair, then immediately springs to his feet again, wringing his hands, pacing. "Everyone calls them werewolves here, so you'll have to deal with it. And you're the one who turned yourself into one with only minor assistance. Got scratched, poisoned, drank a tonic that . . . well. Tia's girlfriend did that apparently."

The last time I saw Nor she was at The Moon, acting funny. She started chatting me up, pleaded with me to sing, brought me that funny tasting beer.

Huh. Well.

It wasn't actually the last time I saw her, because the last time was in the woods, with the others. I felt her. I felt them all. All but Virgie Kyle, wherever she may be. When I flex hard enough I can feel them now, but whatever medication I'm on's cocooned my brain or something, because everything's blurred like a vaselined camera lens. Or maybe this is me dying. Maybe I never left the hole.

I shift against the bed to feel the softness of the mattress and settle my eyes on Josh like he can anchor me.

"Nor probably saved your life." Josh sits.

I frown at him, pull up my texts. "*You saved my life. Brothers, right?*" A peace offering, to let him know it's all right. He came to get me. That matters more than my fucked up fantasies about him. I need him to know that.

But it doesn't have the intended effect. Josh pales. I've made him uncomfortable. I reminded him of something he'd buried.

He's thinking about the hot tub now, about lips that feel like worms crawling over his skin, and hands that could be covered in pus. Like I felt with Pam.

He smiles, and it's tight. "Yeah, brothers." He looks down at the end of the bed. "Song stuck in your head?"

I stop tapping the foot I was apparently tapping. I make myself smile and text a thumbs-up.

We've gone awkward.

Josh smiles. "Gene's planning a party for you for when you're better." He looks behind him at the door. "Man, that guy has a serious crush on you."

The sun's so bright and light and free coming through the windows. It's almost bright enough to bleach out the shitty feeling buzzing in my brain. Josh still feels weird about me, weird enough he's trying to set me up with a man in his forties because it's the quickest way to create distance between me and him. "*I don't want to be with anyone. I just want to go home.*"

He looks at me, full of sorrow as he tugs at a hangnail. He takes an audible breath. "You can't go home. This is home now."

No. No, that was all pretend. I picture the hole, and Pam's room, and even The Moon. I can't be here, in this place that broke me into pieces. This can't be where it ends.

But I feel the truth of it. Deep in my bones and in my blood, the earth and the air and the water all tethering me to something greater than one tiny person in a sea of persons. The island has its own song, and now it's singing that song to me.

My heart beats very fast.

2

THE MAN BEHIND THE CURTAIN

"M r. Kyle."

I'm sitting up in bed. Josh told me earlier it'd been two days. I've been asleep for most of that.

I can talk again, but though it doesn't hurt physically, some small, sick part of me misses the silence. And when I'm sleeping, I dream of Pam. She comes to me, perfumed and with a full face of angel make-up. She says something terrible and true, and it doesn't matter what the specific words are—they're different each time, and I never remember them—because I feel the terrible true thing all throughout my body already. I feel myself cum when she shoves that pillow over my face and I know I'm wrong deep inside. A part of me still lives in the dark.

I don't want to talk and I don't want to sing. I don't want to stand on stage every night of the rest of my sad little life psychically drugging people into wanting to listen. I don't want to die here, old and burnt out, playing bridge with Tia or Gene or whoever's survived long enough to turn eighty—assuming I make it that far myself. I don't want to walk past the house of the woman who manipulated and raped me and cut out parts of me I didn't know I had every *fucking* day of my life and know the furthest I'll ever get from it is a twenty-minute walk.

I don't want to be my mother.

But the man who's going to tell me to do just that is sitting across from me in a white, bejewelled cowboy hat, his hands clasped on his lap as he regards me with a seriousness so textured it's flaked into the air and the furniture's growing cowhide.

"Mr. Uphill," I droll, because after all, the show always goes on, whether you wanted it to or not, and shouldn't you, at the end, bend over and thank them for the opportunity? My role in life is to entertain, only it was never specified whether I was part of the audience.

Uphill uncrosses and recrosses his legs. He regards me with that same flat smile. "I've been told Mr. Likens has filled you in on the details of your werewolfery." He's obscenely unbothered as he says "werewolfery" aloud.

I smirk. "Don't you mean lycanthropy?"

Uphill sucks his teeth. "We prefer werewolfery these days. Lycanthropy was medicalized by eugenicists in the early twentieth century and it has problematic undertones."

"You still called this place Arcadia," I point out.

That's right, Josh caught me up to speed, and not only about werewolf history, but about Pam. He brought me her journal, explained how she was trying to lure him here. I made him take the journal away without reading it. It's not something I ever want to touch. I'd rather he burned it.

"This will go much easier, Mr. Kyle, without the verbal jabs. I'm well aware of how you feel about me, but we're both professionals, and I hope we can cooperate." He reaches for a glass of water on the table and sips. My attention's drawn to the see-saw surface of the water as he lays the glass back down, a shark scenting blood.

"Mr. Kyle." He snaps his fingers and tears my attention from the glass to him.

The rest of my life won't be this way, will it?

There's only one reason he can have come here: to beg me to sing and not let everyone on Echo Island die one by one. I look outside at the groomed gardens of his estate. Nor, Mary, my mother—I might have saved them if I'd known about this place and what I was. What I am.

A wind-up toy. One Mom never wanted to come here. One she doomed all these people to death for.

I wasn't worth it.

"I'm not going to let people die. And what else would I do here, anyway? I'm too much of an attention whore not to get up on that stage again." My lip quivers. I stare at my hands. I hate them. I hate every part of my body.

The thought brings tears to my eyes and I don't know why. Maybe it's that every bit of me's going to get ripped apart and discarded each night until the Dog Days end. Maybe it's the worry I'm not the same me at all, but a simulacrum. Something *like* Tyler Kyle, turned at an angle. A skin to be sewn together and stuffed for Uphill's museum of horrors.

Uphill holds out a handkerchief. Not a tissue, but an initialed fucking handkerchief.

I take it.

He clears his throat and stands up. "I'll return later. You have my sympathies. I hope you know I didn't wish any of this for you."

"No, but it sure is convenient, huh?" I glance at him. "Get on with what you were going to say. Unless it's a speech about skin, or conversion therapy, or living your truth. Then you can fuck right off."

Uphill cracks a smile. He sits down, holds his hat in his hands. "The truth is, Mr. Kyle, there's more to what the Nightingales do for this place than the others realize." He pauses, as though he's wrestling with something painful. "Us Nightingales have never been trapped on the island. That's the truth your mother discovered, and one I tried desperately to hide. Oh, we need to be here during the Dog Days, for safety reasons as much as anything, but if I wanted to throw away the lives of my fellow experiments, I could hop on a plane with Gord and ride a taxi to Avalon. So could you." He sighs. "But I hope that you won't. I won't make you stay here against your will, Mr. Kyle. I did that to your mother for years and it turned me into a shell. It was wrong."

Part of me wants to say fuck it and run. The way Josh was talking in Babel, he made it sound like he wants me back on the show and I—I want to be. I want to take back my phonecall break-up and be close to my friends however I can. I want to hold something in my hands.

"Couldn't I record some songs and send them over?" I ask. "Or come back every summer?"

Uphill smiles sadly. "I wish it were so simple. The Nightingales don't just sing to the islanders; we sing to the island. When the founders made this place, they tethered us to the soil and the trees. It was meant to be a temporary fail safe, in case exactly what did happen, happened. The island's song sustains us, and the Nightingales sing the island's song back to it. You may not feel it immediately—it's been a very long while since I changed for the first time, and I can't remember exactly what that experience was like—but you'll feel it eventually. The song saves us, and the song traps us, because the founders wrote it to trap us. A long time ago, your mother and I were trained to work the song, to change its message. You've noticed, I'm sure, that while the other islanders lose most of their human selves when they transform, you and I do not. You were able to recognize Mr. Likens and defend him. We are shepherds, Mr. Kyle. When I die, someone will need to shepherd the community for me. *If you choose to do so.*"

I snort. "And I can cut the community off from the real world like you have. Not let them engage with culture, or art, or science."

He smiles. "Is it kindness, or is it cruelty to set a chocolate cake outside the bars of a starving man's prison?" He pauses. He knows what he's saying and who he's saying it to. "You might disagree with how I've done it, but we've made this a home of our own. For all the horror, we're happy here. I will never leave this island, Mr. Kyle. If I allow myself the indulgence of

Arcadia and its pleasures, it's because I've given everything to my people."

I'm sure that makes sense to him, but no matter how he frames it, he's a despot. "Well, I won't be like that. As soon as I'm in charge, everyone's getting WiFi."

Some of the hardness drains from him. It's because we both know I've relented. And how could I not? He knew I wouldn't leave. It was always a false choice.

"You can do what you like when I'm gone, Mr. Kyle. I won't be around to complain, except in the summer, and even wolves breathe final breaths."

King of shit castle. Great.

"So what's this song I have to sing? Please not 'Baby One More Time.'"

Uphill laughs. "Of course not. It's not a song like a human song. If it helps, think of it as a spell."

I shrug. "It doesn't."

"Then how about a chemical formula? Alter one small piece and the entire recipe changes. But keeping the formula intact reinforces its bonds, creates stability. You're creating the stability of the forms of the people here. When you're well enough, I'll teach you, the way the founders taught your mother and I."

Something he said sticks in me like a thorn. "The song can be changed."

His brows pinch together, and he tucks his cowboy hat into place. "It would be like tugging a thread from a spider's web and expecting the web to survive. The founders were careful in its construction, and without access to the proper machinery, altering their tapestry would risk unraveling the masterpiece. The Saint Serge experiment ended when we rebelled. Captivity of another kind was the price of our freedom."

"Machinery." I'm latching onto keywords here—a thousand video game fetch quests have trained me well.

"*Yes*," says Uphill. "But that lab is inaccessible. It's not in Babel, but under the hatch you found in the woods."

I wrinkle my nose. "Wait. So, you're saying, if you or me had access to that hatch, we could . . . change the song and everyone could go wherever the fuck they wanted and not be stuck on this cursed fucking island? Buy a fucking bulldozer or something."

"Really, Mr. Kyle. Language." He sighs. "Its walls are too strong to penetrate. There's another entrance, but I've been unable to find it. None of the extant blueprints show it. Do you really think I haven't tried?"

I sit up straighter, feeling a twinge of pain in my stomach where the bite wound is only mostly mended. "My mother's video suggested she'd found something that would let her *and* Tysha leave. There's her coded journal—the map." I frown. "Why not let me figure out what my mom knew and open this thing?"

Uphill frowns at me. "Virginia discovered I'd been manipulating her, that was all. She left on seven thirty, when her abilities were at their height. She thought she could undo the song and help Tysha leave with her, but it didn't work."

I snap my fingers. "But something she found made her *think* she could do it. Maybe she worked out the song on her own or made up a song." I have no idea what I'm talking about, or if this makes sense. I think I felt something like "the song," when my hearing first started to change, but with nothing to compare it to, I can't be sure. I haven't exactly been in my right mind. "At least let me try. You haven't seen Josh work. He's a boss."

Uphill stands. "Mr. Likens is free to boss around whomever he likes, but whatever Virginia discovered is lost with her."

And with Pam maybe. "Pam found something out about it. When I was with her in Babel, she made it sound like I was the key to her escaping."

He chuckles. "I think we can both agree that Pamela Matheson was dangerously delusional."

True, when it came to certain things, but it doesn't mean she was delusional about everything.

3

THE SECRET DIARY OF VIRGINIA KYLE

I 'm sitting cross-legged on my hospital bed, papers fanned in front of me. Josh has cobbled together a conspiracy board out of garish construction paper and glittery wool from fuck knows where, and Kayla is communing with a pile of rocks to determine which of mom's diary pages contain pertinent information.

So, basically, I'm working alone.

"Maybe we should film this?" Josh asks. "We can put some montage music over the top. 'Eye of the Tiger' is too expensive, but—oh man, what about some Beastie Boys?"

"'Intergalactic?'" I suggest without looking up.

"Nah, I'm saving that for an alien episode. If werewolves are real, what does that tell us about aliens?"

"Nothing."

I skim another of Mom's gossipy journals. I guess when you're stuck on the world's dullest monster island, the question of whether Susan knows Deirdre is sleeping with Pru in exchange for her collection of contraband Sarah Mclachlan is a world-shattering scandal.

"'Sabotage!'" Josh shouts. I look up, thinking he's unearthed something—sabotage, presumably. But then: "Shoulder holsters are hot. We should wear shoulder holsters for the promo."

He's talking about the Beastie Boys video.

"And those seventies wigs." I whistle.

I shove another journal in the useless pile. Then I get to one that mentions me.

She has already—mostly casual references, as if I'm something she's trying not to think about. At a certain point she started wondering what I was up to, what kind of person I was, if I was married, if I had a good job, if I had kids of my own. Mostly the answer is no, no, and no. No Mom, I didn't do anything with the life you gave up everything to give me.

Like most of her diary, this entry's written as though to Tysha.

> I've worried a lot about Tyler. All mothers worry, but my worry feels special. Connie would tell me it's because I always have to be special, but he has no leg to stand on. We're a couple of bitches barking at each other. Tyler's always been alone. Even when he was a child. So much of that was my doing. I didn't want a child, and when I looked at him sometimes, my resentment was all I could see. I'm sure he saw it in my eyes, and maybe that's why I wasn't attentive like I should have been. We are all human though, aren't we? I think I should forgive myself for not being perfect, but there's a gulf as wide as the moon between should and can, and now that I've lost him, he's most of what I think about. Him, and you. I've turned into the cliche I never wanted to be in my old age: bad hair dye, bad perm, constantly talking about a son who never calls and a wife who deserted her (not that it was your fault, but it hardly stops me hating you for it, baby doll). When I watch him on his television show the worry disappears. The way that Joshua boy looks at him is the way you looked at me. Do you remember the May Dance? You were so shy I

had to drag you onto the grass and even then you made a face. I'm still not convinced I didn't bully you into marrying me. Oh, but that's not a fair thing to say. You were shy, and I was a hussy, but we made it work. We were great, weren't we baby doll? We could have stormed the whole world if the world hadn't decided our fates long ago. The day we took back the island I felt like Boudica reborn. When you looked at me, I felt the same rush. The way this boy looks at my Tyler is like that, and the way Tyler looks at him is like that too. I only hope they figure it out before time figures it out for them. People waste too long being afraid. When you find something special, you should nurture it. Maudlin, I know, but there it is. My father used to say that: but there it is. My father was an unpleasant man, but he had some good sayings. For all I know, that's what my son says about me: she was an unpleasant woman (often true), but she had some good sayings. I want to know my son is happy. When he smiles at that boy, I know everything will be okay. He won't have a mother, but I was a terrible mother to begin with. Still, I hope we had fun while we were together. I wasn't the most dependable woman in the world, but I might have been the most fun. Oh, but you and I, we had such fun, didn't we baby doll? We were whirlwinds in a world terrified of rain.

Do I want to reach across the void and tell my mom she was a great mother? Sure. Is it completely true? No. Do I want to tell her I did have fun, that I wasn't alone? Yeah, and that part's more honest. But I can't do anything. It's all tracing living fingers over cold graves, and letters written long ago by dead people to other dead people. And maybe she was wrong about Josh, but she was right about me. And maybe I should take Josh seriously and try and be happy here with Gene, or someone like Gene. I should stop assuming everything Josh says is a dig.

There's a grunt from Kayla's circle of pricey nonsense.

"Any luck?" I ask her.

She shushes me. Josh and I share a look.

"I mean, I've decoded the secret message," Josh offers, sheepish. "It's not all that helpful. But it does mean Discovery Bang's discovered something, so that's a first."

I start to get up to examine what, admittedly, is a very impressive craft project on Josh's part. He practically leaps the five feet to the bed to stop me.

I hold up my hands. "I'm not going to crumble to pieces. Promise."

Josh inhales sharply. "You weren't there. You didn't see your guts spread all over the forest floor."

I was there, and I did see, but I know what he means. "It's all healed." Mostly. "I'm saving myself for that anaconda."

That gets a smile out of him, but then he glares. He turns back to his work, which, as I approach, is way more than a collage with string. He's decrypting the couple journal entries Mom wrote in numbers.

"It's a simple book cipher," Josh explains, pointing from the diary entry to a photocopied page from *A Case of Conscience*, which I guess he must have photocopied specifically so he could pin it on the board. The actual paperback is on a table next to it, a fluffy pink bookmark tucked inside that could easily be Pam's.

I remember the pictures in her trash—the wolf and the fox, the skull. Were they supposed to be me? I shudder, taking an involuntary step back.

Josh is staring at me, so I must have made a weird face.

"I'm fine," I say. "Tired. Being a werewolf is very tiring."

"Uh huh. You've spent most of your time as a werewolf high on morphine or unconscious, but okay." He turns back to the board. "It talks about how Uphill's keeping her here. How she's going to change the song so it thinks Tysha is a Nightingale too."

I comb my hand through my hair. "Fuck everyone else, I guess." Not Mom's best look.

Pam comes to mind again—she was trying to turn herself into a Nightingale, I think, or somehow ingest enough of one to take its powers.

"She was a complicated lady," Josh agrees. "What's interesting is she says they need to leave on seven thirty, or during the Dog Days at least. When werewolves," Josh says, holding his hands out like the Ancient Aliens guy, which I'm sure he doesn't know he's doing and which is adorable—fuck, I need to stop thinking of Josh like that.

"I'm explaining werewolf science," Josh is saying now. "You need to listen."

"Right, werewolf science. Go." I nod. I'm out of it. I'm a mess. I'm probably still somewhat high.

He clears his throat. "During the Dog Days, did you notice the werewolves all have your crazy hypnosis powers, but in their eyes? Well, in the same way regular werewolves—" Yes, he did just say *regular werewolves*, "develop that ability when they change, Nightingales get stronger."

I nod. I'm following. "Uphill did mention that."

"Exactly, so your mom thought she could change the song during that time and not any other. *But also,* she says she knows where the door is, that she tried to open it but couldn't do it alone. You need two Nightingales, and she didn't think Conrad would help her."

Fuck. What? "Then where the fuck is it? And why didn't she open it once she was back again and all pal-y with Uphill?"

This is ridiculous. I want to cry. And throw things. The lesson here is not going to be that friendship is fucking magic and people should trust each other. It's not. I will not let it. Even though both of those things are true, but still. Fucking dumb fucking shit.

"She doesn't say where it is," says Josh. "Just something about squirrel balls."

Fucking dumb fucking shit. The map. Gene's place with a code underneath it, the hatch circled in the forest.

"It's Mr. Nuts." I grip my head, which aches with the pain of a thousand hangovers. "It's in Gene's basement where he was keeping Ru." And because Uphill never fucking told anyone about all this, Gene had no fucking clue.

My chest is electric, my blood is electric. "So I'll go there tonight. Down the hatch and I can fix this in like, five minutes probably."

Five minutes, to undo something Uphill and my mom spent forty odd years trying to work out.

I'm so exhausted. But I'm free. I'm a free bird. "So why didn't Mom show it to Uphill once she got back?"

Kayla gets to her feet behind us. "Me! Me! Me and Lazaria have this one." But when I turn to look at her she's holding out a folded notebook, frowning. I don't like the look on her face. "Sorry, it's not something to be excited about."

"Just tell me," I say, long-suffering at this point. Part of me already knows what she's about to say.

She grimaces. "You know I always really liked you, Tyler? I like how you employ me, and will hopefully continue to do so because, you know, student loans?"

"I won't shoot the messenger." Am I terrifying or something? I should buy her flowers for, uh, saving my life.

Josh's fingers lace in mine. I squeeze back. We're good. We're cool. We're platonically holding hands like normal. I'm fine with this.

Kayla winces across the room. "It was because of you, Ty. She didn't want anyone else to leave and find out about you and make you come back here."

And fucking hundreds of people have probably died for it.

4

ISLAND SONG

"We're not going to fit," I tell Gene as we stand above the hatch with Uphill and Josh. The cellar looks terrifyingly small for one "werewolf," let alone two. Ru was horrifically scrunched against the walls in that little room. The image is frightening now for entirely new reasons.

Conrad sighs and descends. "It's no time to be precious, Mr. Kyle."

I cross my arms, contemplating the repercussions of stomping on his fingers. "Can you please call me Tyler?"

Uphill looks up at me and grins. "Why I thought you'd never ask."

Ugh.

Gene pats my back, dirty dishrag in hand. "You'll be fine. You were on the smaller side. Ru's taller."

Really? Now I'm getting werewolf body-shamed?

Josh elbows me in the side. "You were pretty cute actually."

Excellent. I was cute. Non-threatening, unremarkable. My brain could come up with synonyms for days. Maybe I can sing myself a song that'll make me fall out of love with my best friend. "Exactly what every guy wants to hear."

Josh goes quiet. I made it weird. *Fuck.* I'm an asshole.

"That does remind me," Uphill calls to us. "Gene, you owe Arcadia the associated fine for Mr. Rajaram's captivity."

Gene throws his dish rag down the hole, and I'm pleased to report that it lands on Uphill's smiling face. Gene stomps into the kitchen. "I'll be wolfing in the woods if you need me."

Uphill rips the rag off and drops it like he's a fancy lady planting a handkerchief for her beau. "Are you planning to join me, Tyler Kyle, or was this an elaborate hoax to trap me in Gene's freezer?"

"Oh, how I wish that were true." I grab the hatch door like I'm gonna slam it shut, but I open it again and follow. Darkness closes around me.

I freeze.

It's dark and it smells of dirt and blood. It smells like the hole in Babel and—I close my eyes. Everyone's going to think I'm crazy. And Josh is there, and Uphill.

Pam's there too though, in the dark of my mind. She glows like a terrible angel under a spotlight. She has a knife in her hand. She has bits of me in tubes. She licks the side of my face.

Someone's skin touches mine and I almost fall.

"Tyler!" Josh screams. He's holding my hand.

My chest is heaving.

"I'm fine." I force a smile, but as I let go of him and continue, the blackness edges in. Josh and the light of the freezer are an ever-diminishing presence.

"Please be careful, man. Okay?" Josh asks. "I'll be here waiting. You're safe."

I'm broken as all fucking shit, but yeah, in the grand scheme of things, I'm safe.

What looks like a long stretch of tunnel continues behind Uphill, its ceiling lower than the room we're in now. I swear I was never claustrophobic before.

"I'm fine." This time my voice doesn't even shake.

Uphill ambles up the tunnel. "We should scout ahead. We don't want to be trapped down here."

Especially not with each other.

I wave goodbye to Josh and follow.

A cramp sends me to my knees as I reach the tunnel. To his credit, Uphill waits. A pained expression is plastered across his face, as though he's not feeling any better than me, but is more practiced at disguising it.

"Does the change get easier?" I haul myself against the rough-cut wall. It's like a mine down here—the kind that doubles as a base from a Bond movie.

Uphill sets his cowboy hat on the ground. "You become more adept at anticipating it. The pain usually fades from memory."

I snort. "Like childbirth."

"Perhaps." He's unbuttoning his shirt.

"Are you stripping?" At least it's a distraction from the pain, which is itself a distraction from the darkness. And the sound—I can hear someone pouring a beer all the way back upstairs. Kay and Josh are talking. It comes to me in waves.

"—maybe he *shouldn't* do the show anymore," says Josh.

Oh.

"—know what he wants? Ask him how he feels about it—"

"Hey, Uphill. Is there a way *not* to hear things?" I ask, trying to talk loud enough that I can't overhear a conversation that's not meant for me. Maybe it's not even *about* me. Maybe it's about some mysterious other "he."

Lazaria's cousin, Bill Crystalis or whatever.

"In time, you'll be able to control it. In the beginning, it's unpredictable. Think of it as a second puberty."

Exactly what every thirty-year-old needs. "What about the strength? When do I start being able to punch holes in cement? Would have come in handy a week ago."

Cracks are running through me. I know Josh and Kayla are talking about me. I know why. I know deep down I was right to leave the show because, I mean, look at me. I can't stop caring about him, and here he is still holding my hand and flirting and all the little things that fucked me up in the first place, or maybe I fucked them up. Either way, we can't be around each other.

Why isn't Uphill answering me?

He crumples against the wall in his underwear, possibly having a heart attack, possibly turning into a werewolf. Who knows! It's always a surprise on Echo Island.

"—tomorrow, at Gene's—" says Josh.

Kayla claps and it echoes in my ears. "What about—"

"Because he's Scottish," says Josh.

A groan escapes me, and it's only partially because Josh wants to keep me around so he can do his Loch Ness Monster episode. The second reason is that my skeleton's trying to claw out of my body to join tonight's moonlight furry soiree.

"Are you all right?" I ask Uphill.

He waves. There are very large, spiked bones protruding from his fingers.

On the list of my favourite werewolf transformations, this one's zero, because it's happening to me, and I don't like that.

I collapse, screaming.

In the distance, Josh is freaking out. Apparently I'm not the only one with A+ hearing.

I'd like to say the rest is a blur, that I pass out, that my brain buoys me along on a gentle eddy of serotonin, but it categorically does not. If you want to know what it feels like to have your skin rip open, your ever-expanding skeleton walk out of your ripping skin, your organs displace themselves or otherwise enlarge at a rapid rate, then I direct you to what I just described because it feels like what that feels like it should feel like.

And now I can't even talk, so there's that.

It's only the second time I've been consciously a werewolf. It's superior to the first on account of not getting disemboweled, but there's still time and I am with Conrad Uphill.

He stalks ahead of me, leaving the pile of clothes and skin behind him in the tunnel. Retrospectively, taking off my clothes would have been a good idea, especially as I'm running low at this point, and there's only so many of Ru's things I can borrow before it gets weird.

As I follow Uphill, these are the wolfy thoughts I'm having. It's a bit disappointing. In novels, werewolves usually think about things like *scent* and *pack* and *prey*. And I am a bit hungry, but really I just want some vegan mac and cheese.

Okay. So the vision's a bit different. A bit intense. And *okay* I can hear the others, or feel them. And *okay*, I guess the island song is flowing above and around me. It's a bit like being bodily jacked into the internet, or how that always looks in movies and anime. It's a bit like Nirvana—the religious concept, not the band. It's a bit like that moment before you die, and your brain's on fire and all it has is one lousy extinguisher to service a whole apartment building. It's a bit like having a pillow shoved over your face by a murderous fanfiction writer with mommy issues.

Easy enough to imagine.

I fold my legs beneath me, crawling like a bat through the cramped tunnel. Water drips from the ceiling, and I shiver as damp soil clots in my fur and rolls over my skin. You don't think about things like shivering werewolves, but maybe we should all take a collective moment to do so.

The song rolls over me, thick as water that's been partly transmuted to jello by the wizardry of seventies dining culture. It pricks every hair on my back, singing like the wolf in the woods on my first night here. Beautiful and poisonous, resonating in my blood.

Obey stay staystaystay edge of trees 9 kilometers 9 kilometers 9 kilometers 9 kilometers sky 9 kilometers stay—

Uphill's back legs kick, showering me in dirt. At first I think he's being an asshole, but no, there's an incline.

A massive network of roots coils across the ceiling. I can smell stone and dead things, bones that were once werewolves, human remains co-mingling with them in decay. I feel mycelia and rhizomatic systems. I feel water trickling all around us and animals in their burrows. The footsteps of the few humans on the island are like thunder, sending shockwaves through the ground, and the footsteps of the islanders are somehow both gentler and louder. The low frequency thrum of their voices is like the safety net below the trapeze.

I try to call to them and ask them to do handstands, but I have no way to test if it worked. Let's pretend it did.

I scrabble up the incline, the ceiling crushing me, the song drowning me. It's like doing the butterfly stroke through soup. But Gene and Uphill weren't wrong. My body folds compactly. I press myself flat against the soil, using my claws as grappling gear.

The narrow tunnel opens into a cavern big enough to comfortably hold both of us.

We're standing before a vast door. "ADAM" is painted in big red letters, letters I'm impressed I can still read. There's a speaker built into the side of ADAM—a name clearly meant to be yelled—and behind both speaker and door, the song. It vibrates through everything, telling us what we are and what we do, what our world is, and how everything on the island is to Be.

Uphill starts singing, softer than the Nazgûl cries, threaded through with sounds I couldn't hear as a human. My body sings with his, though I make no conscious choice to.

The door opens.

It's not dramatic, or momentous. It just opens.

There are machines inside. The controls are intended for human hands, so there's a lot of absurd clicks of claws and delicate prodding of instruments. But we reset it—the instructions are clear enough. We set it to let us go.

And when it comes time to set a new song, to build the parameters of our world in vibration and tune, Uphill steps from the machinery. I don't need to hear him speak to know he wants me to do it.

And I know exactly what to sing.

5

A SONG FOR TYLER KYLE

"No way, man. You didn't." Josh grins. He's beaming, and not just because a variation of his show's theme has been immortalized as the fabric holding together both space and time—okay, that's a bit dramatic, but it is functioning as an audio network interconnecting a modest population of werewolves and their weird gay town.

The second reason is that he's drunk, and the third is that I get to leave. It's August 9th and the moon has risen. Starting today, the whole island is free.

Tia and Kayla are sitting with us at a table inside The Moon and the bar's full of dancing patrons. Gord's on stage doing "Mr. Roboto," directing most of his attention Gene's way. One of the two of us won't be lonely for long.

Flap snap. "Fuck," says Tia. She's flipping beer coasters against Kayla and losing badly.

Josh whistles. "Where are those werewolf reflexes, Tia?"

"They're up your ass," Tia spits. *Flap snap*.

"I PUKED IN YOUR SINK I'M SORRY," Kayla blurts.

Where did that come from? Whose sink?

Tia looks up at her, so I guess it was Tia's sink. I'll assume it's not innuendo, either, even though both of them avert their eyes or giggle when the other so much as walks in the door. It's unlikely anything'll happen so soon after Nor, but there's hope on the horizon. It's nice. I'm glad people are getting nice things.

Tia reaches across the table, jostling everyone's beers and Kayla's Shirley Temple. She snags Kayla's pile of coasters. "Then I get to win."

"That's not how that game works," says Josh. "No games work like that."

Kayla smiles as Tia stacks and counts her coasters.

Tia pushes her chair out and rests her feet on the table, boot buckles jangling. "It's how my games work."

"Feet off the furniture, Tee!" calls Gene over the noise. She pretends not to hear him.

I'm supposed to sing tonight. I still don't want to, but whatever Uphill and I did, we all still need the music. We'll all still have to come back every summer. I've agreed to record some material before I go, for people to carry with them, though most of the islanders want to stay. And fair enough. Maybe I'd stay if not for what happened to me here.

Josh shoves Tia's boots off the table. "*Germs.*"

"What are you going to do, Tia?" I ask. She knows I mean leaving because it's all anyone's talking about.

She picks at her nails. "Dunno." But she smiles, weakly. "I kind of wanna go? But Gene'll never leave this place. I don't know if I can let him stay here by himself."

"Sisters of the Moon," I say.

Tia jumps from her chair and points at me. "Hey. Wait here." She runs off.

A minute later she returns. She stands behind me. "Close your eyes, Kyle."

"I already have my back turned, so closing my eyes will do nothing." Also, it's obvious she's going to give me a jacket.

"Just do it, you jerk." She nudges my shoulder.

I close my eyes. What's obviously a jacket flops over my face.

"Ta-Da!" Tia lets go. It slides under my chin and I open my eyes.

It is, in fact, a jacket. But it's still incredibly thoughtful. I smile. I don't pretend to be surprised. "This is really cool, Tia." I mean every word.

She winks at me. "You won't say that when Gene puts you on cleanup."

I get up and try it on, do a little spin, be something like what Tyler Kyle is supposed to be like. Everyone smiles. I'm doing this right.

I sit back down. "You know," I nod at Gord, "I think Gene'll be okay." I take a drink. "You should leave with us. We'll all be driving back together, and you'll need somewhere to crash. And I—" It's so much harder to do without the barrier of the phone. But it's better than having Josh break it to me again that I'm not right for the show, that he's uncomfortable around me. "I'm moving out sometime soon, and if you want it, Josh'll need a new co-host. You guys have a good dynamic. Maybe you could even tempt Kayla out from behind the camera."

When I look up, everyone's staring.

Josh is bug-eyed. "Y-yeah. I was going to say, you should get back to auditioning. You're wasting all that talent, man." He smiles wide, but his lips are pressed together. I don't know how to read what's happening to his face.

"I don't think so," I say. "I don't really want that anymore. I thought I might go back to school. Something low-key—"

"Like what?" Josh snaps. "You're not a low-key person, Ty."

I wave my arms, a little penned in.

Kayla noisily sips her Shirley Temple through a red and white novelty straw.

"Like logging," I say. Logging?

"*Logging!*" Tia snorts. She clinks her glass against mine. "Have you ever chopped wood before? Or seen a log?"

"I've seen logs." I have.

Josh is tapping either side of his glass. "You're joking, right?"

I look him in the eyes. He deserves that much, after he gave me a platform, supported my ambitions for years, worked alongside me on stage and very small screen. "I'm not. It's not working. Whatever I had in school I lost it. I'm not just pushing thirty, I *am* thirty, and that's not going to get easier once I'm . . . out. If that happens."

Josh starts moving his glass around, tongue poking his cheek like he does when he's mad. "Fuck you, man."

"Josh." Kayla lays her hand on his.

He shakes her off. "*No*. You're the most talented person I know. You don't get parts because you don't audition. You don't have an agent, you never talk to the contacts you made in university. I wish I had half of what you have. It's a waste."

"Josh, I can't. I don't want to." I stare at the table. His chair screeches against the floor. "Everything's different now. I'm not the same person."

I'm not fully a person, and I don't mean the werewolf part. Something crept inside me while I was here. It lives there now. All I want is to run away somewhere it won't be so loud. I want to forget about Tyler Kyle and be somebody different. Make new friends, get over Josh's handholding and the hot tub and the flirting and that e-mail. Let myself love the friend who saved my life and deserves so much better than what I can give him.

He throws his beer in my face.

Tia hauls me onto the dance floor. I barely catch a glimpse of Josh as he storms from the bar, Kayla at his heels. I dab my face with my t-shirt.

Queen Cee's on the radio singing pop jams, but I can't focus on the lyrics. Tia hangs her arms over my shoulders, slow dances with me to a fast beat.

"Is this about that e-mail?" She links her hands behind my neck.

"Sort of," I say. "You saw it?"

"Found it with your stuff." She lays her head on my shoulder. "I'm not gonna take your place on your show. Josh can find someone else if he wants to, but I'm not gonna be the shit friend who steals your job."

I shrug. "It's a job."

"You're in love with him." She kisses my cheek. "That e-mail was shit."

"Yeah, well, maybe we're both shit." That was juvenile.

I want to get trashed.

When the song ends I head for the bar and order a shot of Booze, then a second. A third.

I still have to sing. I don't want to.

I order a fourth shot and Gene shakes his head. "You need to slow down."

"You know," I snap at Gene, "when you want to fuck somebody, don't act like their dad. Just a pro-tip."

Gene's face falls and I feel like the last shaving of toilet paper when the roll runs out. I'm a waste, like Josh said, like Pam knew I was. She saw it. She understood all about the real Tyler Kyle.

Tia glares as Gene hurries to the other side of the bar. "That was real ugly."

"I'm an ugly person."

"No." She spins me round. "You're not, and that's why I'm pissed. Apologize to Gene."

I start to cry.

"Jesus, Kyle." Tia pulls me against her. "Okay. It's okay. After tonight, you and me are gonna have a real good talk about what happened, all right? Maybe you don't want to tell Josh, but you need to tell someone. Do you want to go back to my place?"

I wipe my eyes. Fuck, that was embarrassing. "No. I'm sorry. I'm not dealing with things that well. I guess."

I break from her, try to get Gene's attention. But Gord's arms are folded on the bar, and they're making eyes at each other. Gord asks him on a date and Gene's mood goes from crushed to flying high.

It's easy enough to fade into the crowd. The bar's full, the room is moving. I've fucked everything up. I still have to sing.

Tia and Josh and Kayla are talking at the bar. There's a lot of gesticulation happening.

I need to sing. I need to apologize to Josh, and also everyone. Two birds, right? On stage, I flick off the music. Everyone's watching me.

I feel sick. I feel small. Sing, and I can make it all go away. Drug them, drug myself, drug Josh. Fuck. I don't want to see that happen to him.

"This one's, uh," I scroll through songs till I find what I need. "For Kayla, I guess. Because she likes Fleetwood Mac, and Josh." I clear my throat. The mic whines. "And Gene. And whoever I pissed off. Which is everyone. Because I guess I'm a piece of shit. So." I laugh because what else do you do? "I just want you to know that you saved me, and when I met you, you were the best friend I'd ever had. That'll always mean something to me, whatever I did to fuck it up." Everyone's staring. "I want you to feel comfortable on the show you made." A bad end to a bad speech. "And not be thinking about how I creeped you out. I'll sing now."

"Go Your Own Way," seems perfect, and hopefully Josh will understand it's me letting him go, as nice as I can. But as I sing, it doesn't matter if he understands, because the stupid science happens, and people get excited, and I get excited, even when I start to cry again.

The glow fades when the song ends, like I knew it would. I hop down, only marginally dizzy. I get right back to dancing with Tia. I can't look Josh or Kayla in the face. Can't wait till that awkward drive home in our one car.

A firm male body dances up close behind me. It's Josh.

I can't handle this. I don't know if my singing did this, or if he's fucking with me, or he thinks this is cute, or he feels sorry for me. Whatever it is, I don't want it.

I reverse mine and Tia's positions, and she's a class act, because she knows exactly what I'm doing and starts dancing with Josh.

Kayla's behind me. She's cocking her head at the stage, but not at me. At Josh.

I turn in time to see him take the stage with a graceful hurdle.

"Hello!" Josh adjusts the mic. I don't want to look at him. "Ty?"

Fuck, now I have to.

"I'm going to sing a song now." Josh's voice wavers. "It's for you, Ty, and I hope it communicates how much I care about you—yes Kay, I see you nodding—and I'm so happy to have you back in my life. And it'll express how I feel." He pauses to tap the screen. "But also apologies, because I can't sing."

Kay's giving him an enthusiastic thumbs up.

"500 Miles," plays.

I feel cold everywhere, and far more sober than I either should, or want to be. This isn't going to stop. It's going to go on and on and on. Josh being sweet, and doing sweet things for me, punctuated by no-homo moments, and me acting out when things don't go how I'd hoped. It'll go on and on and on.

So as people resume dancing, I let the crowd swallow me and head for the door. The usual guilt remains. Josh made a grand gesture and I'm being rude. What if he noticed me leaving, and it guts him?

Across the lake-moat, the trees are watching me. Somewhere out there, the rest of the wolves are watching too, at least until Uphill sends for more dogs. If I wanted, I could walk right into the forest, and maybe I'd even make it for a little while. I could sing to the others, build a treehouse, live off blueberries and roots. Take up logging.

I retreat around the back of the bar and slouch against the wall. There's a stomped-out cigarette on the ground and I stick it in my mouth, forgetting I don't have a lighter. "Shit."

"Ty?"

Shit.

"I really needed some fresh air. Sorry." I pause. "That sounded sarcastic, but I meant it. You're my best friend." I spit out the cigarette.

Josh holds up a paper. It's crumpled in a way that suggests smoothed-out garbage.

It's the fucking e-mail.

I stand up, ready to bolt. "Please don't say whatever you're going to say."

"I didn't write this e-mail, Ty. I'd never say these things to you." He stares at it, then crushes it and tosses it at the open dumpster. It bounces off the rim. "Pam wrote it."

Oh.

I swallow. Try to play it cool. "Right. I mean, that makes a lot of sense, now that you say that."

"I want you on the show. It doesn't work without you." He pauses. "But only if you want to be. And only if you start auditioning again. I get this feeling sometimes, like I'm holding you back? If I am, I don't want to. I meant what I said. You're the most talented person I know. But if you ever didn't want to act, or sing, I wouldn't hate you. I'd be mad, but I couldn't ever hate you, man, okay?"

I kick a stone across the asphalt. My shoulders slump. The fight's gone out of me. I've been so erratic. "I want to be on the show," I say, slow. "I don't know about the rest. I felt like I did want it. I wanted it so bad, but after Pam." I crack my knuckles. "She fucked me up, or I was fucked up already and she pulled it out."

Like my guts, turned to silly string across the forest floor.

Josh walks up to me. He shoves his hands in his back pockets. "You're not fucked up. Not in a *bad* way. We're both pretty fucked up. Can I hug you?"

He's just Josh. Regular, harmless, sincere Josh. "Mmhm."

He puts his arms around me, and I pat his shoulder. And we're good, just like that. "I'm sorry for being drunk and dramatic." I laugh. "Almost like I'm traumatized or something, right? Wild."

"Yeah, I'll believe it when I see it," he jokes back.

It's nice holding him, being held.

"I was shitty to Gene," I admit. "So when a firing squad executes me tomorrow, you'll know why."

Josh doesn't let go, so I don't either. "A firing squad's too good for you. You deserve thumb screws, maybe an iron maiden. I'm sure Conrad probably has a rack somewhere."

Joking about torture and morbid shit should suck, but it's a healing tonic.

"What was that e-mail responding to? It said there was a message?" Josh pulls back, meeting my eyes.

He never even heard my stupid confession. He doesn't know how I feel.

"I don't. Know." I'm very convincing.

Josh pulls out his phone. I can't let him listen to that fucking message. I can't hit repeat on the e-mail. Sure, he'd be nicer about it, but Pam didn't fake what happened in the hot tub. When Josh said he didn't want me, that was real.

I grab the phone.

"Hey. I want to listen." He tries to snatch it and I spin round.

All Josh's passwords are the same, and also they're consecutive numbers. *A-ha.*

"*Ty.* Seriously. I want to hear it—I forget to check those, and also my password. Kay?!" he calls out, like she'll hear him. "What's my password?"

"It's 1-2-3-4," I tell him, still facing the wall.

Josh lunges for the phone.

I shove him and run.

"*Ty!*" Josh's feet stomp after me as I tear down Rivers Road, the objectively worst named werewolf road. "Can you come the fuck back?"

"Nope!" I feel sick, but I keep running. I fumble with the phone, trying to figure out his inbox. Delete's usually 7.

"Playing message," says Majel Barret.

Shitshitshit

I go flying, and with me, the phone.

"*Ty!*"

I'm flat on the pavement. My face, I can already tell, is bleeding. The phone is far away, playing the message. I roll onto my back and stare at the night sky.

Josh comes to a stop at my feet. He bends down, brushes his finger over my lower left cheek, then my chin. It stings.

"God, Ty. Are you okay?" He brushes gravel off my face.

"I don't think I want to anymore," says the phone, perfectly audible and perfectly out of reach. I close my eyes, smooth my hair down. "Look. Fuck. I'm in love with you, Josh. It's not a joke for me. I need to step away. Just try and call back when you get this so we can hash it out. The rental's phone line should work—if you leave a message, we can set up a time to talk. Or we can wait till I get back. Don't bother with Uphill. I think I need to do this alone. Talk soon."

This is it, the moment I've been dreading. I open my eyes.

Josh is leaning over me on the ground, very close to my face. He kisses me.

A piece of bloody gravel rolls into my mouth and I spit instinctively.

Josh draws back, brushing beer-infused road off his cheek.

"You don't have to do that." I spit out more gravel, wipe my face, prop myself up with my elbows.

"Tyler, I'm gay."

I blink. I stare at him, trying to determine if this is residual science from The Moon, if I've drugged Josh with Fleetwood Mac, if he's Pam in an Oscar-winning costume and she's about to peel off her mask.

Josh does none of those things. He looks scared. "Say something?"

I swallow. "What does that mean. Exactly."

"You want me to define gay for you? I want to fuck men. I'm romantically interested in men."

"The island helped you work that out?" I just want to say I know I'm being obtuse right now, but I'm also terrified. If I let myself think he means me, he's going to laugh and wave the notion away and make a distinction between me and other men, me and hot men, me and men he wants. He'll call me cute like that's a compliment.

"You," he says. "You helped me work it out. I'm going to come over by you again. Is that all right?"

"Why wouldn't it be?"

"You're staring at me like I'm a giant spider, and I'm a little worried you're going to run away and accidentally drown in the river. That'd be pretty tragic."

I make a face. "It's not a river. That water's barely moving. It's like a lake. I've been calling it a lake-moat. But yeah, you can come over I guess."

He leans over me, one hand propping him up. He's almost lying on me. He holds my face with his other hand and feels out the shape of my lips with his thumb. I watch his skin touching mine, and when I find the courage, I look him in his brown eyes. I'm wary, but it's hard to be. It's not like before.

This time, he's not going to pull away.

I kiss his cheek, the side of his mouth, put my arm around his neck. It's a hard pose to hold, so we kind of . . . deflate onto the road, my tongue sliding past his lips, his nose nudging mine, our hands going many places. I'm touching him, and he wants me to.

"I'm sorry, Josh," I say, hand on his ass. "I'm actually straight."

He punches me in the shoulder.

We're making out again, and my mouth is full of bits of road and blood, but it's very high on my list of good moments, probably number one actually, and I grab his hair, and he grabs my cock through my pants. Distantly, I'm worried about public indecency laws, but not that worried.

Josh's cheeks are wet against mine.

He's crying.

That doesn't seem good.

I pull back slightly, though that's hard, because I'm hard, and the last thing I want is distance. "If you don't want to do this."

He shakes his head. He reaches for mine and grabs my hair, pulls us back together. "No, I. I just love you. I've loved you for a really long time. I made you seductive vegan risotto." He lays his hand on my chest. "It didn't work."

"I promise if you make it again I'll be seduced."

"I'm not making it again; it was hard." He kisses me. "Maybe if you do a sexy dance."

I laugh against his skin, bite his cheek. "Why would I do that?"

"Because cryptids are real, and I have a werewolf boyfriend."

Ten minutes ago I was chewing a gross alley cigarette and contemplating my future in logging. Now I'm somebody's werewolf boyfriend.

"No one wants a dance, Josh." I push my hand under his shirt, pull it off.

He pops my jeans, slides his hand inside. "I want a dance."

I bend back against the road, kiss his neck, his shoulder, his chest.

Me and Josh don't *quite* fuck on the road, but we don't exactly not, either.

And I tell him I love him again, and why, and that I want him, and he tells me the same thing, and what's weird about it all, is I believe him.

6

MOONLIGHT DESIRES

W hen you want good beer, mediocre cocktails, and baller company, you visit The Thunder Moon. When you want quiche, you go to Ziggy's. And apparently, when your two future co-hosts set you up on a candlelit dinner date in a private room with red velvet curtains and a giant Gothic Victorian bed, they book it at The Squeaky Duck.

Josh is wearing his favourite tuxedo t-shirt and the shorts he considers high-class because there's a logo for an extinct 1920s cigar company on them. I'm in my faux leather jacket over a t-shirt because it's the only thing I have anymore with sleeves, and a pair of black pants Gene promised me weren't Ru's pajamas and which are 100% Ru's pajamas.

There's a bottle of champagne in a bucket on the round, be-cloth'd table where Josh and I are struggling to seem sophisticated, and the plates in front of us are occupied by dots I'm sure if I asked would be "emulsions," "reductions," and "coulis."

They're also probably delicious, but the only thing I'm looking at is Josh.

And he's looking at me.

"Wow," he says. "First date."

I reach for the wine, pop the cork. It's satisfyingly phallic. "So I'm a scorpio, my birthstone's geranium, I like long walks on the beach, and the poetry of Michael's craft store decals. I know it's cliché, but 'When Life Gives You Lemons' was a peak in their creative output."

Josh makes a face, watching me as I carefully spill wine over his glass. "You're not a scorpio." He shakes his head like a disappointed tutor. I'm not sure whether it's because I still can't pour liquids or because I don't know my star sign.

We toast. I sip. Josh tosses it back like a shot and it comes out his nose. You can't take some people anywhere.

We stare at our plates. We pick at the food.

"You know," he says, "it's not really our first date."

I shoot him a look. "Yeah, but all 50 of the others took place on camera."

Josh grins and makes another toast. "To date 51."

I lean back in my chair, not hungry, despite the obscene effort Tia and Kayla went to. All I can think about is kissing him, about his cock in my hand and mine in his, about the punctures still lining my back from the gravel on the road two nights ago. I tip my head at the bed. "And you're living your vampire castle fantasy."

"Yeah, but it's ruined because my boyfriend's dumb and he turned himself into a werewolf."

"If you want me to leave, you can hang out alone till Dracula shows up, but the vampires get the island in December, and they're not big on Jesus from what I hear, so, you know, no Christmas."

Genuine distress distorts Josh's face. "Shit man. Do you think the werewolves get Christmas?" He shakes his head. "Before you fixed the magic song thing, I was thinking maybe I'd get Tia to turn me into one, but I dodged a bullet."

I shrug one shoulder. "I'm sure Uphill's invented a psychopathic Christmas substitute. Merry Nightwell—let 80 turkeys loose and shoot them with bazookas, that kind of thing." Wait. "Wait wait wait. You were gonna get Tia to curse you?"

Josh blushes, he stares at the massive window with its dramatic curtains. "Can't make more episodes if half of Discovery

Bang's stuck on this island. It's all or nothing. Josh and Tyler, or Josh and nobody . . . no, wait. Nobody. It would be nobody without us both, that's what I was trying to say."

"Don't ever do that." I'm looking at him too hard for how good this dinner feels, for how darkly good what he's told me feels. But I can't be Tia or Gene, watching Josh walk off to die in the forest one day.

He smiles at me. "Well I won't, now I know they don't have Christmas."

The food's just . . . sitting there. And he's sitting there, and he's sexy, even in the terrible shirt and Addington's cigar shorts.

"I feel bad for Tia and Kayla, but I'm really not that hungry," I say.

His eyes are fixed on mine, round and dark in the dim mood lighting. His Adam's apple bobs. "You wanna just fuck?"

We're halfway to the bed before it registers how we got there, how I got my jacket and shirt off, how he took his shorts off between the foot of the bed and the table.

I remember the dinner, and the waiters who'll eventually be coming back up. I dash for the door, slip the Do Not Disturb sign on and lock it.

When I turn back, Josh is positioning a camera so it's facing the foot of the bed. I'm mostly concerned about where he was hiding it.

I tilt my head. "Wasn't expecting that."

Josh pulls his shirt off and tosses it aside. We've seen each other naked before—it was hard not to in theatre school or on the road—but this is different. I'm staring at him, despite the shock of the camera. He's poking out of his underwear, beautiful and absurd in front of the canopied bed, thick plains of light casting bright slashes across his pecs.

"Special episode on werewolf mating rituals?" Josh suggests.

"You're lucky you're hot."

Josh walks up to me. He kisses my neck, lips soft, like he put something on them. He tugs on Ru's "fancy" pajamas. I hook my fingers on either side of his underwear, hands resting on his hips. I rub my cheek against his jawline.

"And you're lucky *I'm* hot," he quips.

I laugh right into his ear. "That's what I said, you have to say . . . ." He tugs on my cock gently. I pull his pants down. "Fuck it, nevermind."

We fumble our way to the bed. I trip on our discarded clothes and fall on him at the edge of the bed. The camera's right next to us as we slide onto the floor.

Of course Josh would have an exhibitionism kink. It's the one thing out of all the things I've learned recently that's made sense.

"Are we really doing this?" I kiss his chest, working my way down.

"Fucking?" His voice is breathy. He's got one hand on my back, digging his fingers into the ridges of my shoulder blade. His other hand tangles in my hair.

As I go lower to lick the tip of his cock, he loses his grip on me, stroking his hand up my spine.

I draw away to speak. "On camera." I smirk. "Discovery Banging?"

He pulls his knee up and kicks my shoulder gently. "You're lucky I'm hot."

"Whatever. Get up on the bed." This sounds sexy, but actually I'm thinking about how my back's gonna kill on the drive home tomorrow.

Josh pulls himself up with some assistance. He scooches toward the headboard and I get on the bed with him, back to the camera. Not the best view. The best view is from where I'm sitting, my knees to either side of him, his body sinking into the red sheets, his cock hard and his eyes a little desperate.

I lean down, inch back, take him in my mouth.

"It's not for other people," says Josh. "It's for like, us, when we get old and we can, ah," I suck on his head, "look back and, ah, see how hot we were." He pauses. "And be sad about it, or horny."

Absolutely nothing bad could ever come of two internet semi-celebrities making a sex tape.

I glance up. Josh's clutching the sheets, eyes closed, head turned to the side. I take him deeper, fold my tongue under him, taste his precum in my mouth. He moans loudly.

". . . is . . . happening. This is—" He makes a lot of indescribable happy noises. "*Ty.*"

I reach up, drag my hand down his hip, along the side of his ass, his thigh.

There's a knock from the side of the bed—a hand on wood.

I stop so I can look up.

Josh glares at me. The drawer to the bedside table's open. He throws a bottle of lube at my head. It hits my shoulder. "Don't stop, asshole."

I bite my lip, sit up, grin. "Just staying on brand."

I pop the lube, squeeze it directly on his cock, jerk him off slow.

Josh tries to prop himself up, but he seems to be having some trouble with that for some reason. I lean over him and he grabs my face, slamming his mouth against mine, our cocks glancing against each other, slippery with lube and saliva. He reaches down for mine and . . . fuck. I curve my back.

He rolls us over, our lower bodies slick as oil. His toes drag against my calf. He straddles me, and for a second I think he's gonna shove my cock in his ass, but he sits on me, holding us together. He cums all over me.

I swallow a laugh. "Meant to do that?"

He scoots back. He grabs my thigh, squeezes, takes all of me in his mouth.

I'm floating in space. My cock's throbbing and wet and that's Josh. That's Josh down there. And he's . . . he's really fucking good at what he's doing. He licks the base of my cock.

"For a straight guy . . . you're really good at . . . sucking dick." I swallow, groan. My fingers graze his shoulder. He sucks faster, tongue working me. I'm making the same stupid noises he was making, probably worse noises actually, and Josh is recording all of it on his stupid fucking home video and what if it gets out and what if Josh's parents see this? But I guess Josh doesn't care about that anymore because he sure is filming himself with my x-inch cock in his mouth and his tongue like a snake around me and—He grips my thigh harder, pushing my leg back.

"*Ah fuck.*"

I cum in his mouth.

He starts licking it up. I slump into the bed, flex my shoulder into the silk.

When he's done cleaning me off, he inches up beside me. I kiss him, long and hard, my hands around his shoulders, his on mine.

"It wasn't my first time." Josh glares, and I realize it's because I'm staring.

"When did this happen?" There wasn't exactly a ton of time between Ashley and hot tub fun times.

In the dazed, happy, after sex place where I'm living now, he kisses my chin. "When I was a teenager. Then . . . ."

I pinch his back and he bucks against me. "Then?" I bite his neck, his collarbone.

"Threesome. Ashley. Some guy who . . . ." Josh squirms against me. "Looked like you. It's most of why we broke up."

I pull back, looking at him, his face in my hands. "Ashley broke up with you over a threesome?"

He bites my thumb, sucks on it, grazing his teeth over it, looking me in my eyes the entire time. "She thought it'd be hot. Which it was."

I smirk. "And you found some guy who looked like me."

"She did."

Huh. "And?" I slide my thumb against the inside of his cheek, pull it back out.

"We fucked a lot."

"You're leaving out some details." I stroke his hair.

"We fucked a lot on and off for a few months." He curls into me, head hooked over my shoulder. "She liked it when she was watching."

Oof.

"I broke it off, but then you . . . ." His back shivers under my touch.

"Only Fans."

He nods into me. "And the award show happened. All I could think about was I was horrible. I'd cheated, sort of, with that guy, and I was depraved."

I snort, grab his ass. "I'm looking forward to meeting depraved Josh."

"You don't even know."

"I want to."

We break apart about half an inch. "What if I fuck this up," he says.

"Why would you?"

"Because my parents fucked me up." He looks down, obviously so he doesn't have to look at me. "They made me go to these church sessions. I tried real hard not to be gay. What if it worked?"

I gesture at us, naked and covered in lube, cum, and sweat. "I'm not worried."

"I love you," he says.

I kiss his forehead, his nose, his lips. "Well if you forget, I'll call up another evil fanfic writer to set us straight. Next season, Discovery Bang takes on the dark obsessions of Pornstar Popsicle. The dark obsessions are mostly my cock, apparently."

Josh laughs nervously. "You don't have to wait till next season for that."

I clench my jaw, trying to read his expression. "Pam was both of them?" The Ao3 plot twist I did not want.

Josh slaps me. "*No.* Her writing was shit. You really can't tell the difference?"

"There was a difference, I just don't understand why you're so invested."

His brows are pinched in incredulity. "Ty, you're dumb as fucking bricks, man."

When he kisses me, I'm still blinking in confusion. He hops off the bed, walks to our discarded clothes, shakes out his phone. It *clunks* on the floor.

I roll over so I can see him, fold my arms behind my head.

"This is something PP was working on last night," says Josh, scrolling and tapping with his thumb.

This is certainly something.

He clears his throat, shifts nervously, as though he's not standing naked at the foot of the bed already. He rubs the back of his neck.

"'*So my voice is an aphrodisiac,' says Ty, back taut and sweaty as he rams into Josh in the spare room where his parents think he's doing Bible study. 'Yeah,' Josh pants,*" RealJosh swallows again. He's swaying. I sit up, walk around the bed, biting my cheek not to laugh. "*'A-And I'm addicted. What are we going to do? When,* uh, *when we're not fucking my head hurts. I get the shakes. We can't do the show like, like this.'*"

He's shaking.

I walk up to him, fold my arms over his shoulders. He stops reading, so I read for him. "'*Or we could do the show like this,' says Ty. Josh's father's footsteps echo in the hall, but he's too horny to stop. He wants to get caught. He wants to fuck Tyler in the ass in the woods and on the couch downstairs. Ty cums inside him, and Josh cums a moment after that. 'You're an aphrodisiac too,' says Ty, as the door opens.*"

Josh breathes in hard, throws the phone on the bed. "Sorry."

"You should be. You didn't finish it." I reach around him, pull him right up against me.

He starts laughing, turns around, kisses me. "So I'm not a creep."

"You're an aphrodisiac." I kiss him back, and we stumble a little on our return to the bed. "And I've never minded a bit of stage direction."

7

THINK BUT THIS AND ALL IS MENDED

"Y ou okay, Tee?" I nudge her with my elbow.

She and Gene spent the flight in complete silence, taking turns in the pilot seat next to Gord, eyes glued to the windscreen. Now that we're standing on the stairs leading from plane to solid ground, Tia's wearing the same shell-shocked expression.

The conifers past the small airport look the same as the ones on Echo Island. Fog seeps over and between them, their branches sloped beneath the weight of a hundred remembered winters. She watches them like they're special, and as I stand beside her the specialness of these mindnumbingly ordinary trees in this mindnumbingly ordinary place infects me too.

We're not on the island. I'm safe.

"I'm good," says Tia.

And I am too, except there's a disturbance at the tree line that sends a shiver through me. The trunks of the pines bend, and I take a step backward, expecting Pam to step out of the forest and onto the tarmac. She doesn't, but it hardly matters.

Last night, I woke up screaming. I didn't even see Josh when he started shaking me, though he claims my eyes were open. I can leave the island, I can restart my life, but she'll never be completely gone. I force it down. For Tia, this is a huge moment.

"Ready to take your first step?" I reach for her hand, squeeze. She nods.

I give her another nudge, about to say something wise and hopeful.

Josh and Kayla plough into our backs, whooping. They high-five as me and Tia fall the remaining steps and land on the pavement.

My wrist breaks my fall and *agggh*. I suck back a scream and Tia hisses in pain.

Above us, Gene ambles into view beside Gord. "Magisterial," he says, watching the woods.

Josh hauls me to my feet. "You fell over," he informs me helpfully. "You should try doing that closer to July so you can heal and everything."

"Mmm." I shake out the kink in my hand.

"Are you sure you don't want to come?" Josh asks Gene.

Gene glances at Gord and smiles. "This is enough of a trip for me. I put my roots down on the island, and it's got its roots in me, too."

Tia hops back up the stairs to Gene while Gord reminds us to take our damn suitcases because his plane's already full of crap and what's he going to do with a boom pole?

The three bags slung over my shoulders are light as coolwhip. I try not to grin too much while I'm being impressive, but I don't try *that* hard. Josh is still in the phase where me lifting moderately heavy things shrinks his pants a couple sizes and I'm perfectly fine with that.

Kayla pulls me and Josh toward the car. "Come on, give them some space."

"Who would ever need space from us?" Josh quips. "We're internet darlings, we're intrepid investigators, we're beloved YouTube personalities, and I'm about to break the internet."

"Like Kim Kardashian?" Kayla slaps his ass. "I thought you getting laid on the regular would make you sufferable, but you're just twice as obnoxious and now you smell sweatier at breakfast."

"He was always sweaty," I point out.

Kayla groans. "I said sweati*er.*"

Tia throws her arms around Gene's neck. He swings her round. I'm not gonna see him again till next summer, and who knows what'll have happened by then: maybe he and Gord'll be happily married. Maybe—

My attention's pulled toward Josh.

Josh catches me looking and kisses my cheek. "Do you think you could lift a car? Oh—no, wait. Could you lift a very large horse? What about multiple crates of beer taped together into a pyramid?"

As we round the small building servicing the airport, Josh's car comes into view—cracked mirror, bumper held on by duct tape. It's the only car in the lot, and I'm not sure it counts as one. I could hug it.

"Now I know this'll be hard," I say, "but try and remember where you parked."

We wait for Tia—she doesn't linger with Gene for too long. Gord hands her a paper, and the last of Kayla's bags. She carries everything over without breaking a sweat, shoving the paper at my face as she reaches us.

Kayla pops the trunk so Tia can unload.

"*Payment to be rendered unto Conrad Augustus Uphill no later than*—fuck. It's a bill. Uphill's billing me $5000 for knocking a fucking picture off the wall of his creepy museum."

I absently hand Josh one of the bags and he falls over.

Tia taps the paper. "And *defacing* the picture. Plus Gene won't give it back, so he's claiming it's theft."

I crumple the bill, ready to toss it, but there's something taped to the reverse. It's a USB. A note written above it in purple glitter pen reads: *The Virginia Kyle Collection. To Tyler Kyle, thanks for everything - Queen Cee.*

I shove the USB in my pocket, then take a moment to unbury Josh.

Kayla's already wedged into the backseat with a massive bag. She taps the window, indicates Tia, then pats the seat next to her luggage excitedly.

Me and Josh turn around to wave at Gord and Gene, but Gene's already headed back inside and Gord's almost to the maintenance building. For an instant, I'm stuck staring at the structure, where years ago Pam learned about Tyler Kyle for the first time. Where she fell in love with Josh Likens and decided not being alone anymore was worth smashing a stranger's face in. There's a pang of sadness there, something shared between me and her that I wish to Pazuzu wasn't. It's raw and hideous and harmful.

Josh punches my arm. "You're driving." He tosses me the keys.

Inside, I immediately go for the radio, but I hesitate, take out the USB.

"Put it in." Josh is smiling at me, wearing Uphill's cowboy hat.

I'm obviously not fast enough for him, so he grabs it from me. As we pull out, Kayla's rattling off "city facts" to Tia, but Tia's still staring out the window, hypnotized.

Kim Carnes starts playing, Virgie Kyle style.

Moments later, we're cruising down the highway toward Avalon, and thence to Montréal.

Tia howls out the window. "This is amazing. I love cars." She kicks my seat. "Hit the gas, Kyle."

At risk of losing the bumper completely, I step on the gas, roll my own window down. Cool air whips my too-long hair, and I hold my hand out, feeling the breeze. I howl along with her.

Josh aims his phone's camera at me. "Welcome, Discovery Bangers—"

"Josh, why are you filming this?" I swat the camera.

"Why not? We have *definitive* proof that cryptids are real." He raises the camera. "And here we are with real-life cryptid, Tyler the werewolf."

I pull my hand back inside so I can drive and hit him at the same time. "Get that fucking camera out of my face. You're not telling people I'm a *werewolf*."

Josh shrugs. "Why not?"

"Because it's—it's *private*."

"Oh so, not, you know, *not true*." He grins at the screen. "Not because cryptids aren't real, but because you're scared of sharing an intimate moment with the very viewers who paid for your plane ticket."

I wish they hadn't. "Uphill made me sign an NDA—the government could step in if we cause trouble."

Josh dismisses me with a wave. "The government's not covering this one up. We're Discovery Bang, we can take on anyone."

"Yeah," I say, "Now we've defeated a mediocre fanfic writer on her home turf, what's stopping us from going after CSIS?"

"I'm glad you see it like I do," says Josh.

Kayla leans forward, starts tapping my shoulder. "OMG TYLER YOU CAN BE ON I SURVIVED."

"Ooo, ooo!" Josh undoes his seatbelt and stretches back, facing Kayla. "And he's got healing powers, and he's a wolf, and they're looking for a new Wolverine for X-Men."

I'm glad someone's having fun. "Audiences are gonna be pretty disappointed when Marvel announces I'm replacing Hugh Jackman."

"Shhh," Josh snaps. "We're fixing your career."

On the radio, "Bette Davis Eyes" fades away, and my mom starts talking.

"*A lot of you know I lost Tysha.*" Josh slides back down into his seat. My mom's pained laughter fills the car. "*I sing all my songs for her. Except tonight. This one's for someone else very special, someone who'll never hear it.*" There's a lull, like she's having trouble continuing. Someone whistles in the audience. It might be Gene, or Mary, or Ru, or Queen fucking Cee.

Josh lays his hand on mine, but I'm staring at the horizon. The sunset is all kinds of purple and orange. The sun burns molten where it meets the ground, a rare fire blazing as it fades.

I flick on our headlights.

"*This one's for you, baby doll*."

"Chiquitita," fills the car. I tap my finger, try not to cry, fail. Josh starts singing along, and his voice and the accompanying shimmy are so terrible it helps. Only when the music becomes a medley and "Thank You For the Music" plays, I start sobbing. Tia reaches from behind me and rubs my shoulders.

"Fuck Conrad Uphill." I sniff. "He did this on fucking purpose."

A car pulls ahead of us, from where I have no idea, but seeing another vehicle calms me down. The song ends, and Josh leans over, lays his head on my shoulder, watching the other driver zoom into the distance.

"I'm tired." He yawns.

"So sleep. I'm good to drive," I tell him.

He clutches my hand. "I don't want to. Every time I do, I'm worried I'll wake up in a universe where I didn't find you in time. I don't know what I'd do if that'd happened."

For a second, I lay my head against his, one hand on the wheel, our fingers latched together. "There's not a world where that would happen. You're Josh Likens. You always get your man . . . animal. Manimal. And what would you have done about next season? Aren't we supposed to hunt some ghost child only other kids can see? Who else would point out the obvious flaw in that plan?"

Kayla scoffs. "Like you're not both man-children."

"Why do we want to find a ghost child?" asks Tia. A valid question I ask myself most days.

"Views," says Kayla. "You'll understand when you have to pay rent."

Josh is silent.

I put my arm around him, holding him close. "There's no world where you wouldn't find me." He doesn't speak. "How about this? We'll put proving the existence of the multiverse on the long-game list, and if we find a world like that, we'll fix it. Or you can have two of me for the price of one. Since I'm free, that's not a *great* deal, but—"

Josh snores. He's drooling. He slumps against me.

We drive through the dark, and when our small stretch of road joins the larger flow, other travellers curve in beside us, passing us by, if only for a moment.

Josh mumbles that he loves either me or pizza, and as the lights of the city glitter in the distance, I pretend it was the first thing. But even if it wasn't, it doesn't matter, because I know both of them are true.

I brush his hair out of his eyes, and he stirs at my touch. He smiles in his sleep, hand folded on my jeans. He needs to shave. With all the hair, someone might confuse him with Sasquatch. Everyone but me, the man who's going to sleep in his arms tonight. The man who'll wake up to him in the morning, knowing the two of us are exactly where we want to be, lying next to exactly who we want to be with.

"I love pizza too, Josh," I tell him. "I love pizza too."

And scene.

ACKNOWLEDGEMENTS

I've been so worried that I'll accidentally leave someone out that writing the acknowledgements has been the reason it's taken me so long to release a print book. So, a massive caveat that I'm sure I *have* forgotten someone very important and that if that's you, then I'm very sorry and please know you were meant to be included. In fact, why not write your own name here (I've even left a space):

Aside from ye of the awesome name (above), a big thanks to my family: Mom, Dad, Agnes, Lucas, Kate and the rest of the Cober clan, as well as my cats! I also wanted to thank Quinn in particular for providing critical care when it came to some of the medical stuff in the book. Any mistakes or exaggerations are my own.

Thank you also to my friends, especially Jackiie (J. Patricia Anderson), without whom the book you hold in your hands would not exist (literally—as I type this, she is helping me navigate IngramSpark and formatting my book in Atticus). Thank you Kat, Fi, Claire, Elliott Gish, Daniel Maidman, Crystal Baynam, and all my friends back in Newfoundland, as well as my SPFBO crew and Pitch Wars and Queeryfest friends. Thank you to Melissa for the insider info on theatre school and Nicole (and her mysterious friend) for the spark that inspired Echo Island.

I had a lot of help from critique partners and beta readers on this one, and would like to thank Irene Morrison-Moncure, Mary (thanks for all the quiche!), Katie Little, Jason Beymer, Alistair Reeves, Emily M. Dietrich, and Marina Viltch for taking an ominous plane ride to Echo Island with me, as well as providing sensitivity readings. And to the Indie Cover Group on Facebook for your feedback (it hurts, but it helps)!

Kola Heyward-Rotimi—you are one of the most talented writers and wonderful people I've ever met. Thank you for being there during some truly painful moments, and for picking me up when I was struggling. Your insights as a critique partner are trumped only by your insights as a friend. Here's hoping Tyler, Josh, and co. have a chance to meet up with Blaze and the gang at the next video awards! Justin—you're a beautiful person inside and out, and your friendship, kindness, and support has meant the world. To Maria Dong—I'm constantly in awe of your talents. Thank you for pushing me to write this book (if you hadn't, I probably wouldn't have got off my ass and done it), as well as for the name *Discovery Bang* and the line "Seven thirty, fingers dirty." And to my fellow Monsters: Samantha Rajaram and Ava Reid.

I'd also like to thank my brilliant and talented #Queeryfest mentor, Mary Ann Marlowe, for taking a chance on my weird queer horror book. It meant a lot to get that "yes" after a sea of nos and the work you put into helping me revise the book was invaluable. I can't thank you enough for everything you've done to support me. To my Pitch Wars mentor, K. A. Doore—thank you for believing in me and for the editorial wisdom you shared on Lesbian Vikings. I took that wisdom and was able to apply it to this one too. I owe you so much! And to Anna Kaling and Carrie Callaghan as well—the best cheerleaders!

Lastly, I'd like to thank all the readers (including reviewers) who've taken a chance on this weird, wild book. I hope you enjoyed it and that when Discovery Bang returns you'll remember to click that like button and subscribe.

   - Steve

ABOUT THE AUTHOR

Steve is a trans author of fantasy, science fiction, and horror (basically, if it's weird he writes it).

He grew up on the eldritch shores of Newfoundland, Canada, and currently lives and works in (the slightly less eldritch) Montreal. He holds advanced degrees in Russian Literature, Medieval Studies, and Religious Studies. His current academic work focuses on marginalized reclamations of monstrous figures and he has published academically on fungal monsters, disability in *Resident Evil*, and zombies. He teaches the History of Satan; Religion and its Monsters; and Magic, Witchcraft, and Religion.

Steve is passionate about queer representation, Late Antiquity, and spiders.

CONTENT WARNINGS

Sexual assualt, physical abuse, emotional abuse, psychological abuse, gore, explicit violence, torture, stalking, vomit, implied ingestion of urine for survival purposes, implied cannibalism, mild dysphoria, discussions of homophobia, discussions of conversion therapy, starvation, eye trauma, body horror

Printed in Great Britain
by Amazon

45794199R00260